Jo Watson is the bestselling author of the Destination Love Series, *Love To Hate You*, which has sold over 100,000 copies, *Love You, Love You Not* and *You, Me, Forever*. She's a two-time Watty Award winner with over 50 million reads on Wattpad and 85,000 followers. Jo is an Adidas addict and a Depeche Mode devotee. She lives in South Africa with her family.

For more information, visit her website www.jowatsonwrites.co.uk, follow her on Twitter and Instagram @JoWatsonWrites and find her on Facebook at /jowatsonwrites.

No one makes you laugh like Jo Watson!

'Witty, enjoyable and unique' *Harlequin Junkie*

'Found myself frequently laughing out loud and grinning like a fool!' *BFF Book Blog*

'Heart-warming, funny, sweet, romantic and just leaves you feeling good inside' *Bridger Bitches Book Blog*

'Full of pure-joy romance, laugh-out-loud moments and tear-jerkers' *Romantic Times*

'It was amazing, it was hilarious' *Rachel's Random Reads*

'An addictive read, it is heartbreaking at times but ultimately a stunning heart-warming read' *Donna's Book Blog*

'Will definitely be reading more by this author' *Captured on Film Blog*

By Jo Watson

Destination Love Series
Burning Moon
Almost A Bride
Finding You
After The Rain
The Great Ex-Scape

Standalone
Love To Hate You
Love You, Love You Not

You, Me, Forever
Truly, Madly, Like Me

Truly, Madly, Like Me

Jo Watson

HEADLINE
ETERNAL

First published in Great Britain in 2020 by
HEADLINE ETERNAL
An imprint of HEADLINE PUBLISHING GROUP

Screenplay for *The Birds* by Evan Hunter
Based on *The Birds* by Daphne du Maurier

1

Cataloguing in Publication Data is available from the British Library

ISBN 978 1 4722 6556 2

Typeset in 11/14.5 pt Granjon LT Std by Jouve (UK), Milton Keynes

Printed and bound in Great Britain by Clays Ltd, Elcograf S.p.A.

Headline's policy is to use papers that are natural, renewable and recyclable
products and made from wood grown in well-managed forests and other
controlled sources. The logging and manufacturing processes are expected
to conform to the environmental regulations of the country of origin.

HEADLINE PUBLISHING GROUP
An Hachette UK Company
Carmelite House
50 Victoria Embankment
London EC4Y 0DZ

www.headlineeternal.com
www.headline.co.uk
www.hachette.co.uk

This book is dedicated to Ozzy. Who, whilst I was writing this book, sadly went to the big dog park in the sky. After sixteen years of hunting, jumping, running, playing, barking, scratching and being my writing companion.

PROLOGUE

$\mathcal{I}$'ve always wanted to be a somebody.

And not just anybody. I wanted to be the somebody that everybody wanted to be. And before you judge me, let me tell you why being a somebody is so important to me.

The year is 1995. I'm four years old, and I have high hopes. I have the highest hopes in the world because each year Mom and I enter the Little Miss Daisy pageant. The biggest pageant in town, and each year we win. It's *our* thing. The one mother–daughter bonding moment that we have. And those are very, very rare.

But then, in 1996, everything changed. Because that's when Jess was born, and my mom was just too exhausted and overwhelmed to even remember the pageant. Not to mention too exhausted and overwhelmed to remember me. I went from existing one day to not existing. Buried under a pile of diapers and bottles and sleepless nights and crying and jars of baby food and extra night shifts and shifts on weekends to make ends meet. It was around that time, somewhere in the "lonely time," as I've come to call it, that I first turned to food for comfort.

I remember it clearly, the transformative moment when I realized that my gran's hot-baked apple pie could push so many bad feelings down; the magical ability of those mouthfuls of tasty, fatty, sugary treats to wash negative emotions away and make me feel like the lonely time was just a little less lonely. I'd had no idea that a huge mouthful of pie could have such an effect.

So when 1997 rolled around and my mom wasn't too exhausted and overwhelmed to do Little Miss Daisy, I was the happiest I'd been in a long time. And I was filled with hope again. High, high hopes. That is, until she took me to the dressmaker. I'll never forget the look on the dressmaker's face. *That look* and the hushed whispers that followed as she held up the measuring tape. And of course, I'll never forget the look that washed over my mother's face either. *Total disappointment.*

We didn't do the pageant in 1998, either. And I quickly discovered that all sorts of other foods, besides baked apple pie, were good for pushing emotions down. This time it wasn't just the loneliness I wanted to push away—it was also the memory of my mother's face, and the shame I felt.

And then 2000 came along and it was the first time my mom entered Jess in the Little Miss Daisy pageant. And she won the crown that I so badly wanted. She carried on winning the crown, over and over and over again. Year after year after year. And with each year that passed, Jess got prettier and I got fatter and my mom looked more and more disappointed and I had more shame, and jealousy and anger to push down.

Things changed again in 2010, and it wasn't just because we went into a new decade, it was because Jess won Little Miss Natal, the biggest pageant in the entire province. By then, I had spent so many years sitting on the sidelines watching Mom and Jess do the one thing that was meant to be *my* thing. Only it wasn't any more, because by then I weighed sixteen stone. *A sweet sixteen of a different kind*, my mom used to say as she pushed a plate of celery my way.

It was also around this time that I truly felt like a nobody. Sure, with each passing year I was being chipped away at. Each time my sister won, and my mom cried tears of joy and I sat on the sidelines and thought about that measuring tape, I felt a bit more of myself being ripped away. But it wasn't really until I overheard some pageant moms talking that all my sense of self was finally flushed down the drain.

"I know," they said in conspiratorial tones. "And Jess is so perfect and beautiful, and the other one, what's her name . . .? Frankie? Well, she's just so fat!" They giggled. "God, it must be so hard on her mother, to have a daughter like that." They nodded. "I think they have different fathers though," the other one whispered. "Genetics! That explains it!" They all laughed.

Until that moment, I had no idea my stepdad wasn't my real father, that my real dad had abandoned me shortly after I was born. I had no idea Jess wasn't my full biological sister. My whole world got flipped on its head in an instant. Those next few years were perhaps the loneliest of all. That is, until I discovered Instagram and the wonderful world of diets. Keto, fasting, paleo, vegan . . . You name it, it was all there. And it was there for the taking.

And I took it. With both hands.

I made myself an account and started posting pictures of my weight-loss journey. I became disciplined and focused and tracked absolutely every aspect of my life—every morsel, every step, every hour I slept. At first the followers were slow, but by the time I'd lost my fifth stone, the likes and compliments and followers started rolling in and I wasn't lonely anymore.

Then I lost the very last stone to hit my target, and that's when @TheKyleWhite101 took notice of me. Only one of the hottest influencers in the whole of South Africa. *He* took notice of *me*. Because I was someone to notice. Finally, a somebody.

Do you know, I started #transformationtuesday? Seriously, that was me. And the more weight I lost, the more I became a somebody. And soon, I was the somebody that everybody wanted to be. The somebody that everybody came to for advice and tips. Brands flocked, and my followers grew and my account became less about weight loss and fitness, and more about #inspo and my amazing, glamorous, perfect life as a social-media influencer with a blue tick next to my name. I still remember the day I got that blue tick, it was one of the happiest of my life. The day the powers that be officially anointed me a somebody, and now the whole world knew that too.

And then 2020 rolled around and I had high hopes all over again, because I celebrated the new year by hitting 350,000 followers. I also celebrated my two-year anniversary with @TheKyleWhite101 as the two of us became the ultimate #couplegoals #powercouple. The couple that everybody wanted to be; him with his motivation "Personal Smash Through™" business, and me with all my brand endorsements. Not to mention our most profitable venture, our "Mega Couple Smash Through Seminars™," where we taught you how to be like us. Because we were somebodies, and everybody wants to be a somebody with hundreds of thousands of followers. Nobody wants to be a nobody and sit on the sidelines while someone else wins the crown.

But soon, my high hopes turned to hopelessness. Because 2020 was also the year that I lost absolutely everything. In a mere seventy-two hours, I would go from being a somebody, to a total nobody. And @TheKyleWhite101 would go from dating me, to dating @Paige_Dreams_, and the whole world would think I was either losing my mind, or just plain mean.

And do you know what I blame for all that?

The elevator.

That's right, people, I blame it on the bloody elevator.

Because if I hadn't got stuck in that elevator on that fateful day, I wouldn't have run late for the important photoshoot that @TheKyleWhite101 had set up for his new #motivational web series that he was launching. And he certainly wouldn't have run into @Paige_Dreams_ who had offered to take the photos with him. He wouldn't have uploaded the photo of them together looking gorgeous and in a matter of minutes have gotten 2,000 new followers. He wouldn't have then decided that @Paige_Dreams_ was better for his personal brand than me and posted to all our followers on IGTV, telling them about our break-up *before* I knew I'd been broken up with. *Can you believe that?* Hundreds of thousands of people knew about my break-up before I did.

If I hadn't gotten stuck in that elevator, and almost lost my life as it plummeted, I wouldn't have felt so bloody emotional and shaken that I also took to IGTV and posted that sniffing, sobbing, angry video of myself having an emotional breakdown, that led me to lose 150,000 followers in a matter of hours because I was no longer #inspirational, #powercouple, #couplegoals #fuckingtransformationalbloodyeffingtuesday. #CRAP!

If I hadn't got stuck in that elevator, I wouldn't have then taken to Facebook Live later that night and cursed @TheKyleWhite101 and @Paige_Dreams_ and all those people who'd unfollowed me, which then led me to lose another 100,000 over the next day. Not to mention losing all my brand endorsements and, finally, my beautiful sponsored car. I'd hung onto the bonnet while it was being driven away, which had been good for a TikTok video painting me as a crying, screaming wild woman.

No! If it hadn't been for that faulty elevator, I wouldn't now find myself here. Alone and lonely. Lonely time 2.0. I was officially a nobody again, lying on a bed in a hotel, because @TheKyleWhite101 had kicked me out of our flat, and glued to my phone as #FrankieFreaksOut trended and everyone who had once looked up to me threw insults my way from the safety of their social media anonymity.

And when I wasn't watching my social-media-self crash and burn, I was stalking @TheKyleWhite101 and @Paige_Dreams_ every five minutes as they grew followers by the second and *they* became the #couplegoals #blessed #gratitude #winning #dreamteam that I was only seventy-two hours earlier . . .

Screw that elevator!
And screw hashtags too.
#screwthem

CHAPTER 1

I hadn't cried like this in ten years, two hundred and seventeen days and—I looked down at my Apple watch—eight hours. Specific, I know. But the thing that happened ten years, two hundred and seventeen days and eight hours ago, has been seared into me, leaving third-degree burn scars behind that have never faded.

Hey, Frankie, they'd all said with such big smiles.

I wasn't used to smiles. But I'd wanted them. So badly.

Wanna hang out after school? they'd asked, still smiling.

I'd never been asked to hang. But I'd always wanted to. So, so badly.

Meet us down by the cricket nets. They'd given me high-fives.

I'd never been given high-fives. But I'd wanted them. So, so, so badly . . .

I suppose a girl like me should have known better. I should have known that there would be no more smiles and hanging and high-fives. I should have known that instead there would be taunts and jeers and spit in my "fat, ugly face" before being shoved into the small shed by the sports fields that no one ever went to.

It took my mom a whole night to notice that I was missing—when she'd come home from her shift at the hospital and my bed was still made. It took the police another eight hours to find me after that. Sitting there alone in the dark shed, shivering from the winter cold, hysterical, bloody fingers and broken nails from trying to rip the door open. I should have known.

I looked down at my fingers and picked at the nail that I'd ripped off in the elevator three days ago and sobbed some more. I always wear false nails, I have to. Because since that day in the shed, I've bitten them. But I would hate anyone to see that. I needed a distraction, so I jumped up and did ten quick lunges across my hotel room, and then logged the activity into my exercise app—only twelve calories burned. For some reason, this made me cry even more. Surely, surely there was a universal limit to the amount of water that can come pouring out of a person's eyeballs. I was going to become dehydrated, for heaven's sake! This wasn't normal. And there was no app to calculate this either, so I was really freaking out.

But the tears had been gushing on and off at steady intervals for the last three days, as if on a timer. In fact, they were perfectly timed with the movement of my hand reaching for my phone, only to discover what fresh post from hell was waiting for me there. What new number of thumbs downs, mass exodus of friends, lack of likes, like lemmings plunging off a cliff. Or maybe it was all the comments that were cutting me to the quick that were really responsible for the tears . . .

I used to look up to @FitspoFrankie, but now I just feel sorry for her.
@FitspoFrankie is a bitch. Hate her!
Who thinks that @TheKyleWhite101 and @Paige_Dreams_ make a much better #couplegoals #hotspocouple
I hope @FitspoFrankie gets fat again!

Have you ever swallowed a pill while hiccupping? It catches in your throat with a bolt of sharp pain. Chokes you, makes you splutter, and then when it finally goes down, leaves your throat feeling raw and assaulted. That's what it felt like every single time I went back to my phone. But I couldn't help it. I kept going back for more punishment. I needed to stop doing this, especially now that the video of me clinging to my car wailing was going viral . . .

@FitspoFrankie hanging onto her car crying is the most pathetic thing I've seen all year. #FrankieFreaksOut

Don't worry @FitspoFrankie, walking will be good for you. LOL #FrankieFreaksOut

@FitspoFrankie is a total loser. #FrankieFreaksOut

I needed a distraction, and lunges weren't helping. I needed someone to talk to. So I went to WhatsApp and messaged Suzanne, a friend I'd met online. But when I saw the two blue ticks next to my message and didn't get a response, the need to phone her kicked in. But you can't just phone someone without first asking them if it's okay to phone them. I typed her another message.

Can I phone you?

I stared at my new message and my hopes skyrocketed when I saw her typing back. I waited patiently for the moving dots to result in letters, but when they didn't and the typing stopped and she went offline, my heart sank. She went offline in the middle of a conversation—she might as well have broken up with me like @TheKyleWhite101 had done. The tears prickled in my eyes and, this time, I did make a call without asking.

"Hey, Jess," I said, when my very busy-sounding sister answered.

"Frances." She was the only person in the world who called me that. "What's up? I'm in the middle of the school run." She was always in the middle of something. Suburban mom in a Suburban, driving my niece Melissa to her myriad of extramurals, both cultural and sporty, so she would be well-rounded, as Jess was so fond of saying. And Melissa was only two. Jess had gotten married pretty young—high-school sweetheart, of course—and they'd actually conceived Melissa on their honeymoon . . . *how perfect!*

"I . . . I . . ." I stuttered stupidly and then the tears came.

"Frances, what's happened?" she asked, sounding more irritated than concerned.

"No one likes me anymore," I found myself wailing. "They've all unfriended me."

I heard a sigh. A long, loud, protracted one. "I really don't have time for this now. Isn't there someone else you can call? One of your

Facebook, Twittery friends or whatever you call them?" she asked, not bothering to hide the sarcasm in her voice. Jess had never really understood my "strange online life," as she called it. She was all about real experiences, with real people, and couldn't understand why I didn't agree with her on this. Well, as far as I was concerned, IRL was not all it was cracked up to be.

"I went to the meeting with the lawyer the other day," I suddenly said, sharing something real with her.

She paused. "That must have been difficult. What happened?" I sensed true sympathy in her voice this time.

"Well, I almost plunged to my death in an elevator afterwards, that's what happened."

I heard another sigh. I could tell she had now gone from feeling sympathy, to something else. She didn't believe me. She was always accusing me of blowing things out of proportion. I'd once had the courage to share with her how I'd felt as a child growing up. How I'd felt utterly worthless, always standing in her perfect shadow. She'd said I was being dramatic and exaggerating.

"I'm sorry to hear that," she said rather flatly.

I peered into my bag, and the white envelope stared back at me. I hadn't opened it yet; I guess almost dying in the elevator and then having my entire life blow up had kind of put it on the back burner.

"He left me an envelope though. It's white."

"What's inside?" she asked.

"I don't know," I admitted.

"You should open it." She sounded so rushed. My sister had always been the one person who still made me feel like a nobody, despite my followers telling me that I wasn't. Well, in light of recent events, maybe she'd been right all along.

"Kyle broke up with me," I moaned into the phone.

There was another pause. She'd never really liked Kyle. She'd once called him a narcissistic user. But that was only because she didn't understand the nature of our relationship. It's more complicated when you're in the public eye and people turn to you for motivation and inspiration.

"Look, I'm sorry he broke up with you and you lost all your . . . *friends*. Although it's not really a surprise—I've always said that guy was no good. But I really don't have time for this now, Frances. I have a parent–teacher conference and then I have to make cookies for the bake sale so I can't deal with you now."

Deal with me?

I nodded. I could see that speaking to my sister was pointless, it wouldn't give me what I was looking for, even though I didn't really know what I was looking for. I momentarily thought of phoning my mother, but I had no idea where she might be. Cruising the Caribbean? The Greek islands? Who knew? I was happy she'd found love *again* and was cruising the world with him—Dan, the retired dentist. I took a deep breath and let it out slowly, still fighting back tears.

"I really need to go!" she said again.

"Sure," I said. "Give Melissa a hug for me—" The line went dead. She'd hung up on me. I looked down at the phone in my hand and as I did, the notifications on the screen started screaming at me again. I shoved the phone under my pillow, hiding it from sight, and reached for the nearest thing I could find to occupy my hands. A newspaper. God, I don't think I'd held a newspaper in, well, forever. *Did they still make newspapers?* With paper and ink. Doesn't everyone get their news from BuzzFeed?

I flipped the paper open. It was so stiff, cumbersome and hard to handle; why would anyone want to get their news from this? Why would anyone want to turn pages when they could scroll? I flipped randomly, peeping every now and then at my pillow which was lighting up with notifications, like dominoes. They came fast and steady, one after the other. The pillow was vibrating now, as if it was possessed.

"Oh my God, oh my God!" I turned the pages faster in panic, in an attempt to sweep it all away. With each notification my heart beat faster because I knew the whole world was turning on me. I couldn't bear the feeling. It crawled over my skin—sickly and sweaty and moist. I gave the paper a massive swat and that's when I saw it. The headline grabbed me immediately. I leaned in and started reading.

Quietest Town in South Africa

For most of us, seeing that no-signal sign on our phones is our worst nightmare. But for the 789 residents of Springdorp in the Karoo, having no phone signal is a part of everyday life. In fact, the residents of this small town have never had cell-phone signal before. Let alone Wi-Fi.

"What?" I widened my eyes and pulled the article right up to my face.

The town of Springdorp and the 100 square kilometer radius that surrounds the town, is a radio quiet zone, just one of a few places in the world like it. The reason for the radio silence is its proximity to ASO, the African Skies Observatory, home to the biggest radio astronomy observatory in Africa. Signals from cell phones, Wi-Fi and even from the radio interfere with the sensitive equipment as it listens to exploding stars on the farthest reaches of the known universe.

Taking a few moments to digest this information, I laid the newspaper down on the table and straightened it out.

But residents say they don't mind the quiet. In fact, they wouldn't want it any other way. They love the peace and tranquility that the town affords them, which really gives them an opportunity to get to know their neighbors. "People here make real connections," one resident said. "This is our little paradise and we wouldn't change a thing about it."

I stopped reading and sat back in my chair. A strange feeling washed over me in slow and steady swells. It was so hard to describe that I bet my mood-tracking app didn't even have a category for it! The feeling started at my head, ran the length of my back and legs and then sort of trickled out of my toes. Each swell became stronger and stronger until it hit me all at once like a massive wave. A tsunami of sudden understanding.

I jumped to my feet. *This was what I needed.* A place to fully escape my cell-phone hell and switch off. A place where I could be completely anonymous. A place to hide from everything that was going on in my life right now! A place where the beeping insults and hateful hashtags wouldn't follow me. A place where I would no longer be tormented by #Kaige, *yes*, that was their ship name. They had only been a ship for seventy-two hours, and had already been ship-named. I felt nauseous just thinking about it. I'd once tried to ship us, and all I'd come up with was #Krankie. Their ship name was better than ours and, *oh God*, that gave me such a pain in the ribs.

"Yes!" I said, rushing over to the phone that I'd wanted to avoid. I would rent a car, and I would drive to this town and that's where I would take refuge until all of this was over. Until they got bored of watching me cling to the bonnet of a car, or crying into the screen, snotty bubbles coming out of my nose, and they moved on to the next big story. And then maybe in a week, a few weeks, maybe even a month, I could re-emerge and #reinvent myself on social media as someone completely new. Someone different. Better! Like a butterfly from a cocoon, I could step out with new, shiny wings. I could start afresh. Maybe I would delete my old accounts and start new ones. Maybe I would start a podcast and dye my hair like an eGirl and do funny sketches on TikTok. I could be funny! The possibilities were infinite and for the first time since leaving that elevator, I felt a little bolt of hope.

CHAPTER 2

"I'm sorry," I said looking down at the car, trying to hide my obvious disgust. "Is this the *only* car you have?"

"Yes," the man replied.

"You sure?"

The man nodded solemnly.

"You don't perhaps have another one in the back, or maybe in a storeroom or—"

"Only one!" It sounded like he was getting irritated now. I didn't blame him. I was starting to sound like a stuck record. But I was also feeling irritated. I'd already been to two car-hire places, both of which had no cars to hire to me. I was itching to get out of Joburg, and the longer I stayed here, the more I felt like I might explode.

"I see." I tilted my head and looked at it, trying to see if I could find its one redeeming feature. Half a redeeming feature would do.

The man sighed. "Look, in case you haven't noticed, the big Design Indaba is happening in Joburg, and most car rental places are fully booked. So yes, this is the only car left and you probably won't find another one anywhere else."

"It's very blue," I stated. "I mean, it's very, *very* blue, isn't it? I've just . . . well, I didn't know a car could be so blue. And what with those big, shiny gold rims—*God, they really are big*—it certainly makes the blue pop, doesn't it?"

The guy nodded, and I started walking around the blue beast.

"And as for that, what would you call it on the back? A wing? A canopy?"

"Fin," he qualified.

"Right. It's very big. So big and . . . *Wow!* So high off the trunk. It really protrudes!" I walked around to the front of the car again. "And what would you call that hole on the bonnet, a nostril?" I crouched down and looked at the bottom of the car. "It's really low to the ground, isn't it? I don't think I could get a piece of paper between this oversized bumper—God, this bumper is huge—and the road. It's almost touching." I looked over my shoulder at the man behind me. "I suppose you'll tell me not to drive over bumps in the road?"

He nodded. "That would be preferable."

"And . . . is this a strip of LED lights on the bumper?" I asked, pointing.

"It gives the car a blue under-glow."

"Blue! Right. Because this car could use more blue." And then something else caught my eye. Blue fluffy dice hanging from the mirror.

I heard the man huff, and swiveled to look at him.

"Look, are you going to take the car or not?" He wasn't bothering to hide his obvious irritation.

I glanced back at it again; it was certainly a strange-looking thing, and under normal circumstances, I would never be seen dead in something like this. But I needed a car and my cute little Mercedes hatchback had been taken away from me.

"And you say it's available on long-term rental?" I asked.

The man laughed now. "Sure, it's not like anyone has ever taken it bef—" he stopped and cleared his throat. "Yes, it's available long term." And then he turned his head and I thought I heard him mumble, "The longer the better."

I put my hands on my hips and started nodding. "Okay! I'll take it for a month. What the hell, right?"

After signing the papers, I was handed the key and a small bag of complimentary mints. I made my way over to the car and tried to open the door.

"You have to press the immobilizer first before you can use the key." He pointed at the small grey disc in my hand.

"Okay." I pressed the grey button and the blue lights flashed on and off. "Wow! They are really bright." I slipped the key into the door and turned. But the second I climbed in, I was hit in the face with the stench. I choked and covered my nose. "What the hell is that?"

"It just needs to be aerated," he said, taking a step back.

I pinched my nose. It smelled like cheese. Blue cheese. Just my luck! I turned the ignition on so I could wind the windows down and blast the aircon, but almost flew out of my seat when the car screamed to life with a loud and violent roar. "What the . . ."

"Performance exhaust," the man shouted to me over the sound of the rumbling, popping engine.

I closed the door and wound all the windows down. "Right," I put the car into drive, "is there anything else I should know about this car before I . . . *AAAAAHHH!*" I screamed as my foot touched the accelerator and the car flew forward so fast that my head was flung against the blue leather headrest.

"Uh. It's fast. Did I forget to mention that?" The man was looking a little nervous now. "Ma'am, are you sure you can't fly to where you're going?"

"FLY!" I banged my hand on the steering wheel and screamed when the thing let out an ear-shattering honk of epic proportions. "No. I can't fly there." I was a bit riled now by this question and the noises the car was making. "If I could fly, why would I be renting the ugliest car in the world!" I had to shout to him over the noise.

The man looked at me curiously. "Okay. Sorry, it's just that maybe, on second thoughts, you shouldn't take this car."

"What?" I stared at him. "Second thoughts? Why didn't you perhaps have this second thought a few minutes ago while you were having your first thought which was to give me this car?"

"Um, sorry," the man mumbled under his breath, looking sheepish.

"I need this car; do you understand me? I need this car because my boyfriend broke up with me via IGTV! *Can you believe it?* And now I need to get away. And I don't have a car anymore. I don't have a car because I almost died in an elevator accident four days ago and they took my car away because I said some things I should never have said because I was feeling very emotional. Have you ever had a near-death experience," I looked down at his name badge, "Dwayne Stevenson?"

Dwayne shook his head.

"Well, it's very unsettling. It makes you say and do all sorts of things that you come to regret pretty damn quickly, let me tell you."

"Uh . . . okay." Dwayne took another step back from the car—I was sure it had nothing to do with the smell this time.

"It's true what they say, Dwayne, you shouldn't share everything on social media. Because if you do, you might also find yourself wearing an oversized hat, sitting in a car that smells of blue cheese and planning to drive into the bloody desert! Do you know how hot it is in the desert, Dwayne? Do you know how hot and sweaty you get under a hat like this?" I pointed at my head. Maybe wearing the giant hat had been dramatic overkill, but it felt like everyone in the world was watching me. And I just wanted to disappear.

"Uh . . ." He was really backing away now. "The car is petrol and you might just want to get the windscreen cleaned, since it's been sitting under a tree for so long, it's . . ." He paused.

"Covered in bird shit, I can see that, Dwayne." I looked at the white dollops of crap that were slipping down the glass. I felt a deep connection with the windscreen immediately. I, too, had been shat all over.

"They say it's good luck," he quickly added, and then forced a smile.

I swung around and glared at him. "Well, in Denmark they believe throwing plates against your neighbor's house is good luck, but you wouldn't want me to do that, would you, Dwayne?" I only knew this tidbit of info because I followed this Danish blogger who took baths in icy water every morning. Do you know how many views she gets for that? Total gimmick, if you ask me. Dwayne gave me one last peculiar look before he turned and walked away. I didn't blame him for this either—he probably wanted to be as far away from me as possible in case my strange behavior was contagious.

I drove out of the lot. The car jerked back and forth wildly as I tried to control the speed and braking. It roared and screamed at me every time I put my foot on the accelerator, as if it wanted to take off at warp speed, and then groaned loudly as I pressed the brake, as if it was pissed off with me that I hadn't allowed it to. It was going back and forth so much that I was sure I would get whiplash, and the blue dice were swinging so much that they almost hit me in my face. I grabbed them, wound the window down and, without a moment's hesitation, tossed them out. I heard a yell and looked to see a pedestrian swatting them out the way as they hit her.

"It's good luck," I screamed as I drove away.

CHAPTER 3

I'd been driving for five hours already, and it had taken me at least three to figure out how to drive this car at a normal speed without unintentionally breaking land-speed records. I'd also had to fill this thirsty, blue beast up with petrol already! But now my ears were aching from the noise of the thing. It sounded like a racecar tearing around a track, and I couldn't fathom how anyone could drive like this. I passed Bloemfontein and the Free State, and was soon heading out onto the open road that led into the Cape. A spray of pink and white Cosmos stretched out on the sides of the road, the South African signal that we were going into autumn. I've always loved Cosmos. I remember one Easter holiday we'd stopped to pick some, and then put them in a vase later that day. But the sad thing about Cosmos is you can't keep them beautiful; as soon as they're picked, they begin to die. I always thought that was so sad.

But the vegetation and scenery started to change as I drove into the Northern Cape, deeper into the Karoo desert. The sun was beating down on me, so hot that a rippling haze had formed at the horizon. The land around me was flat. Not a tree, not a building, not an anything rose up to break the desolate flatness. Bleak. That was the only way to describe it. Hot and bleak and far, far away. I hadn't seen a car for hours and this place felt like the loneliest, most remote place in the entire world. I felt so alone out here, driving in the blue cheese, that I wasn't surprised when the salty prick of tears formed in the corners of my eyes and I felt one trickle down my face. I wiped it away with the back of my hand and pushed on. But another half an hour later I needed to pee. Badly.

I pulled my phone out, ignoring all the blue notifications, and went straight to Google Maps. I typed in "Petrol Station" and waited for Maps to present me with the nearest one. But when it returned the result, my shoulders slumped. It was three hours away. At the town I was headed to. That's how in the middle of nowhere I really was. I was in no-man's nowhere land. A place where petrol stations and pitstops were about as few and far between as trees. And now I was going to be forced to pee on the side of the road.

The road was single lane—it had no emergency lane and the sun had warped its surface so badly that it was falling apart at the edges. Simply crumbling away on the sides and falling into little piles of sand and rocks. I needed to pull over, but the blue cheese wasn't built for any kind of off-roading, and one of those small stones was sure to rip the bumper clean off. Since I hadn't seen a car in hours, I took my chances and stopped in the middle of the road. I dug through my handbag for a tissue or something to make this roadside pee experience as pleasant as possible. My fingers brushed past the white envelope and I paused on it momentarily, a lump forming in my throat.

Should I open it?

I pulled the envelope out and held it up to the light, hoping to get a sense of what was inside. But the paper was thick and no matter how many times I angled it, I couldn't see more than a vague outline of something.

"Whatever!" I pushed the envelope back into my bag because it was making me feel . . . *feel what?* I opened the mood-tracking app on my phone and started scrolling.

Angry. Annoyed. Anxious. Apathetic. Blah. Calm. Confused. Confident. Content. Cute. Depressed. Eager . . .

I sighed. All of the above. None of the above. The stuff in between? Maybe there wasn't a name for the emotions I was feeling at the moment, or maybe they were spinning and cycling so quickly that from one moment to the next I didn't know what I was feeling. A sudden sharp pain in my bladder told me that I'd ignored it for far too long, so I reached back into my bag and pulled something out. *Purena Moisturizing Facial Wipes.*

"Mmmm." I turned the package over in my hands and read the ingredients. Not that I knew what any of them were, or whether they posed a serious threat to my lady parts. Not that that was necessarily a problem either, because that area wasn't going to be getting much action anytime soon . . .

I paused, lowering the packet of facial wipes, trying hard to remember the last time that @TheKyleWhite101 and I'd had sex. I honestly couldn't remember. It's not like our relationship wasn't filled with romance, though. We were very romantic! *Very!*

There was that time we went to a game lodge and took those photos of ourselves in the Jacuzzi, sipping champagne together. God, that had been a difficult picture to take because of the lighting and the soapy bubbles. But it had been soooo worth it: 10,000 likes!

And then there was that time we'd put red and white variegated rose petals on our bed. We'd made a giant heart with them and lain in the middle of it wearing matching fluffy white bathrobes and slippers. That photo had gotten 12,000 likes. So, it's not like we weren't romantic, but, still, I couldn't remember the last time we'd had sex . . . or kissed, for that matter. *Really kissed.* Not just kissed for the camera, which we often did. Photos of him kissing me on the cheek cheekily got lots of likes, especially if I pulled a silly, cute face and made a peace sign. But it had been ages since we'd kissed. You know, the kind of kiss that melts your kneecaps and gives you pterodactyls in your stomach.

I sat there for a moment, looking down at the facial wipes and running over the relationship in my mind. The urge to look at my phone was overwhelming again. I wanted to know what #Kaige were doing so badly that my fingers tingled. This was the longest time in years I hadn't posted anything on social media. Usually by this time of the day I would have Tweeted something inspirational and carefully crafted, choosing an appropriate and trending hashtag to accompany it. I would have Instagrammed my breakfast and some of my workout, today was #DumbbellDay after all. Kyle and I would already be thinking of a couple post for the evening, and I would have done some kind of cute Snap, and would be preparing for my weekly vlog. But it had been four days since I'd posted anything, and that feeling was almost unbearable. I'd been thinking nonstop about posting. Especially today. Under normal circumstances I might have taken an ironic photo of the car for Insta, #uglycars. I might have posted a time-lapse video of me driving through the Karoo. I might have Tweeted about feeling such a sense of peace in the great, vast expanse (even though that was a lie), and then Snapped a fun photo of myself on the side of the deserted road with a cute bunny ear filter. And maybe, for humor's sake, I might have also done a whole *Need a toilet stop but don't have tissues! Think it's okay to use #Purena #facial wipes?* (I tag them in case they want to do a brand collab with me.) *#methinking #girlproblems #roadtrip*

My shoulders slumped. The feeling of emptiness in the pit of my stomach was acute, huge and vast, like a sinkhole pulling everything into it. But I couldn't dwell, my bladder felt like it was going to explode. I climbed out of the car, not bothering to shut the front door, and made my way to the side of the road. I looked around. Not another car in sight. I would have to do it quickly though. And so I did.

But just when I'd finished, Purena face-wiped and all (which I must say was actually rather refreshing), I felt a definite, looming presence. Someone, *or something*, was watching me. The feeling was so strong, so overwhelming, that I didn't second-guess it. This was not in my imagination, and so I jumped up, pulled up my panties and looked around. I swung my head from side to side, my stomach bubbling with panic and my heart racing.

Something was there.

And it was watching me!

CHAPTER 4

"*Hellooo* . . . Who's there . . .?" I scanned the sides of the road . . . no one. Not a car, not a person, not an insect as far as I could see. I looked behind me. Still nothing. I felt the sudden need to arm myself, but all I had was a packet of facial wipes and the car key. I held the key in my hand, pointy side out—not that it would inflict any kind of a significant wound should I need to defend myself. Maybe a small poke at best. But I gripped it nonetheless and tiptoed along the side of the car. I could feel I was getting closer to whatever was there. I could feel it in the air, some unspoken communication was happening between us. I knew that it was there, and it knew I was there. *We knew.* I carried on tiptoeing and when I finally reached the front of the car . . .

"Oh God!" I jumped onto the bonnet so quickly that I must have grown wings. I scurried up the windscreen, breaking a wiper as I went, and half pulled myself onto the roof. My heart was beating in my throat as I looked at the thing standing in front of my car.

It was huge.

It was huge and black.

It was huge and black and had one big, yellow eyeball fixed on me.

It was huge and black and had one big, yellow eyeball fixed on me and a massive tooth sticking out of the side of its mouth.

Oh God. I didn't want to die. And certainly not at the hands of this big, black dog that was staring at me with its one eye . . . *Where was his other eye?* I wanted an open coffin when I was dead. I wanted to be beautiful in death. I've worked too hard in this life to be thin and beautiful, and I didn't want to die mangled and ugly. Is that too much to ask? I took a deep breath and tried to relax a little; can't they smell fear?

"Hey, doggy, doggy, doggy," I whispered sweetly.

"WOOF!" it replied loudly, a long trail of spit dripping through the big open gap on one side of its mouth where it had the worst snaggletooth I'd ever seen. And then something happened. The beast and I locked eyes—*well*, eye and eyes or whatever you would call it—and I swear it was trying to look *into* me. Trying to scan my insides with its one yellow eye. We stared at each other for a while. Locked in some kind of stare-down, like we couldn't pull away if we tried, and then it stepped towards the car. I closed my eyes tightly and shook my head.

"Please don't bite me, please don't bite me," I repeated over and over again with my eyes tightly shut, as if closing them would somehow minimize the pain of those huge teeth sinking into me! I don't know how long I stayed like that, eyes closed, perched on the windscreen, hanging on for dear life, but, finally, I forced my eyes open. And when I did, he was gone. *Gone!*

I whirled my head around again, left to right, front to back. No sign of him. Unless he was under the car, ready to nip at my ankles with his horrible snaggletooth. I looked over the side of the car, hoping to get a sense of his whereabouts, but couldn't. Okay, I would have to do this quickly. I would have to slide off the bonnet, climb into the front seat—the door was still open which would make it easier—and then drive away. I could do this, in 3, 2, 1 . . .

In one swift movement, moving faster than I think I'd ever moved, I jumped off the bonnet, climbed into the front seat and slid the key into the ignition. It didn't start. Shit! Immobilizer! I looked down at the key ring, and it was no longer there. I looked out the windscreen and there it was, right in the middle of the bonnet, glaring at me. I glanced around again for the dog, but like something that had never actually been there in the first place, it had disappeared. Just to be safe though, I didn't climb out of the car. Instead, I climbed out the open window and reached around with my arm, grabbing the little grey thing as quickly as I could. I pressed the button, turned the key and then skidded off, leaving an impressive dust cloud behind me. When I was a little way away, I slowed down and looked in my side mirrors. The dog had completely vanished and for a moment it made me question if I'd really seen it. Maybe I was hallucinating under the hot, desert sun. Was I? Honestly, I wasn't sure I knew the answer to that question anymore.

I pulled my phone out and went back to my mood-tracking app.

I pressed the crazy face emoji.

Then I pressed the confused face emoji.

And then a cold shiver ran up my spine and made the hairs on the back of my neck prickle.

Scared emoji.

I was definitely feeling scared.

CHAPTER 5

Three hours of driving later, I stopped my car and looked at the sign in front of me. It stared back at me, with a kind of ominousness foreboding. As if it were threatening me, or pointing an accusatory finger at me.

> You are entering a radio quiet zone.
> The use of cell phones, radios and Wi-Fi are strictly prohibited by
>   the law.

I couldn't believe it had come to this. That I was willingly entering a small town in the middle of an actual desert that had no internet and no way of getting it. Was I that desperate? Had my life really spun so far out of control that I was willing to do this?

I looked down at my cell phone. There were red and blue notifications signs everywhere. Twitter, Snapchat, Insta, Facebook, all lit up like Christmas trees, flickering lights, waiting for me. Beckoning me. Usually those notifications filled me with joy and a sense of excitement, but now they simply struck ice-cold terror into my veins. I closed my eyes and thought about it all for a second. About what had happened to me over the last few days. *How had it all gone so wrong?* And then I opened them again, and took a long, slow, deep breath. I had to do this. I pulled the mirror down to look at myself. I was a mess. I was never a mess. I always strived for perfection.

I reached into my bag and pulled out a hairbrush and my bulging make-up bag. I freed my bleached blonde hair from the messy bun it had been confined to for the past four days. It tumbled down to my shoulders looking wavy and unruly. Brushing it just made it worse, because now it was poodle puffy too. My natural hair is mousy brown and curly. But I'd been bleaching and straightening it for the past two years. @TheKyleWhite101 preferred it like that—he said it was better for our personal brand, and looked good in pictures with him, since he's also blond. I gave up on the brushing and put my hair back into a bun, this time taking care to make it less like a bird's nest. I unzipped my make-up bag and tipped the contents onto the seat next to me. It filled the entire space. Doing my make-up in the morning usually takes at least forty minutes. I have to conceal and contour and bake and blend and highlight and that's just the foundation. Today, looking at myself in the mirror, I just didn't have the strength to do it. I needed to at least get rid of the freckles, though. At least contour the sides and tip of my nose. And put some highlighter on the cupid's bow of my lips, because without all that . . . well, I'm pretty ordinary. I'd discovered the transformative power of make-up some years ago, and then learned everything I could via YouTube tutorials. Make-up has the power to turn the ordinary into the extraordinary, and I need that. Brown curly hair, brown eyes, brown freckles, a rounded face lacking cheekbones and non-pouty lips. That was all I had on offer really, until I put make-up on. So, I gave myself a quick makeover and looked a million times better, if I do say so myself. Then I placed my phone on the dashboard of the car carefully, looked at the road in front of me, and drove forward. Slowly. Very slowly. I inched my way towards the sign, glancing down at my phone, watching and waiting. Waiting for the signal to die, waiting for that dreaded "no signal" exclamation mark to light up my screen, waiting for it to all finally come to an end. But when it did, even though I was expecting it, I hadn't expected the intense rush of emotions that flooded me.

I pulled over onto the side of the road and took my phone in my shaking hands. And then I held it to my chest and wept. I don't know why exactly I was crying, and I didn't even have my app to tell me. But it had something to do with the fact that, to me, this little palm-shaped lump of wires and glass and metal and buttons, had been my everything for years. It had taken me out of the lonely place when I didn't think it was possible for a human to feel any lonelier. It had given me friends, status, fame, a whole life, a network that I could plug into twenty-four hours a day, seven days a week, from anywhere in the world . . . except here. But then, just like that, like some fickle beast, it had turned on me. Blown up in my face and now . . . *now I had to turn it off.*

* * *

It was already eight p.m. when I arrived at the only hotel in town and checked in. I lay on the bed, looked up at the ceiling and watched the lonely fan going round and round and round, like some kind of hypnotic thing. It had been dark by the time I'd arrived—except for the ridiculous blue light that illuminated the road beneath my car, making it look like some futuristic UFO—so I hadn't really had much of a chance to look around, other than the few things I'd seen on the main road. My only concern had been getting to a bed, a place where I could lie flat on my back and rest.

I'd driven for eight hours straight and I was exhausted. Physically, emotionally, and also on some other level that I wasn't even sure I understood yet, and probably never would, since I couldn't check Google to find out. I turned over on the bed and looked at my phone. I had placed it on the side table to charge, like I always did. At night it usually came alive. Lighting up with DMs and likes and comments. I liked falling asleep to that, knowing that while I was sleeping, people were still there. But this time the phone was not lighting up. It was just . . . *dead.* For the first time in its life it really was just a lump of metal and wires and glass.

I sat up and sighed. I needed a distraction. This silence was too damn deafening. I reached into my bag to pull out my AirPods, only to realize I'd left them in a rucksack on the backseat of my car. I moaned loudly and made my way out again. The hotel I was staying at was old—the plaque at the reception said 1899. The architecture—not that I was some architectural expert (but I did have a very popular Pinterest board of interesting buildings)—was a mixture of Cape Dutch and Victorian. Some of the antiques in the room looked like they were actually from the 1800s and had been perfectly preserved and refurbished. A wooden wash-basin stand with a ceramic jug, an antique bedside table, and what looked like original black and white tiling in the bathroom with one of those old baths with claws. All in all, not really my taste, I preferred a more boho-chic vibe—it really photographs well for Insta—but I could still appreciate this. I walked out into the small street where I'd parked the blue cheese. I pressed the immobilizer and the blue lights under the car flickered on and off. #cringe. I opened the backseat and was just about to reach in when . . .

"Oh my God! How did you . . . What . . . CRAP!" I raced to the other side of the road, tripping over my feet as I went, and took cover behind a tree. My terrified heart thumped in my chest, pouring pure adrenalin into my veins. I stuck my head around the tree and looked back at my car. The faint overhead light was illuminating the horror in the backseat.

"You!" I hissed, squinting at the dog who'd clearly hitched a bloody ride with me. And he was not a dog you wanted hitching rides. This dog looked like it came straight from the fiery pits of hell.

"Rrruuufff," Satan's snaggletoothed helper yapped back at me.

"Out! Shoo. Go away. Out." I waved my arm at the thing, but he just cocked his head to the side and looked at me out of his one eye. God, he was an ugly mutt. Not something you would ever post on social media. Those influencers who post photos of their dogs and cats are smart. People like dogs. People like cats. They like dogs chasing their tails and getting confused when their owners disappear behind blankets. They like cats that fall off things and jump when they see cucumbers. But this dog . . . No! Nobody would like him, least of all me.

"Get out of here," I shouted across the road, but he didn't move.

"OUT!" I yelled, and this time, he climbed out the car. He stood there. Staring at me. Still as a statue.

Fear filled me. Tearful, panicky fear.

"Go away!" I jumped out from behind the tree and flapped my arms, hoping that would intimidate him. But it didn't. He was the biggest, blackest, meanest-looking devil dog I'd ever seen. If this dog was a person, he'd be one of those mean, tattooed-faced guys from a late-night mugshot—not that hot one that went viral and became a model—but the kind that if you looked into his eyes for too long, your blood curdled.

"What do you want from me?" I whimpered at him.

"Everything okay?" I heard a voice and whipped around. An older couple were looking at me.

"Who were you talking to, dear?" the old lady asked.

"That dog." I pointed. "It won't leave me alone."

They both turned in the direction I was pointing. Their faces were still for a while, and then they frowned.

"What dog, dear?" It was the little crouched-over man who spoke this time.

"That one." I turned and looked at the empty spot in the road where Snaggletooth had been only seconds ago, but he was gone. Again! I looked up and down the street like I had last time. Nothing.

"He was just there!" I said defensively. I didn't want them thinking I was seeing things.

They smiled at me. "Good night," the old woman said, before they both walked away.

I turned back to my car. The backdoor was still open, but the dog was gone. And for the second time that day, I had the same thought. *Was there even a dog?* Was I hallucinating? And if I was, what did it mean? And, oh crap, I so needed Google right now to find out.

CHAPTER 6

$\mathcal{I}$ woke up the next morning, rolled over and reached for my phone. I yawned, all warm and comfy and cuddly. I had slept well and felt relaxed as I lay in the bed. I opened Facebook, my usual morning ritual, to flip through the news while I woke. It's important for someone like me, a public figure, to know what's going on in the world, so I can make appropriate social commentary when necessary. Like when Notre Dame Cathedral burned down and I changed my profile picture to have that French flag filter. I scrolled a little, but nothing new came up on my feed. I kept scrolling. Still nothing new. I had seen this a few days ago. Why was my news feed not updating?

"*Shit!*" I sat up in bed and looked around. I really was here. This wasn't a bad dream ... I was in Springdorp, in the middle of the desert, in the only hotel in town, with no internet. I sighed loudly and flopped back down in bed. And then I remembered *why* I was here, and that same feeling hit me in my stomach. Icy at first. Then hot. I climbed out of bed and paced a few times.

My morning routine was disturbed, and I felt wildly unsettled. There were certain things I did in the morning when I woke up: check Facebook first, then Insta, Twitter, then check my emails, WhatsApp. Then go to my list app to see what I had planned for the day. Log my mood. Start the pedometer to count my steps. Then go to the app that planned my social media posts, my app that prior-itized my daily, weekly and yearly goals, my motivational app that provided me with thoughtful daily motivation, the app that tracked my heart rate; I might even check the weather for the week to start thinking about the kinds of outfits I could wear for my posts, and then, if there was time, spend some time interior-designing a room . . . *but I needed the internet for all of those.*

"Shit!" I paced some more. Everything felt wrong. I felt like I was free-falling. All the things that held me together and kept me in place were gone. And I needed to be kept in place. For most of my life I had felt out of control, and it wasn't until I decided to lose weight that I finally understood the importance of control. The importance of routine and repetition and all the small things that I did every single day that kept me focused and made me feel calm. And now all of that was gone, and I felt like I was falling apart.

Screw that elevator!

This had been the elevator's fault. If I hadn't run late for that shoot, I would still be with @TheKyleWhite101. We would be happy and I would still have my car and my followers and I wouldn't have made such an embarrassing public spectacle of myself, and I would *not* be here in this dark and dingy room with no bloody internet feeling like I was quickly unraveling. I walked over to the window and flung the curtains and—

"Youuuuuu," I rasped, dragging the word out as I caught the dark, lurking figure on the opposite side of the road. He was sitting there right by my car, as if he'd been there the whole time—which really made me question my mind. He was looking at my room, waiting and watching like a creepy little stalker. I mustered my courage and walked over to the door. I flung it open, but it hit the wall and then came flying back towards me and hit my arm.

"Crap! Ouch," I winced and looked down at my arm. A small cut had appeared and it was bleeding. I rushed to the bathroom and ran water over the cut and then dabbed it with some tissue paper. But then, I froze . . .

I turned slowly. *He* was sitting in my doorway now.

I grabbed onto the bathroom door, ready to slam it if he came rushing towards me. Only he didn't. He stood up and started wagging his tail. I wondered if this was some kind of ploy to lure me into thinking he was a nice dog. I didn't trust that tail wag at all. And when he stepped towards me, I slammed the bathroom door shut. I stayed there for at least five minutes before I opened it and peered outside. And when I did, I wasn't surprised to find him mysteriously disappeared once more.

* * *

I went to breakfast at around ten a.m. I'd spent an hour doing my make-up and straightening my hair—I needed to play out at least one of my usual morning routines to make me feel somewhat normal. But, even so, I was feeling anything but normal by the time I dragged myself there. Breakfast was one of those buffet vibes. Sausages, mushy scrambled eggs, bacon and mushrooms—nothing that looked Insta-worthy at all. Usually breakfast for me was a two-hour affair. I would wake up early to make it, usually a smoothie bowl. Do you know how competitive the #smoothiebowl art world is on Instagram? Getting likes takes hours of planning; cutting your fruit into cute heart shapes and placing it together perfectly with edible flowers, sprinkled chai seed patterns and then lighting it and getting just the right shot at just the right angle!

But lately it had been getting harder and harder to get likes. I mean, this one girl was making bloody unicorns out of frozen yoghurt. And this other vegan blogger was making her bowl look like a beach scene with turtles made of fruit on a beach of granola next to a swirling green and blue spirulina smoothie sea, for heaven's sake! It was no longer enough to put frozen berries on your smoothies, and that's why I'd been thinking of going keto—you can do a lot with an avo, you know!

I looked down at the pile of food on my plate; it didn't look appetizing at all, and a sudden need came over me. The need was so strong it was hard to resist. I tapped my fingers on the table and bit my lip, trying to push the need back down. But I couldn't. I took my phone out of my handbag and tapped it against the palm of my hand—this was usually something that calmed me. But not this time. It only made the need so much worse. So much more intense, too hard to resist. So. Bloody. Hard! I couldn't fight it any longer, and I wasn't going to.

I reached for another plate and started putting the food onto it in a more Insta-worthy way. Lining the bacon up by size, smallest to biggest, trying to make the mushrooms into something that resembled art. The sausage, I had to confess, was not photogenic at all. It was fat and oozing and its porky skin had burst open on one side, displaying its insides like a mass of intestines. I moved the decorative vase of wildflowers closer to my plate, hoping it would distract from the sausage. I looked around the room for something, anything, to make this breakfast shot better.

There were only two other people in the restaurant, and I recognized them as the couple I'd met last night. I tried not to make eye contact with them as I rushed over to one of the free tables and grabbed another small vase of wildflowers. I put my plate in the middle of the table, wildflowers flanking it on both sides, salt and pepper shaker on the right, a napkin tossed next to the plate—it took me ages to get that napkin just right. To make it looked tossed, but in a perfect, pretty way.

The light in here was bad. I looked around again—one of the curtains was closed so I walked up to it and pulled it open. A shaft of light rushed towards my table, casting a warm glow across the plate. I scurried back to the table, a manic, frantic energy seizing me, and held up my phone. But the angle was all wrong. I moved around the table, taking different photos, but nothing seemed right. I needed to take the shot from above, so I climbed onto my seat. I turned when I heard whispers behind me. The couple quickly looked away and went back to pecking at their heinous-looking breakfasts. I heard another noise and swiveled my whole body, only to find what looked like the chef standing in the corner of the room. His arms were folded and he was eyeing me curiously. I gazed at them all, and then had another consuming need. To share my thoughts with them in two hundred and eighty characters or less. The need to share something with them felt overwhelming, like the need to make the things on my plate look pretty and take a photo of them. I hadn't shared what I was doing with anyone in five days, and I usually shared everything! And in that moment, I felt like I was going to burst if I didn't tell someone something. Anything.

"Hashtag blogger's life." The words flew out of my mouth. They just looked at me blankly. So I shot them a thumbs up emoji, expecting some likes back in return, only I didn't get any. *What was wrong with these people?* Had they never seen anyone take a photo of their breakfast before? If you went out for breakfast in Joburg these days, everyone was taking photos of their food. No one ate their food when it arrived at the table anymore because everyone was trying to get the perfect #foodporn pic to post and . . .

The realization hit me again. Hit me like a kick to the gut. Why did I keep forgetting this? I looked at the almost-perfect picture of my breakfast and realized that I would *not* be able to post it. I would not be able to share my breakfast with the world, and for some reason that was once again hard to explain (especially without my mood-tracking app), this thought made me cry. I climbed down off the chair and slumped in my seat. I pushed my plate away and buried my head on the table and wept like a total idiot.

CHAPTER 7

"*A*re you okay?" I heard a voice behind me and peeped around. The chef was standing there.

"I'm thinking of going keto," I said, and then suddenly didn't know why I'd said that.

The man smiled. "I'm not sure I know what you mean."

I lifted my head and looked at him. "Hashtag keto life." I said this almost under my breath.

His smile grew; it seemed genuinely warm and sympathetic. "Again, I'm not sure I know what you mean. But is the breakfast okay?" He indicated my plate, and I looked at it and sighed.

"I actually don't eat breakfast," I said.

He scrunched his face up. "Now I really don't understand."

"I don't eat breakfast," I repeated.

"But you just spent ten minutes taking a photo of it?"

I nodded. "Yes."

"Well, is there something special you would like me to make you instead of this?" he asked.

I shook my head. "No. I really don't eat breakfast. I just take photos of it."

"What do you do with the breakfast after you've taken a photo of it?"

I shrugged. "Sometimes my boyfriend eats it, but now . . . now . . ." I moaned loudly. "I don't have a boyfriend anymore because he's probably taking photos of his special couple breakfast with

@Paige_Dreams_. I bet they're keto now too, you know how popular going keto is? I bet they tagged it hashtag breakfastgoals or hashtag foodgasm or hashtag ketocouple. You know they have a ship name already? It's Kaige. Can you imagine that!"

The man reached out and laid a hand on my shoulder. It was a massive hand. The man was huge. One of the tallest people I'd seen. But not in an imposing way. Like a gentle giant. "There, there," he said, and passed me a serviette.

"Our ship name would have been Fyle or Krankie. How terrible is that?"

The man continued to pat my shoulder. "I'm sure I should know what you're talking about, but really, lass, I don't. But I can see you're upset. Would you like to have a coffee with me and chat for a while?"

"You want to have coffee with me and chat?" I was taken aback.

"Sure."

"What kind of coffee?" I wondered if he could do those things with the colored frothed milk that made it look like you had dolphins and flamingos in your cappuccino. Those made such good Insta pics.

He smiled at me. "Nothing fancy. But it looks like you could do with a friend right now."

I almost opened my mouth and told him that if he wanted to be my friend he could follow me on @FitspoFrankie, but didn't. I shook my head. "I'm okay," I said. "I'm going to be okay. Everything is okay and perfectly normal and fine and okay."

The man gave me a slow, sad smile. "Lass, when you're taking photos of your breakfast and not eating it, something is not okay."

It was the first time I'd taken note of his accent. It was thick and had a sing-song quality to it. I didn't know exactly where he was from, but I was guessing the Scottish Highlands. For a moment I imagined him in a kilt, but pushed the image out of my mind.

"Something is definitely not okay," he repeated and then I seemed to hear his words for the first time.

If I was taking photos of my breakfast and not eating it, something was not okay!

The strangeness of it hit me all at once. I had never thought about it before. But having someone point it out to me, in a place like this, it suddenly sounded so absurd. For years I'd been taking photos of my breakfast—and not just any photos, ones that were perfectly crafted and curated and styled and filtered—and in all that time I'd never eaten any of it. Not once. Not one tiny morsel of my perfect breakfast had ever touched my overlined lips. I threw my hands up in the air, looked over at the chef, and then I started laughing. He looked nervous for a few moments, as if trying to decide whether it was okay to laugh along with me, or whether my laughter was a sign of bad things to come. But then he threw his head back and also laughed.

"Now that's the spirit, lass," he said. "Laughter is the best medicine, isn't it?" He had this big, hearty laugh, the kind you would expect from a red-bearded Scotsman type. It was deep and throaty and felt like it was the kind of laugh that could reverberate through walls. It wasn't forced or fake either. It was authentic and genuine and suddenly I felt desperately sad. In the face of his obvious authenticity, I felt so suddenly inauthentic. *Posting pictures and not eating breakfast.* I was a fake breakfast eater! I was a liar, sharing my #nom-nom breakfast and telling everyone how delicious it was, but never actually eating it. My laughter stopped abruptly and the Scotsman also stopped. I felt the tears in my eyes again, and I tried to bite them back.

"Now, now, that's less of the spirit, lass," he said, as tears started rolling down my cheeks. I was getting quite hysterical. I could feel it like a rubber band inside me being pulled until it was about to snap. I turned and watched the couple in the other part of the restaurant get up and walk out, eyeing me suspiciously as they went.

"This was a bad idea," I finally said. "Coming here, to this town. This was such a stupid idea."

"How do you figure that when you haven't even been here for twenty-four hours?" he asked.

"How do you know how long I've been here?"

"Small town. Tiny hotel."

I nodded and slumped back down onto the table again.

"You know what you need?" he asked.

"What?" I looked up at him from my face plant on the tablecloth.

"You need to go outside and get some fresh air. A walk in the Karoo fixes everything."

"Does it?"

He nodded. "There is a quiet magic here in the desert—it has a way of seeping into your soul and making you new again."

"Really?" I asked thoughtfully.

"Truly. There is something very spiritual about this place if you just tune into it."

"I see," I mumbled under my breath, even more thoughtful now. *Mmmm . . . Spiritual. Soul seeping. Making you new.*

I lifted my head a little.

"Spiritual?" I repeated slowly.

"Very," he said.

"I see." I sat up straight now.

"You have to be open to it though." He almost whispered this part, as if it was some great secret.

"Open, you say . . ." I stood up out of my chair when it dawned on me. Going out into the desert on a kind of sojourn of self-discovery would make amazing content! I could take photos of myself out there in the quiet emptiness under the setting sun. #soulsearching

"You know what, you're right. I am all about making myself new. I'm all about inspiring and discovering and exploring and getting to know myself and nature. And my followers love journeys of self-discovery, hashtag spiritualawakening."

"Uh . . . yeah, no!" he said flatly and then that giant hand reached out again. That huge one with the red fluff on the freckled knuckles.

"I'm not really sure that's what I meant, lass. I meant something spiritual that was just for you."

I looked at him and scrunched my face up. "Why would I do something just for me?" I shook my head. What was the point of doing something if it couldn't be shared? Not that I could share it right now, but I could keep it for later. Kyle always said that if we did something that wasn't worthy of posting about, then we might as well not do it.

"So, how do I get into this desert?" I asked.

He smiled again; this time it did look forced. "We're sort of surrounded by it."

I nodded. "So I should just walk out this door and, what—carry on walking out of the town and into the desert?"

"Exactly."

"Right!" I nodded at him. "I can do that! I am going to go and find myself and have a spiritual awakening in the desert." And with that, I walked straight out.

"Good luck," he shouted after me.

Luck! I scoffed. Why would I need luck if I was walking towards enlightenment?

CHAPTER 8

I could see my new vlog. It would be amazing. It could start when I got back from my spiritual awakening in the barren desert. Alone, under the sun, only the grasshoppers to keep me company. Instead of posting workouts in the gym, squatting in my new gym clothes and wearing the latest make-up, I would take photos of myself meditating and doing yoga at sunset. I would definitely go vegan, maybe even raw vegan. I would stop bleaching my hair, let it grow and embrace the curls. Maybe I would even add blue mermaid streaks to it and beads. I needed a new wardrobe for this, obviously. I couldn't wear Adidas sports gear anymore, I needed something flowing, something that spoke to my new spiritual vibe. I could partner with essential oil companies, and do yoga retreats and all that stuff, and I would no longer be fake and inauthentic.

Yes, I was determined to have a spiritual experience out here and let that be my new defining brand voice. Frankie, who ran away from it all, who turned to the solace and quiet of the desert and found herself. Ha! I bet you @TheKyleWhite101 would hate that, if I swooped back in with a totally new angle. It would be me saying that I didn't need him anymore because I had found me. The real me. And then people would like me again and I would be somebody once more.

I excitedly started writing new posts in my head; I would need a completely new vocabulary for my new persona. I would need to be all chakra and chi. Mantra and mindfulness. Awakened and looking out of my third eye with crystal healing clarity. I would need to change my name, of course, @FengShuiFrankie maybe.

I walked to the end of the main street in town. It ended abruptly and the tar crumbled away into sand and rocks. I loved the sound of the rocky ground under my shoes; it would make a great ASMR video. But my gosh it was hot out here, and it was autumn! Heat pressed down on me like an iron to clothing. It was suffocating and I could really do without it while trying to have my spiritual reawakening—it was very distracting.

I walked some more. The ground was flat and small, dry bushes were the only things that dotted the landscape. Some shoots of yellow grasses seemed to be clinging onto life. In front of me, huge mountain ranges rose up. Everything was a reddish brown here, no green in sight. The sky was blue and completely cloudless. I wiped my brow as I walked. Crap, I didn't know how much longer I could put up with this weather. My spiritual awakening better bloody come soon, because all I wanted now was to be in the shade, a glass of iced water in hand. I shielded my face from the sun with my hands—I should have brought a hat. And worn sunscreen! But I hadn't thought of any of that as I'd marched out the restaurant and straight into this godforsaken place.

God, it was quiet out here! Unnervingly so. I looked back over my shoulder; the town was still right behind me, I hadn't even gone that far. And then, out of the corner of my eye, I caught a streak of black movement. I swung around so fast I almost lost my balance. It was Satan's Little Helper, and he was watching me.

I held my hand up at him. "Oh, you would, would you? Come out here and follow me like this."

"Rrruuuff!"

I glared at him. "Whatever! I don't care anyway, because I'm about to have a spiritual reawakening. Besides, I'm not even sure you're real! I think you might be some kind of figment of my imagination!" I looked away from him and then threw my head in the air and marched as fast as I could into the dry, brittle shrubbery. He started walking too, about ten meters away from me, mirroring my steps. I stopped, and he stopped. I walked again, and he walked. Stopped. Walked. Stopped.

This was getting ridiculous. I was being followed around by the world's ugliest dog, who might or might not be a hallucination. Or wait . . . maybe this was all part of my spiritual experience. Maybe the black dog was actually a metaphor for something else? But let's get real—what the hell would a hideous black dog be a metaphor for anyway?

I started jogging now, jumping over prickly shrubs as I went. God, it was hot. I didn't know how much longer I could keep this up. Satan's Little Helper was also jogging, and then, all of a sudden, he changed pace and started racing towards me. His tongue was hanging out of his mouth and he was panting. He looked determined and started barking frantically. I ran faster and faster, but then he was in front of me. I almost fell over him as he came to an abrupt stop. A massive cloud of red dust shot into the air and I could feel it in my eyes and taste it in my mouth.

"What are you doing?" I groaned, wiping the dust out of my eyes. His barking grew louder and now it had been joined by deep, throaty growls. With the dust out of my eyes, I could finally see what he was barking at, and when I did—

"SNAKE!" Mother-effing, head-rearing, fang-showing, scaly and coiled, bloody snake. I froze for a second. It was very inconvenient. I had wished that my innate, instinctual response could have been more of the "flight" variety, but I guess I was a freezer. Luckily, some common sense finally kicked in a few seconds later and my freeze ended with a very fast turn and run the hell out of there!

I ran as fast as I could, not caring that the dry grass and shrubs were scratching at my ankles. And I didn't stop running until I reached my hotel room. When I got there, I looked back over my shoulder for the first time. Satan's Little Helper wasn't behind me, and neither was the snake. I threw myself into my room and tried to catch my breath. I was so relieved to be out of that stupid desert.

Spiritual shmiritual awakening, my bloody ass. What awakening can you have out there amongst the dry, decrepit landscape with a snake in your face? There was nothing spiritual about the desert, nothing spiritual about me. What had I been thinking, reinventing myself as some kind of enlightened, guru blogger? I looked down at my ankles which were now streaked red with blood, the color looking hideous against my now fading Tropical Days spray tan, one of my former product partners. I was pouring with salty, sticky sweat and gasping for air. I wiped my face with the back of my hand and a brown smear of foundation came off on it. I was sure the skin on my face was sunburnt too, because it was stinging. I was sure a thorn had pierced my foot because I could feel something pricking there, and I was sure that I absolutely fucking hated it here. *I needed to get away from this place.*

What had I been thinking? A social media detox?! I hadn't heard of anything more stupid in my life and yet, here I was. What was wrong with me?

I couldn't do this! I needed reception and Wi-Fi like I needed water to drink and air to breathe. I had never needed anything so badly in my entire life and I felt like I was drowning in this intense longing for something I couldn't have. I couldn't stay here a second longer.

CHAPTER 9

⌒

$\mathcal{I}$ rushed over to the cupboard and pulled out my suitcase, grabbing fistfuls of clothing as I went. Shoes and shirts and dresses all shoved into the bottom of my case. I'd once done a Smart Packing Life Hack video on my vlog, one where I showed everyone how to pack effectively by rolling T-shirts into little Swiss rolls, which got over 500,000 views. But now, I couldn't be bothered.

When the suitcase was packed, I turned my attention to my scattered make-up bags and brushes and lip kits. I gathered up the beauty debris and shoved them into my oversized handbag. One last look around the room, then I threw some cash down on the bed for my stay and I ran. Out the door, leaving it wide open—I wasn't going to waste a second more closing it. I raced across the street and straight to the bright blue cheese. I rummaged through my bag for the car keys and found them. Then I went back in for the immobilizer and rummaged some more . . . and rummaged some more . . . and rummaged some more . . . and mother-effing more! Where the hell was that stupid little grey thing?

"Nooo," I whined loudly and raced back into the room like the Road Runner. You remember that cartoon, right? Where Wile E. Coyote is always trying to catch Road Runner as he tears down the road; a flurry of feet and feathers and smoke trailing behind him, *"Beep, Beep!"*

Well, I was like that as I arrived at the room and began turning it upside-down. Under the bed, bottom of cupboard, under pillows, duvet, down the side of the small sofa, I even pulled the corners of the carpets back. I was sweaty and desperate and on my hands and knees peering under the night stand when I felt it . . . again!

"Oh nooooo." I hung my head and shook it. I knew what I was going to see when I turned around.

"What do you want this time?" I asked sarcastically, turning to face the black dog. "And don't just say *bark!* Not that I would understand you if you said anything else, not that you can say anything else . . . Oh God, whatever! I can't be talking to a dog now. I'm in a hurry, I need the immobilizer—*what car still even has one of those anyway*—and you know what? I actually don't care what you want, or if you're even real. I don't care if you are a weird figment of my imagination." I stood up and started walking towards the dog. It straightened up. "You know what? You are far too big for your own good! Your fur is way too wire-like and you have one eye, you creature from the bog or wherever you come from—" I stopped and gasped in shock when I saw it. Because there, dangling from Satan's snaggletooth . . . the little grey immobilizer.

I smiled down at him, changing my tune immediately. "Doggy! Pretty little cute, uh . . ." I held my hand out tentatively, moving it closer and closer to the grey button that was dangling from the big, ugly tooth. "Preeeettty please, big guy. Give me the key. I'll give you a yummy treat. Yummy for your tummy." I rolled my eyes. Okay, I didn't know how to talk to dogs. This was very obvious. I had never owned one. I crept a little closer and then deliberately made eye contact with him. I tried to communicate with my eyes to his eye (singular), that I really, really needed that immobilizer. And it seemed to be working because he cocked his head to the side and his jaw loosened somewhat, as if he was about to drop it to the floor.

"Thank Go— NO! NO!" I yelled, watching in horror as he threw his head back and the immobilizer vanished down his black mouth.

"You didn't!" I rushed over. I was no longer afraid of him, he might not even be real, after all. I reached for his mouth and pulled it open, looking inside. (Although that did feel very real.) It wasn't there though, and because I think I had watched something like it on a medical drama, I ran to the back of the dog, put my arms around his body and began some animal version of the Heimlich maneuver. But he was heavy, and I was only able to jerk him ever so slightly.

"Spit! It! Out!" I said with each pull. But nothing happened. He simply sat there, looking at me over his shoulder as I tried to shake the key out of him. At last, my arms could no longer handle the weight of him, and I collapsed onto my back and lay there looking at the ceiling.

"You swallowed my car immobilizer," I whimpered. "And now I can't get out of here. I'm stuck!" And then, for the one hundredth time in the last couple of days, I cried. And then I laughed. I laugh/cried. I laughed so hard that I choked on the tears, and snorted and hiccupped until my ribs hurt. I looked to my left. Satan's Little Helper sat there looking at me with his one yellow eye. I stopped laughing and wiped the tears from my face. I propped myself up on my elbow and glared at him.

"God, you are so damn ugly."

"Ruufff!"

"Did you do this to me because I didn't thank you for saving me from that snake?" I asked. "Is that why you're punishing me?" This time he didn't bark. "You know, I would have seen that snake anyway. It's not like you saved my life." I glared at him again and he glared straight back. "Fine, thank you for saving me from that snake, now will you please give the immobilizer back?" I held my hand out and watched and waited for him to miraculously spit it out. He didn't, so I flopped back down to the floor and lay flat on my back again. And then something strange happened. Satan slid down too, lying next to me. I watched as he carefully rested his head on my foot, and then breathed out as if he was relaxing. We lay there for a while, until it hit me and I sat up again. It hadn't even crossed my mind, until now.

"Wait, you swallowed an immobilizer! Oh my God. You could die!" I jumped up and rushed over to my phone, only to realize that I couldn't call 112. Do you even call 112 for animals? What the hell was I supposed to do? I rushed around the room a few times. Uber, I could call an Uber to take me to a ve— Shit, no Uber. I raced some more—I could post on Quora: 'What to do if your dog swallows an immobilizer?" Wait, no Google, and there was probably a subreddit for this too! I threw my arms in the air and called out to no one in particular. And then I stopped rushing as my sister's face flew into my mind. I could see her rolling her eyes at me now, at this "Frances fiasco" as she was so fond of calling them. She was younger than me and yet she had this uncanny ability to make me feel like I was a child all over again. Blowing things out of proportion. Making mountains out of molehills. So I took a long, deep breath and calmed myself down.

What the hell do you do without the internet? "Right! Be calm," I told myself as I looked down at Satan's Little Helper. He'd raised his head and eyed me curiously.

"Can you walk?" I asked, which was ridiculous. Why was I talking to a dog as if it were a human? A dog I still wasn't one hundred percent sure was even real. I'd seen a small vet's practice on the main road when I'd driven into town, it was only a few blocks away, on the same road as the hotel now that I thought about it. I clicked my fingers together a few times and Satan's Helper rose to his feet as if he understood me.

"Okay, let's go." I turned and walked out the hotel room, the dog hot on my heels.

CHAPTER 10

*W*e arrived at the house that had the small "Vet" sign hanging outside it. Like all the other houses, it was a typical Karoo home; blue and white Victorian, with a tin roof and a big wraparound veranda. This veranda was crammed full of pot plants so there was almost nowhere to sit. The door was closed, and an old brass bell hung from the wall. I rang it and waited for an answer. I didn't have to wait long and soon the door was being opened by a short, very pregnant-looking woman. I glanced down at the name badge on her white coat. Doctor Samirah Shaik Umar.

"Hi, are you the vet?" I asked, although the presence of the name badge did seem to render this question rather redundant.

She smiled and nodded. "As far as I know."

"Right! Okay, weird question, before we go any further: can you see this dog?" I pointed down at him and held my breath in anticipation of her answer. The moment where I would discover, beyond a reasonable shadow of a doubt, whether or not I was losing my grip on reality.

She looked at him and smiled again. "Of course."

"Phew!" I breathed a sigh of relief and then giggled. "That's good." She looked at me strangely so I quickly cleared my throat and added, "Just checking, you know?" I'm sure she didn't know, but anyway.

"What can I do for you?" she asked breezily.

"This dog needs a doctor," I said.

"Well, come in then. The practice is out back." She held the door open, and I followed her down a long, narrow passage, wooden floorboards creaking, as if there was something trapped in them, wanting to come out. We walked out the house and into a small garden cottage out back. Not exactly what I'd been expecting, but this was a small town.

She pushed the door open and we entered a little white room with a big silver table in the middle of it. I'd never been into a veterinary practice before, my mom hadn't believed in animals, growing up. Too dirty. Too costly. Too unhygienic. My mother was a nurse before she retired, and she was always pointing out how full of germs something was or wasn't. Not to mention how full of calories something was or wasn't.

"So, you must be new here." She extended her hand for me to shake. "I'm Samirah, and you are . . .?"

I grabbed her hand and shook it. "Frankie," I said quickly. "How do you know I'm new?"

She smiled at me. "Small town. I know every person and every pet in this entire town."

"You do?" I asked.

She nodded. "And I treat them all. There are seven hundred and eighty-nine residents here with six hundred and thirteen pets of some kind."

I nodded at her, although I wasn't sure why she was telling me this.

"Although," she leaned in and whispered, "I definitely prefer some over the others. Denis Gutterman's parrot, for instance," she shook her head, "every time you turn around it says, 'Nice buns, sweetie.' Total pervert! And then there's Dottie's Persian, Babushka; she gives that cat so much catnip, it's always bumping into tables or falling off the roof." She shook her head and turned her attention to Satan's Helper. "And who's this handsome guy?" she asked.

I laughed. "Handsome? That would be the last thing in the world I would call him."

But she nodded. "He looks like he's really lived. Seen and done it all. What's his name?"

"It's Sat—" I stopped. I didn't think I could say that out loud. "He's not my dog. I saw him on the side of the road, and then he climbed into my car and came here with me. I have no idea who he belongs to. And now he's following me around. Not my dog."

She stopped talking and eyed me strangely. There was something very mystical and guru-like about the way she was looking at me. Perhaps it was her eyes. She had huge eyes, outlined in thick black liner. She had an olive complexion, but her eyes were a pale green color. That, combined with the dark lines around them, gave them a very mysterious look. "He's adopted you," she said.

I shrugged. "Against my will and totally by accident."

"There are no such things as accidents," she mumbled, as she opened Satan's mouth and started inspecting his teeth. "This is clearly your dog. He has chosen you. And, therefore, you have chosen him too."

I shook my head and rolled my eyes as she looked inside his one upright ear. The one that stood up and didn't flop down.

"No. No. Trust me, I did not choose him. If I had to choose a dog, it would not look like this. I mean, I can't even photograph him. He is so not hashtag dogs of Instagram, if you know what I mean?" I said.

She looked at me strangely again, and then a slow massive smile seemed to spread across her face. "Definitely your dog!"

"Definitely *not* my dog, but anyway," I said defensively.

"So why have you brought him here?" she asked.

"Because he swallowed my car immobilizer, and I need it back so I can leave. I have to get home," I said, even though technically I no longer had a home, but that was just a tiny detail I would need to iron out later. My sister did have a spare bedroom and if worse came to worst, I suppose she might let me stay there for a while . . . or would she?

She chuckled. "Maybe he's trying to tell you something by keeping you here."

I tutted. "Keeping me here, that's ridiculous. Dogs don't think like that, he just swallowed it because he's a dog. That's what dogs do. They swallow stuff."

Her smile grew even more. All mysterious and mystical again; who was this woman? A vet or some pet psychic?

"He's not my dog," I mumbled one more time, starting to get a little pissed off that I kept having to explain myself.

"Suuuuure." She really stretched that word out and then bent down and stroked his head. "Hey, big guy, did you swallow your mom's car keys?"

"Not his mom," I interrupted her.

She seemed to ignore me and rubbed his belly. She did it slowly and carefully and then gave a loud, "Uuummm."

I stiffened. "What? Is he okay . . .? I mean . . ." I cleared my throat uncomfortably and looked down at him. This sudden pang of concern I was having felt very strange and wildly inconvenient.

"For someone who isn't his mom, seems like you care a lot."

"I don't. I just want the thing back so I can leave this place."

She stood up again. It looked like it was hard for her to get around, and she confirmed this when she grabbed her belly with one hand and the table with the other. And that's when I noticed just how pregnant she was. I mean, I knew she was pregnant, but she was huge. "How big was the immobilizer?" she asked, sounding out of breath. I stared at her stomach for a moment and wondered if it would be rude to ask how big her baby was.

"Twins," she offered.

My eyes flicked up to hers quickly, embarrassed I'd been staring. "Sorry." I blushed. "It's just you're so . . ." I stopped talking and zipped my lips together.

"Big? Huge? Massive? Beachball-like?" she asked, a smile on her face now. It was clear I hadn't offended her.

I nodded. "Yes!" I matched her smile. "I mean, you really are."

She nodded. "I know. And I'm only going to get bigger." She rubbed her belly and looked down at it. That was hard to imagine. "So, the immobilizer," she said, coming back to our previous conversation, "how big did you say it was?"

"Small. One of those small plastic things." I demonstrated the size with my fingers.

She nodded. "Should be fine then. We'll just have to wait for it to pass. I don't feel any tenderness or swelling in the belly, he seems to be in no pain, so it's just a waiting game for now."

"What do you mean, waiting game?"

"Well, he should pass it naturally."

"Pass it?" I looked at her and blinked. I think I knew what she was saying, but I needed it confirmed.

"With a bowel movement," she added.

"Umm . . ." I stared down at the dog now, the picture starting to form in my mind. The fact he would need to crap out my car immobilizer. I cringed at the thought.

"It should take about twenty-four hours or so. Depending."

"Depending on what?" I asked.

"Depending on the size of the bowel, how much is in the bowel, how long it takes for it to travel down the bowel."

"When will you know when it happens? How long will you keep him?"

She smiled. "I'm not keeping him. He's not sick. Besides, I don't have any space for him."

"Well, how am I meant to . . . you know. When he's . . . you know."

"Passed the immobilizer?"

"Yes."

"I would recommend a sieve," she said.

"A WHAT?"

"You can buy one at Jim's Everyday Store. I'll give you some gloves too—"

"WAIT! No!" I cut her off. "I am not sifting through Satan's Little Helper's poop! I am not doing that."

"Satan's little what?"

"Helper."

She frowned at me.

"You know in *The Simpsons* they have that ugly dog called Santa's Little Helper?"

"No, not really," she replied.

"Well, he reminded me of him, only he looks like he works for the guy with the other name that starts with an S—you know what I mean." I looked down at the floor and her eyes followed me. "The guy downstairs," I added.

She looked up at me after looking at the floor for a while and then shook her head. "That's a terrible name for a dog. Truly terrible."

"He's not my dog!" I was getting very frustrated. "And, as such, I am definitely not looking through his poop, or giving him a better name!"

"Do you have a spare immobilizer then?" she asked.

"No. It's a rental."

She shrugged. "Well, then . . ." She grabbed some gloves out of a box and planted them in my hand. "Bring him back here immediately if he starts vomiting or showing signs of lethargy and not eating."

"I'm not feeding him," I said. "I found him. He's not my dog."

She smiled again. "I'll give you some food and a bowl, you can bring the bowl back once you're done."

"Wait, you don't understand. This isn't my dog. He must have an owner somewhere. They are probably looking for him. I bet there's someone out there right now calling his *real* name over and over again."

Dr Samirah picked up a kind of scanner and waved it over his neck. "No microchip, no collar, he's still got his goods." She pointed

at the dog's backside and I looked, only to see the goods she was talking about hanging there. "His nails look like they haven't been
clipped in forever, he could do with a good bath and a general trim.
I don't think anyone is looking for him, or has been for a very long
time. I think he's found his someone."

"Me? You think I'm his someone?" I shook my head. "No."

She smiled again, all sagey and guru-ish with her mysterious
green eyes. "Try and keep him confined to a small space so he doesn't
wander off and do his business where you don't see it. And you may
want a collar and leash so you can keep him close. I have a spare one
hanging on the back of the front door, you can grab it on the way out.
Also, taking him for a long walk can stimulate the bowels. Good
luck! Keep me posted and bring him back the second you have any
concerns."

I was trying to take this all in as I walked out of the practice, grabbing the leash and collar she told me about. Apparently, I had a dog
now and apparently, I was meant to run around with a sieve and . . . I
cringed. I couldn't even think about it. And twenty-four hours or so,
what the hell was I meant to do to keep busy?

I felt itchy just thinking about all those hours stretching in front
of me with nothing to do. What does one do without a phone? I felt
so alone and disconnected from the world once more. As if someone
had unplugged me from it.

CHAPTER 11

I stood on the street, feeling a deep sense of loss and aloneness in the pit of my stomach. I looked down at Satan's Little Helper and sighed.

"I guess we're stuck with each other, but only for a while." I wagged my finger at him. "Don't think this makes you my dog, regardless of what she says. Okay?" I waited. "Now would be a good time to bark so I know that you understand what I'm saying."

Still nothing.

"Great, *now* you're silent." I turned away from the vet's house and started walking up the street. I had no idea where I was going, or what I was going to do for the next day, but I supposed buying a sieve would be the first thing. I surveyed the street; you couldn't get lost in this place, it seemed so small—well, I hoped so, because I didn't have Google Maps with me, a thought that left me feeling even more uncomfortable.

At the end of the street, like all these small Karoo towns, a huge church steeple rose up and dominated the view. Small, pastel blue-and-yellow-painted houses with little verandas lined the streets. No one had fences here, or if they did, they were waist high at most, you could easily climb over them. The road was empty, apart for an old double cab that drove past me. It was ancient, rusty and the exhaust pipe spluttered. In the back, a boy sat and, on his lap, a sheep! A big, fluffy sheep! I reached into my pocket and scrabbled for my phone, this would make such a great Instagr—

I stopped scrabbling and stood still. I didn't have Instagram. I couldn't take a photo of this and share it with the world. I couldn't shout it out to the universe that I had seen a boy sitting in the back of a double cab with a sheep. Anxiety bubbled up inside me and this desire to take a pic and post it made me want to scream out loud. I needed to share it with someone. Because if I didn't tell someone—anyone—about it then it felt less real in some way. Almost as if I hadn't seen it at all. Or that seeing it wasn't important or interesting, until someone told me it was. I looked down; Satan's Little Helper was looking up at me curiously, as if he was wondering why I'd stopped walking. I rolled my eyes at him and continued my stroll down this empty, lonely street. At least I would get some extra steps in today, #tenthousandstepsaday. Unfortunately, I wouldn't be able to tell anyone about this either. So what was the point?

It was so quiet here. Quiet like I'd never heard quiet before. Quiet in a bad way. I liked to feel like something was going on around me at all times, it kept me feeling a part of something. Here, I felt a part of nothing, other than silence. If I was disconnected from all those hundreds of thousands of people, did I even exist? Existential questions that I really wish I wasn't thinking seemed to be bashing about in my brain, and I didn't like it one little bit. They were on a par with questions about sounds of trees falling in the forest and all.

I finally found the general dealer, and because the shop was so small, I quickly located a sieve and some snack bars, the healthiest things in the shop, although I couldn't use my calorie-tracking app to check. I walked up to the counter. An older woman with long hair and lines etched into her face looked up at me.

"Hi, you must be new here," she said, as I placed the stuff on the counter.

I nodded at her. Did everyone in town know each other?

"Oh, and looky here. Who is this guy?" She walked around the counter, reached down and stroked Satan's head. He rubbed it against her knee like a cat and I glared down at him. Where was the loyalty? He hadn't rubbed his head against my knee and look what I'd done for him. He turned and looked at me with that single eye, and I narrowed my eyes at him.

"What a great dog," she said. I almost laughed. "So much character."

"Character" was right.

"I'm Jim's wife, Natasha, but you can call me Tash—everyone does. I run the store in the mornings." She held her hand out and I looked at it. Then I reached out and took it tentatively. She gripped it hard. "And you are?" She leaned in.

"Frankie," I said.

"Frankie! What a unique name. Is it a nickname or does it mean something special?" she asked.

"Uh, it's a nickname. My real name is Frances."

She looked me up and down and then gave the biggest smile. "I love it. Suits you much better than Frances. Of course, my husband is actually James, but everyone calls him Jim. I think that nicknames often suit people more than their real names, don't you?"

"I suppose. I haven't really thought about it," I replied rather flatly, feeling confused by this sudden, unprompted conversation.

"So where are you from?" she asked, not even bothering to ring up my sieve and snacks. In fact, she'd put her elbows on the counter and was resting her chin on her hands as if she had all the time in the world to talk to me. "What brings you to our special little town?"

I shrugged. Because right now, I didn't fucking know why I was here.

She smiled and nodded at me. "Looking to get away from the rat race, from all the chaos and noise?" she asked, not letting it go. Why was she so determined to have a conversation with me? Under normal circumstances I might have picked my phone up and looked at the screen, to give her the impression I was far too busy for this conversation. If she wanted to talk to me, DM me, for heaven's sake! But I didn't have a phone to hide behind and that left me feeling very exposed. I had never been comfortable with social interactions. Being an overweight teen will do that to you. Each social interaction becomes an opportunity for bullying, so you just land up avoiding everyone altogether. I had found that hiding behind my phone had been a great way of avoiding things, only now I didn't have it.

"How long do you think you'll be staying with us?" she continued in a merry, chirpy voice.

"I don't know yet." I looked down at Satan's backside. "That depends on a few factors," I said rather pointedly to the dog, and he looked up at me as if he understood.

"Well, welcome to Springdorp. We love having visitors here with us. Have you been given the town social schedule yet?"

I shook my head.

She turned and reached behind the counter, pulling out a handwritten piece of paper that looked like it had been copied. "Here." She passed it to me.

I scanned the words on it. *Games Night. Quiz Night. Movie Night. Murder Mystery Night.*

"What is this?" I asked.

"Our social activities."

"Wait, you all get together and do things?" I asked. "The whole town?"

She nodded. "Sure. Not all of us all the time, but most of us."

Murder Mystery Night. A chill ran up my spine. Where was I? Please tell me I hadn't wandered into one of these spooky, serial-killer towns full of axe-wielding people that did that thing where they welcomed in strangers with big open arms, only to slice their arms off days later? In fact, now that I thought about it, everyone in this town did seem rather friendly. *Too* friendly. The man willing to cook me a custom-made breakfast, who comforted me when I'd cried. The vet with her big smiles, and now this lady. Alarm bells went off in the back of my mind. People were *not* this friendly. People did not smile so much and want to know so many things about you—not IRL anyway. I took a step back from the counter and then pulled my wallet out. It was thick with cash as I'd drawn as much money as possible before coming here, after reading the warning about there being no ATMs in town.

She looked down at my wallet and smiled again. "Came prepared," she said.

I pulled out some notes and put them on the table.

"Most people who come here don't know that we don't have any ATMs. If you're prepared, are you planning on staying a while?"

"I don't know," I mumbled under my breath.

"Do you like books?" she asked suddenly.

I looked up at her suspiciously. "I guess. Maybe."

"Some of us ladies have a book club on a Thursday evening. We don't put it on the calendar because then everyone will come, and we like our little group. But if you'd like to come?" she asked me.

Why was she asking me? She didn't even know me. "I haven't read a book in ages," I said. "Well, not one with pages anyway."

She gave me a curious, confused look. "What kind of book doesn't have pages?" she asked.

"An eBook," I stated.

She cocked her head to the side. "What's that?"

"Um . . . you buy them on Amazon."

"The Amazon?" she said, sounded utterly intrigued.

"Yes."

"What kind of books are those? From the Amazon?"

My jaw dropped. My eyes widened. My mind boggled. "So, you were born and raised here, I take it?" I asked, already knowing the answer to this question.

She nodded proudly. "Our family are direct descendants of the original Ackerman family who settled here in 1859 and founded this town."

"How interesting," I said, although I didn't mean it at all, but this seemed to be the right response, because she smiled at me.

"Here." She turned around and took something else off the shelf. "If you're interested in it, you should come to our annual town festival." She passed me the piece of paper.

"The Spring Festival," I read. "But it's autumn."

She laughed at my joke, a joke I wasn't even sure I understood. "It's a yearly festival that celebrates the arrival of the Ackermans to this town. They suffered a terrible drought on their original farm. So they took the whole family and what remaining livestock they had and headed out into the desert in search of water and a place to build a new farm. They were almost on the brink of death when they finally arrived here and found the spring."

I nodded. "So, spring, as in *water* spring."

"Exactly. And each year the whole town reenacts their journey down the main street, and we end it at the spring with some music, a large braai and a party."

"I'm sorry . . . you reenact it?" Oh. My. God. More alarm bells went off in my head. This sounded totally cultish, and I wondered what they braaied at the spring. A human sacrifice?

"It's a tradition we've kept going for over fifty years. My father started it. But if you ask me, these days it's more an excuse for a big party." She winked at me. I hated winky face emojis, I always thought they showed no imagination. So generic. I mean, put some effort into your emojis, for heaven's sake. Personally, I spend hours thinking about what emojis to use and under what circumstances. I choose them according to color and theme and what message I want to convey. But I found myself responding to her winky face with an even more generic emoji, by giving her a thumbs up.

I looked down at the sieve and snacks on the counter now, very pointedly. I really wanted her to ring them up so I could get out of here. She looked down at them too.

"Is that all you're taking?" she asked.

I nodded.

And then she did something strange. She simply pushed them,

and the notes I had put on the counter, back to me, without ringing anything up. "It's on the house, as they say." And then she smiled at me, so big and genuine and kind that I felt a little tug inside. I was used to getting free stuff from people, but they usually wanted something in return for it. A post on Insta, a mention on Facebook. But I could see that her offer didn't entail this.

"Are you sure?" I asked.

Her smile grew. "Think of it as a welcome present."

"Thank you. So much," I said, taking my stuff. "That's really kind of you." The last word in that sentence caught in my throat just a little, for some reason.

"It's a pleasure, Frankie."

I gave her another small smile and then walked out the shop and back onto the lonely street outside. I looked around again. Twenty-four hours to wait. A whole day! I kicked some stones as I ambled along the pavement, trying desperately to kill time. But time felt like it was murdering me. Pulling my phone out I checked my step count. Only 2,476 steps! God, it felt like I was walking miles out here. Suddenly, I felt a jerk. My phone fell from my hand, so did the leash, and Satan started running.

"Stop!" I yelled after him, as I picked my phone up. "Stop!" I shouted as I tore down the street after him at breakneck speed. I hated this dog. He had been nothing but trouble since I'd discovered him on the side of the road. He left the main street and turned down a small alley.

"Get back here!" I shouted as he gained speed with those big, black, bounding legs. And then suddenly he turned sharply and he was gone, disappeared into a small open door.

"Shit!" I hissed under my breath. I made the same sharp turn, and without thinking, raced into the shop after him, jumping over an orange sign as I went.

"OH, CRAP!" I yelled as I entered and saw the large shelf in front of me. I tried to put on brakes but the soles of my shoes skidded across the floor, making a loud squeaking noise as they went. Flapping my arms in the air, I couldn't stop my forward motion. Like skidding on ice. The floor was just sweeping me away as if it was . . . wet?

It was wet! It was soapy and wet. My legs lost their footing and finally I tumbled to the floor and connected with something hard. I crawled onto my hands and knees. A spilt bucket lay on the floor in front of me, and there was water everywhere!

I reached for something and pulled myself up, and that's when I noticed I wasn't alone. A man holding a mop stood on the other side of a counter looking very pissed off.

"Shit," I mumbled and then gave the man a small smile.

He did not smile back.

"Sorry, I didn't mean to—" I took a step back and as I did, more disaster struck.

CHAPTER 12

There was nothing I could do as I stood there helplessly and watched the DVDs fall off the shelf and hit the floor like hailstones. Every time I thought it was done, another one toppled off and landed on the floor by my feet. The man and I looked at each other while the slim boxes fell around us, and when it was finally over, we both looked down at the mess at my feet. Our eyes must have lingered on the floor for exactly the same amount of time, because when I finally looked up again, he looked up too.

"Sorry. I'll help you put them back," I offered quickly.

But he said nothing. Instead, he simply stared at me. And then something curious happened. His eyes seemed to drift down to my chest area. His face reddened slightly and after lingering there for a second too long, he looked away and cleared his throat.

"It's okay," he said, moving off, sounding defensive now. He bent down and started picking up some of the DVDs. Why was he suddenly acting like this?

I looked down at my chest and that's when I realized I had two big, round wet patches around my boobs. The rest of my shirt was somehow dry. I pulled my shirt away from them, but there was just no way of hiding what was going on there. It was as if I had two bright beacons on my chest drawing your eye in.

"It was the dog," I said, trying to draw attention away from me and my wet boobs. "He ran in here and . . ." Wait, where was the bloody dog?

"Satan?" I swung around and looked for him.

The man in the store turned and raised a brow in query.

"Uh . . . like Santa's Little Helper but . . ." I started.

He nodded. "I get it. Still, not sure I would name my dog that."

"Not my dog," I barked and then walked around the shelf to see if I could find him. And there he was, lying in a puddle of water as if trying to cool himself down. I marched up to him and grabbed the leash.

"Naughty dog! Naughty!" I scolded, and then pulled him to his feet. The man's eyes widened when he saw him and I quickly shook my head.

"He's harmless," I said, and then quickly corrected, "Well, not totally harmless, as you can see. But he won't bite your leg off, if that's what you're thinking!"

"Cujo," he said.

"What?"

"You could have named him Cujo. It's a book by Stephen King that became a movie." He walked over to a shelf, pulled a DVD off and passed it to me. I stared down at the image of the massive dog jaws and nodded.

"I see." I passed the movie back to him and then gave him a serious once-over. He was nerdy. Kind of cute though. In that glasses-wearing, floppy-haired kind of way. He was wearing an old, worn T-shirt that had a small hole at the collar and said Nirvana across it. I didn't know what that meant at all; wasn't that something you said during yoga? He took his glasses off and looked down at the splashes of water across the lenses. Then he lifted his T-shirt and started cleaning them. I watched intently, somewhat hypnotized by this cleaning process. When the lenses were clean, he held them up to the light and, before putting them back on, he looked at me and our eyes locked and . . .

Huh? Something about him . . . Something about those eyes made him look familiar. But then the glasses went back on and that split second of familiarity disappeared. He turned away from me and I studied him a little more. He was probably around my age, a bit older maybe. Somewhat pale, even though he lived in the middle of the desert. Not very muscular, didn't look like he enjoyed outdoor sports . . . *And then a thought hit me!* A big thought!

There was no way someone like him didn't have internet access. He looked like the kind of guy who was into playing those roleplay strategy games on his phone. He looked like the kind of guy who played Fortnite in a basement somewhere. *Maybe there was Wi-Fi here after all?* A secret Wi-Fi that you had to tap into. Black-market Wi-Fi. You just needed to know how, and where, and with what password. And I intended to find out.

"So, do you work here?" I asked with a smile. Maybe it was a little flirty, I don't know. At least I hadn't pushed my chest out (not that I needed to).

He scrutinized me for a while, and then bent down and picked the bucket up. "Looks like it," he said. It was obviously sarcastic, or maybe that was just the Australian accent he had. Hard to tell really. I ignored whatever it was though and persisted.

"Soooo. You live here then?"

He nodded as he started mopping up the water on the floor.

"Live here long?" I asked.

"I suppose."

"I've only been here for a day," I continued.

He stopped mopping and eyed me. He reached up with one hand and scratched his head. His hair flopped about and fell into his face. It had this cute, natural wave to it, giving him a rather boyish look.

"Very quiet here," I said, also scratching my head. I'd listened to a podcast about leadership and influencing people and it had said that mirroring people's movements made them like you more. It didn't seem to work, because he just looked at my hand strangely.

"I must say, I'm super bored already." I tried another smile on him, but it didn't seem to work. My roundabout way of questioning also seemed to be going nowhere. I might as well stop beating around the bush. I took a deep breath. "So, what's the story around here anyway?" My tone had changed from sweet and flirty to straight-up direct.

"What do you mean?" His accent was thick, and I almost expected him to throw a "mate" on the end of the sentence. It made me think of that social media influencer, Ozzy Man, who did reviews of seemingly banal things in an Australian accent which made them hysterical. I wondered how he would review this moment, which was getting more awkward by the second as this man in front of me regarded me with a very confused look on his face.

I fiddled with the leash in my hand. "What I mean is, does this place really not have any internet?"

He shook his head. "Nope."

"But there's got to be some way of getting online, right? A way that they don't advertise."

He looked confused. "Advertise?"

"Yes. Like some secret internet that you can only log onto from a certain place with a secret password?"

At that he half-smiled and shook his head. "No."

"Oh, come on!" I said a little more loudly. "There has got to be something, right?"

He pointed behind me and I swiveled round.

"You can try hiking up that mountain, if you like. You might get signal there. Might not."

I squinted off into the distance. The mountains were so far away that they looked like smudges on the horizon.

I turned back to him. "But say I didn't want to hike across the Karoo and then up a mountain." My tone was very conspiratorial now and I narrowed my eyes for added mystery. "Say I just wanted to check my Instagram quickly, what would I do?"

"I wouldn't know, I don't have Instagram."

"You don't?"

He shook his head.

"But you have Facebook, right? Everyone has Facebook. Even my mother has Facebook. God, she even has a Tinder account—that's how she met Dan the dentist."

But the man in front of me shook his head. "No Facebook."

"Impossible," I said. "Let me see your phone."

He looked at me incredulously and then walked over to the counter. He picked up a landline and held it out to me.

I rolled my eyes at him. "Your cell phone."

"Don't have one."

"You don't?"

"Can't use it here, so why would I have one?"

"For the games, maybe. For reading on. Counting your steps. Tracking your mood. Your heart rate. Taking photos. Listening to music. Counting your calories . . . I mean . . . *everything!*"

He smiled slowly at me. This time he looked amused and I wasn't sure how to take it. "I usually read this thing called a book. Listen to music on a CD player. I've got a camera for taking photos and I don't count calories. Don't need to. Fast metabolism."

"But what if there was an emergency?" I asked, feeling flustered now, thinking about all the things I couldn't do.

"Like what?" he asked.

"Well, I could have hurt my leg when I slipped here—you should really have a sign up saying that the floor is wet, by the way."

At that, the man pointed behind me to the doorway. I turned and that's when I noticed the sign I'd jumped over.

Slippery When Wet.

"Oh," I said, nodding and feeling very sheepish now.

"Carry on, though," he said, a clear smile in his voice. "You slipped and hurt your leg?"

"Yes! And then what would I do? I can't go online and Google what to do."

"Why would I do that when I could just phone the doctor? He lives a road away."

"But . . ." I stopped talking and thought about it. "Okay, but maybe I didn't hurt my leg. Maybe I choked on something."

He looked around the place, his smile growing. "What would you choke on?" he asked.

"I don't know. Something! I could choke on something and maybe the doctor is not available and you have to do an emergency tracheotomy and you would need to consult the internet for that!"

I heard a small chuckle escape his lips now. His glasses slipped down his nose as he did and I didn't know whether I hated him for chuckling, or whether I liked him.

"Everyone who lives in this town manages just fine without the internet."

"Well, I am not managing." I heard myself spit the words out—they were louder than I had intended. His smile fell. "I am not managing, okay? So, please, if there is some kind of secret underground internet here, will you please just tell me?" I could hear the high-pitched desperation in my voice.

He shook his head now, a strange look on his face that told me nothing of what he might be thinking. "I'm sorry, there is no internet here. No cell-phone reception. Nothing."

I sighed and looked away from him. I felt a tightening in my chest again, and I didn't want him to see.

"So, if someone like me were stuck here for twenty-four hours or so, what would I do to pass the time?"

The guy looked confused for a moment but then pointed around the shop. "Well, you could hire some movies, for starters."

"I thought you couldn't watch TV here?" I said.

"You can't tune it in and get any channels, but you can use it to watch movies on."

I nodded at this. "What else?" I asked.

"You could buy some CDs, listen to music." He pointed to the other side of the store, and I could see it was dedicated to music.

"What would I watch the movies on? It's not like I can slip a DVD into my phone or iPad."

"You could try a television set—you know those, don't you? They are sort of like books in that you look at them too."

"Ha, ha. I know what a TV is. I don't have one myself. We watch everything on our phones."

His lips twitched into a tiny smile and our eyes locked for a moment and that feeling rose up inside me again . . .

Familiar. Something about him was familiar.

Very familiar.

CHAPTER 13

I tilted my head to the side and looked at him from a different angle. But the brief moment of familiarity I'd just experienced disappeared quickly when he too tilted his head to the side and his glasses slipped down his nose. I looked around the store again.

"Okay, fine. What do you have?" I walked up to one of the shelves, careful not to slip on the still wet floor.

"What movies do you like?" He came up to me; it was the closest we'd been until now, and I noticed his smell immediately. He smelled minty, as if he'd been chewing gum. And also spicy and woody and . . . *Oh my God*, he smelled bloody amazing. Like the best smell I'd smelled in a while. I leaned in a little and took a deep (subtle) breath. It felt terribly wrong to go around smelling strangers, but I couldn't help it, the guy really smelled good.

"So?" he asked.

"So what?"

"What movies do you like?"

"Oh, yes, that." I'd almost forgotten what we were talking about. "*The Kissing Booth, To All the Boys . . ., The Princess Swap*, you know."

"Sorry, never heard of any of those. Who directed them?" he returned quickly.

"I don't know, they're on Netflix."

"Aaaah," he said and then tutted.

"What does 'aaah' mean?"

"We don't have those here. We have real movies."

"Those aren't real?" I asked.

He shook his head.

"I like TV series too?" I added.

"Like what?"

"*YOU*, *Stranger Things*, *The Witcher*, but mainly only for Henry Cavill, you know?"

"Not really." He looked at me blankly over the rim of his glasses. They did give him quite an intellectual look. Young, sexy-professor vibes.

"Are those all Netflix shows too?" he asked.

I nodded.

"Before Netflix, what kind of movies and series did you watch?" he asked.

"Before?" It was hard to imagine a time before Netflix. A time where you had to wait to watch the next episode or something archaic like that. Or where you actually had to leave your house to watch a movie.

"I watched *Pretty Woman* once," I remembered. "It was sweet. I like Julia Roberts."

"So, classic romance?"

"Yes. I like romance, well . . ." I tailed off as an image of Kyle came into my head. *Bastard!* Breaking up with me like that. Maybe romance wasn't such a great idea right now.

Video Store Guy leaned in and seemed to inspect my face. "Not romance then?"

"I don't know. Should you watch romance if you've just been broken up with?" I asked.

He seemed to consider my question. As if he was really taking the time to think it over. "Watching romance after a break-up is probably the best time to do it."

"Why?"

"Well, isn't that when you need to believe in love again the most?" he asked.

His question caught me off guard because . . . Something about the word "love" struck me as odd and I couldn't really connect with it. *Wait* . . . A semi-thought started bobbing about in my brain. Had Kyle and I ever actually said we loved each other? We had said it online, on our platforms.

Hanging out with my #love.

Love my #bae

Happy #valentinesday love

But had we actually ever said it to each other IRL? With our mouths? Words and vocal cords? I wracked my brain. I wasn't actually sure, now that I thought about it. Was it weird to not know if you'd told your boyfriend you loved him, and vice versa? My sister had certainly thought so. She was always implying that our relationship wasn't real, despite all my assurances to her that it was. Despite me telling her that just because we were public figures, that we had a carefully constructed personal brand and that we worked hard on it together . . . it didn't mean it wasn't real.

"So?" Video Store Guy pressed, and snapped me back to reality.

"Sure. Romance. Why not?" I shrugged.

He nodded and then graced me with another smile. Small smile. Tiny even. But it made his nose wrinkle a little, which made his glasses creep down and, soon enough, he was pushing them back up his nose again. He walked over to a shelf and I followed close behind him, walking in the invisible train of his intoxicating scent. I waited and watched as he started pulling DVDs off the shelves. Something had changed in him. He'd gone from slouchy, low energy to looking almost perky. Once he'd finished, he walked over to the counter and laid them out.

"What about watching some of the quintessential Hollywood romances then?" he asked.

"Okay." I looked at the boxes and then pointed at one. "But this is in black and white. I can't watch black and white. It's like watching an entire movie through a bad Insta filter."

He shook his head at me. "But this is *Casablanca*. It's one of the greatest love stories ever written."

I shrugged.

"Humphrey Bogart, Ingrid Bergman, 'Here's looking at you, kid!'" he exclaimed.

I shrugged again. "Have you got anything that's not black and white?"

"How can you not want to watch something just because it's in black and white?"

"It's boring," I said. I never used a black and white filter on Instagram. That's just lazy.

"Boring!" he exclaimed and then looked at me questioningly. I held his gaze and eventually he just shook his head.

"Fine, what about this?" He showed me another one. "It's a must-see romance."

"*An Affair to Remember*," I read, taking it in my hands. "It looks soooo old."

"It came out in 1957."

"Nah, I don't think I'll relate to it then." I waved my hand at the DVD dismissively.

He shook his head again, hair flopping from side to side. "That's where you're wrong. The thing with a good romance is that it's timeless. A love story today is just the same as one from long ago. Love is love, no matter the time and place and language." I watched him as he talked; he came alive when he spoke about movies. Like this was his passion, and, for some reason, this won me over ever so slightly.

"Okay, I'll give it a go. What else is here?" At that, his face lit up even more, his smile caused his glasses to slip down again and he popped them back up on his nose, a move I was starting to find rather endearing, for some reason. He started passing me DVDs: *Grease, Sixteen Candles, Sleepless in Seattle, Love, Actually.*

"I'm giving you one from every decade." He sounded pleased with himself.

"How do I watch these?" I asked. "I'm staying at the hotel."

"They have TVs there, from before the observatory moved here. They're pretty old, but still work."

"How do you know?" I asked.

He suddenly shrugged and looked a little sheepish. "I've been there. You just have to rent a DVD player from me and plug it in."

"Okay," I said.

"Here, take this one." He walked over to a shelf and picked one up. "It's small enough to carry."

I eyed this strange black box in my hands and squinted at it in disgust. "I can't believe we actually used to use this to watch movies on," I said with a tone of amusement in my voice, but when I looked up at Video Store Guy, he didn't seem amused by my comment and I think I had offended him.

"Do you know how to hook it up?" he asked flatly.

"No, but I'm sure if you give me the instruction booklet I can work it out," and then I chuckled as a thought crossed my mind. "Is it printed on papyrus?" I carried on chuckling but stopped when I saw the look on his face. Okay, maybe I had pushed that a bit far.

"Fine." He sounded brusque and then walked off to the counter, picked up a booklet and almost slapped it down on top of the DVD player.

"Thanks," I mumbled. I looked around the shop again. "What music can you recommend?" I asked.

"Music is such a personal choice, I can't really recommend any-thing," he said, not looking at me now.

"Okay, I'll just take these then." I pulled money out of my wallet and passed it over once he'd added up my total. But when I tried to leave, Satan defiantly planted himself down and wouldn't budge. I pulled at the leash. But it was like pulling a brick wall. Immovable.

"Come, boy! Come!" He just looked at me.

"For heaven's sake!" I hissed. "Five minutes ago you were raring to go! What happened?"

At that, he rolled over onto his back, put his legs in the air and his belly on display.

I huffed. "You can't be serious."

Video Store Guy walked over to him and gave him a belly scratch. Satan's legs wiggled around, as if he was running. And then, just like that, he rolled over, jumped back onto his feet and shook his head.

"He just wanted a belly scratch," the guy said.

"Come, Satan!" I called and started walking again. He still didn't move. I sighed.

"Come, Cujo!" At that, he turned all the way around and trotted after me, out the shop.

"I told you that was a better name," Video Store Guy shouted, sounding amused.

CHAPTER 14

I arrived at my hotel after a hot and sticky walk from the DVD store. I was carrying a heavy bag and pulling a huge dog along, who didn't seem to want to go. This just made the whole experience that much sweatier and I was really looking forward to the cool shade of my room. I opened the door and Sata—*Cujo*—slipped in, just as I saw the manager of the hotel walk up to me.

"Hello!" She waved at me.

"Hi," I replied with a smile.

"How's your stay going?" she asked cheerfully. Everyone around here seemed very cheerful.

"Good," I said.

"I'm so sorry to have to ask this, I don't want to sound like I'm prying or being nosy or anything like that."

"What?"

"It's just, we have a strict no-animal policy here, and one of the other guests said they saw a big black dog hanging outside your room?" She looked me in the eye and I subtly dropped the leash from my hand and threw it into the room. I gently pulled the door closed with my toe.

"Oh my God, I think I saw that dog too," I said, trying to tap into some nonexistent acting skills I hoped I had. I needed Cujo firmly in my sights, what with that thing firmly lodged inside him. "Do you think he's dangerous?" I asked, in my most sincerely concerned voice.

"So he's not yours?"

I shook my head. "No. God. Have you seen him? He's terrifying. One eye!"

"Really?" Now she also sounded concerned.

"I hope he doesn't have any diseases or anything," I added to my embellishment.

"Me too," she half whispered under her breath.

"In fact," I continued—perhaps I was having too much fun with this—"now that I think about it, I'm not so sure it was a dog. Could be anything, what with the desert here and all."

She looked at me uneasily. "The other guest did say it was abnormally big."

"Could be a coyote?" I offered up.

"We don't have coyotes here."

"Wolf?"

She shook her head. "Although on some nights when the moon is full, you can hear distinct jackals calling."

I clicked my fingers. "Yes! I bet that's what it is. A jackal."

She shook her head, looking concerned and then irritated. "That's all we need around here. I better put up some warning signs. Make sure you don't leave any food out."

"I won't!" I said emphatically.

"Sorry for thinking you would have a dog here," she said apologetically and for a moment I kind of felt a little bad for lying. She was really pretty. Creamy pale skin, red hair, blue eyes and a great body—not wearing a stitch of make-up. A pang of jealousy wracked me.

"No worries. Don't stress," I assured her and then walked into my room and closed the door behind me. Cujo was sitting in the corner, and when I looked at him, I swear he shook his head at me. I stepped forward.

"You know, it's like you understand English or something, but that would be crazy, right?" I asked him. He cocked his head to the side, as if posing that same question to me.

"Me? You think *I'm* crazy?" I pointed at myself and thought about it for a while, then started nodding. "I mean, I can see why you would think that, but it's not fair to make that assumption now. I'm not usually like this. I haven't been myself these past few days. And, sure, it's making me feel a little mad. Like I'm losing it. Losing control. Losing . . . everything that meant anything to me." I took a deep breath and paced the room a few times. "I shouldn't be here with you. I should be back home. I should be posting to my followers, which I would still have if things hadn't gotten so messed up after the elevator and . . ." I stopped talking and shook my head. *What the hell was I doing?* God, Frankie, get a grip and stop talking to a jackal dog, for heaven's sake. I walked over to the TV. God, it was old. Like those old box TVs you had back in the eighties. I turned around and looked at Cujo as a thought hit me.

"You're not a jackal, right? I shouldn't be worried that in the middle of the night you're going to take one of my legs off?" I looked at him for the longest time and then sighed. "Of course not. You saved me from a snake. You like me. You truly, madly, like me!" I laughed at the rather lame joke I'd just made. "Truly, Madly, Love Me" had been one of my favorite songs, by my all-time favorite band back when I was a teen.

Cujo stretched out his legs and collapsed onto the carpet. He put his big head down on his paw and gave a loud sigh, as if he was completely and utterly relaxed. It seemed to be contagious, and soon I was also sighing. But as I did, a feeling of relaxation didn't come over me. A deep feeling of loneliness and sadness descended, once again. And this feeling only intensified when I realized I would not be able to watch anything. Thank you, DVD brochure writers, for using what was clearly a very bad version of Google translate. I read out loud to Cujo.

"*For placing blacky machine box in instalments sockets, making wires with electricity color matching for keeping safely.*" I tossed the brochure onto the bed and lay down next to it.

"Now what?" I asked the empty room. I asked the universe, the ceiling, the bloody dog and the strange silence of this small town. But I didn't get an answer. I hadn't been this alone in years. Not since I was that chunky teenage girl climbing into bed after school with a tear-streaked face from all the bullying. My sister and I had gone to the same school, and what made the whole thing worse was, even though she was younger than me, she was in the popular, pretty crowd. The crowd that for the most part did the teasing. She never teased, per se, but she certainly didn't try and stop them.

I looked over at the snack bars on the bed next to me and reached for one. At one point in my life, food had been my best and only friend. And now it was really more of an enemy. Something to be wary and suspicious of. I pulled the bar up to my face and read the calorie content on the back. The desire to enter the calories into my app and then work out how many minutes of exercise it would take to render this null and void was overwhelming. I felt like I needed to track calories. I felt like I needed to track everything in my life. Every aspect of my life needed to be recorded and tracked in a neat and ordered manner, or else it would all fall apart.

But I was hungry. So I ripped the wrapper off the snack bar and then tossed it into the air. It landed on the bed next to me and I stared at it for the longest time before I defiantly took a bite, trying to tell myself that untracked calories would not derail me, even though I wasn't sure I totally believed that, and didn't have Google to check either.

CHAPTER 15

*E*vening came around. I'd spent the entire afternoon trying to entertain myself. I pulled all my false nails off, and tried to salvage the things below. I'd given myself two facial masks and bathed for over an hour, but still I was so bored that I simply had no other choice. I walked over to the video store, leaving Cujo in the room. I arrived just as Video Store Guy was leaving for the night. I stood behind him and watched as he locked the door, slipped the keys into his pocket and then finally turned. He jumped when he saw me standing there and did an actual hand-to-the-chest gasp.

"Sorry," I said, holding my hands up and smiling, amused that he had gotten such a fright.

He gave me a small, embarrassed smile that told me he didn't like the idea that I'd seen him like that. It was kind of adorable.

"What's up?" he asked. I could hear he was trying to be deliberately casual.

"Uh . . . turns out I actually don't know how to hook the DVD player up," I said, flashing him a grimace. "The instructions for the 'blacky machine box' were hard to follow."

He smiled again. Not as boyish this time. It was a self-satisfied smile that spread all the way into his eyes.

"You knew that those instructions were written in gibberish?" I folded my arms and his smile grew even more.

He shrugged. "Maybe. Maybe not."

"That's not funny," I said. "Or fair."

"I'll come help you," he said quickly, and started walking.

"Uh . . . thanks. I didn't mean you needed to help, you can just tell me how to do it."

"It's okay," he said. "I was on my way to help you anyway, since I suspected this would happen."

"Oh. Thanks." I was slightly taken aback by this.

He seemed to pick up pace as he crossed the street. I tried to keep up with him, but he was surprisingly fast.

Why did he walk so fast . . . and then I noticed his height. I hadn't noticed it before. He was tall. Long legs and long arms. Each step he took was like three to me. When we got to the hotel, he stopped and looked at something on the wall. I leaned in too.

"Well, how about that," he said, reading the handwritten note pasted on a pillar.

WARNING: Suspected jackal activity in town. Please keep windows and doors closed and make sure no food is left out.

I burst out laughing and he swung around and looked at me questioningly.

"There's no jackal," I said.

"There isn't? How do you know?"

"Because," I slipped the key into my door and pushed it open, "that's the jackal." I pointed at Cujo as we walked inside. He was lying on the carpet, fast asleep. His paws were crossed and his head was lying on them like a pillow and, for a moment, a split second, a tiny part of a split second, he actually looked a little cute. *Cute?* The bowl of food I'd put down for him earlier was completely gone; in fact, I had never seen anyone or anything eat so fast before. As if his life had depended on eating as fast as he could. As if he would never see food ever again. My heart had broken a little, wondering how long it had been since he'd eaten anything.

"He was mistaken for a jackal?" Video Store Guy asked.

"Well, I might have planted that seed."

"You and your dog are troublemakers," he said teasingly.

"Not my dog," I replied. But at the sound of my voice, Cujo tipped his head up, opened his one eye and looked at me. He started wagging his tail so vigorously that it made a loud noise as it hit the wall.

"For a 'not my dog' he seems rather happy to see you."

"Well, you know dogs. They will wag their tails for anything." I eyeballed Cujo and then, suddenly, he was on his feet walking towards me. And before I knew what was happening, he'd pushed his face into my stomach and nuzzled it there.

"Totally your dog," he said.

I shook my head again and gave Cujo a brief pat and then pushed his head away. "Yeah, yeah, that's enough." I looked at Video Store Guy and rolled my eyes; he gave me the slightest smile again. He actually had an incredibly nice smile. Perfect white, straight teeth. The way the corners of his mouth turned up and gave a little twitch. The way it wasn't straight at all, the way it curved up on one side more than the other. His smile disappeared when he turned his back on me, picked up the DVD player and started fiddling. I watched curiously as he simply plugged one thing into the TV and then turned it on with a remote. It was that easy.

"Thanks. You didn't have to come all this way and do this."

"It's okay, like I said, I was coming here to help you anyway, and I also wanted to give you some more DVDs."

"Why?"

"I felt like I may have given you the wrong movies," he said.

"Why?' I asked again.

"I thought about your situation again, and thought that maybe you didn't want to watch romance after all." He pulled the old worn rucksack off his back and pulled some DVDs out.

"My situation?" I asked, making eye contact with him.

He paused. "Sorry, you told me you'd just broken up with someone?"

"Oh. That. Well, he broke up with me, actually," I corrected.

"Sorry," he offered. "That sucks."

"Sucks," I repeated, thinking about the word, and then I started nodding. Because it really did suck. It sucked big time. "You know! That is a really good word and it describes my situation perfectly. But I must say, him breaking up with me didn't suck as much as *how* he did it. I didn't even know I was being broken up with, can you believe that? Hundreds of thousands of people knew before me. And you want to know why he broke up with me?" It was a rhetorical question, I didn't wait for an answer. "Because she was better for his personal brand than me." That thought really, really stung. It made me feel so many things; mad and sad and not so glad and all the other emotions on my mood app. "Apparently, I'm now a *nobody* and she is a somebody, and now I have a strange dog living in my hotel room in the middle of the Karoo desert. And I'm going to have to internet date again and that is just such a minefield, and the creeps you come across are next level. I once went on a date with a guy and halfway through the meal, his fiancée came up to the table and poured his glass of wine over his head."

"Uh . . ." He looked at me blankly.

"Sorry. Overshare. Sometimes I need to share. You know."

He nodded.

"And I literally haven't shared a thing in days which is making me feel a little crazy. So crazy that I have been talking to a dog."

He nodded again and his face seemed to soften slightly.

"Sorry, again. I'm oversharing. I'll stop. I'll just stop talking." I put my hands over my mouth.

He shook his head. "No worries. Sometimes you just need to talk, I guess."

"Just ignore what I told you, I didn't mean to blurt it all out like that." I looked down at the DVDs in his hands and decided to change the subject. "So, what's this?"

"Well, I was broken up with once too, and it also sucked and I remember that the last thing I wanted to do was watch anything romantic, so I brought you this." He smiled and passed me the movie.

"*Saw*?" I asked, looking down at it.

"It's bloody disgusting and terrifying and if there's one thing that will make you forget a broken heart, it's this. And this . . ." He passed me another one and I took it.

"*The Grudge*?"

"Also, will defo scare you shitless."

"Defo?" I smiled. He was so Australian right now, it was kind of cute.

"So you reckon I should watch these instead?" I asked, turning the covers over in my hands.

"I reckon," he said.

"Well, thanks for these, and for hooking up the machine and for listening to me rant, even though I didn't mean it." I sat back down on the bed; it felt awkward me sitting on the bed and him standing there, but there was nowhere else to sit. "I would offer you a seat but . . ." I tailed off.

"I should probably go," he said, moving towards the door.

"Thanks again," I called after him.

"You know, if you enjoy these, you should come to movie night tomorrow. We have it at the old barn at the bottom of Church Street."

"Let me guess, that's the street with the church in?"

"You can't get lost around here," he joked. "It's very casual."

I nodded. "Thanks, but I'm hoping *not* to be here tomorrow night."

"Okay," he said and then started walking out the door.

"I'm Frankie, by the way," I called after him for some reason.

He turned. "Mark."

"Cool, nice meeting you." He walked out the door and I thought he was gone, but then he popped his head back in. "Um . . . so, I don't mean to be rude, but . . ." He paused.

"But what?"

"The jackal." He pointed at Cujo. "Kind of smells."

"Really? I hadn't noticed."

"You've probably gotten used to it," he said. "Try walking outside, taking a few deep breaths and then walking back in."

"Okay." I walked outside and filled my lungs with air, while Mark watched me. I smiled at him, gave him a nod and then walked back inside and took a deep breath in through my nose.

"Oh God. Yes! Gross." I looked over at Cujo. "Can't believe I didn't notice."

"I have a sensitive nose," he said with a smile.

I smiled back. "Well, then, I've learned two things about you today. Fast metabolism. Sensitive nose."

He gave a small chuckle, those glasses of his slipped down his nose again and he pushed them up.

"Ever considered contact lenses?" I heard myself say without thinking.

"Yeah, but then I would have to touch my eyeball."

"True!"

We looked at each other for a while, and that little feeling of familiarity niggled again. I was just about to open my mouth and say something, when he turned and started walking away.

"Thanks," I called after him again, and then turned my attention to Cujo in the corner.

CHAPTER 16

"Look, if we're going to share a room for the next day, we're going to have to do something about the way you smell," I said. He was sprawled out across the floor. Lying on his back, his legs flopping in the air, clearly enjoying the feel of the breeze from the overhead fan on his exposed belly. He turned his head and looked over at me, tongue hanging out of his mouth. His tongue was so long that it hung all the way to the carpet where a small puddle of drool had gathered. *Gross!*

I walked to the bathroom and ran a bath. When it was full and the temperature was a perfect lukewarm, I clapped my hands together and, within seconds, Cujo was standing by my legs. He looked up at me, as if waiting for me to tell him what to do. I sat on the side of the bath, moving my hands over the water. He approached the bath tentatively and eyeballed the water with great suspicion.

"Come on." I splashed the water, trying to make it look enticing, but when he didn't budge, I hiked my skirt up and climbed in.

"Come on, come on." I clapped my hands together again, standing calf deep in the water. He moved a little closer, until he was standing right next to the bath. Cautiously, he stuck his nose over the edge and sniffed. He looked up at me with his one eye and I nodded at him. A reassuring nod that hopefully conveyed that it was okay to come on in. And then he lifted his paw and touched the water, patting its surface gently, hardly moving it, and then, as his ease grew, he slapped it, sending drops flying. He barked and tried to catch the drops in his mouth, his tail started to wag and then . . .

"Oh my God!" I shouted and covered my face as an avalanche of water slammed into me. He'd jumped straight into the bath, sending most of the water flying out. I swatted the flying splashes as he thumped about excitedly, as if he'd never been in this much water before. Maybe he hadn't. I climbed out and dried my face with a towel and watched him cavort around.

He looked so happy. Full of joy. As if this simple thing, a bath of water, was the best thing he'd ever seen before. He bit the water with his mouth, buried his entire head in it and blew bubbles, surprising himself every time when the bubbles popped on the surface. Finally, when he looked exhausted, he flopped down onto his belly and rested his head on the lip of the bath. He looked up and me and I swear he was giving me a snaggletoothed smile.

"Right." I picked up a bottle of shampoo and poured a stripe of pink liquid from his head to his tail. "We are going to have you smelling like jasmine in no time," I said, as I lowered my hands to his coarse, wiry fur and began rubbing. It took ages; he was huge and long and his fur was as thick as anything I'd ever felt before. The lather built up so much, that at some stage I was scooping out handfuls of the stuff and dumping it into the sink. The water was now stained a dark brown. Small twigs, dry leaves and dead beetles were floating on the surface of the brown goo.

When it was time to rinse him, I pulled the handheld shower off the wall. I was just about to turn it on when I heard a noise. He'd fallen asleep with his head on the lip of the bath. I watched him, this big, sleeping dog, and something about this scene made my stomach clench. He looked so peaceful and content that I felt bad when I turned the water on and woke him. He didn't seem to mind though, and when we were finally done and I'd let all the water out, I wrapped a towel around him and rubbed until he was as dry as I could get him.

"There! All done." I removed the towel and immediately regretted it when he shook his body so hard that he coated the ceiling in drops of water. I took him back to the bedroom, pulled out my hairdryer and set about drying him while I brushed him with a brush (I would throw it away after this, obviously). But there was something about the repetitive movement of the brush over his coat, and the continuous sound of the hairdryer droning on, that made me start talking. For some reason, I spoke about things I hadn't spoken about in years. The things I hadn't told anyone. The things I was scared and ashamed of. I told him about my fears and my childhood and the lonely time and the teasing and bullying and how all those words somehow seeped into me and ate away from the inside like a cancer. Eating away at my self-worth, my self-esteem. I told him how I found out that my stepdad wasn't actually my real dad and that in a way I'd felt relieved; it certainly explained the way he treated my sister and me differently. How he favored her more than me and never bothered to hide it. I told him about my mother's love life, how she was on her fifth marriage already. Dan the dentist was lucky number five, and then I told him all about Kyle and me.

I'd been so flattered when Kyle had slid into my DMs that fateful day. I'd admired him from afar for years, listening to his Monday motivation videos about self-improvement and Personal, Massive, Explosive Smash Through™, watching his workout videos and ogling his hot pictures. He was everything that I wanted to be with his fame and followers and brand endorsements. And so when he'd messaged me and asked if I wanted to do a brand collab with him, well, I'd jumped. Having someone like Kyle say he admired me, it was all I'd ever wanted. So, I'd been more than happy to take all his advice over the years about how I could better myself, do better and just *be* better.

Explosive Smash Through™ better.

And then I told him about the elevator and the white envelope and by the time I was done, I realized that I had tears streaming down my cheeks. Cujo never looked up at me while I talked, but his good ear was constantly pricked up and pointed in my direction. Talking to him felt strange, but good. And I realized that I hadn't spoken to anyone like this in person for years. I poured my heart out to him and I knew that he was capable of holding it and keeping my secrets safe inside. He would never tell anyone; instead, he would absorb them and they would be a part of him and, in some way, this immediately made me feel lighter and less alone. By the time I was done, he was fast asleep on the floor. I leaned in and put my nose to his big neck and took a deep breath—he smelled of soft, powdery jasmine and I smiled. I popped in the *Saw* DVD and pressed play and then looked down at the dog.

"Need the toilet yet?" I asked.

But he didn't budge; instead, he started snoring.

CHAPTER 17

I woke up the next morning and jumped out of bed. I'd barely gotten any sleep and my sleep app wasn't working so I had no way of knowing how long my REM cycle had been, which made me feel very unsettled. I like to know and track how many good quality hours of sleep I get. But even without it, I could tell it hadn't been long.

Saw!

Why would Mark have given me a movie like that? I needed to talk to him about that and take all the others back. Clearly, he had questionable taste in films. But in my sheer terror last night I'd forgotten to take Cujo out to the toilet. I smelled the air. I didn't smell anything and I couldn't believe I was actually doing this. Me, sniffing the air for dog shit, and actually *wanting* to smell it. I walked the room, checking the corners, checking under things, checking on things. This was impossible—this dog hadn't taken a crap in a day. What dog doesn't do that?

"You didn't do it!" I said to him, putting my hands on my hips. This was unacceptable. This dog needed to go! I still wanted out of this place and he was my ticket to freedom.

* * *

I knocked on Samirah's door and she opened it almost immediately. I'd had to sneak Cujo out of the hotel room so the manager hadn't seen us.

"Is everything okay?" she asked, looking a little tired, as if she also hadn't gotten much sleep; she could do with a sleep app. I glanced down at her belly which looked bigger today. How was that possible?

"No!" I said emphatically. "It is certainly *not* okay."

She looked down at Cujo. "Is he okay?"

"Well, he's still holding onto the immobilizer, so NO, I would say that is not okay."

She gave him a pat on his head.

"And I watched a terrible, I mean truly awful, movie last night and . . . can't you make it come out faster? Isn't there something you can do to speed up this process?"

"It's better to let these things take their course naturally," she said. "I could give him a laxative, but then he might really go . . . everywhere."

I cringed. That didn't sound like a good idea. "Can't you squeeze it out of him?" I asked, looking down at his long body and wondering whether I could wring it out like a wet cloth.

"No," she chuckled. "You can't squeeze it out. How would you like it if I came over to your house and tried to squeeze you ou— Oooowwweee!" Samirah winced and reached for her belly.

"Are you okay?" I pointed at her belly. "One's not about to come out, is it?"

She forced a smile, shook her head and held her breath for a moment as if she was in pain. "I hope not. They aren't due for another month."

"Oh." I looked at her stomach, unable to imagine how much bigger it would be in another month.

"She just likes to kick me in the ribs from time to time, remind me that she's still here." She pressed her hand to her stomach and looked down. "And he likes to push on my bladder at the most inopportune times." She moved her hand to the bottom of her belly now.

She waited for a while, staring down at her belly. "Okay, they've settled. Bring him to the back and I'll examine him anyway." She waddled down the passage, as if she had a watermelon between her thighs. God, I couldn't imagine four more weeks of that.

Samirah examined Cujo and again gave me the all-clear to take him home and "wait."

"I'm sick of waiting," I said. "There is literally nothing to do here. I don't know how you people survive without your phones. And I'm certainly not in the mood to watch another movie. I'm sure that guy at the video store gave me that on purpose, knowing how horrendous it was!"

"Perhaps you should try doing nothing," Samirah offered.

"Nothing?"

She nodded. "Absolutely nothing."

"That's impossible," I said, trying to think of how one is able to do nothing at all.

She shook her head. "It's very possible. A few of us get together and do some guided meditation. It's very therapeutic. You should come. It's today at three."

I shook my head. "I've already tried to have a spiritual experience once. It didn't work. I almost got bitten by a snake. I think my days of trying to be spiritual are over."

She looked at me strangely again. "Aaaaahhhhh," she mumbled in a long, slow, deep voice.

"Aaaaahhh what?"

"It's just interesting," she said.

"What is?"

"Interesting that you saw a snake while trying to have a spiritual experience."

"Why?"

"Well, in some cultures snakes are a symbol of transformation. They teach us how important it is to shed what we no longer need. If a snake doesn't shed, it dies."

"Uh . . ." I looked at her blankly; her green eyes were locked onto me like laser beams.

"So, if you think about it," she continued, "the snake tells us to let go of the things that restrict us, in order to grow. What are the things you need to let go of?"

I stared at her for a while, not sure how to respond. "Yeah, but they also bite," I said.

"This is true too," she said in a low, mysterious voice. I leaned in a little, because it sounded like she was going to expand on this thought. Like the act of biting was also some metaphor for something. But she didn't. She just graced me with a big smile.

"So you still think I can't speed this whole bowel movement along then?" I asked, trying to move the conversation away from the spiritual and back to the physical.

She shook her head. "Patience."

"Mmmm, so I should do nothing and be patient?" I said sarcastically.

"Exactly."

"Those are two things I'm not very good at," I said.

"Think of it as your chance to practice them."

"I'm not sure I want to practice them."

She wrapped her stethoscope around her neck and looked at me for the longest time.

"I think that everything that's happening at this moment is happening for a reason. I think that you finding this dog, bringing him here, him swallowing your keys and keeping you here, it's all part of the universe's plan."

"The universe?"

"Or God, or karma or whatever you want to call it."

"God's plan?" I chuckled, thinking about the name I'd given Cujo in the first place and how opposite that was from anything godly. I looked down at him. Surely, if this was all part of some divine, magical plan, God could have brought me a better-looking dog. Not one that looked like this!

"Here." Samirah pulled out a piece of paper and started scribbling on it. It seemed to take her ages, but finally, she passed it to me.

"This is the address of the meditation. You should come. Seriously. It can't harm you."

"I don't have a car, so I can't get there," I said.

"It's in walking distance. And the walk will do him good—it might even speed up the process."

I shrugged. "I don't know."

"Bring him, and I promise that if he decides to go while he's there, I will personally sift through it for you."

At that I perked up and looked down at the paper.

"Or I could fetch you if you want?" she asked. I looked up at her. Was she really this nice?

I shook my head quickly. "It's okay. If I come, I'll walk. Like you said, it may speed him up."

I started reading the directions. *"Go down Church Street, turn left into Berg Street, at the second house take a left, at the big jacaranda take another left. Pass the blue sign, and it's the second rusted gate on your left."* I looked up at Samirah. "Huh? These are the directions?"

She nodded.

"There is this amazing thing called Google Maps, trust me, you guys would love it," I said sarcastically.

"This seems to work for us," she said with a smile. "We never get lost, and if we do, it's for a reason."

I put my hand on my hip. "What's up with you anyway?"

Samirah laughed. "What's up with me?"

"Yes, you're very friendly and you like to give strange advice and say things about the universe and snakes and how Cujo belongs to me and things happen for reasons."

"I thought his name was Satan?" she asked.

"It got changed."

"That's still a terrible name," she said.

"Well, it is better than Sat—"

"Yes!" She cut me off. "But only marginally."

We both looked at each other for a while. She had a kind, round moon-shaped face. It was so open. Welcoming.

"Do you really believe in that stuff you were talking about? The universe and plans?" I asked.

"Yes, I do."

"Can I tell you something weird then?" I asked.

She smiled at me, open and welcoming, and she didn't need to say a word, because I could see I could talk to her.

"I think I might have almost died a few days ago." The words flew out of my mouth. They had sort of been on the tip of my tongue the entire time. Not that I'd been consciously thinking about it, but on some level, it hadn't really left me.

"That's awful, what happened?"

"I was in an elevator with two other women and suddenly the thing plummeted. I thought I was going to die, but then it just stopped."

"Was anyone injured?" she asked.

"Yes, actually! One of the women was hit on the head, she passed out. They took her away on a stretcher."

"Is she okay?" she asked, looking genuinely concerned for this stranger.

I shrugged. "I have no idea." And then a thought hit me. "Oh God, she could be dead, couldn't she?"

Samirah looked very solemn for a moment. "I hope not," she said softly.

"Me too." I thought about the way her eyes had glazed over just before she'd fallen and a shiver ran up my spine.

I shook my head, trying to get rid of that thought. "Anyway, it's weird, because after the elevator, everything changed. And I mean *everything*. And in a matter of seconds."

She observed me for a while before speaking again. "And now you are here." It was a statement, not a question.

"I guess so."

"Are you okay?" she asked.

I was taken aback by the question. "What do you mean?"

"Well, having an accident like that can leave you very shaken up. It can change your perspective on a lot of things, it can . . ." Her voice got soft and suddenly she looked like she was remembering something herself. "A near-death experience, well, it can change everything about you. Your whole life."

"What happens if I didn't want my life to change?" I asked. "What happens if I liked my life and it was perfect?"

"Was it?" She raised a brow at me.

"Was it what?"

"Perfect?" She leaned closer to me and I didn't answer right away. In fact, I didn't answer at all. I couldn't.

"Sometimes we can't stop the change," Samirah said, breaking the silence that we'd fallen into. "The change happens to us whether we're ready for it, or not."

I looked down at Cujo, who looked like he was getting restless. And then I looked back at Samirah. "I wasn't ready for it," I said softly, and then walked out.

CHAPTER 18

"*T*urn left at the . . . What?" I looked down at the piece of paper in my hands. I'd decided to go to this mediation thing after all. Not because it was something I desperately wanted to do, but because I was so bored I wanted to cry. On the way, I'd stopped over at the video store, hoping to catch Mark and reprimand him for the movies he'd given me, only he wasn't there. A young guy with splotchy stubble and a squeaky voice had replaced him.

"Um, left at the . . ." I squinted at the piece of paper again. It was so hot and bright out here and I wished I hadn't walked, but I was almost there. I looked around. I had just walked off the main road and I felt like I was in the middle of bloody nowhere again. This place was a place of vast nowheres and nothings.

"Rusted gate. Blue sign. Rusted bloody gate." I scanned my surroundings for this rusted gate. "Nope," I said to Cujo who was now looking at me. "Let's walk a little more." We kept on walking in the heat, why was it so hot at this time of year? I was sweating and just when I thought I couldn't walk anymore, I saw it. A rusted, buckled gate that was falling apart in sections. Tied to the gate was a bunch of brightly colored purple feathers. I assumed this was a place for meditation.

I opened the gate, closed it behind me and then proceeded to walk down the long, red sandy driveway that led to a small, purple-painted farmhouse. I was covered in a thin layer of sweat and dust by the time I reached the house, and a few flies were buzzing around me. A few cars were parked outside. One of them was Samirah's, I could see that from the giant "Vet" sticker on the bonnet. I walked up to the front of the house and knocked on the door. But when I got no answer, I pushed the door open and jumped at the sound of the wind chimes that suddenly rang out. Cujo gave a loud bark, as if the sounds had frightened him too.

"Come in, come in," a soft, sing-song voice called. "We're out back."

I entered the small living room. Crystals and dream catchers and feathers and a lot of purple ribbons. I walked through to the patio outside: crystals and dream catchers and feathers and a lot of purple ribbons. But there were also people there.

"Hi." I gave Samirah a small wave. She quickly walked up to me and introduced me to Cheryl, clearly the person who'd decorated this room. She was covered in purple tie-dye from head to toe. Her long dreadlocks were perched on the top of her head in a massive bun with a purple ribbon tied around them. I extended my hand for her to shake, but instead she gave me a little bow. So spiritual.

"And who is this?" she asked, turning to Cujo.

"This is *not* my dog," I said flatly, casting a look at Samirah who shook her head, as if amused.

"Well, welcome to both of you." She gestured for me to sit. "Human souls and animal souls all welcome." I frowned; her name didn't really match her persona. Cheryl seemed like such a mom name. The kind of name that drove an SUV and hosted book clubs, not the kind of name that had a purple stud through her nose.

I walked past Samirah and whispered a quick, "The sieve is in my handbag. And it's for you," at her. She chuckled so I turned around and shot her a very serious look, so she knew I wasn't joking. If anything came out of that dog's butt in the next hour, it was all hers.

"Do you have a mat?" Cheryl asked, as I took my place between the women sitting on the floor.

I shook my head and she handed me a soft, squishy purple mat. Cujo looked at me, as if asking a question.

"You can go there." I pointed to the side and he walked off and did exactly what I said. I caught Samirah gazing at me out of the corner of my eye and I flashed her another serious look. I knew what she was thinking.

"Not. My. Dog!" I mouthed to her, but she only smiled in that sage-like way that she did. It was wildly irritating, yet her smiles kind of warmed me too. I couldn't remember the last time a smile had warmed me like that. I couldn't help but return it.

"Greetings and salutations, ladies and animal," Cheryl said in a whispery voice. "We have two new souls joining us today on this journey, please join me in welcoming her and her canine companion."

"Not my—" I started and stopped when I saw all the faces around me smile. Some of the faces even reached out and placed hands on my shoulders, whilst others gave me waves and one even gave me a praying hand emoji. They all looked so serene. I don't think I'd ever seen such a serene bunch of people before. Maybe this was what meditation did for you? I'd once downloaded a meditation app, but I'd found it extremely boring.

"Please, lie back and get comfortable on your mats and start breathing deeply and clearing your minds."

I lay back, feeling a little uncomfortable with this communal lying about. I closed my eyes but flicked them open when a very strange sound rang out. I looked over at Cheryl who was rubbing something that looked like a rolling pin against big brass bowls. A noise like I'd never heard before settled into the air around me. I closed my eyes again and took a deep breath. *Go with it, go with it, Frankie*, I told myself, even though I still wasn't sure I wanted to go with it. This all seemed a little too spiritual for me, despite my previous wish to have a spiritual experience, but I guess it beat being bored in a hotel room. I focused on the soothing noise and Cheryl's mystical-sounding voice. I bet she practiced that voice when she was alone.

"Now," Cheryl continued, calmly and softly, "I want you to think of a time that you felt a negative emotion." Wait . . . Why did she want us to think of this? I thought this was all about *not* thinking. I re-adjusted myself; I was starting to feel more and more uncomfortable.

"Get comfortable, take your time," the voice said. I was sure she'd seen me wriggling.

"Deep breath in," she coaxed and I tried to do what she was asking. I took a deep breath and suddenly, without my permission, and without having to dig that far into my mind, the negative feelings flooded me. My stomach tightened. I didn't like this one little bit and I wanted to stand up and leave.

"Now think of that feeling washing away. Think of a bright white light rushing into you. A warm light sweeping over you and sweeping all the negativity away. Imagine that negative thought flying out of the tips of your toes and leaving you."

I rolled my eyes in my head. It was all a little ridiculous for me . . .

Wait! What was that? I tightened my eyes and heard something deep inside my head. *A song.* My song. My favorite song in the world. This song had been the only thing that had made me feel better as a teen. I'd listened to it over and over again. It had been there for me in my darkest times.

I shuffled again on my mat as the sound of the song started creeping into me, mingling with the strange sounds of the bowls and with her voice. The song was by my favorite childhood band, a boy band. There had been posters of them plastered across my walls and ceiling, and on some days they had been the only smiling, friendly faces I had seen. The lyrics of the song I was thinking of had meant everything to me when I was younger.

"*Special girl. You can be anything in the world.*"

The five singers had crooned in their melodic voices, harmonizing as one. They were the only people in the world who told me I could be anything I wanted to be. If it hadn't been for that song, and their music, I don't know if I would have made it through my teen years. I felt something wet and cold slip down my cheek and it dawned on me that I was crying.

"Go with that feeling." I heard that voice again. I felt a terrible tightening in my chest as more wetness slid down my face.

"NO!" I sat up and scrambled to my feet, grabbing at my bag as I went. Cheryl walked over to me, placed a hand on my shoulder and gripped it.

"It can be very overwhelming at first, but it's worth it."

I looked around the room. Everyone was sitting up now, looking at me with concern in their eyes, especially Samirah.

I wiped my tears away. "This is stupid," I said. "I can't do this. It's . . . it's . . ." I shook my head and could hear I was crying again. Well, some version of me was crying, a version I felt very disconnected from. A version that had been residing deep inside that had been neatly tucked away and pushed down, until now. God, I wanted my phone so badly. That soothing feeling of my fingers rushing over my screen, distracting me. Logging, and recording, and tracking things until I felt all this disorder melt away. Control. I wanted control again.

"This is . . . I shouldn't have come, it's . . ." I started to leave.

"Where are you going?" Samirah called after me.

"Away," I said.

"Let me drive you," I heard her call after me.

"No! I want to walk!" I shouted over my shoulder as I rushed through the house and ran outside. I raced back up the dirt driveway as fast as I could, Cujo hot on my heels. Reaching the gate I pulled it open, not bothering to close it behind me this time. I ran up the road and as soon as I was far enough away from the house, I stopped and bloody wept.

I wept loudly and wildly and it was ugly. I felt so emotional. All those memories of my early years that I'd worked so hard to push away, were back. I was the "fat" lonely girl in my room all over again, listening to the same songs on repeat. The terrified girl in the shed that no one had even noticed had gone missing. I leaned against the big jacaranda tree on the side of the road and held my face in my hands. I'd tried so hard to escape all of that and be someone else, but it had all failed, hadn't it? I'd lost my boyfriend to an influencer who had more followers than me. I'd lost all my friends and likes and status and brand endorsements and everything in my life that meant anything and now I was just Frankie. A nobody. A girl with an ugly dog in the middle of the desert on a dirt road to nowhere.

Suddenly, I felt something. I looked down to see that Cujo had put his massive head against my leg and was cuddling into me. For some reason this made me chuckle ever so slightly. I lowered my hand to his head—God, his fur was as prickly as wire—but I stroked it and his massive tongue came out of his mouth and gave my hand the wettest, longest lick.

"Ew," I giggled and wiped it on my shirt. I slung my bag off my shoulder and reached into it for the face wipes; the salty tears were making my skin sting. But as I opened it, the white envelope tumbled to the floor. I stared down at it. I'd forgotten all about the envelope . . .

CHAPTER 19

Six days ago

*T*he man with the moustache pushed the big, white envelope across the table towards me. It seemed to move in slow motion, as if there was something very heavy inside. I guess in some ways there was. I reached out and took it in my hands. It felt heavy. Not physically, but heavy with something else. I stared at it. Trying to look through it. Trying to see inside but couldn't.

"Well, aren't you going to look at it?" the moustached lawyer asked.

"Aren't I going to . . .?" I continued to stare. For some strange reason, it hadn't even crossed my mind to open it. But what did occur to me was that this was the closest I'd been to my father in years. I couldn't even remember the last time I'd seen his face. But now, I was holding something that he'd touched. Something that was smeared with his DNA. His handwriting on the front looked messy and was almost illegible.

Frances.

No one called me that anymore. Except my sister. I didn't like that name. I'd shed it and every connotation that went with it years ago. Frances wasn't who I wanted to be.

"Open it," the lawyer urged.

I finally tore my eyes away from the pristine envelope and looked at the man with the bushy white handlebar moustache that made him look like Santa had taken up biking.

I shook my head. "No," I said, and slipped it into my black handbag.

He nodded at me, as if he understood what I was feeling. He probably did. He probably saw this sort of thing all the time. Just as I was closing my handbag, my phone rang. It was Kyle. A stab of panic hit me in the ribs. I needed to leave or else I was going to run late. Kyle had stressed to me how important this was for him . . . *us*.

"I have to go," I said, standing up.

"You can't go yet, there are a lot of papers that need signing, and I need to get a copy of your ID too, please."

"Uh . . . okay." I sat back down and pulled my ID out. He took it and smiled.

"I'll get the papers." When he exited the room, I pulled my phone out and called Kyle.

"Babe, where are you?" He didn't even bother to say hello. He sounded frantic.

"Still at the lawyer's," I said.

Huge sigh. "Are you going to be late?"

"I'm trying to hurry. But they have papers they need me to sign."

Another huge sigh. "That's why I told you to postpone this meeting. Lawyers always take ages."

"I'm going as fast as I can," I said, feeling more panic rise inside me.

"Do you know how important this shoot is for me . . . *for us*," he corrected.

"I know."

"I booked the photographer and everything. The whole studio is set up. Everyone is here, except you."

A stab in my ribs again. I wanted to tell him how important this was to me too, but he didn't seem interested. Or seem to care. This was something from my dad. The man who I shared half my DNA with. The man who was now gone, and who I would never have a chance to meet. This was a huge day for me too, and he was just disregarding it.

"I need you by my side for these photos—research shows that people are much more likely to relate to someone who has a girlfriend. Besides, I don't just want to appeal to the male demographic."

"I'll be as quick as I can," I said, feeling pissed off but trying to hide it. But really I wanted to shout in his face. I usually hid those feelings from Kyle, though. I was always so scared that if I showed him how I felt, really felt, he might leave me. I hung up as the lawyer came back with the pile . . . *Oh God*, that was a serious pile of papers.

My hand was sore by the time I walked out of the lawyer's office. I hadn't written that much, with an actual pen, in years. I rushed back to the staircase that I'd walked up to get here. I never took the elevator. I couldn't be in small spaces, not since the shed incident. Besides, taking stairs burned five to ten calories a minute. But when I got to the stairs there was a "No Entry, Slippery When Wet" sign blocking them. I looked at the elevator, took a deep breath and walked over to it. Just thinking about being inside was making me nervous. I pressed the button and before the doors opened, I checked my lipstick and smoothed my hair back in the steel panel that was now doubling as a mirror.

I looked like a real businesswoman today, that's for sure. I'm not sure why I'd dressed like this, to be honest. A full suit, black heels and matching black bag. My hair scraped back neatly as if I worked in an office. I'd tried on about ten outfits that morning, but it was hard to decide what to wear to the reading of your dead father's will. A father who'd abandoned me in life, but decided to leave me something in death, even though I'd never gotten so much as a birthday card from him.

I didn't know how to feel about this. And my mood-tracking app had given me no insight either. I suspected that if I did figure these feelings out, I might crumple to the floor in a heap of tears. Perhaps that's why I'd worn the clothes I had. Black and smart and strong and sophisticated. Clothes that didn't crumple to the floor in tears. My outfit was cool and calm and didn't show emotion. It was a suit of armor to protect me from the emotions of that meeting. I looked up at the elevator light but it didn't seem to be moving and, in frustration, I pressed the button five times in a row. This didn't make it move faster, though. The elevator finally stopped, and as the doors were about to open, my phone rang again.

"I'm on my way!" I said immediately, because I knew it was Kyle and I knew why he was phoning. The lift doors opened. "I'm leaving now, okay?" I walked into the elevator, briefly registering that someone was inside. "I'm walking into the elevator. I'm in the elevator. I'm pressing the button. I've pressed the button. I will be there on time."

"You better be," Kyle said down the phone and I just felt like crying. Kyle often said things that made me want to cry.

The elevator doors finally started closing. "Elevator doors are closing now. They've closed. I'll be there soon . . ." The phone delivered a loud hiss into my ear. "Uh, hellooooo?" The hiss continued and it was now joined by a static crackle. "Losing reception, sorry . . . uh . . . See you soon." I hung up and looked down as the screen delivered a no signal exclamation mark. A bolt of panic grabbed hold of me. I hated it when I had no signal. And I hated it inside this lift. I tapped my phone on the palm of my hand, partially because I felt like I had a cramp in my hand from all that writing, and partially because the nervous energy inside me was coiling and bubbling and needed to come out.

Something caught my eye. A big, smiley emoji. I glanced to my left. The woman I was sharing the elevator with was wearing a smiley emoji on her shirt. I lifted my eyes to her face; ironically, she didn't look smiley at all. She was fiddling with the strap of her handbag and looking as agitated as I felt. She gave me a small smile, but I looked away. I felt this nauseous sense of panic rising up in me and I was sure if I tried to smile back, I might get sick. I looked down at my phone again, no signal. I tapped it against my hand a few more times while I thought of that envelope in my bag. I thought of Kyle and the photoshoot and how important this was to him . . . *to us*, I corrected mentally.

I looked up at the floor numbers, but they seemed to be going so slowly and I wanted to scream. I wanted to be out of this lift so bloody badly and it was moving so slowly. And then, to my horror, it stopped and a hurried-looking woman strode in. She pressed the button once, and when the doors didn't close immediately, she pressed it another five times.

"It's not going to work faster if you push it more than once," I said to her, remembering my failed attempt with the exact same technique. But oh crap, she must have read my tone wrong, because she swung around and glared at me angrily. *Oh wow!* I inhaled sharply. This woman looked a little wild in the eye. She did have good eyebrows though, high and arched and black. But they did give her a very stern look.

The doors finally closed and she turned back. I was grateful when she did, because I felt like I was disintegrating under her intense stare. I turned and tried to catch Smiley Emoji's attention, and hopefully share a look of acknowledgement in solidarity of what had just happened, but she was too busy fingering the strap of her bag. Another noise caught my attention—it was the woman who'd given me a death stare. She was tapping her foot on the floor in a way that made my agitation boil, and made me tap my phone on my palm even more. We were each in our own worlds, tapping away. We were so physically close to each other, and yet so far away. All alone in our own worlds and—

Fuck!

A loud screeching noise ripped me from my thoughts. My stomach flew into my head, hot and red and choking as the lift plummeted.

I opened my mouth and screamed as we fell so fast I felt like I was going to pass out.

I was going to die!

I was sure of it. And in that moment the only thought I had was that I would never see what was inside that envelope. And never know what my father had said to me . . .

CHAPTER 20

I gripped the envelope in my hands tightly and turned to Cujo. He was looking at me as if waiting for something. As if there was food in the envelope. I shook my head and slipped it back into my handbag.

"I guess meditation is not my thing," I said to him, pushing myself off the tree trunk. "Guess we'll just go back to the hotel and sit there. And sit there and stare at the ceiling. And sit there and wait and wait and wait . . ." The need to reach out and touch my phone was so overwhelming again. The thought that I would go back to an empty room, alone, and have no way to contact the outside world, or distract me from what was going on inside, was killing me.

"You know, screw space! I mean, really? What the hell is so special about it anyway that we have to point these temperamental satellites at it? What kind of high-tech satellites get disrupted by a little Wi-Fi anyway? And what more do we need to know about space? It's a bunch of stars, okay! Stars!" I said to Cujo and started walking. He followed right behind me. I walked faster as this feeling of messy anger started rising inside me. I didn't know what I was angry about, exactly. Maybe everything. "And screw meditation. Thinking about nothing . . . What is that? Bashing brass bowls about, what good does that do? I can't believe I ever thought I could be some kind of spiritual blogger. Screw crystals. Screw tie-dye and definitely screw purple. And it's not like we were thinking of nothing anyway. That Cheryl was making me think of things I don't want to think of."

I took a deep breath to continue my rant. A rant that was making me feel slightly better. Cujo was a good listener. "The past is in the past, right? Motivation Monday, let's move on! Let's look to the future and better ourselves. That is what people expect from us. No one wants to come to my Insta and see me dwelling on the past. People want to see me smiling and squatting and eating smoothies and kissing Kyle. That's what they want and that is what I give them! Kyle says that we have to project an image of success at all times. We need to be aspirational and motivational and always strive to be the best people we can be. Our Massive, Explosive, Smash Through Best™! That's what's important, right?"

I walked faster and the muscles in my legs started burning and it felt good, because at least it was distracting me from the painful feelings that were swelling inside me. And all this thinking of Kyle and our relationship was making me feel somewhat mad. But it was also making me think. My sister's words echoed in my head . . . *narcissistic user.*

I stopped walking for a moment and turned to Cujo. He sat down and looked up at me. "Maybe . . ." My voice was softer this time. Less frantic, more thoughtful. "Maybe, okay I'll admit this, *maybe* things with Kyle weren't as good as I thought they were. Maybe I shouldn't have been so surprised by the break-up." My stomach knotted and I suddenly felt bad for saying that. I felt like I needed to defend Kyle and our relationship in some way. And so I did. "It's just that he was very driven and ambitious, okay? We both were. He was always pushing me to be a better person. Is that so bad?" I asked Cujo, who obviously didn't respond. "It's not that he didn't like me the way I was, though . . . he just wanted me to be better. For us both to be better. To have more followers and grow our businesses and focus on the things that really mattered, like what others thought of us!" Sadness. Sudden and hard and cold. Nibbling away at me as I spoke. I stopped walking and stared ahead of me.

"Nobody likes me anymore," I whispered softly to myself, my heart breaking in my chest. "They all hate me."

"Ruff! Ruff!"

"I don't know if you liking me counts. You just like me cos I feed you and let you sleep inside." I turned and looked at him as I walked back onto the main road and headed for the hotel. His one yellow eye looked full of compassion, his mouth was open, tongue hanging out as if he was . . . smiling?

I reached down and patted his head. "Thanks," I said. "You like me, and you're a good listener." The thought brought the smallest smile to my face and made me feel just the faintest bit better and less alone. No one had ever just let me vent like this. Not my sister, definitely not Kyle. And it felt good to finally voice out loud everything that I was *really* feeling inside. Even if it was all *very* confusing, and I didn't have a bloody app to un-confuse me either.

CHAPTER 21

After an entire afternoon spent in the hotel room with nothing to do again, other than popping to Jim's store to buy some doggy treats, I was utterly bored. And because of this boredom, I once again found myself walking down the street. This time it was not towards spiritual enlightenment, but rather towards movie night.

I walked down the street to the barn at the end of the road, Cujo next to me on the leash. He was surprisingly good, he never pulled and seemed to walk in perfect unison with me. If someone was looking at the two of us, they would think we'd been walking like this for years. Perfectly in tune with each other's movements.

The walk through the town was a pleasant one and the air was much cooler now. It was bearable being outside in the evening like this. And, at this time of day, the town really looked like it was something out of a picture book. It almost didn't look real, and certainly not of this time; it looked older and more historic in the warm lights shining from the streetlamps and out of people's windows, a place frozen in time. Like it was trapped in a snow globe, this perfect little place that was somehow separate from the rest of the world outside. If I could, I would have taken a photo of it and posted it on Instagram with some well-thought-out hashtags, but obviously . . . *not!* This thought saddened me. Sharing what I saw with others was an important part of my life. And now, it was gone. And worse than that, there was probably no one left to share it with anyway.

I found the barn at the end of the street, and automatically pulled my phone out of my bag to check how many steps I'd taken. I was still keeping my phone on me, even though I couldn't use it. Just knowing it was there made me feel better in some way.

The barn was a big structure with a high roof and no sides. It was full of people sitting on colorful blankets draped over hay bales. A screen had been made on one side by tying a sheet between two poles. Some people were sitting, others were milling about talking, and some were standing in queues ordering hot dogs, beers and milkshakes. I walked over to the milkshake stand and looked at it for a moment. No way to check how many calories were in it. But I was starving and the big, bright pink things seemed to be calling to me. I looked down at Cujo, almost asking for his permission, like I might have done with Kyle. He of course would have shaken his head and told me to "keep my eye on the prize"; keep my goal firmly in sight and don't let temptations pull me away from my true purpose. Smash Through™ temptation and step into my Massive, Explosive Purpose™.

But Kyle wasn't here. He was with @Paige_Dreams_ and they were probably both sitting on the sofa right now, the one I used to sit on, phones out, planning their social media posts for the week ahead, or filming some motivation video #couplegoals #screwthem!

So I ordered a strawberry milkshake. I hadn't had one in years, and it came just how I liked it, thick and creamy and bright pink. Cujo looked up at me and I shook my head at him.

"Not for you." I reached into my bag for the treats I'd bought him at Jim's earlier. While there, Natasha had invited me to book club again. I'd politely declined, again.

I glanced around the barn, looking for Mark. But when I couldn't see him, I walked over to a big hay bale and sat down. Cujo sat next to me and looked at the screen as if he was watching. I was late, the movie had already been on for a while, so I folded my arms and settled in to watch, as an older lady wearing a grey hat was talking to a blonde on screen.

"*I think they were after the children,*" the blonde was saying, looking somewhat terrified.

"*For what purpose?*" the older woman replied.

I found myself leaning in as the blonde paused and looked at her.

"*To kill them,*" she said.

My eyes widened and I twisted my body and looked at Cujo. He was looking at me too. As if he was thinking the exact same thing I was. *What the hell kind of movie was this?* I raised my brows at him in query and his one good ear stood to attention. Murder Mystery Night, Creepy Movie Night . . . My brain went back to the thought I'd had yesterday in Jim's store. I looked around the barn; everyone here seemed quite normal-looking, but I guess if I was someone in a murderous town, I would also look normal in hopes of luring people in. Suddenly, the screen filled with hundreds of flapping birds, going for a man's head, and I jumped in my seat. I didn't much care for birds, not since that time a dove had flown into the house and flapped around frantically for hours, trying to escape, flying into the window over and over again until it died. I shuddered at the memory, just as Cujo rose to his feet.

"What are you doing?" A sudden jerk from him and I was also on my feet. It felt like my shoulder had just been pulled out of its socket, the tug was so hard. He put his nose to the ground and started sniffing.

"Oh my God, yes!" I grabbed the sieve out my handbag just as Cujo took off. This was it! This was it. I ran behind him as he sniffed and wove his way through the seated crowd.

"Sorry, sorry, coming through," I said, as I bumped into people, sieve in hand, chasing after the dog. I had his backside in my sights and I wasn't going to let him get away. But then, he picked up pace. He jumped over a group of picnicking people on a blanket and I almost ran into them.

"I'm so sorry, I'm so sorry," I frantically apologized but kept on going. People around me were starting to get pissed off, I could hear their murmurs growing louder and louder. A few shouted "Sit down, we can't see!" but I couldn't let him out of my sights. I was going to get my immobilizer come hell or high water. And I didn't really care how many people I had to jump over, stand on, or irritate in order to do it!

CHAPTER 22

The general disgruntled chatter around me got louder as Cujo ran straight up to the front of the barn, casting a massive shadow over the screen and then, *then*, he started squatting. Right there in front of everyone! Loud boos rang out, but I didn't care. I ran up behind him with an outstretched sieve and then I heard a familiar voice.

"Frankie! What the hell are you doing?" I turned as Mark rushed up to the screen. More boos rang out, and some popcorn came flying my way.

"I have to get the immobilizer," I said, pointing at Cujo who looked like he was seconds away from it.

"But you're blocking the movie!"

"I can't move him," I said. "He's almost there."

"You have to move him, everyone is watching." He sounded rather frantic, with an air of sharp embarrassment in his voice. He was looking at the sieve in my hand. "I can't watch." He turned away. "This is beyond—"

"Disgusting!" someone yelled.

I tried to block out the noise and concentrate on the task ahead. But then as quickly as he'd started, Cujo stopped. He stood up. He looked at me over his shoulder and walked off.

"No, no, noooooo," I called as he scratched his paws on the ground pointedly.

"Get down, lady," someone else yelled.

"Aren't you going to do it?" I called off after him. "Please do it. Please," I begged, but he kept on walking.

"Go away!" More yells.

"You're ruining the movie," another one shouted.

I turned to face the crowd, the light from the projector blinding me, and I shielded my eyes with my arm. "What's wrong with you all, never seen a woman with a sieve?" I held it up and shook it at everyone, just as a piece of popcorn connected with my face.

Someone grabbed me by the hand and pulled me. It was Mark.

"Come," he urged, pulling me out of the light and away from the screen. A massive cheer rang out from the crowd. I turned and gave them all a death stare. I'm sure I heard one guy shout, "Go away, sieve lady." So much for this little, social, friendly town. .

"What are you doing?" Mark asked, when we were both far away from the screen.

"He swallowed my car immobilizer. I'm trying to get it back."

"Who swallowed your what?"

"Him!" I pointed.

"*Your* dog?" Mark replied.

"*Not* my dog swallowed my car immobilizer and it's a rental and I don't have a spare and I would like to use the key to get the hell out of here!" I was feeling overwhelmed now, and I could hear that my voice had risen a few octaves.

"Right here, right now. At movie night. In front of the whole town?"

"Excuse me, it's not like I planned for him to . . . you know."

He cleared his throat. This was such a bizarre conversation to be having and I think we were both aware of it. I shuffled my feet around awkwardly.

"Do we have to talk about this?" he asked.

"No! NO! We don't," I said, relieved that he was putting an end to this conversation. "I'll just go." I walked over to Cujo and picked up his leash. "I'll go back to the hotel and, I don't know," I sighed, "do whatever I need to do with a sieve. Maybe. If it ever happens." I shot the dog a look and he seemed to lower his head in embarrassment.

"What?" I asked him. "You're embarrassed? Well, I was the one trying to catch your crap with a sieve in front of half the town. I should be the one embarrassed." I turned away from Mark and started walking.

"You know he doesn't understand English, right?" Mark sounded amused and I swung around again. He was smiling at me now, his irritation seemed to be gone.

I walked back over to him and then leaned in and lowered my voice. "Can I tell you something?" I asked.

Mark leaned in. "Sure."

"Sometimes, I swear he bloody understands me. And I'm sure he's been messing with me since the day I met him. And I'm not sure why, but sometimes I get the feeling he has ulterior motives."

Mark laughed.

"I know, it sounds weird!"

But Mark shook his head and gestured to the screen. "Who am I to argue with that? We're watching *The Birds* by Alfred Hitchcock, after all."

I looked at the screen again as more murderous-looking birds filled it.

"In this movie, the bird population starts attacking humans. They become coordinated and plan staged attacks."

"I see." I looked at Cujo suspiciously. He didn't look like he had some grand, malicious master plan; now he just looked lazy, lying there on the floor, his head propped up on a hay bale as if using it as a pillow, as if he was about to fall asleep. I tugged on the leash and he opened his one eye lazily. I sighed. He couldn't fall asleep at a time like this.

"I have to go," I said, hauling Cujo to his feet. I was having to pull him along with me now. He was no longer being good on the leash. Instead, he was lazily dragging his paws on the ground, as if he didn't want to leave, as if he was trying to keep me here. But I wasn't going to let him.

"You can stay if you want!" I heard Mark say and I turned. He was smiling at me again, a small, curious smile, and my stomach gave the tiniest little flutter. A pitter-patter of feet running across my diaphragm. I looked back at him and noticed for the first time that night that he wasn't wearing his glasses.

"You're not wearing your glasses," I said.

His smile grew. "I touched my eyeball."

I smiled back at him. "Well, it looks . . . you look . . ." I stopped talking when I had that feeling again.

Familiarity? Where the hell from though?

"You know, this is probably going to sound weirder than dogs understanding me, but . . . I don't know. You look familiar."

Suddenly, Mark's entire demeanor changed. He lowered his head and turned his body away from me. "I have one of those faces," he mumbled. He briefly looked up at me again, but then walked away. "See you around."

I stared at his back. I hadn't expected him to get so touchy and irritated.

"Bye. Whatever!" I said, and walked away briskly, while the pitter-patter on my diaphragm turned to stomping. I noticed a woman walking purposefully in my direction. Well, I thought she was walking in my direction until she crossed her arms angrily and moved past me. I turned around and watched as she stamped up to Mark and stopped in front of him.

"I thought you weren't coming here tonight?" she asked with what was clearly an accusatory tone.

"Um . . ." He ran his hand through that hair of his. Slightly long, slightly wavy. "I changed my mind. But it was too late to let you know." I smiled to myself. That sounded like a lie. He sounded guilty. Boyfriend-guilty.

"Really." She had her hands on her hips now. Clearly, she also didn't believe him.

I scoffed and rolled my eyes, as he gave her what looked like a fake placating smile. And then his eyes moved past her and he caught me watching. His smile immediately disappeared and he narrowed his eyes at me. He obviously didn't want me seeing this. Whatever! I turned and walked away.

I can't believe I'd had a pitter-patter over him.

CHAPTER 23

I was having a strange and disturbing dream. I was running down the road in the town and was being followed by a flock of blue Twitter birds. They were raining brown poop emojis down on me and I was frantically weaving from left to right to avoid them. And then I heard laughter and turned to see #Kaige riding on the back of a giant Twitter bird. I felt a hard thump on my head and realized that they had tossed my iPhone 11 Pro in rose gold at me—the one that @TheKyleWhite101 had bought me for my birthday last month; he'd filmed that amazing unboxing with me and then Apple had sent us another one free. I stopped and picked up the phone and it melted in my hand like mercury. All my pictures and videos and messages and friends and likes and followers, melting through my hand like mush and falling to the ground. I tried to grab up the liquid and make it solid again, scrabbling for all those years of work and sharing and posting, but it was gone. And then, the evil Twitter birds started shooting giant Pinterest pins out their mouths like missiles. They flew through the air and one caught me, pinning my skirt to the ground. I tried to get away, pulling at my skirt, but it wouldn't budge. I was stuck. Trapped by the physical manifestation of social media come to life to torment and torture me. And then, just as a giant screaming ghost-face emoji started rushing at me, I opened my eyes.

I sat up in bed. Drenched in sweat, panting hard. I grabbed my phone and squeezed it. Thank God, it was solid. Everything was still intact. I breathed a sigh of relief and flopped back onto the bed. I was just about to roll back over and go to sleep again, when I heard a whimper.

"Cujo? Are you okay?" I looked over at him. All I could see was a black shadow stretched out across the carpet. I flicked the lights on. He was lying on his side, his head down on the ground, tongue hanging out.

"Hey! Are you okay?" I climbed out of bed.

He tilted his eye up to me, tried to raise his head, but it flopped back down again as if he couldn't hold it up.

"Oh no!" I rushed over to him and shook him. He barely stirred. "No, no, no! Don't you dare!" I slipped my arms under him and heaved with all my might, trying to get him onto his feet. He teetered there for a moment or two, and then slipped back down onto the ground like something without bones. Shapeless like jelly, melting into the floor, like the phone in my nightmare.

"Come on!" I repeated the action, and again, boneless, he slipped back down.

"Shit, shit!" I walked in a circle as I decided what needed to be done. And right now, there was only one thing to do. "Right!" I heaved him up again, this time using every ounce of my strength. He was so heavy, like a deadweight, and it took everything inside me to finally hoist him off the ground.

"You've gotta help me here! Okay! I can't do this alone," I urged, huffing and puffing from the exertion. He seemed to understand, and put his paws on my shoulders, slipping his legs over them like two great arms. I wrapped my arms around his back and hoisted him onto me as best I could and then rushed for the door.

"Oh my God, you are heavy," I said, as I walked as fast as I could down the road towards the vet's. Each step I took felt like torture, as his weight held me back like a gale force wind might do if you were trying to walk into it. My back ached from being bent backwards, my knees ached, my fracking spine felt like it was going to snap in two.

"Almost there, almost there, almost there," I said to myself, to him, to whoever as I shuffled up the road. One tiny step in front of another tiny step. Soon I could see the house. But the closer I got, the more he was slipping from my grasp. I stopped and tried to reposition him, his legs over my shoulders, my arms wrapped tightly around his back, holding him onto me, pressing him tightly against my body like glue. I could feel his heart beat, feel the weight of his head on my shoulder and the hot rush of breath against my neck. Finally, after another exhausting few meters, I arrived at the house. I kicked my foot against the wooden door over and over and over, drumming at it repeatedly and loudly, calling out until a light went on and the door was finally opened. A sleepy-looking Samirah looked at me through hooded eyes.

"Something's wrong with him!" I exclaimed.

Samirah nodded and flung the front door open, and then without saying a word, grabbed hold of Cujo, making him instantly lighter in my arms. We walked like that down the hallway, and out into her practice. We lifted him onto the steel table and he flopped down on it like a sack of potatoes with a loud thud.

"Oh my God!" I gasped when his one eye started to close.

"How long has he been like this?" Samirah asked, placing a stethoscope to his side.

"I don't know. I went to sleep. I . . . and then he made this noise and I found him like this. Is he okay?" I felt frantic. Hysterical.

"I'm going to take an X-ray and let's see what's going on inside." And with that, she wheeled the great steel table out the room and around the back. I bit down on my nails as I paced the room a few times. A mass of feelings was building up inside me, consuming me . . . and I didn't really know what they were, or why I was feeling them and I bloody wanted my mood-tracking app to tell me. I needed an emotive emoji face to explain to me my feelings, but in my haste, I'd left my phone at the hotel. My heart was pounding and the desire to check my heart rate and make sure I wasn't having a heart attack was also overwhelming.

Samirah finally appeared around the corner again. "I'm going to have to operate to get the immobilizer out."

"What?" I gasped. "You're going to have to operate?" And then, like something I couldn't control, I burst into tears. "Is he going to be okay?"

"He will be if I operate now," she said, sounding calm but hurried.

I shook my head, tears streaming down my face. "You can't let him die," I gushed, so unsure of where this emotion was coming from. This wasn't even my dog. I didn't even like him. And yet, the idea that he might not exist in the world anymore was making me feel like I couldn't breathe.

Samirah walked over to me, laid her hands on my shoulders. "Can I call someone to sit with you while I'm busy? This might take an hour or so and I don't want you to be alone." She sounded so concerned for me and this made me want to cry even more.

I shook my head. "There's no one. I don't have friends here."

"Is there really no one?"

And then for some reason, and I don't know why, maybe it was because he was the only person I knew, the only name I knew, I said it. "Mark. I don't know his surname. I don't even think he likes me, but he's the only person I know here, other than you. From the video and music store."

She nodded and smiled. "Sure, I'll call him." She reached for an old landline that was attached to the wall. "You can wait inside the house, help yourself to a cup of tea, I'll be done as soon as I can."

"Can I see him, before you operate?" I asked, tears streaming down my face.

"Sure." She put the phone back and led me around to the back. Cujo was lying on the steel table, looking so lifeless and alone. My heart broke for him. I rushed over and grabbed his paw. He looked at me, one eye connecting with mine and I swear, he smiled a bit.

"Don't die on me. Okay!" I squeezed his paw and he picked his head up with what looked like great effort and then he licked my hand. He was comforting me, even though he was the one who needed comforting.

"Okay, I'll see you soon," I said and exited, leaving Samirah to do her work. I walked out of the small cottage and into her house. I stood there in the middle of the passage and for a few moments didn't know what to do or where to go. She'd told me to go into her house and wait there. Make myself at home. Was this small-town hospitality? So trusting of her, and she didn't even know me. The gesture was both comforting in some way, and almost too much to bear. As if she had entrusted me with something I had no right to be entrusted with. And then, like some dull pain, it crept up on me again. The feeling that I'd spent my whole life running from. The feeling that I could usually swipe away with my thumb, that I could smile away with a selfie stick, that I could vlog away with my recorded words and likes and shares . . . Loneliness. Big and cavernous and so vast that it echoed deep inside me. It hurt.

I shook my head, physically flinging the thoughts from my mind. A photo on the wall caught my attention and I walked over to it. It was of Samirah and her husband on their wedding day. The two of them were standing arm in arm, smiling and laughing happily, as if truly enjoying having their photo taken. Not like when I took photos. Taking photos was work. It took effort and time. But this one seemed so natural and unrehearsed. You rarely see photos like that anymore. Photos that capture a happy moment and freeze it forever. No filter necessary. No Photoshop.

Honestly, I couldn't really remember the last time I'd taken a photo like that. I turned away from the framed photo and walked into the kitchen and . . .

"Oh!" I said. A massive dog bed lay on the floor and it was filled, and I mean *filled*, with five small dogs. I'd never noticed dogs here before. They all looked up at me, but didn't move. I sat down at the table and laced my fingers together, and then unlaced them. I did this over and over again, thinking of the lick Cujo had given me.

Satan, Cujo . . . *what the hell?* The sound of those names in my head suddenly felt so wrong. Because he was anything but Satan's Little Helper, or Cujo the horror dog. I'd been so wrong about him, and I vowed right there and then that as soon as the surgery was over, I would give him a proper name. A real name. I heard the bell ring, and I rushed over to the front door. And when I pulled it open, there was Mark.

CHAPTER 24

"You're actually here." I stared at the man standing there in what looked like clothes you would sleep in. A ruffled, old creased T-shirt that said Pink Floyd across it, with a neckline that had been stretched with what looked like years of wear and tear, and an old pair of tracksuit pants.

"Samirah called. She said I was needed, so I came."

"Just like that. You came here?" I asked.

He nodded.

"Well," I looked away, "thank you, I mean, I didn't think you would really come. In the middle of the night and after what happened at the movie." What I wanted to say was, *After your mood totally changed and you turned your back on me*, but didn't.

"Are you okay?" he asked gently. His voice was full of warm sympathy, and it made me feel like crying all over again.

I nodded, and then shook my head. "I don't know. I mean, I feel . . . I don't know. He's not even my dog and yet I feel . . ." I walked back to the kitchen. I could hear Mark following me. I stopped and swung around. "I don't even like dogs. And definitely not that one. He is the ugliest thing I have ever seen and yet . . ." I lost the words and started walking again, and then stopped once more and swung around. "I should be pissed off with him. I mean, he hitched a ride with me without my permission and then swallowed my damn rented car immobilizer just as I was trying to leave this place. Like he knew. He knew I wanted to go and he did it on purpose and I should be so mad with him that I . . ." The words left me again and I started walking, then repeated my dramatic swing around. But this time, I pointed at Mark. "You know what? I am mad at him. So, so mad at him. Because now I feel like this, all worried and stressed and like I want to cry, and I don't like feeling like this and he made me feel like this. So yes, I'm mad at him!" I put my hand on my hips and exhaled loudly. At that, a small smile tugged at the corners of Mark's lips.

"What?" I asked.

"For someone who doesn't have a dog, doesn't even like dogs, thinks this dog is the ugliest thing they have ever seen, you sure care about him a lot."

I threw my hands in the air. "Could people stop saying stuff like that to me! I think I would know if I cared about something." I said it, even though at this stage I knew that was a blatant lie. I flopped down at the kitchen table again and held my head in my hands for a few seconds. And then I shrugged.

"Fine. I care, I guess," I said into my hands, almost inaudibly. "I don't want him to die. That would suck."

I heard a small chuckle and looked up. Mark was turning the kettle on and pulling two cups out of the cupboard as if he knew his way about this kitchen.

"Why are you laughing?" I asked him.

"It's just funny listening to you going around in these circles. When it's so clear to everyone."

"What's clear?"

He looked over his shoulder at me as he dropped two tea bags into the cups. "You love that ugly, one-eyed, immobilizer-swallowing mutt out there." His Australian accent suddenly sounded so strong. I'd almost forgotten it until now.

I held his gaze as he smiled at me, and then my face started contorting and my lips started to quiver and my eyes started to go all blurry and . . .

"I'm sorry." He stepped forward, looking slightly panicked and concerned. "Did I say something upsetting?" A tear rolled out of my eye and waterfalled down my cheek. He looked around the kitchen and then grabbed a big roll of heavy-duty kitchen tissue and passed it to me.

"Thanks," I managed. I tore a piece off and wiped my eyes and then didn't care that I blew my nose and it sounded like an elephant trumpet. I paused for a moment and then the words came flying out of my mouth.

"I love him," I moaned loudly. "Against my will though. Trust me, I don't want to love him. He is not the dog I would choose to love. If I was going to choose to love a dog it would not look like that. It would be one of those teacup poodles that you can put into tiny things like shoes and handbags and take cute photos of; do you know how many likes teacup poodles get, or French bulldogs? I once saw this video of a French bulldog in a bowtie, it went viral. That's the kind of dog I would love, not Cujo!" I slumped onto the table again, overcome by my very inconvenient feelings.

It occurred to me, right there and then, that Cujo was the first creature that I'd cared this much about in a very long time. I didn't even care this much when @TheKyleWhite101 had gone in for his pec implants. He'd threatened me with death if I ever told anyone about them. He had a genetic deficiency, he called it. All the men in his family had small pecs, no matter how much they worked out, and he needed pecs for his personal brand. It had been a long surgery, but I'd mainly spent the time weighing in on some Twitter war that was happening. And when they'd finally wheeled him out of surgery all groggy from the anesthetic and moaning from the pain, in truth, I hadn't really felt that much.

But now, I was feeling a lot. I didn't want Cujo to be in pain, I hoped Samirah would give him painkillers. I hoped he would remember me. I hoped he would lick my hand and bark like he used to, because right now, he was the closest thing I had to a friend.

A real friend.

And maybe he'd been more of a friend to me in the last few days than some of my other online friends had been to me in years. Like Suzanne. When I needed her the most, she'd ghosted me. Same as my sister. But Cujo was still here, and I felt closer and more connected to him than I'd felt to anyone in a very, very long time.

"What's going on?" Mark burst my bubble.

"Why?" I looked up at him.

"Looks like you are having some big aha moment there?" He poured the boiled water into the cups and then walked the tea over to the table and sat down across from me.

I shook my head. "Aha moment. I don't think so." I grabbed the tea and took a sip, and this time I kind of knew I was lying to myself again too.

Because I was having an aha moment. An aha moment about the kind of life I'd been living up until that point. The kind of relationships I'd had. And I didn't much like it.

CHAPTER 25

I'm not sure how long Mark and I sat there in total silence sipping tea together. But it felt like forever. Time seemed to be dragging on in a way that was making it feel like it had stopped altogether. The silence between us was strange. Comfortable, but strange. It was as if we'd both decided not to speak to each other at all, even though no such agreement had been made. We had fallen into it naturally, for some reason. The only noise in the room, other than the occasional sipping of tea, was the snoring of dogs in the corner.

Finally, Samirah's head came around the corner. I jumped out of my seat and raised my brows in question.

"He's out," she said with a smile.

"Is he . . .?" I let the question hang in the air and she gave me the biggest, warmest smile I'd ever seen.

"Absolutely fine."

At those words I felt a sense of relief flood over me. I held my head in my hands for a moment or two, because it felt like it was spinning.

"And here." She held her hand out.

"What's that?" I asked, reaching out.

She opened her hand and I saw the immobilizer; I had totally forgotten about it. Somewhere along the way, that had become the last thing on my mind.

"Th-thanks." I stumbled over my words. "Can I see him?"

"Sure."

We followed Samirah out the house and into the small cottage outside. Cujo was lying on a big bed on the floor. His one eye was open slightly, and when he saw me, his tail made the slightest attempt at a wag and my heart felt like it might explode. I walked over to him and was about to reach out and pat his head when I saw his stomach and the scars across it. And I don't mean the fresh scar that Samirah had made. His stomach was shaved and it looked like it was crisscrossed with lines and deep wounds. I looked up at Samirah with wide eyes.

"What's all this?"

She bent down next to me and started pointing to the marks. "I would say these are from jumping over a wire fence, this looks like it's a bite from another animal, this could be from a porcupine."

"But there're so many." I stared at the map of lines on his belly.

"And I bet if I had to shave other parts of his body, you would find more. This guy has had a long, hard life. I think he might have lived out in the wild his entire life. Maybe he belonged to someone once, but he hasn't belonged to anyone in a while."

A tear rolled out my eye. I reached for his paw and he lifted it up to me.

"Still think he's not your dog?" Samirah asked. I looked up at her and rolled my eyes.

"Perhaps it's time to give him a real name now," she said.

I heard Mark come up behind me now. "Yeah, you can't keep calling him Cujo."

"What should I call him?"

We all kept quiet for a while and then Samirah spoke.

"In Arabic, we have a boy's name that comes to mind."

"What?" I turned and looked at her.

"Harun. It means warrior lion. Fighter."

I turned and looked at the big black dog on the floor. Full of the scars of a hard life lived and I couldn't think of a better name to describe him.

"Hey, Harun," I said, as I laid a hand on his big head.

Suddenly, his whole head lifted and he gave a feeble bark.

We all laughed. "That's his name," Mark said.

"That's his name." I agreed.

Samirah reached out and laid a hand on his nose, as if taking his temperature. "And it seems that Harun here has plans of his own."

"What do you mean?" I asked.

"Well, you can't travel with him now. He needs some rest and recovery time. He's going to be tender for a while and needs to be kept still and calm for a few days. So, I'm afraid you're not getting away from us that easily." She glanced at me and then her eyes drifted over to Mark and then back to me again.

"Oh," I said flatly.

Samirah gave me another one of her guru-ish smiles with that mysterious twinkle she had going in those hypnotic green eyes of hers. Her eyes and smile that seemed privy to some kind of cosmic information that none of us were privy to. Like she was tapped into something that none of us saw. "Seems that someone is telling you to stay right here, aren't they?"

I sighed. Something about that statement seemed right on some level. For the last few days it had felt like something had been pulling me in a weird direction I didn't quite understand yet. From elevators, to here. I didn't know what it all meant right now, but I was starting to think that it might actually mean something.

"You can come back in the morning to fetch him," Samirah said, pulling a blanket over him. "I'd like to keep him here overnight just for observation."

"I'll come and fetch him with you," Mark muttered.

"Oh, thanks," I smiled at him appreciatively, "but I do have a car now."

He shook his head. "I'd like to come and see how he's doing anyway."

My smile grew. He was nice. A nice guy. Only a nice guy would come here in the middle of the night to comfort a total stranger who had almost ruined his movie night with a shit show, so to speak.

I gave Harun's paw a big squeeze and then stood up and eyeballed Samirah. "Take care of him tonight! Please."

She nodded. "I'll look after him as if he was my own," she said, and I believed her. And then she turned to Mark. "Perhaps you would be kind enough to give Frankie a lift back to her hotel?"

"I can walk," I said quickly. "It's literally a few feet away."

"I don't know if you're aware, but there seems to be a jackal on the loose. Perhaps it's safer if Mark drives you."

I smiled. I slowly raised my eyes to Mark's. He was also smiling at me. We locked eyes and our smiles grew and then my cheeks felt like they were heating up. I put my cool hands to them and looked away, a strange feeling roiling in my stomach.

"I should defo give you a lift, what with the jackal on the prowl and all," Mark said, and I could hear he was fighting back laughter in his voice.

"Defo?" I asked, feeling amused.

"Sorry, my Australian need to abbreviate coming out."

"He usually tries to keep it hidden until he gets to know someone," Samirah added.

"Really?" I felt somewhat touched by this.

"And then it's all brekkie and footie and Chrissie!" she teased.

Mark laughed. "Let's get out of here, before she makes me look like a total fool." I got the feeling from this interaction that Samirah and Mark knew each other well. I started walking out when something caught my eye.

"What's that?" I asked, pointing at it.

Samirah walked up behind me and sighed. "I need an assistant. It's getting too hard to work being this pregnant. And I'm sure I'll need some extra help when the babies arrive too. I was planning on sticking it up in the town hall."

"Oh." I looked at the poster for a moment. "Good luck. Hope you find a good person."

CHAPTER 26

$\mathcal{W}$e pulled up to my hotel, after what was a literal thirty-second drive. But for some reason I didn't want to get out the car. I was agitated and I didn't know why. I'd been feeling so relieved a few moments ago, and now I wasn't. I shuffled about in my seat a little and then, without thinking, reached into my bag to grab my phone, only to realize that it wasn't there. This made me feel even more agitated.

I caught Mark looking at me out of the corner of my eye. I turned and our eyes locked. I took the opportunity to study them for a while. He was wearing his glasses again. His eyes were brown, nothing spectacular or out of the ordinary and yet . . . *yet?*

Something familiar about them I couldn't place. Maybe he was right, he had one of those faces. A generic, nice-guy face with generic, friendly brown eyes. He wasn't the kind of guy you would find on Tinder posing at the gym with his pecs or sending you dick pics.

"Weird not being able to use a phone?" His question caught me off guard.

I nodded. "It is. More than weird. It's . . ." I didn't finish the sentence, because I didn't really have the words to describe this feeling of not having it. And especially at a time like this. I would usually have told everyone about my dog's surgery and everyone would have reached out with good wishes and praying hand emojis and emojis with tears. That would have made me feel better . . . *I think?*

"Do you know why there is no reception in this town?" he asked, as if he could hear my thoughts.

"Some satellite looking at space," I offered up. "Something like that."

"No. Not a *something like that* at all." His voice had taken on a slightly harsh tone.

"Then what?"

He leaned forward and looked out the windshield, casting his eyes upwards. "We can't see it here. Because of the lights from town. You up for a short drive?"

I looked at the time. It was already two a.m. But I didn't really feel like being alone right now, and I probably wouldn't be able to sleep if I was.

I nodded and he smiled at me. "Right, let's go." He pulled off and started driving again.

* * *

We drove out the small town and left the lights behind us, and soon we were on a dirt road heading into the middle of the desert. I briefly wondered if I should be scared, driving out into the middle of nowhere with a virtual stranger. These kinds of things rarely ended well. I looked over at him as he drove and decided that all indications so far suggested he probably wasn't a threat . . . I hoped not anyway. Soon the flat road we were on started tilting up, going higher and higher, and soon it felt like we were climbing up the side of a high mountain. We drove slowly, right on the edge of it. I plucked up the courage to look down only for a moment . . . instant dizziness and swelling nausea. We were higher than I'd imagined.

Finally, we stopped and Mark turned off the lights of the car. I was suddenly hit by how black everything outside was. I stared into the blackness. It was impenetrable. Like it was a solid wall. Or a thick, black mist. It seemed like the blackest black I'd ever seen before.

"It's so dark here," I whispered, a shiver running down my spine.

"This is called a dark site." Mark opened the car door with a creak and climbed out.

"What's a dark site?" I asked, also climbing out into the cool night.

"This is!" He threw his arms into the air and I looked up, and when I did, I gasped.

"Oh my God." I stared up at the sky in absolute awe and amazement at the stars spread out in front of me. I didn't even know so many stars existed. And they were so clear. Like perfect, bright pinpricks. A massive arm of them stretched across from one side to the other. I'd never seen that formation before.

"What is it?" I asked, lifting my hand into the air and tracing the line from one side to the other with my pointed finger.

"That's the Milky Way," he said, staring up at the enormous arch that cut the sky in two. "And down in that valley, there are ten massive radio telescopes that are studying it right now, and even the slightest disturbance from a cell phone, a TV or a radio signal could interfere with what they're doing."

I ran my eyes over it, from one side to the other, inspecting it, and soon I wasn't just seeing stars and sky, I could clearly see colors. Faint purples and pinks formed what looked like massive clouds encasing the archway of stars. And in the middle of the archway, a thin vein of black ran through.

"It's huge." I knew I was stating the obvious, but it really was massive.

"I know. And we're such a tiny part of it." Mark's voice sounded a little distant, as if he was really thinking about this. "They think there are 100 billion planets in the Milky Way."

"Wow." I let that number sink in for a while. It was a number so big, it was hard to truly comprehend. "Do you think there are other life forms out there, like us?" I asked, putting my hands on my hips. "Like somewhere in the Milky Way there are two other people like us staring at the night sky wondering the exact same question?"

Mark turned and grinned at me. "I don't know. Probably. Maybe. It's very possible."

"Or maybe there is a future version of us and a past version," I said thoughtfully.

"What do you mean?"

"Us, but in a different state of evolution. For example, there could be a planet out there that is less advanced than us. And there's a prehistoric version of us, all loincloths and making fire with sticks. But somewhere else, there is a futuristic Frankie. Some AI cyborg version of myself with technology integrated into my brain."

Mark turned all the way around now and faced me. He looked surprised. "I had no idea you were so . . . deep?" He seemed completely amused.

I shrugged. "I used to read a lot of books when I was young and spent a lot of time alone thinking."

"Oh?" That was definitely surprise in his voice.

"What? Don't I look like the kind of person who reads books and thinks a lot?"

His grin grew. It seemed to wiggle its way up into his eyes, and suddenly those plain brown eyes that seemed less than extraordinary just a short while ago were looking pretty extraordinary now.

"Well, what?" I heard myself ask again.

He just shrugged. "Nothing." And then he turned and walked over to the bonnet of his car and climbed on. He lay all the way back and looked up into the sky. He patted the bonnet next to him, and he grabbed my arm as I climbed up, helping me. I lay on my back and looked up at the sky. We were almost shoulder to shoulder, and it was so quiet here that I could just hear his breathing next to me.

We lay there for a while, until a breeze picked up and made me shiver.

"Cold?" Mark asked.

"A little," I confessed.

He shuffled closer to me, our shoulders now touching, and the warmth coming from his body was a very welcome surprise. He gave my shoulder a nudge, as if to ask if it was okay that he touched me with it. I nudged back, letting him know that it was okay through some kind of magical shoulder speak that I think we were just making up.

"So what do you think?" he asked, after a long moment of silence.

"About what?" I asked.

"You think you can sacrifice some cell-phone reception and Wi-Fi for this?" He swooshed his hand across the night sky again.

"Mmmm." I turned my head towards him, only to find him looking at me. Our eyes locked for a moment and my once audible "mmmm" became a breathy, whispered "mmmm" which had not been the intention at all. He raised a brow at me in query. I shrugged my shoulders, forgetting our shoulders were touching, and they dragged against his, slowly.

"I guess this is a sort of vaguely okay reason not to use a phone." My voice was a little playful and sarcastic. "I mean, this would make an amazing Insta pic though." I also swooshed my hand across the sky.

He laughed a little and I found myself suddenly feeling very attracted to him, something which surprised me.

I looked away from him and back up to the sky. "Do you know what any of them are called? The stars and constellations?" I asked.

"Not really. I mean I know Orion's belt, that's about it."

"If we had the internet I could download an app that would probably tell us exactly what everything was."

"Yeah, but where's the fun in that?" he said.

"I like to know things," I said. This was an understatement, obviously. Not knowing things was not an option for me. I needed to know and I needed to know now, and Google always told me. Knowing was always an instant hit of relief. But now, I found myself knowing nothing.

"Sometimes knowing everything isn't all it's cracked up to be."

His voice was smaller and more serious than it had been a few moments ago and I turned to him again.

"Also, it's more fun to guess the names." His tone was suddenly back to being light and playful. "For instance, that one over there looks like a lamb shank." He pointed up to the sky and traced the stars with his finger. And when I saw it, I had to agree. I chuckled softly.

"And that one," he continued, "a llama."

I leaned forward and looked as he traced another series of stars with his finger. I chuckled again. "Or an ostrich," I said.

"And that one?" He pointed all the way across the sky again, I followed his hand. "The one starting by the big orange star at the horizon?"

"Mmmm." I stared at it for a while, joining the dots. "It actually looks a little like Harun. See, the one big eye."

This time Mark chuckled. "Totally Harun."

And then he turned his head to me again. "See? Much more fun than looking on an app."

"I guess," I said thoughtfully.

CHAPTER 27

"*A*aaahhhh!" I threw myself off the bed, tripping and falling as I went. For a second, I was on my hands and knees, but quickly stood up as Mark flew off the bed and almost bolted to the other side of the room, as if I was contagious.

"Oh my Go— Sorry!" he said.

"Me too. Me too. Sorry!"

"I didn't mean to—" he exclaimed.

"ME NEITHER!"

"I mean, I really didn't mean to!"

"Trust me, neither did I!"

(Awkward silent pause between us.)

"Ummmm . . ."

(Even longer awkward silent pause.)

"Let's just forget that happened."

"Already forgotten," I said quickly.

"Me too!" Mark reiterated.

(Awkward laugh from both of us followed by another awkward pause . . . AGAIN!)

"Right, shall we fetch Harun?" I finally said, breaking the ear-shattering silence in the room.

"YES! Right. Let's do that!" Mark looked so happy that we were changing the subject from the huge elephant that was clearly in the room with us now.

"Let's go then," I said as we both rushed for the door, only to bump into each other as we went. We both jumped back at the same time, as if we'd run into an electric fence.

"Shit! Sorry!" I said, moving even further away from him.

He stepped back. "Sorry!" He shook his head and then rushed out the door, as if he didn't want to be in that room a moment longer. As if he wanted to be as far away from me, and that bed, as possible. Which I did too!

We drove in silence and my cheeks burned red and hot as I thought about it. Thought about falling asleep during the movie we'd watched together last night after coming back from star-gazing. About waking up tangled—and I mean *tangled*—in each other's arms. His arm around me, pulling me close to him. His one hand pressed against the skin of my back where my shirt had crept up, my head buried deep into the crook of his neck, breathing in his smell, my lips against the rough skin of his neck. Even our feet and toes were tangled together, as it seemed like our bodies had melted into each other's. It had taken me a few seconds to realize what was happening when I'd woken up, but when I had, we'd both disentangled ourselves as quickly as possible, and now we were enjoying this incredibly awkward moment in the car.

We arrived at Samirah's and both flew out the car, careful not to look at each other. We rushed for the door as if our lives depended on getting to it before the other one and then . . .

"Sorry!" I said as our hands connected, fingers slipping between each other's as we reached for the door handle at the same time.

"Sorry," Mark said hurriedly, as if he couldn't get the word out fast enough. We both pulled back and then . . .

"Crap! SORRY!" I said again as we both reached for the door handle again at the same time, mashing our hands together once more. We both pulled away and stood there quietly staring at the door handle in silence. No one moved.

"You open the door," I said, pointing at it.

"You sure?" he asked.

"Yes. You open it," I replied.

"Okay," he said, but then paused and did nothing at all . . .

"Alright. Fine. I'll open it," I said with force, but didn't make a move either.

"How about I open it?" We both jumped when we heard a voice coming from behind the door. The door opened and a man was standing in front of us, a smile plastered across his face.

"Hi," I said, shooting him a lame, wave-emoji hand.

He was still smiling at us. "Reminds me of when Samirah and I first started dating," he said in a big, friendly voice. He was the man from the photo I'd seen the night before.

"Sorry, what does?" I enquired.

"You know . . .'Oh, you hang up,' 'No, you hang up,' and then you just land up sitting on the phone even longer because neither of you wants to end it." He burst out laughing. Samirah walked up the passage and joined him, followed by the five scrappy-looking dogs I had seen the night before. They looked like a real motley crew.

"What's so funny?" she asked.

"These two trying to decide who should open the door, like we used to try and decide who hung up the phone first."

Samirah glanced over at us and smiled; we both looked away, which I know must have made us look as guilty as hell. But guilty for what? Accidentally spooning each other in our sleep? No, let's be honest, it wasn't exactly spooning. Spooning is neat and ordered, this had been all over the place and twisted together and . . . *whisking!* That's what it was. We'd been in bed together whisking. I forced my eyes up to Samirah's so she would stop looking at us like we were kids on the naughty seat.

"HOW'S HARUN?" Mark and I both said at the exact same time (maybe a little too loudly). This caused Samirah and the man to burst out laughing together.

"See what I mean?" the man said, placing a hand on Samirah's shoulder.

She nodded. "I do see," she replied, and then eyeballed me with one of her strange, meaningful looks. The kind that burns through your soul like a flaming sword through a watermelon (which I've seen on a YouTube video btw! The Sword vs Watermelon #challenge)

"Frankie, this is my husband, Faizel," she said, introducing us.

I shook his hand.

"So! You're here to fetch Harun?" Samirah asked, moving down the passage.

"Yup," I said as we followed behind her.

I found Harun lying on the big dog bed exactly where I'd left him. He looked so much better this morning, and on entering, he lifted his entire head and wagged his tail at me.

"He's doing excellently," Samirah said. "Dogs heal much faster than humans, but he'll still be tender for a few days. I'm going to send you home with some medication, and, I'm afraid, no traveling for at least three days, even if you do have your immobilizer back."

I bent down and laid a hand on his fur. It really was coarse. Rough and prickly and scratchy, despite the fact that a few nights ago he'd gotten lathered in a very pricey tub of jasmine-scented hair mask.

"Hey, boy," I said, running my hand through his hair. And then I slipped his collar and leash on and was just about to pull when Samirah stopped me.

"Oh, he shouldn't walk just yet," she said.

"I'll get him," Mark said, bending down.

"I'll help." Faizel jumped in and he and Mark lifted Harun up. We all walked like that out the house and to the car, where Harun was placed carefully in the backseat.

"So, will we see you at quiz night this week, or are you going to chicken out since you're one person down?" Faizel suddenly asked Mark.

Mark gave a sarcastic chuckle. "Oh, we'll be there," he said, in a jokey tone. "Trust me, Risky Quizzness can still take on Beyoncé Know'Alls, even though we're a player down."

"Risky Quizzness and Beyoncé what?" I burst out laughing.

Mark shot me a really cute, coy kind of smile and then a shrug.

"Hey, we like Beyoncé," Samirah piped up.

"We do!" Faizel gave her a high-five.

"Wait, you guys are all in quiz teams and do quiz nights?" I looked at them all.

"Well, I'm not sure that Risky Quizzness can call themselves a team anymore, they're more like a duo, now that Emma pulled out." Samirah narrowed her eyes at Mark, a look of meaning passing between them.

"Perhaps if you stopped dating your teammates—" Faizel started, but Mark cut him off.

"I didn't date her," he said quickly.

"She had a huge crush on you, though," Faizel said matter-of-factly.

Samirah nodded. "That she did. Mind you, half the town has a crush on you . . . except me."

"I should hope not," Faizel joked, placing a hand over her big baby bump.

"Half the town has a crush on him?" I asked. I hadn't meant for my voice to take on that skeptical tone and for my eyes to run up and down his body, twice.

Samirah nodded.

"Okay, let's stop this," Mark said, closing the door.

"No, this is interesting." I folded my arms and looked at Samirah.

She smiled at me. "It's as if he wields some magical power over all the women in this town that no one quite understands."

"Fascinating."

"I've seen it many times. It usually happens after the second or third time people meet him. Something changes around then."

Faizel burst out laughing. "That is so true! Remember Sally . . ."

"And Zoe," Samirah added. "She didn't even like him when she first met him, and then a week later she kept saying that he looked familiar and she couldn't take her eyes off him, and then a week after that she was smitten."

"Okay, that's really enough." Mark walked around the car to the front door.

"And you know, he never really dates any of them. Not for any good length of time, anyway." She looked at me and shook her head, tutting. "So sad!"

"I'm just fine on my own."

"No one should be on their own," Faizel said.

Mark stopped and swung around. He glared at Faizel now. "You should stop worrying about me, and start worrying about Risky Quizzness smashing the Beyoncé Know'Alls!"

"Oooh," Faizel teased and folded his arms. "You hear that, Samirah? Sounds like a challenge."

"It is a challenge, so bring your game face!"

Faizel swished his hand in front of his face and his expression suddenly changed. His forehead wrinkled and creased and he squinted his eyes. "Already have it on!"

Samirah laughed and I looked around at the three of them. I hadn't realized they were all friends, but I guess this was a small town. A small town that for some reason seemed to be infatuated with Mark.

CHAPTER 28

‍ climbed out of Mark's car; he'd pulled all the way up to my
hotel door so we didn't have to carry Harun too far. He was heavy,
and because he was groggy from the operation, he was like a big,
floppy dead weight, with a long tongue. Mark hoisted him out the
backseat in one swift move, as if he weighed nothing. I was impressed
and my eyes drifted down to his arms where I was surprised to see
some muscle bulges. I hadn't noticed any muscles before. *Where had
they been hiding?*

I looked at him again as he walked to the door. I started to rumin-
ate on what Samirah and Faizel had said, about his effect on women
in the town. I wasn't totally sold on it. I mean, I guess I saw it, kind
of, just a little. But clearly, I wasn't smitten with him like everyone
else was. A loud angry voice snapped me out of my thoughts.

"AHA!" the voice bellowed.

I swung around to find the manager of the hotel standing there,
staring at us.

"So you *do* have a dog," she said in a very accusatory tone.

Mark stopped walking and turned around, and when he did, her
face fell.

"Mark, what are you doing here?" she asked in a hurt-sounding
voice. I rolled my eyes.

"Uh . . . Hi, Selma." He sounded sheepish AF. The same sheepish he'd sounded last night with that woman from the movies.

"Why are you carrying that dog?" she demanded.

"Do you guys know each other?" I asked.

Selma whipped her head around and glared at me. Angry eyes. Angry eyes that had nothing to do with bringing a dog to her hotel. Her angry eyes were way too icy for that.

"You could say that," she said snappily, now turning her glacial eyes on Mark.

Mark averted his gaze. I looked from him to her and back again.

"I mean . . . I thought we might know each other better but I guess that can't happen when the guy avoids you after what I thought was a nice date," she said, sarcasm cascading off that sentence like a waterfall over rocks. "And what with it being such a small town, you really have to put a lot of effort into avoiding someone, you know."

I tried to hold back a smile. This was interesting. This was the second woman in two days who was pissed off with Mark. And after what Samirah and Faizel had said, this magical power he seemed to wield, it was becoming clear that Mark was Springdorp's most eligible (yet reluctant) bachelor.

Mark looked up at Selma and met her gaze for a second, and then gave an apologetic look.

"Sorry," he said lamely. "I was busy."

"Busy!" she repeated, clearly not believing him. I didn't either. What was he busy with?

"And you?" Selma now turned her attention to me. I wiped the smile off my face so damn quickly. "What do you have to say for yourself, lying to me about having a dog?"

I shrugged. "Sorry."

Something in her expression suddenly changed, as if she was realizing something for the first time. She looked from me to Mark and then back to me. I knew what she was thinking.

"Oh no, we are not together, if that's what you're thinking. Trust me. I don't even know him. We just met. Three days ago. I don't even think he likes me that much, to be honest," I finished, and gave Mark a satisfied grin.

"I didn't say I didn't like you," Mark said to me, undoing the good work I'd just done.

At that, both Selma and I glared at him. There was an uncomfortable beat for a moment or two and then Selma turned and looked at me, definite venom blazing in her beautiful blue eyes.

Oh shit! Things were about to go south. More south than they already had.

"No dogs allowed! I'm going to have to ask you both to leave," she said in a low, firm tone.

"He can't go anywhere though," I said quickly. "He's just had an operation. Can't you make an exception?"

She shook her head.

"What am I meant to do then?" I asked, a little panicked.

She shrugged. "You could stay in the other hotel in town," and then she giggled. "Oh, I forgot. I'm the only hotel in town."

I looked at Harun and then at my hotel room. What the hell was I meant to do now? I guessed I could ask Samirah to look after him at her practice for a few days. But I immediately discarded that idea because then I wouldn't be able to be with him.

"Fine," Mark piped up and started walking back to the car. "You can stay at my place for a few days."

At that, Selma's mouth dropped open. Mine did too.

"Go pack your things," he called out to me, putting Harun back into the car. "I'll wait here."

"But . . . Uh . . . I . . ." I didn't know if I wanted to stay with him. But he was looking at me, and Selma was glaring at the dog, whilst also flashing Mark angry-woman eyes, and the tension in the air was so physically palpable and it was getting tenser by the minute. It felt like a stick of dynamite had just been lit and we were all standing there watching the flame travel down the string getting closer and closer and—

"OKAY!" I shouted at Mark then rushed into my room and started grabbing my things.

CHAPTER 29

*W*e pulled up to Mark's house. It was a little way outside town, and was reached by driving along a dirt road for about five minutes. And when we got there, I couldn't quite believe my eyes. I climbed out into the hot, unyielding desert sun and took in the view around me.

"You live here?" I asked, staring at the house in front of me which was truly and utterly in the middle of nowhere.

"Yes," he said casually, as if this was completely normal. As if living in a tiny, cute house in the middle of the desert was a perfectly normal thing to do.

The house was small. Painted a bright shade of white with tiny blue shutters on little windows. A shaded veranda ran the entire length, and on it a wooden table and two chairs. Next to that, a large, comfortable-looking daybed was pushed up against the wall. There was no fence or wall and the house simply stood there, tiny against the massive backdrop. Flat lands surrounded it, no trees, and in the distance, a massive mountain range spread across the skyline. To the left of the house, the only other thing that was taller than the house, was an old windmill pumping water into a round reservoir.

Two big tractor tires lay flat on the ground. They had been painted the same bright white as the house and flowers of cactus and succulents burst out of them. A small path of brightly colored pebbles ran up to the front of the house, to the bright red front door—this place was so quaint and picture-perfect it looked like it belonged in a book of fairytales.

"Oh my God, you should totally put this place on Airbnb, people would love it here . . ." I stopped talking. "Oh. No Airbnb." I kept forgetting this one important fact. And then another thought hit me. I looked around again; we really were in the middle of nowhere, and honestly, I didn't know Mark very well. I watched him as he carried a sleepy-looking Harun from his car.

"I don't really know you, do I?" I blurted out. "And now I'm here. At your house. In the middle of nowhere, and I don't really know you."

He looked at me and nodded. "I suppose."

"So should I be . . ." I chose my words carefully, "worried?"

"About me?" he asked.

"Well, yes."

He smiled. "Were you worried about going on dates with people who you met online who were, what did you call them, next-level creeps?"

"Hey, how do you know that I online dated?"

"You told me. When I came to hook up the DVD player."

I had to think about this for a while. "Aaaah. Yes. I did. But I also told you to ignore everything I said to you."

He smiled. "Sorry."

"That is not a good example though. Firstly, this is not a date. And secondly, I do know the people I meet online. More so than I know you."

"I didn't say this was a date." His smile grew.

"I didn't say you said it was a date. I was just acknowledging that it *wasn't* a date." I wished I'd never used the word date, because now things were just getting awkward.

Mark kept smiling. "I think you know me better than some guy you met online."

"How do you figure that?" I asked, folding my arms. Blocking that smile of his.

"Well, we've spent actual real time together. I mean, we even spent a night together."

At that, my face went a little blushy and flushy and, without thinking, I gave it a quick fan with my hand, which caused Mark to smile even more—I assume he was also remembering that wildly awkward moment this morning. Not every day you wake up tangled in the arms of a stranger.

"I'm sure that's more than you can say for all the people you met online. I bet you've never met the majority of the people you know online. And I bet you went on dates with people you knew less about than me."

I paused. He did have a point, now that I thought about it. I hadn't met most of my online friends IRL. But that didn't matter, did it?

"You can know someone online though," I said, feeling defensive.

"No, you can't." He started walking towards the house with Harun, and I followed behind him.

"Uh, yes, you can," I argued.

"No, you can't. Until you've sat across from a person and looked them in the eye, face to face, you can't ever truly know someone or call them your friend."

"Um, yes, you can. I have about ten thousand friends like that. We are all very, very close."

At that, he burst out laughing and kicked the front door open with his foot. It wasn't even locked. I followed him inside and was met by a small, cozy-looking sitting room that seemed to be centered around an old stone fireplace. Mark walked across the room to a sofa under a window and gently placed Harun down on it.

I inspected the place some more. It was a strange mix of old and new furniture. A huge, modern flat-screen TV took up a massive space on one wall—obviously it was just for movie watching—and on the opposite wall a shelf covered in old books and antiques.

I could only see three doors leading off this room, so I walked around and peered into each one. A small kitchen with a little wooden table and chair. An old bathroom, stone walls, bright blue

painted ball-and-claw bath, and in the other room, a small bedroom.
I swallowed.

"Uh . . . where would I sleep?" I asked.

"You can sleep in my room," he said.

"Where would you sleep?"

"I sleep outside on the veranda when it's warm."

"Oh. Okay." I looked around, feeling very strange all of a sudden.
I rubbed my arm.

"Look, if you would feel more comfortable, you can go back to the
hotel and I'm more than happy to look after Harun for a few days
while he recovers."

"No. It's okay. I think . . ."

"I'm not a serial killer, by the way."

"I didn't think you were. You don't look like one."

He was smiling now. "Isn't that what everyone says when they
catch one? 'But he didn't look like a serial killer.'"

"So are you saying you *are* a serial killer?" I asked, a little amused.

He waggled his eyebrows. "I could be."

"Nah, I don't think so," I said after studying him a little longer.

"Well, thanks."

"Pleasure."

"I'll take that as a compliment." His smile broadened, as if I was
amusing him greatly.

"You should. *Not* being a serial killer is a really good thing, or so
I've heard." I smiled back at him.

He nodded. "I reckon *not* being a serial killer is actually kind of
an essential human quality. Don't you think?" he asked and I
laughed and ran my eyes over him. Mark was funny and nerdy. It
was a good combination, not that I was under his magical spell or
anything. Far from it. But I was certainly starting to see the Mark
appeal.

Mark looked over at Harun. "You think he needs anything?"

"Maybe a bowl of water. Samirah said he probably wouldn't be too hungry today. We should just keep him comfortable and hydrated and make sure we give him his painkillers."

He nodded and walked into the kitchen. I followed behind him and looked around. The kitchen was amazing. It looked like it had been restored perfectly.

"Did you do all this?" I asked, looking at the bright yellow painted shelves and the old Granny Mazawati tea tins that lined them, as if they'd been collected.

He looked around. "I like to collect things," he replied a little sheepishly.

"I can see that," I said, also noting a collection of old tin cups in bright colors hanging from the walls. "How long have you lived here?"

He reached for a bowl, filled it to the brim with water and then walked back into the lounge and placed it next to Harun.

"Four years."

"WOW! Four years. No internet."

"But look what else I have here." He walked onto the veranda and flopped down on the comfy-looking daybed outside.

I stood on the veranda and gazed out over the strange, desolate landscape. It was so still, and the air seemed to throb and pulse with heat, even though it was meant to be autumn. My clothes felt sticky on my skin and I could see little perspiration dots breaking their way through the surface, leaving rather unsightly marks on my clothes. I took my shirt between my fingers and flapped it back and forth, trying to get the air to circulate. Otherwise I might soon have unsightly underboob sweat marks.

"You get used to the weather here," Mark said, looking up at me.

"Do you?"

"Eventually," he said with a smile. "I've taken to sleeping naked outside when it's hot like this."

I flashed him a look.

"Don't worry, I'll keep my pants on when you're here." He said this with a smirk. Ever so slightly naughty, and I couldn't help blushing at the innuendo, whether it had been intentional or not.

"Uh . . . thanks." Suddenly images of a pantless Mark flashed through my mind, and I couldn't help wonder what it all looked like. I indulged this thought for a while until . . .

"You okay?" Mark suddenly asked.

"Huh? What?" I jumped in fright.

"You looked like you were deep in thought there?"

"Oh, no! Nothing! Just . . . you know . . . nothing," I trailed off, embarrassed. Hoping he wasn't some kind of mind reader.

He narrowed his eyes. "Something I should know about?" he asked.

"No! Definitely . . . NO!" I said, a little too emphatically, which of course made him smile even more.

That smile of his though . . .

Was I imagining it, or seriously, was he familiar?

CHAPTER 30

"So, what do you do out here all day?" I finally asked Mark, when I'd unpacked all my things into his wardrobe and we'd both gathered back in the kitchen.

"I have a lot to do," he said.

"Like what?"

"Well, I run a store during the day."

"Not every day, though," I said.

He raised his brows at me.

"I went round and you weren't there. This other guy was."

"You came round looking for me?" he asked.

"Well, no. Not like that." For some reason I suddenly didn't want him to think I went looking for him. "I wanted to return the movies," I added quickly.

He nodded, seeming happy with this explanation.

"What else do you do?" I asked.

"I have a band on the side," he replied.

"You have a band?" I was totally taken aback.

"Yup!"

"What kind of music do you play?"

He shrugged. "Mixed genres really. It's not a very serious thing. But we do have a gig tonight, if you want to come?"

"Yeah?" I perked up at that. I was very curious to watch Mark play in a band. "What else do you do here?"

"I make my own gin," he said.

"Really?"

"You want to see?"

"Uh . . . Sure."

We walked around the back of the house. A cottage caught my attention, and behind that, a small shed.

"What's that used for?" I pointed at the buildings.

"I used to rent the cottage, but now it's just a storeroom."

He opened the door to the shed and we walked in. The small room was dominated by a brass pot, and then behind that, rows and rows of bottles with handwritten labels. I felt uneasy in the small space, but tried to push that feeling away.

I walked up to one of the bottles and picked it up. "Do you drink all of this?" I asked.

"No," he chuckled. "It's not for me. I supply The Reservoir."

"The what?"

"It's a little restaurant. It's where I'm playing my gig tonight. I also supply the hotel."

"Ohhhh, so that's how you know Selma?" I asked.

"Um . . . Sort of." He sounded sheepish once again. A coy quiver in his voice.

"She's pretty," I said, but I don't know why.

He shrugged. "I guess." As if he hadn't noticed!

"You seem to know a lot of people in town . . . *sort of*." I hadn't meant for that "sort of" to come out in such a strange tone. But it had.

"Small town. Small dating pool," he finally said after a while.

"So you've dated a lot of women in town then?" Why was I asking this? I sounded like some jealous wife, which I wasn't. Obviously.

"Not that many, but if you do go on a date here and decide not to go on another one, it's awkward, because you'll defo bump into them again."

There was that cute "defo" again.

I thought about that for a while. "I guess you can't just swipe left on them or unfriend and block them."

I turned my attention back to the bottles of gin.

"Want to taste some?" he asked.

"Oh, I'm not drinking at the moment," I replied.

"Why?"

"It was just something that Kyle thought would be good for extra content, you know?"

"No, I don't know." He looked at me with a blank expression.

I took a deep breath and started. "Well, there is this #NoWine-OClock-Challenge. You know?"

He shook his head.

"It's this thing that people are doing, it's a really popular hashtag at the moment. You take photos of yourself before, during and after one year of no drinking. It's something a lot of influencers are doing. You can get a lot of new followers from that. There is a whole community of people online doing it."

"Wait!" He held his hand up. "Let me get something straight. Do you have a problem with alcohol?"

I shook my head. "No."

"Ever had a problem with it?"

"Nope."

"So, you're only *not* drinking so you can post pictures of yourself and hashtag it because it gives you more content and likes. And you are doing it because your ex-boyfriend thought it would be a good idea?" he asked, looking appalled.

"Yes," I said.

"You know how ridiculous that sounds, right?"

"What? No. It's not, it's—"

"Ridiculous," he cut me off.

"Hey, our followers really went up when we started the challenge." I pointed a finger at him.

"So you make actual life decisions about important things, based on whether or not it makes good content and gets you more followers?"

"Um . . ." I thought for a while. When he put it like that, I mean, I admit, it didn't sound great. "Sort of," I said, backtracking.

He nodded slowly. As if taking in every single word I was saying. And thinking about them too.

"What?" I asked, feeling uncomfortable under his prying eyes.

"What brought you here? You mentioned the break-up and someone else being better for your ex's personal brand or something?"

I sighed loudly.

"Sorry, you don't have to talk about it if you don't want to. You sort of implied that you did want to talk about it the other night though, when you started talking about it."

I nodded. "My ex broke up with me for someone who has more followers than I do. And then because of that, and some things I might have done and said online that sort of went viral, I kind of lost all my followers, so . . ."

"You're running and hiding from it all in a town without internet?" he asked.

"I'm not running and hiding." I put my hands on my hips in a defensive pose.

He rolled his eyes. "You're not the only person who's come here with this idea of having some great social media detox."

"Really?"

"A while ago some guy came here because he did something online that went viral for all the wrong reasons. He lasted about ten minutes before he left. Before that a group of girls came here too—they also left quite quickly. You're the only one who's lasted this long."

"Against my will. And I'm still leaving as soon as possible," I reminded him. "As soon as it's safe to travel with Harun, I'm out of here."

"So, you taking Harun with you?" he asked with a smile.

"Well, what am I supposed to do with him? He's kind of my dog now and . . ."

"You love him."

I sighed again. "Also against my will."

"I wonder where he came from?" Mark pondered. "What his story is? Where he lived before? If he ever lived with anyone, or whether he's just a traveler."

"A traveler," I echoed.

"Yeah, maybe he moves around, going from person to person, maybe he's had tens of different families, but only for a while."

"Maybe." I considered this; there was something about it that rang true. For some reason, I couldn't imagine him staying in one place for long. A thought tugged at me and made my stomach tighten. I hoped he wasn't going to leave me as soon as he was better! The thought made me uneasy.

'Don't worry." Mark put his hand on my shoulder. "He's clearly not going anywhere! Looks like he's never had it so good before."

I forced a smile. I seriously hoped not.

"So," Mark sounded like he was changing the subject, and I was glad for that, "you want to come tonight?"

"To your gig? You think Harun will be okay here alone?" I asked.

"I'm sure he'll be fine. We'll give him his meds. Make him a comfy bed. We can even put a movie on for him. Something with dogs in."

"Mmmm . . . I'm not sure."

"You don't want to leave him?" Mark asked softly.

I shook my head. "I don't know. I'm worried about him."

"We can call Samirah and ask her?" he suggested.

"Okay."

We walked back inside and Mark bent over and picked a landline up from the floor, as if it had just been discarded there. He held it out to me.

"I can't remember the last time I used one of these," I said. "And look, it has buttons. How cute."

Mark gave a sarcastic chuckle. He flipped open a small book full of telephone numbers and ran his finger down the list.

"Cute. Phone contacts," I mumbled, looking down at it.

"I never use this phone. No need. Everything is such a short distance here that people usually drive when they want to get hold of you."

"It's like living in the past," I said, as he dialed the number and passed the phone over to me.

"Hello," Samirah answered.

"Hey. It's me. Frankie," I said.

"Is Harun okay?" she asked immediately.

"He's fine. I just wanted to know if it was alright to leave him for a little while tonight. Will he be okay?"

"Yes, just give him his meds and keep him confined," she said.

"You sure?" I asked.

"Totally. You going out tonight?"

"Mark invited me to this gig tonight," I said dismissively.

"Oh great! I'll be there too. Will be cool to see you."

"Really?"

"Faizel also plays in the band. It's nice that you and Mark are getting close."

I looked over to see where Mark was, and when I was sure he was out of earshot, I cupped my hand around the mouthpiece and whispered, "Mark just asked if I wanted to come, that's all," I said. "We're not that close."

"Where are you?" she asked as if she already psychically knew the answer.

"At Mark's. I got kicked out of the hotel with Harun. Mark said I could stay here for a little while."

"Cool," she said. But she said it in a strange tone that I wasn't very fond of. "See you guys soon." She hung up before I could say anything else.

CHAPTER 31

*T*here was a knock on the door, and I opened it. It was weird being inside Mark's bedroom. It looked like a guy's bedroom, in that it was very minimally decorated, no scatter cushions—in my experience lack of scatter cushions usually indicates a male presence. The room was small, but the bed was bloody huge. It took up most of the space and I couldn't help but wonder if that was for all the ladies in town, and how many ladies in town had been in this bed? I eased the door open and peered out. The smell hit me immediately. It was Mark and it was amazing.

"You smell really good," I said, before I'd even had time to think about the words and what they might mean and whether they were appropriate to say.

He smiled. "Thanks. Another thing I collect."

"What is?" I asked.

"Cologne. Perfume."

I opened the door even more. "You collect perfume?" I was amused now. It seemed like such an unusual thing for him to do. Although, there was something cute about the idea.

"Wanna see?" he asked.

"Sure." I followed him into the bathroom, and he opened one of the cupboards on the wall. It was large and when he did, I gasped. I'd never seen so many bottles of smelly stuff in my life. There must have been at least thirty or forty bottles in there. And OMG, the bottles were amazing. They were like works of art themselves.

"I've collected one from every country I've been to," he said, pride in his voice.

"You've been to that many countries?" I asked, shocked.

He nodded. "I traveled a lot before I came here." His words sounded dismissive now, or laced with something that he was trying to hide. I don't know. That was the feeling I got, anyway, as he seemed to toss those words out, as if he was deliberately trying not to draw attention to their meaning.

"Which one are you wearing tonight?" I asked.

He picked a bottle up. It was exquisite. It resembled a crystal ink-well with an amber liquid inside.

"What is it?' I asked. The bottle didn't look familiar at all; not the usual DKNY, or Armani or Cool Waters by Davidoff or the things you see in the shops. In fact, none of his bottles looked familiar.

"It's from Barcelona. By Ramon Monegal."

"Never heard of him," I said, rolling the beautiful bottle around in my hands.

"Well, I don't collect Aramis and Old Spice," he said with a smirk in his voice.

I smiled at him. "You collect the niche stuff that no one has heard of then? This is the artisanal gin version of perfume," I said in a slightly mocking but playful way.

"You could say that." He took the perfume from my hand and opened it. "Ramon Monegal is a master perfumer from Spain. One of the greatest, if you ask me."

"It smells *really* nice," I said.

He shook his head. "It doesn't smell *nice*." He stretched out the word "nice" and placed a lot of emphasis on it. "It smells complex and rich. It has citrusy top notes. It has some peppery middle notes and then finally fades to warm base notes of sandalwood and cedarwood."

I blinked. "Wow. You really know a lot about this stuff."

He shrugged, maybe a little embarrassed. "My mum had a perfume shop. That's how she met my dad. He had a music and video shop in the same mall. I used to work there during summer holidays, so she taught me some things about perfume."

"I'm impressed," I said. And I genuinely was. I'd never met a person who knew fragrance like this, let alone a guy. I looked at him again. Floppy-haired, glasses-wearing, intellectual-looking, with a seemingly endless knowledge about gin and scents, and a collector of quirky antique tins. Mark was unique. I don't think I'd ever met anyone like him. And then suddenly, the fact that this guy who lived in the middle of the desert knew about fragrances and collected cute things and was passionate about movies and cared about my dog, made him very, *very* attractive. I looked away quickly when I realized that I'd been staring at him a little too intently.

"My mum used to say that everyone had their own signature fragrance. That there was a perfect smell out there for everyone that captured who they were."

"What was hers?" I asked, looking up again.

"Easy. Chanel No 5. I can still smell it if I think about it. You know, your sense of smell is the sense that is most linked to memory."

"Really?" I said thoughtfully.

"You can probably recall a moment in your life, or a person, and remember the scent that goes with it," he said.

I thought back to my mom and tried to remember her scent. "My mom wasn't as fancy as Chanel—I don't think she could have afforded it—but when I think of her, it's latex mixed with something sweet and rosy."

"Latex?" he asked.

"She was a nurse. She's retired now. Which she deserves, I guess. She worked really hard when we were young. Lots of night shifts, because those paid more." And then a smell hit me. A smell thought. It wasn't pleasant and I didn't know where it came from at first, until I did.

"I think my dad smelled of cigarettes," I said pensively.

"You think?" he repeated.

"I don't know. I last saw him when I was a toddler. But I think I remember cigarettes." I tried to shrug off what was starting to become a painful memory. "But that's impossible, right? You can't remember smells from when you were that young."

"I don't know." Mark sounded thoughtful. "Smell is a very powerful memory."

I thought about that for a while and then thought about all the smells in my life. Kyle always smelled of that specific hair gel, the one he liked to use. My sister always smelled of mint, she chewed gum a lot, and I remember how my niece had smelled when she was first born.

"What's your signature fragrance?" I asked him.

"Don't think I've found it yet," he said, gesturing to the cupboard.

"What would mine be?" I asked, and then a lump formed in my throat. God, why did that question seem so strangely intimate? It felt like I was asking him what kind of lingerie he thought would look good on me.

"If you had a fragrance it would be . . ." He paused and looked at me for the longest time. His face looked searching at first, and then slightly blank, as if something was dawning on him.

"What?" I asked defensively. "Are you trying to decide what my personality is?"

"I am," he said.

"Looks like you're having trouble?" I felt a little hurt that he wasn't able to see me and my unique personal scent.

He nodded for a moment and then agreed with me, much to my horror.

"I . . . I have a personality," I said, broken. "It's uh . . . um . . ." I stumbled over my words and then stopped talking. *Did I have my own personality?* Holy crap! I shook my head at the thought.

"What are the things you like?" he suddenly asked. "Other than likes and popular hashtags?"

"I . . . I like, well, um . . ." I stopped talking and wracked my brain. What were the things I liked? My likes always seemed to be dictated by the current hashtags, and things that were trending or whatever was going to get me more likes and shares. I squirmed. Suddenly this conversation was making me feel very uncomfortable. I turned and walked out of the bathroom, wanting to be as far away from those bottles as possible now. They seemed to be mocking me. Each with their own bloody unique personality and me with my lack of personality, or so it seemed. I had a personality, didn't I? I had done those online personality tests before! They had told me I had a personality. Wasn't there an app I could use to figure out what I liked? Shit! My fingertips itched and I needed my phone. It was plugged into the wall next to Mark's bed and I started moving towards it.

"Where are you going?" Mark asked.

"To get ready for tonight." I walked into the room and closed the door behind me.

"Cool, we have to leave in about five minutes," Mark shouted through the door to me.

CHAPTER 32

ive minutes turned into ten, turned into fifteen, something that Mark pointed out to me several times through the door.

"I'm just contouring," I shouted out.

"What's that?" he asked.

"Never mind," I shouted back, not wanting to explain what contour was. When I was still a lot bigger, I'd done a YouTube tutorial on contouring, giving a chubby face cheekbones. It had been one of my breakout videos, the one that had put me on the map as an influencer to watch. I still remember that feeling I got when I woke up and saw how many times the video had been viewed. The feeling I got as I read through all the positive comments telling me what an inspiration I was for losing so much weight and how beautiful I looked. It had felt so exhilarating. To have something I'd done acknowledged so publicly, when nothing I'd done for years had garnered any attention. Well, any positive attention. I got a lot of attention from my mom when I was young, but not the kind I wanted. She was always trying to put me on a diet, which inevitably made me feel worse about myself, which made me eat even more.

I finally stepped out the room when I'd contoured, done my brows and over-lined my lips. I walked out and looked at Mark. His jaw fell and he stared at me in a way I did not know how to interpret. I felt self-conscious.

"What?" I asked.

"Um . . ." He stood up. "I think you might find it hard to walk there in those." His eyes trailed down to my feet.

"These?" I was wearing my favorite heels. Super sexy, super high.

"We're walking there," he said.

"Why would we walk there?" I asked.

"Drinking and driving. There's no Uber here."

"Oh. Right." I nodded.

"So you'll definitely need some comfy shoes."

"I can't wear comfy shoes with this outfit," I protested. "It's too cute for comfy shoes."

Mark tilted his head to the side, as if trying to point out the obvious solution to this.

"Well, what should I wear then?" I asked.

"The most casual thing you have."

I sighed. "Comfy and casual." I walked back into my room and closed the door behind me. I slipped the dress off and rummaged through my suitcase. I found a casual top and one of my ankle-length boho skirts and slipped that on with a pair of sneakers. I looked at myself in the mirror: the whole ensemble looked ridiculous, the sneakers with the skirt. Usually I would wear a strappy sandal with them, but snakes! I looked from the outfit to my face. My highlighted cheekbones and red lips now totally clashed with this toned-down version of myself. I grabbed some facial wipes, but then hesitated. I never left the house with a face that wasn't totally made up, because inevitably there would be lots of photos that would be posted of whatever I was out and about doing. I looked at the facial wipe in my hand and sighed. There would be no photos posted tonight. I raised it to my face and wiped the red off my lips. Then I took it between my fingers and pulled some of my thick mascara off. Then I took a tissue and rubbed my cheeks a little, some of the blush and highlighter came off and I hadn't looked this barefaced for an evening out in forever.

I turned my attention to my hair and I took it out of the perfect, messy bun on the top of my head and let it tumble down to my shoulders. I didn't bother to brush it. I walked out again and Mark did the exact same thing he'd done before, only this time the look on his face was totally different.

"What?" I asked again. I expected things to play out the way they had before, him telling me something about my outfit was wrong. But they didn't.

"You look . . . great," he said.

"I do?" I asked, bewildered.

He nodded. "Really, you look great."

"Thanks," I said, smiling, feeling buoyed up by this compliment. I could never really tell how I looked, until someone told me I looked good. Usually it was via a thumbs up or a heart emoji . . . *but this felt better.*

"Okay, we really have to get going now," he said.

"Let me just get my phone," I said automatically, and ran through to the room.

"Why are you getting it when you can't use it?" he shouted to me.

I ignored his comment and grabbed my phone off the bedside table where it had been charging. I ran my hand over the screen and it was black.

"Shit," I muttered.

"Oh, I forgot to tell you that plug point next to my bed doesn't work."

"Oh my God." I rushed over to the other one and plugged the phone in there. Nothing happened.

"Yeah, the other one doesn't work either," he mumbled. I turned and looked at him.

"My phone's dead," I said, feeling panic.

He nodded.

"My phone's dead," I repeated slowly, letting those words sink in. I don't think it had ever been dead in its entire life.

"Leave it. You can't use it anyway."

"But I . . . I . . . never go anywhere without it." I looked down at it.

"Be a rebel," he said. "Leave it behind."

"But . . . but . . ." I looked at the dead thing in my hand. It felt heavier than usual, like a deadweight.

"Toss it on the bed," Mark said. "Do it."

I looked at him, then the bed and then my phone.

"Do it. Come on!" he urged.

I looked at my phone again and then at the bed and then, as if tossing a Frisbee, I let it fly out my hand. It landed on the bed with a soft thud. I gazed at it for the longest time, caught between wanting to pick it up, and wanting to leave it.

"We're going to be late," Mark said again and I knew we needed to go. As I walked out the room, Mark put his hand in the air.

"Fiver," he said with a massive smile that was so contagious I found myself smiling back, despite the circumstances.

I gave him a high-five as I walked out without my phone, for the first time in as long as I could remember.

CHAPTER 33

I watched Mark on stage. He seemed to be completely transformed. The version of Mark I knew before he slung that guitar over his shoulder and climbed onto the tiny stage that wobbled when you moved, was completely different from the man I'd come to know.

There was something so loose about this version of Mark. Like a scarf in the wind, being blown about by something else. Something wild and free that was unraveling in the corners and coming apart because it wasn't tethered to anything. He was lost in the sounds the instrument was making. Lost in the thud of drums and the wail of vocals that Faizel was belting out. Look, they weren't going to be winning any battle of the bands anytime soon, and Faizel was no great vocalist. But it didn't seem to matter. Because on that little stage, in the small cramped restaurant, with the bad purple lighting, they were rock gods. They were the best band in the world and their songs were Billboard chart toppers, even though they were basically covers of eighties rock ballads.

I moved my eyes away from Mark and looked at the crowd around us. Everyone was seated at small tables around the stage and something soon became very apparent. All the women were looking at him. Every single one watching him getting lost in his guitar. They all had similar looks on their faces of adoration and awe and . . . God, they all looked like they were in love with him. I stifled a giggle and then glanced over at Samirah; it was clear she knew what I was thinking.

"I know!" she said biting into one of her fries. "Half the town is in love with him."

"Why?" I asked.

She shrugged. "Personally, I don't get it, but everyone else seems to."

"I don't get it either," I said, amused as hell.

But the look Samirah gave me made me think she didn't quite believe me. "Just wait. His power seems to know no limits."

"Not going to happen," I protested. But I didn't believe that as much as I would have liked.

"Wait. It usually kicks in around the third or fourth time someone meets him."

I shook my head. "I've met him more than that and I'm totally fine."

I looked down at Samirah, who was counting on her fingers.

"What are you doing?"

"If my calculation is correct, by the end of the night, you should be madly in love with him and you'll have no idea why. That's what everyone says. That they have no idea what it is about him."

I burst out laughing. My laugh was so loud that a few people turned and looked at me.

"Sorry," I mouthed when someone gave me a dirty look.

"This is their best song," she mouthed back, and then held her finger over her lips and shushed me.

I looked back at the stage. Faizel and the drummer had left. Mark was alone and he'd changed over to an acoustic guitar. I watched, fascinated, as he pulled a stool up towards the front. He sat down on it and started strumming. A soft, sad, haunting tune came out. The lights dipped lower, the room darkened. Small beams from the footlights shone all patchy and uneven, casting dappled shadows across his face. He strummed the guitar with so much feeling and my eyes were drawn to his fingers, dragging slowly over the strings.

There was something so erotic about watching the tips of his fingers gliding and catching on the strings like that. I looked around the room, and it was clear that almost every female there was thinking the exact same thing.

A collective in-breath was taken as every single woman in the room gazed at him. This acoustic guitar solo was clearly more than simply that. It was one of those elaborate mating dances and displays that birds of paradise give while trying to lure a mate. This was like an advertisement for more . . .

Oh shit, it was working on me a little bit. That pitter-patter on my diaphragm was back. Tiny and furtive, fairy feet. I felt my body leaning in, watching him, every single move he made. The small flick of his hair, the way he moved his neck back and forth to the beat, the way he tapped his foot on the ground. I felt a nudge in my ribs, which zapped me back to reality.

"Told you," Samirah whispered to me.

I turned to her. "Isn't there something about him that looks familiar to you?" I asked.

She shook her head. "Nope! So many people have said that, though I don't see it."

I looked back at Mark and tried to place this strange feeling of familiarity that he seemed to wield. But couldn't. I scanned my mind, but it was nowhere. The veil of almost-familiarity started to lift though and soon something else started to emerge. An entirely different picture of Mark. An entirely different Mark. I was totally shocked by this revelation, because trust me, I had not seen this coming, at all.

Suddenly, strangely, Mark was just about the hottest man I'd ever seen in my life. Not hot in that typical way, but hot in a way that seemed to rise up from the inside and spill out of him. His once unremarkable brown eyes were like pools of warm, melted dark chocolate now. Thick and creamy hot chocolate on a cold night. His floppy hair was suddenly something I wanted to sink my hand into, run my fingers through. I wanted to grab a handful of it so badly, like that feeling when you see something cute, like a chubby baby, and want to bite its foot.

I was overcome with a wildly irrational need to bite him on the neck and then squeeze his cheeks so hard. And his body . . . Oh my God. His height suddenly seemed sexy and dizzying and you just wanted him towering above you, looking down at you, pushing strands of hair out of your face. And his soft hands, the way they strummed the guitar strings—well, you could imagine them strumming all sorts of other things.

I looked around again and a part of me felt terribly embarrassed to be clearly feeling the exact same thing every woman around me was feeling. I shook my head, tossing all these ridiculous thoughts out.

I scoffed loudly. I would *not* be taken in by any of this Mark silliness . . .

Oh, who was I kidding? I was totally taken in.

CHAPTER 34

"Can I get you guys some drinks?" Mark asked, after he'd finished playing. He was standing by our table now, hair a little wet around the hairline from sweat, cheeks reddened and his eyes wide and shining brightly. It had taken him ages to even get to our table. He'd had to weave his way through an army of adoring female fans. There didn't seem to be any particular demographic to the adorers either. From younger fans who were all red-cheeked and coy-smiled, to older ones who seemed equally smitten.

"Sparkling water for me," Samirah said.

"Same for me," I echoed.

Mark leaned across the table and looked at me. "Hashtag NoWine-OClock doesn't exist here," he said with a teasing smile.

"What's that?" Samirah asked.

"Some internet meme thing that Frankie has fallen victim to." He gave me a playful wink and my spine felt like it straightened.

"It's YOU!" I heard a voice behind me and turned. The accent was unmistakable, it was definitely Scottish. Thick and sounding like all kinds of smooth, silky honey. The chef from the hotel was standing by the table. He placed a massive hand on my shoulder.

"How was your spiritual awakening. Are you woke?" he asked with a smile.

I shook my head. "But I nearly got bitten by a snake."

"Aaaah, yes. Those pesky things in the desert. You have to be careful of them."

"You could have warned me," I said pointedly.

He smiled apologetically. "As long as you're okay, lass."

"Why wouldn't I be okay?" I asked, a little defensively, somewhat embarrassed by how I'd behaved the last time I saw him.

"Ye was in quite a state that morning," he replied, softer this time.

I shrugged, trying to be nonchalant about the whole thing.

"What happened?" Samirah asked, as Faizel came to the table and slipped an arm around her shoulder.

"She was taking photos of her breakfast," he declared loudly.

Everyone looked at him blankly, as if this needed further explanation.

"She was standing on her chair, taking photos of her breakfast. She even made the napkin look pretty. She doesn't even eat breakfast!"

Samirah and Mark looked at me, both raising their eyebrows.

I looked down at the table and laced my fingers together. "My breakfast photos are the highlight of my social media feed, okay? Do you know how many likes they get?"

Samirah shook her head. "You see, this is what I don't get about this whole social media thing. Why would you share a photo of your breakfast with the world? Who wants to see it?"

"A lot of people. Especially when I make those purple smoothie bowls with the blueberry hearts."

Samirah laughed heartily now. "Who has time for that?"

"Not me," the chef piped up and Mark also laughed at this. "I'm too busy frying up everyone's bacon."

"I did, okay. I did! I had the time for that!" I hadn't meant to say it with such a sting, I hadn't meant for the words to come out with such a bite to them, and they'd silenced the laughter at the table now. I took a deep breath. "That's what I did. That was my job. I woke up every morning and made the most Insta-worthy breakfast; sometimes it would take two hours to make. And then I took a photo of it and posted it. Three hundred thousand people were waiting to see what I ate for breakfast every morning, okay!" I paused at that. "Well, that's not really quite true, is it? Because I don't eat breakfast. But I act like I eat breakfast, because breakfast is #mostimportantmealoftheday . . ." I trailed off, totally aware of the blatant lie in all that. The deception that I'd been putting out into the world. Showing them this side of me that didn't even exist. This breakfast-eating side that they'd all bought into, so much so that many of them attempted to recreate my gorgeous spreads, sharing pics of their attempts on social media.

For some reason, saying those words out loud in this environment, in this place that was so far away and disconnected from the rest of the world, made them sound absurd. The whole idea suddenly seemed absurd. As if it was an idea and concept that didn't exist, and had no right to exist here either. Like bringing some prehistoric beast back to life and popping it in a modern-day zoo. Out of place and time. Strange and foreign.

"Why?" Samirah suddenly asked. I turned to her. "Sorry, I'm not being funny or trying to put down what you did, but why would someone want to see what you ate for breakfast? And why would it be so important to show them? What does everyone get out of it?" She sounded genuinely intrigued, as if she really did have no idea why anyone would want to look at my homemade granola swirls.

Her question wafted across the table and by the time it reached me, it truly confused me. I shrugged. And then I shook my head. "My breakfast always looked pretty. If it was a pink smoothie bowl I would decorate the scene with pink things, you know? Like maybe a pink napkin or pink flowers or . . ." I tailed off as I heard the words and then I shrugged again. "I don't know," I said softly, almost inaudibly, almost to myself. "I don't know," I repeated a little louder this time. There was a lull in the conversation, a beat of sadness or aloneness, I could feel it, and I'm sure everyone else did too, because for a few seconds they all kept quiet and waited for me to speak again.

"I know what you need." The chef finally spoke up. "You need a good ol' gin and tonic." He clapped Mark on the back, and Mark jerked forwards a little. It was clear that those massive hands wielded some considerable power. "You know this man makes the best gin? And they stock it here. So what do you say?" he asked.

"I'm not drinking at the moment, I'm doing Hashtag No-WineO—" I cut myself off again. This was such an automatic response to this question and, suddenly, it didn't seem like it needed to be. #NoWineOClock didn't fucking exist here. It was the furry mammoth in the normal zoo. And then I nodded with conviction. "Okay. Sure. I mean, why not? When in Rome with no internet, right?"

Everyone looked at me as if my statement had confused the hell out of them, but the chef obliged and soon he returned with the most beautiful-looking gin. His name, I soon learned, was not "chef", but Logan. He placed the big, beautiful glass in front of me; floating pomegranate seeds, a long copper straw, mint leaves and twisty bits of orange rind and suddenly, it was just all so funny. I burst out laughing. It was the kind of laughter that bordered on hysterical, but it was also clearly contagious, because soon everyone at the table was laughing too.

I pointed down to the gin. "It would make such a good photo on Instagram," I said, wiping a tear away. "But I don't have my phone." And then I was hysterical with laughter again. "And even if I did, I wouldn't be able to post it." More laughter from me. I got the feeling that the people at my table were starting to feel less amused and more concerned with my current state. But I wasn't stopping.

"Hashtag ginology!" I said, almost snorting, and then I looked up at everyone at the table. "Hashtag night out." More laughter from me. Snorts of sharp, ugly-sounding laughter. "Hashtag blessed. Hashtag happy. Hashtag fucking hashtag . . ." And then the laughter turned to tears, and soon, I was weeping like a blithering idiot at the table in front of a whole bunch of strangers.

God, this was so embarrassing. But it wasn't the first time I'd done this. I felt an arm come up around me; it was Samirah and she gave me a firm, empathetic squeeze. I looked up at her and she smiled. She didn't say a word, but something in her caring and calm eyes told me that she wasn't judging me for this outburst. And I'm sure I must have looked terrible. Some unhinged woman, crying into my pretty gin.

"Here." Logan pushed my gin closer, until the copper straw touched my lips. "Have a big old sip, lass," he urged. I wrapped my lips around the straw and sucked. It was tasty as hell.

I looked over at Mark. "It's good," I said to him.

"Thanks," he said and then grinned. "Look at you . . . such a rebel. Drinking gin without taking a photo of it."

"And tracking how many calories it has in it," I added. I smiled back at him while I sucked on the straw as if I hadn't had a drink in months—which I hadn't. Our eyes locked over that glass, over that gin of his that was all silky and warm and delicious. My eyes trailed down to his hands, lying loosely on the table. His beautiful hands, mournful-guitar-string-strumming fingers. And then I looked back up at him, our eyes locked again and he held my gaze with such intensity that I was sure I might fly off my seat and then—

"Hi." I heard a voice behind me and turned, the moment that I'd just shared with Mark was over. Because standing behind me was the hottest man I'd seen in a while. Hot in a completely different way to Mark. This guy was the epitome of generic, model hot.

"Hi," I said back, a little whispery.

"I'm Zack," said the extremely large and attractive man.

"Frankie," I cooed back in an embarrassing tone that I wished I didn't possess. But this man was really good-looking. He was big, strapping and tanned and had the most amazing dimples in his cheeks when he smiled.

"You must be new around here," he said, slipping into a spare seat next to me, ignoring the others completely.

I nodded and sucked on my copper straw, the warm liquid slipping down my throat and making me feel a little tingly.

"And you?" I asked. "Are you from around here?"

"I have a farm. On the other side of the hill."

"A faaarmer . . ." I hadn't meant for it to come out like that, and I heard Samirah give a small chuckle under her breath. I'm pretty sure I saw Mark roll his eyes and then move away from the table.

"Can I buy you a drink?" this Zack god asked with a smile that was sexy as hell.

"I've already got one," I said, although I started sucking on the straw a little faster, because I really wanted this strapping farmer with the sexy dimples to buy me another drink. I heard myself giggle, when he put his elbow on the table and leaned towards me in a very flirtatious way.

CHAPTER 35

"*L*ook at me, look at me," I declared loudly, tottering down the street. "I'm walking and I don't even care how many steps I've taken." I turned to Mark and waved my arms about. "One, two, five hundred and eight, one thousand and . . . WHO CARES? Not me! I don't even have my phone on me. Hashtag ten thousand steps a day, who knows?"

Mark laughed as I kept on walking, taking small steps and then long strides. It was about two hours since the gin had started flowing, and I was about three big, beautiful glasses of gin down—zero photos taken. I'd landed up chatting to the delicious Zack guy for about an hour, but then he'd had to leave. And now Mark and I were walking home.

"Oh my God." I stopped walking and faced him. "And I don't even know what my heart rate is! How about that! And you know what? I have no way of checking." I burst out laughing. "No way of knowing how many beats per minute my ticker is taking. No way of knowing how many calories were in that delicious gin, no GPS to guide me home and no way of knowing if it's going to rain, or not!" I threw my hands in the air and looked up. The sky was completely clear and cloudless and I looked back down at Mark. "Okay, so I could probably guess that it isn't going to rain, but I have no idea what the temperature is today, or the humidity. And more than that, I have no idea how I feel about that! Happy emoji face? Sad emoji face? Who the hell knows?"

"What a novelty," Mark teased. "Looking up at the actual sky to gauge what the weather is, simply through the keen skills of observation alone. Revolutionary."

"HA HA! Don't diss my weather app," I said sarcastically. "You would want to know if a hurricane was approaching."

"We don't get hurricanes here." He was smiling at me. He had a nice smile.

"Use your imagination, Mark. Say there was an approaching hurricane . . . you guys wouldn't know. But my weather app would and then I would be able to warn the entire town and I would be a local hero! You might even write about my heroics in your local paper."

Mark laughed at this. I'd encountered the local paper today at the bar. A small two-pager written by a local, printed and then distributed. It contained really arb news, but Harun had made the front-page headline. "Warning, suspected jackal spotting in town." Mark, Samirah and I'd had a giggle over that. I stopped walking, tipsy enough to feel the wobble in my legs. The one that told me if a policeman pulled me over and asked me to walk a straight line, I would stumble.

"It's like, I know *nothing* about *anything* right now!" I said thoughtfully.

"What?" Mark asked.

I shrugged. "I don't know how to explain it."

"Try," he urged.

"I always like to know things and plan things. All the time. Like what time the sun is setting, and how many hours of work versus exercise I do. How many carbs versus proteins are in my meals, and calories I've burned from walking and what kind of sleep I have, and how deep my sleep is and how productive my week has been and how many goals I reached."

"Which you do on your phone?" he asked.

"Exactly!" I clicked my fingers together. "And now that I don't have my phone, and I can't do them, it's like I'm not missing them."

I paused. "Although, maybe that's because I drank too much of your gin."

Mark laughed again but it wasn't a mocking laugh. It was sweet and playful.

"And you know what else, I can't even stalk Zack."

"Why would you want to stalk him?" he asked, his voice not as light-sounding as it had been before.

"Because that's what I do when I meet new people. I stalk them. You never know someone until you look at their photos, and their Tweets. Know what I mean? You can tell a lot about a person by their Tweets!"

Mark shook his head. "Not really. I guess I always assumed you can get to know someone by having a conversation with them." He paused. "Like this. We're getting to know each other now, aren't we?" His voice had taken on a slightly strange tone and I wasn't sure what it was. But I had to agree with him, we were getting to know each other, and I hadn't even looked at his first Facebook profile picture yet to make sure he wasn't a creep in disguise.

"I guess we are, Mark, I guess we are." I walked down the road, swaying my arms from side to side happily. I felt so strangely free all of a sudden. Like I was a bird that had been caged, but now I'd been released and was stretching my wings for the first time. This idea of freedom was exhilarating, albeit a little terrifying too.

Mark and I turned off the tarred road and back onto the dust. It was starting to look familiar here. In the beginning the elements of the desert all looked the same to me, but now I was noticing little details that made it unique; like that little bush there that looked like a rabbit, that rock with a vein of bright orange running through it. I started humming something and then stopped when I realized how loud it had gotten.

"You're a really good guitar player," I said.

"Thanks."

"You're really good. Like, really good. You should quit your day job," I said. "Pursue it professionally and get rich and famous."

Mark smiled at this, but it looked forced. I stopped walking when I saw the expression that flashed across his face. The little dark clouds that moved over his eyes briefly.

"Nah, I'm not that good." He was brushing me off.

"I'm being serious. If you posted TikTok videos, you'd be TikTok famous," I said and waited for him to respond to this. But when he didn't, when he strode ahead suddenly and I had to rush to catch up, I dropped it. I was feeling too happy to talk about something he clearly didn't want to. I carried on humming, I didn't even know what song it was, and I didn't have Shazam to tell me, but I didn't care. I was in that nice buzzy state of fun, intoxication. The kind where you are still totally in control of your faculties. You're just happier and chirpier than usual. Alcohol is like that. Just the right amount and it's like Prozac, the wrong amount and it sends you spiraling into weeping, sad hell. Crumpled on the floor, calling ex-boyfriends. But I wasn't like that tonight. I turned to Mark again.

"If you were my ex-boyfriend I wouldn't call you now!" I declared loudly, even though I knew that only made sense to me, thanks to the lively conversation in my head.

Mark burst out laughing. "I'm not sure whether I should be flattered by that, or offended."

"Flattered," I said thoughtfully, but then quickly changed my mind. "No, actually! You should be offended, because I broke up with you, Mark. You're my ex and no matter how drunk I am, I am not phoning you."

He laughed even more, a big smile spread across his face. "Why did you break up with me?" he asked, playing along with the strange and nonsensical conversation in my head.

"Because you rented me some seriously terrible movie. Why would you do that, by the way? Why would you give me a movie about someone having to saw off their foot!"

"Nah," he said, "I don't think our break-up had anything to do with the movie, I don't think you really loved me," he teased.

I shook my head. "Perhaps I didn't. Perhaps I was just taken in by your spell."

"What spell?"

"Oh please!" I stopped and put my hands on my hips. I looked him up and down for added effect. "Let's not pretend you don't know that half the town is practically giddy in love with you, because you have some sort of . . ." I waved my arm around in the space between us and he looked down at my hand. "Some sort of . . . magical, voo-doo thing going on."

"Voodoo?" He sounded really amused now.

"Don't act all innocent. You even got me for a moment!" I realized what I'd said and quickly corrected. "But only for a moment. I am totally over you now."

"I didn't know you were on me?"

"I was. For about five seconds while you were strumming your guitar all sexy, moody vibes."

"Sexy, moody vibes?"

I nodded and then whirled around again, did a full 360-degree playful pirouette of sorts. It kicked up the dust around us and I stopped to watch it settle back down on the ground. "I was too big to do ballet when I was young. And I wanted to do it so badly. I loved how ballerinas looked, so long and elegant and beautiful, and I wanted to be a ballerina so badly, but I couldn't," I heard myself say.

Mark stopped walking and his eyes swept over me, as if he was trying to reconcile this person with a bigger person.

I flapped a hand at him. "You can see my throwback Thursday pics on Instag— OH!" I laughed. "You can't." I twirled around again. "I used to be 'fat'!" I said. "That's how I became an influencer; I lost shitloads of weight and suddenly everyone wanted to know who I was, and what I was eating for breakfast." I twirled again. "My sister was a beautiful ballerina." It was meant to sound light and frivolous, but landed with an air of iciness that I hadn't intended.

"That's . . . terrible," Mark suddenly said and I stopped twirling.

"What's terrible?"

"Terrible that people only wanted to know you after you'd lost weight. That seems . . ." He stopped talking, as if thinking about his next word carefully. "Shallow."

I blinked at him. Gob smacked. I'd never thought about it like that. I'd always thought about it as a positive thing, but the way Mark had just put it . . . it didn't sound that positive after all. I didn't like that thought, and distracted myself by humming and walking again. And then I realized what song I was humming.

"Ice Ice Baby," I sang and heard Mark laugh behind me. His amusement only seemed to spur me on even more, so I started rapping, totally fucking up the lyrics.

"Like a harpoon nightly and daily and tightly and will it ever stop?" I pointed my finger at Mark and raised an expectant eyebrow at him.

"YO! I don't know," he shot back to me. I clapped and giggled happily at this, our masterful attempt at nineties rapping. But when our laughter tapered off and everything around us was silent again, our eyes found each other. We froze.

It seemed like the entire world froze too. The crickets went quiet and the breeze stopped blowing.

CHAPTER 36

*I*n this light—the light that was coming from the stars and the now faint town lights, the light from the small torch Mark was holding—his brown eyes seemed more black. A dark and stormy sort of black. A black that seemed to wipe all those cute-boy looks straight off his face. The color aged him and gave him a streak of something else, something that was the complete opposite of the slightly unkempt, nerdy guy from the video store who was wearing a faded Metallica shirt now.

I cocked my head to the side and looked at him, as that strange familiarity bubbled up inside me again. I tilted my head the other way, looking at him from another angle.

"You know, in certain lights you really do look familiar—"

"Shhhhh," Mark cut me off, putting his finger over his lips. "Listen," he said quietly, under his breath.

"Listen to what?"

"Just listen," he urged.

"I can't hear anything," I said to him, leaning in a little.

"Listen again."

I held my breath and listened. It was so silent here. Well, at first, anyway. The sounds were subtle though. The buzz of a beetle, the sound of something walking, maybe a small rodent, over the dry sand. Something rustling in a bush. The slight movement of sand as a light breeze picked some up and dropped it somewhere else. I closed my eyes and the sounds seemed to fall into a predictable, rhythmic pattern now. Slow and long and . . .

"Oh wow." I opened my eyes and looked at Mark. "It's breathing. In and out. The desert is breathing. It's alive." I gazed around into the dark, dark night. "You really love it out here, don't you?" I asked, turning back to him and his stormy eyes.

"I do. There's nowhere on earth quite like this place. And I've been to a lot of places. I have traveled all over the world, but I would come back here over and over again."

"It's your signature fragrance," I said. "The sound of the desert is your signature fragrance. You know some people can smell in colors, or hear colors. Maybe with you, you smell in sound."

"What?" He moved closer to me.

"I think it's called synesthesia, I read about it once. I used to read a lot when I was young, you know!" I blew my cheeks up to a much rounder face. "I read about this girl who could see colors in sounds and could touch them too."

Mark took another step closer to me; he was looking at me intensely now. His eyes boring into me.

"What?" I asked.

"You're not what you seem, you know that?"

"Aren't I?"

He shook his head. "No. You have these bursts of strange, yet somehow profound thoughts about parallel universes and inanimate objects breathing."

I laughed. "My ex used to tell me to keep those thoughts to myself. He used to say they were off brand."

"Off brand?"

"Yeah, our brand as a couple was to be inspirational and aspirational. I was supposed to say motivational things, like 'Find your purpose and step into it,' and 'Visualize your goals and don't let anything stand in your way,' and 'Own the day!' Not weird things."

"Supposed to say?" he asked, looking concerned now. "Your ex sounds like he was very controlling?"

Controlling? The word hit me in the silent night . . . hard. "I mean . . . I guess . . . he was clear about what he wanted." I felt defensive again.

"What about what you wanted?" he asked.

"I mean, I wanted it too."

Mark looked skeptical. "Did you?"

"You know, when Kyle and I started going out I only had one hundred and fifty thousand followers, and now I have over three hundred thousand." I shook my head. "Had! Had," I quickly corrected. "I don't have those anymore." My shoulders slumped suddenly.

"Well, I think your ex sounds like a total moron. I hate him."

"Really?"

Mark nodded. Slowly and deliberately. And then the nod stopped, and he just looked at me. It stole my breath. "I think I know what your signature fragrance is now," he said, his voice a little husky-sounding.

"What?" I was suddenly feeling very transfixed with this man in front of me. The spell! I was succumbing to the spell.

"Well, it's hard to tell with you at first. You're closed. Everything is very measured, and controlled. But then you open up slightly. Slowly. Showing only little parts of yourself. Pops of color and little eccentricities. That's what your fragrance would be like. Subtle at first, almost something you can't smell, and then you get bursts of bright fragrances, citruses and then something fun and irreverent like tuberose. Bright and breezy. Quirky."

"Wow, okay . . ." I said breathily, looking straight into his eyes. Everything suddenly changed between us; even the desert wasn't breathing like it had been a few moments ago. It seemed to be breathing faster, a little shallower—or was that me? I couldn't quite tell.

"You're looking at me like you like me," I suddenly blurted out, all gin courage.

He smiled. Small. "Maybe I do."

"Do you?" I asked, perking up a little.

He nodded.

"Not many people like me at the moment," I said. "In fact, about two hundred thousand people don't like me anymore. They don't like me so much that they unliked me. Some even blocked me."

"That's a lot of people."

"Mmmm," I mumbled. "It is."

We continued to stand there, looking at each other in the desert.

"And do you care if they don't like you?" he asked.

I scoffed. "Of course I care. That's why I came here. To get away from all their hateful comments and shitty words all over my feed."

"Why do you care so much about a whole bunch of people you don't know not liking you?"

"Because caring about what a whole bunch of people think about me is how I make my living . . . living. Wait, *my living*." I opened and closed my eyes a few times. Why had this not dawned on me before? How had I not thought about this? "Oh my God! I just realized something."

"What?"

"I have no way of earning money anymore. I am literally going to go broke!" I put my hands on my hips. "Huh! What do you think of that?"

"Is that a rhetorical question?" he asked.

"Um . . . no. Not really." I stood there and thought about it for a while. I knew the idea should have frightened me much more than it did right now. It was probably the gin smoothing over those rough edges of reality. Making them just a little less rough.

I shrugged. "What can I do, right?" And then I did another ballet spin again, almost falling on my ass. I flapped my arms to stop myself from falling and Mark rushed towards me. I stopped him with my hand though.

"I'm okay," I said to him.

"Good. I'm glad," he said and smiled at me.

"Can I ask you something?" I said.

"Sure."

"When I first came into the video store, you didn't seem to like me that much. I mean, I know I basically broke your shop, but . . ."

Mark glanced away. "That." He started walking again and I followed behind him. "Sorry," he said over his shoulder.

"Why didn't you like me?" I asked.

Mark paused for a moment, as if trying to figure out how to say it. "You know that song 'Video Killed The Radio Star'?"

I shook my head. "No."

"My dad ran his music and video store for over forty years. In that same spot in the mall. It was such a huge part of our lives growing up, it's how he met my mom, it's where we would spend our holidays helping out and listening to music. And then one day, people started coming to it less and less until they stopped coming altogether and it closed." He sounded sad now. "Spotify, streaming movies, Netflix . . . It killed his business. It was really sad."

"Sorry," I said softly, understanding now why he might have been so offended when I'd told him what my favorite movies were. "I see why you came here. So you could open a video and music store in the one place on earth you can!"

"That's not why I came here," Mark said, his tone totally changing now. It was colder and harsher than I'd ever heard it before. It gave me a shiver and I stood up a little.

"Why did you come here?" I asked nervously.

He looked at me for the longest time. As if weighing something up. And then he shook his head and started walking. "Some things are best left alone," he said, striding back towards the house. I watched him and something inside my stomach twisted into a knot. The entire mood of the evening had changed and this saddened me. I had liked the mood, but now it was clear it was over. I rushed after him so I wouldn't be left behind as he walked off towards the house at speed.

CHAPTER 37

"Good night, Mark," I said, lingering at my door, perhaps a little too long. I was lingering because I was hoping he might speak to me again—he'd been silent since we'd arrived.

"Good night, Frankie," he said. He'd hardly said my name since we met and I must say, it sounded nice coming from his lips. He had nice lips, actually. But there was also a gravity to him I hadn't seen before; something looked like it was bothering him. But then he shook his head and gave me a smile.

"I'll make sure I don't sleep naked," he said jokingly.

My cheeks flushed. "Good idea. Don't the insects bite?"

He smiled. "I burn citronella candles."

"How romantic!" I said sarcastically and Mark laughed at this. I looked down at Harun, who seemed to be watching us out of his one eye. His head was down, but his eye and one good ear were definitely tracking our conversation.

"Do you mind if he sleeps with me on the bed?" I asked.

"Sure. No problem."

"Harun," I called, and clicked my fingers at him. He got up slowly and walked over to me, wagging his huge tail so much that I was worried it would knock things over.

"It looks like he's been your dog forever," Mark commented. "He listens to everything you say."

"Not everything. Otherwise he wouldn't have had his belly cut open."

"Sleep well," he said. "If you need anything, just call."

I reached down and patted Harun on the head and he nudged my leg. I don't think he knew his own strength, because whenever he did this little gesture, it rocked you back and forth on your feet.

"Good night then," I said, and Mark started to walk away.

"You know where the bathroom is, right?" he stopped walking and asked.

I smiled at him. "We were in it earlier, remember?"

"Oh. Yes. Right." He took a few steps again, and then stopped once more.

"Kitchen, if you need a midnight snack or anything."

I smiled. "I think it's past midnight."

"Well, if you need a three a.m. snack or whatever, you can just scratch through the cupboards."

"Thanks," I said.

"Make yourself at home."

"It's very kind of you to let us stay here."

"It's a pleasure," he said quickly.

And then, without thinking, I walked up to him, and hugged him. I wrapped my arms around him and pulled him close. He immediately reacted, wrapping his arms around me too. I had intended it to be a short hug. Quick. The kind of hug you give when you say hello to someone. But it wasn't. It lingered. I closed my eyes for a second. He was warm. He smelled so good. And he was . . .

"You're very kind," I said, finally pulling away from the hug and smiling at him. "Letting me stay here. Helping with Harun."

"I like Harun." He smiled back. The light in the room was dim and warm. It cast a golden glow over his face, and suddenly I felt sad for some inexplicable reason.

"You look surprised that someone is kind," he said.

I shrugged. "I've had so many people be unkind to me lately that, I guess . . . I don't know."

"I think I know what you mean," he said softly.

"You do?"

"Let's just say that kindness can be in short supply sometimes." He sounded sad when he said that. And that gravity he'd shown a few moments ago was back again. Something was bubbling just below his surface, I could see that, but didn't know what. We looked at each other for a moment, and it felt like something inside me knew something inside him. As if a part of me understood him in a way I wasn't conscious of.

"Good night, Frankie," he repeated softly. He had such a nice voice too. Deep and gravelly and I wondered why he didn't also sing when he played the guitar.

"Night." I closed the door behind me and climbed onto the bed. I didn't care about removing my eye make-up or my clothes at this stage. Harun climbed up next to me and spread out like pancake batter being poured into a pan. God, I used to love pancakes. I hadn't eaten one in years. And I mean, *yeeeeeaaaarss*. I almost didn't know what they tasted like anymore. Harun readjusted himself and stretched out even more, until he took up most of the bed.

"Oh, so that's how it's going to be," I said, squashed into a small corner, almost clinging on. But Harun did nothing, except sigh loudly as if he was completely content.

I reached out and put a hand on his head. "It's okay, boy," I said. "You've probably never been in a bed before." I lay there next to him in the silence and again he elicited that feeling in me, as if I could say anything to him.

"Can I tell you a secret?" I whispered, not really expecting a reply. "I think I like Mark. He's nice, isn't he?" I turned to Harun, to find him snoring.

I sat up and looked across at him. "Some help you are." I yawned and then lay back down and shut my eyes.

CHAPTER 38

⌒

"What the . . .!" I flew out of bed, my heart thumping in my chest. The sun was streaming through the window and it looked like it was already late morning. Why hadn't my alarm gone off? I scrabbled for my phone on the side of the bed, only to remember it was dead. I stood there in the room looking around. It took me a few seconds to recognize where I was. My body felt stiff and tight, mainly thanks to Harun. During the night he and I had been engaged in a battle for space and blankets. I'm afraid to say, he'd won. This was evident when I woke up and found myself at the bottom corner of the bed, *a là* fetal position, barely clinging on. A clock on the wall caught my attention; it said ten and my heart thumped again. I never woke up at this time. Waking up at this time threw my entire morning routine out. I yawned, still not fully awake.

I was determined to find coffee. I wasn't hung-over or anything, but I did have a slightly heavy head that sat a little stiffer on my shoulders, the kind of head that told me I'd drunk the night before. The sticky coating over my tongue and mouth also told me that before I went to the kitchen, I needed to make a serious stop at the bathroom for a rendezvous with my toothbrush.

Mark was already in the kitchen when I got there. The smell of coffee came strong and delicious at me as I walked into the room.

"Morning," he said. I was taken aback by this word, and it struck me as odd. A guy saying "morning" to me. Usually when guys say "morning" to you, it's because you've spent the night together. Mark and I had not spent the night together. Well, not in that way, anyway. Suddenly, without trying to, I wondered what it would be like if Mark and I had spent the night together in *that* way. I bet it would be good. The way he'd played that guitar so slowly, and passionately, and with such feeling, made me think he would be much better in bed than Kyle. Sex with Kyle had been okay, I guess. I'm not sure I would write home about it. And I never felt completely comfortable doing it either, I never took my clothes off fully and always made sure the lights were off.

Sometimes I'm convinced I'm being cheated out of good sex. You're always reading these articles about multiple orgasms, or orgasms that last for days, and this multitude of different orgasms that we're all supposed to be having. I'm not sure whether there's a day-long orgasm out there waiting for me, but it would be nice to at least experience more of them in general. Not that I haven't had one, but honestly, no ground has shaken for me yet, no mountains moved, and heavens opened and explosions happened. And it would be nice to feel more comfortable doing it in general. To be completely naked and feel utterly sexy . . .

"You okay?" he asked and I jumped, as if I'd been caught with my face in the cookie jar.

"Wh— fine?" I replied quickly.

"Looks like you were really pondering something there."

I shook my head. "I'm just slow to wake up in the morning."

"You feeling okay? Need some paracetamol?"

"No, I'm actually fine."

"Good," he said and handed me a cup of black coffee. "I don't know how you take it. There's milk and sugar on the counter."

"Thanks." I reached for the sugar and then stopped myself. I didn't eat sugar. Not since I was fat. I glared at the sugar bowl, the little white, crystal-like beads staring back at me. Glinting in the sun . . . No, they weren't glinting, but they should have been, because they were seriously calling my name right now. *If I ate sugar and didn't record it on my calorie-tracking app, did that mean I had really eaten it?*

"It's just sugar," I heard Mark say behind me.

I shook my head. "Trust me. This is not just sugar, this is a gateway to very bad things."

He laughed a little at this. "What bad things?"

"Fat cells," I said flatly.

"You're not going to eat one spoon of sugar and put on ten kilos," he said.

"Mmmm, I wouldn't be so sure about that," I replied.

Mark walked up to the bowl and before I knew what he was doing, he had shoved a spoon of pure sugar into his mouth. I shook my head and laughed.

"But it tastes so good," he said, mouth full, bits of white sugar flying out of it onto his chin. He wiped it with the back of his hand. This morning he had what was a little more than a five o'clock shadow. It made him look totally different. Not so boyish. More manly. A tiny, white grain of sugar had perched itself on one of the small tufts of hair. I pointed at it and he wiped his face some more. And then he filled another spoon with sugar and passed it to me.

I took the spoon in my hands and looked down at it for a while before tilting the spoon over my coffee. I watched the grains trickle off the spoon, cascading into the black liquid. I looked up at Mark, almost for reassurance, and he nodded. I dunked the spoon in and stirred until it felt like all the grains had dissolved into the liquid. And once that was done, the excitement to get it to my lips was almost too much to bear. And when I sipped . . . *When I sipped . . .*

"Oh God, that's goooooood."

He nodded at me. "Breakfast?" He moved off to the stove and lit one of the gas hobs, but then turned back to me. "Oh, I forgot, you don't eat—"

"Breakfast." I nodded in agreement.

He gave me a smile. "Good decision. Most important meal of the day, you know."

I scoffed. "And most stressful." I took a long, slow sip of my coffee.

"How's that?"

"Trying to think of the most Insta-worthy breakfast to make. Trying to get the perfect picture of it. By the time I'm done and it's posted, I'm exhausted and then I have to reply to all the comments on it."

Mark paused. He turned the stove off and then looked at me sternly. "Let me get this straight. Because you put all this pressure on yourself to make the perfect breakfast and take a picture and then post it and wait to see what the response is . . . Because of all that, you don't really have the time and energy to eat it. Is that correct?"

I nodded.

"I see."

"See what?"

"Are you hungry at breakfast?"

"Um . . ." I thought about it. "I guess. But by the time I'm done, it's time for lunch."

"And do you take pictures of your lunch too?"

"No, breakfast is a way more popular hashtag."

"I see," he said again, slowly and thoughtfully. "Do you do anything for yourself?"

The question stumped me. "Of course I do."

"Doesn't sound like you do."

"I do," I said defensively.

"Really? Seems like you don't do anything for yourself, you only do things for the benefit of others, or for likes and comments and whatever your ex says you should be doing."

I shook my head. "I do a lot of things just for myself."

"So you have a wide variety of hobbies that you don't post and share with others?"

"Um . . . no, but I do . . . that is, that I . . . um . . ." I slowed down and then finally stopped talking.

"Name one thing that you do in your life that you don't share with the world. One thing that's just yours that you do purely for your own enjoyment!"

I looked at him, and my mind went blank. And then I shook my head. "Nothing."

"And don't you think that's absolutely ridiculous, now that you think about it?"

I considered his question very carefully. "You know, it's funny," I started solemnly. "Since coming here, a place that is so cut off and far away from it all, where social media isn't part of every minute of your day because it can't be, I guess I've wondered about that myself. Because when I say these things out loud here, they do sound . . ." I paused, looking for the words.

"Ridiculous?" he repeated.

I nodded.

"Ludicrous?"

"Hey! That's taking it too far," I said. "Are you calling me ludicrous?"

He shook his head. "No. I just think it's sad that you live your life for thousands of other people who you don't even know and don't even—"

"Hundreds of thousands," I corrected.

"Fine. Hundreds of thousands that you don't even know. That you do nothing for yourself. If you think about it, your entire life is just a show for someone else's benefit." Something in Mark's tone changed. He seemed to be getting angry, maybe too angry, and I got the feeling that he'd stopped talking about me and my life, and was talking about someone else's life . . . *maybe his own*? "Your entire existence is this careful, thought-out performance for everyone else's benefit. But where are you in all that? Where is your sense of self? Instead, you're just getting lost in a show that is supposed to be your life. But it's not, because none of it is real and it's all just this carefully curated, thought-out thing for someone else's enjoyment, not yours."

I stared at him and I think he could see what I was thinking, because he stopped talking abruptly and then turned away from me. His cheeks seemed to be a little redder than they'd been a few moments ago.

"Sorry," he mumbled quietly. "I didn't mean to . . ." He moved back to the stove and lit the gas again.

Something strange had fallen over him, I could see it like a dark cloud around his head, same as last night.

"Where did you say you lived before coming here?" I asked curiously. He ignored my question and turned to me with a smile.

"I'm thinking bacon and pancakes," he said cheerfully.

I looked at him for a moment; it was clear he'd put an end to this conversation, and it was clear that it wasn't for my benefit either. I took another sip of coffee, the sugar firing up a whole bunch of neurons in my brain that had been lying dormant for quite some time. They tantalized my taste buds and make my mouth cry out for . . .

"Pancakes. Yes. Please." I sat back down at the table.

"Good choice." Mark turned back to the stove and, moments later, a large plate was pushed in front of me. I stared down at it and images of my childhood breakfasts came back to me. Breakfast was always my favorite meal of the day and I used to pile the plate with food and eat as much as I could. Kind of like a tranquillizer, taken before an operation to calm you down. That plate of food I ate in the morning was like that to me, something to calm me down before the inevitable day of relentless teasing at school. Ironically, the thing I was turning to in my moments of pain was also the thing causing me to be teased. The vicious cycle continued, and went around and around on itself, like that image of a snake eating its own tail.

"I only eat pancakes and bacon on the weekend," Mark suddenly said, and I looked up, confused.

"What?"

"During the week I eat muesli with yoghurt and fruit." He stabbed a pancake and put it on his plate. "Point is, pancakes on the weekend doesn't make you unhealthy. It doesn't make you a sugar junkie. It makes you normal."

I watched as he tipped the syrup over the pancake and it dripped down the side.

"I learned many years ago that being too extreme about one thing isn't good for your mental health." He cut the pancake with the side of his fork and popped a piece in his mouth. I nodded at him. That did make sense. He looked at my plate and seemed to urge me on. I sighed.

"Well, here goes," I said, sticking my fork into a piece of crispy bacon and fluffy-looking pancake. I raised it to my mouth and looked at it. It looked back at me—well, that's how it felt anyway. I bit into it. It crunched between my teeth and the delicious salty taste was instant, followed by the sweet syrup. It made my body scream out for more. Within minutes, I had devoured everything on my plate and when I looked up, Mark was just watching me.

"Would you like more?" he asked, as if he'd been waiting to ask this question.

I simply nodded. No words needed. Mark slid his plate over to me.

"What about you?" I asked, looking down at the kind offering.

He shrugged. "It's fine. Looks like you need breakfast more than me."

I nodded at him and carried on eating, eating as if I hadn't seen food in years. My phone, and Kyle, had always made me feel guilty about what I ate, and now that they were not here, the guilt was melting away, much like the syrup down the side of the pancake.

CHAPTER 39

I stood on his veranda, looked out over the nothingness and started to feel a little scratchy and itchy all over. It had nothing to do with the warm, full sensation deep in my belly. This was the scratchy itchiness I'd become familiar with over these last few days. It was that uncomfortable feeling of having nothing to do, nothing to fill those moments and gaps of silence with. The gaps that I would usually fill with my phone.

When nothing was happening around me, I would pick up my phone. I'd scroll through it with no intention of looking at anything in particular. I saw nothing. I read nothing. I stopped at no pictures. But just the act of doing it and knowing that there were people, right below my fingertips, that I could reach out to at any time, usually made me feel better. It made me feel less alone, like my phone was a portal to a place I could visit any time I wanted to.

I crossed my arms over my chest as Harun came up next to me. He stood close, his giant body pressed into mine. We both looked out together over the nothingness, and I felt like I knew him well enough to know what he was thinking.

"Sorry, boy. Still no running around until you heal properly."

I glanced down at him. He seemed to be staring out over the land with a kind of far-away longing and I wondered where he'd been before me. If he'd had a family? If he'd ever had puppies, or what he'd been like as a puppy? I wondered if he'd ever been loved before and had slept in a bed? Three chickens suddenly walked past us and

I quickly looked down to see if Harun had seen them. He had, but they didn't seem to bother him. I heard Mark come up behind me and I turned and looked at him.

"You have chickens!" I stated, pointing at them as they wandered past, clucking and pecking the ground.

"I do!" he said with a smile. "So, you ready?"

"Ready for what?"

"Saturday," he stated.

His statement confused me. "How is one ready for Saturday, exactly?"

"My Saturday hobbies," he said, sounding full of cheer and pep.

"Hobbies?"

"Yes. Things you do for fun and enjoyment," he teased.

"Aaaah, I see," I teased back. "Those things."

There was a small pause, a beat between us in which I felt myself getting a little closer to Mark. Feeling that I could talk to him openly.

"I don't have hobbies." I sighed. "You were right. I don't do anything for myself. I don't even know what I would like to do for myself. I wouldn't know where to begin."

Mark smiled slowly at me. "Well, let's see if we can't find something you like doing."

"Okay," I agreed. "What's your plan for the day?"

"While the weather is still warm, I have to collect more fynbos for my gin."

"Fynbos?" I'd heard of it, but wasn't sure what he meant.

"It's this vegetation that only grows in a tiny part of South Africa, nowhere else in the world. And it grows on our doorstep. I use it in my gin."

I looked around. "Where is it?"

"I get mine from a small fynbos farm about an hour and a half away. You want to join me?"

"Um . . ." I hesitated. I don't know why.

"You totally don't have to though," he said.

"No. I'd love to," I heard myself say.

He smiled. Big smile. Contagious smile and I smiled back. That little tug in my chest happened again, the one where I swear, just for a second, he looked familiar. But then it was gone again.

"Let's just get Harun comfortable, give him his medicine, set up some food and water, and then we can go," I said.

Mark gave a chuckle.

"What?" I asked.

"It's just cute the way you care about him so much."

"Cute?"

"Yeah, a few days ago you were telling everyone and anyone who would listen that he wasn't your dog, and now look at you. A dog mum."

"A dog mum!" I let those words sink in. "I guess I am." Was it strange that in a matter of only a few days, this creature had bloody wriggled its way into my heart in a way that I now couldn't imagine him not being there?

* * *

We'd been driving for an hour when we finally stopped. Like I'd seen before in these parts, there was just an old rickety gate on the side of a dusty road. All the fences and gates here looked like they could fall apart at any moment; they leaned over, like old men on walkers. The gates were not locked either, and you could simply push them open, which made me wonder why they were even there. At this particular gate, a small rusted postbox hung from a skew pole, and I doubted very much that this was on the postman's route. A small, rusted sign announced:

Opperman's Fynbos Farm

We pushed the gate open and then drove for about another half an hour, until we arrived at a farmhouse. It was very much like

Mark's, except it was bigger. But it still had that same picturesque quality as his did. We were greeted by a couple who seemed to know Mark well—clearly he did this often. After that, we went around the back of the house and then proceeded to walk over a small hill and when we reached the other side of it and emerged into the valley, I gasped.

"This is amazing," I said, looking at the massive fields in front of us in the valley. They were bursting with the most vibrant colors I'd ever seen before. Oranges and pinks and reds and greens and sky blues and little pops of white that seemed to make all the other colors stand out that much more.

"Incredible, right?" Mark said, standing next to me.

Their shapes were the things of Dr Seuss books. Round and fat flowers, strange long grasses with fluffy, cloud-like, cotton-candy tops, spikes and bushes and things that looked delicate and petaled and things that looked like they would prick.

"It's kind of alien." Mark started moving into the field and I followed him.

"Completely," I agreed.

"You know, these flowers and plants grow nowhere else in the world except here. They are unique to this area."

"I didn't know that." I reached out and ran my hand over a huge pink protea. It felt soft and fluffy to the touch.

"Most people only know the protea, since it's your national flower, but there are over 9,000 different types of fynbos; the protea is just one of them."

"I had no idea." I was in awe of everything around me. It was like I'd driven off this dry and dusty road, straight into a paradise of bright plants that I couldn't—in my wildest dreams—have imagined.

"Pick what you like," Mark said. He was holding out his arms, running his fingers over the riot of colors. "I like to experiment with different types of fynbos. They give the gin a different flavor each time."

"Okay, I will."

I continued to walk along the path that had been created through the field, and then something caught my eye. I bent down.

"These," I said, pointing to the bright turquoise flowers that stared back at me. Their centers were round and yellow, and reminded me of Harun's one good eye.

"Pick a few." Mark walked up to me and bent down. I picked them delicately and gently, careful not to damage them. They were gorgeous, and when I was done, I held them out for Mark. He took them and slipped them into a small basket he was carrying. We stood up together at the same time, and when we were fully upright, our eyes zoned in on each other's. There was a breeze around us, warm and soft, blowing through the flowers and bushes, making a soft rustling sound. Without warning, Mark reached up and touched the side of my face. The sensation was hot and sticky, like lava or something molten rushing over my skin. I briefly closed my eyes; well, I let my blink last a few seconds too long.

"There," he said.

"There what?" I opened my eyes and looked into his. Brown. Kind of hazel. With flecks of gold. Complex. Not plain brown like I'd previously thought.

"The flower." He pointed at my head and I raised my hand to feel the flower he'd pushed behind my ear.

I reached into my pocket immediately to take out my . . .

"Oh. That's right," I said blankly. No phone. "I can't see what it looks like."

He smiled at me. Small. Gentle. Just a flicker on the corners of his lips.

"Looks perfect," he said softly.

CHAPTER 40

*W*e sat on the veranda and watched the sun set over the great, endless Karoo. The sun here seemed to paint the sky all sorts of different colors when it set. It saturated it with shades of dark purple and maroon and then, on the edge of that, lavender-colored clouds. I sighed as I settled into the daybed, sipping my glass of gin. One of Mark's gins. When we'd gotten back, we'd put the blue fynbos flowers into the gin to infuse and I couldn't remember having a day like this in a long time. A day actually spent doing things. Kyle and I used to "do things" but not really. We didn't do them because we enjoyed them, we did them for everyone else. But today, I'd just enjoyed it. For no one else in the world other than me.

"I can see why you like it here," I said, as Mark walked outside and sat next to me.

"Yeah, she's a real beauty, the desert," he echoed, sounding very Australian again. He made himself comfortable on the bed, only a little way away from me.

"She is," I repeated with a smile, suddenly thinking of this place as female.

"But not in an obvious way," he said.

"What do you mean?" I looked at him.

"Not everyone can see beauty in a desert. It's not obviously beautiful, like rolling green hills or a waterfall. Her beauty takes a little more finding, but once you've found it, you've got it for life."

"She, eh?" I teased him.

"Well, what do you think?" he asked.

I looked out again. Then stood up and walked to the edge of the veranda and scanned the vista in front of me. It was harsh, but there was something soft about it. I guess you could say feminine.

"She!" I declared and then walked back and sat down. I thought about everything Mark had told me up until this point. He'd traveled a lot before coming here, but where? And for what reason? I was trying to form a proper picture of him in my mind, but he was still a rather large mystery to me.

"Is that why you came here?" I asked. "Because of her beauty?"

He shrugged. "Not really, but that's part of the reason I stay. Maybe that's the reason that all the others stay too."

I thought about this for a while. The idea that you could come here for one reason, by accident even, like me, but then land up staying for another reason entirely.

"What kind of people live here?" I asked.

"What do you mean?"

"Well, I've met you and Samirah and Faizel and Logan, and you all seem fairly normal. But if you think about it, it's pretty extreme to choose to live in a place with no internet. So what kind of people choose to live here?" I posed this question generally, but really, I was still trying to get a better grasp of him. There was so much more to Mark than met the eye—I could see it and sense it, I just had no idea what it was.

Mark smiled at the question and then turned to face me. The move caught me off guard and my body stiffened a little in response to it.

"A lot of Wi-Fi refugees live here, as they call themselves," he said.

"What's that?"

"People who choose to live without the internet. Or live without it because they think it makes them sick."

"Oh!" I'd never heard of this before.

"And there's this one guy who moved here because he believes that aliens are mind-controlling people through the radio, or micro-waves or something."

"Really?"

He nodded. "He's a nice guy, but has some strange beliefs. There's this other family who moved here accidentally a year ago."

"Accidentally?"

"Story goes, they were on their way to AfrikaBurn and took a wrong turn and just stayed here. Proper hippies. Full on tie-dye poly-amory love."

"Oh yes?" I sat forward, interested and listening.

"They live in a teepee compound just on the outskirts of town, sometimes they come to town every now and then. But they mostly stick to themselves. And then there's Bob and Betty-Sue."

"Who?"

"They identify as people from the 1950s."

"Sorry, what?"

"They choose to live as if they're in 1950. They moved here some years back. You see them out and about quite often. She always looks amazing, full 1950s make-up and hair and outfits. She drives a pink Cadillac."

"Oh wow! That would make an amazing Instagram account!"

Mark smiled at me in a sort of endearing way. "And then there's an author who lives here, she's really famous: Emelia King."

"I know her," I replied.

"Everyone knows her. She releases one book every ten years, writes on a typewriter and hates modern technology. She's lived here for a while too."

"That's amazing. This town is really . . . weird," I said.

He smiled. "You don't know the half of it. Wait until the spring festival. Which is coming up soon."

"Why?" I was curious now.

"Well, if you plan to stick around, you'll see."

That sounded like a question. Was he asking me if I was planning on sticking around? Was I?

I looked at Harun; he was sleeping happily on the blanket that Mark had put down for him. He looked completely content to stay exactly where he was. And we would be staying for a while until he recovered fully, but when he was better . . . *Was I going to leave?* I'd desperately wanted to leave only a few days ago, and now I wasn't so sure.

"I don't think I could get used to the dry heat here, though," I said, fanning myself. "I can't even imagine what it's like here in summer."

"It can get brutal in summer. And I'm from Australia. I know hot weather." He paused and watched me for a while, as if concocting a plan in his head. "Want to cool down?" He had a mischievous grin on his face.

"Sure."

"Come." He stood up and started walking off the veranda.

"As long as it doesn't involve nudity!" I said.

He laughed. "Funny you should say that, sometimes it does, but I'll spare you that."

"Thanks." This conversation seemed to be getting a little flirtier. Or at least, that's how it felt to me.

"Come on," Mark called as he walked into his sandy garden.

I followed him slightly tentatively; I wasn't sure what was about to happen. He made his way over to a small rusted tap in the succulent bed and looked at me.

"What are you going to do?" I asked.

"I'm going to turn on the sprinkler and then run through it."

I laughed. "Seriously, you do that?"

"Often."

"Okay. I'm ready," I said, preparing myself for the shower of water.

"Okay . . ." Mark turned the tap on and a sprinkler sprang to life.

The water was still warm from the hot day, but soon it was cool and refreshing. I laughed as it rushed over me.

"When last did you run through a sprinkler?" Mark shouted, running and jumping over the gushing water.

I burst out laughing. "I can't remember. Maybe never." I copied him and ran directly at the sprinkler and then jumped over it, wetting myself entirely.

I stopped running and stood there, letting the cool water rush over me. I looked up at the night sky, it was incredible. Like someone had thrown silver glitter across a black canvas. I looked back down and found Mark standing right in front of me. The water was dripping down his face, and he was smiling. Smiling so much that water was pooling in the corners of his mouth. And suddenly, I wanted to kiss him so badly. Kiss that water off his lips . . .

And so I did.

CHAPTER 41

And he kissed me right back.

The kiss was hot under the cool water. But it was slow and soft, unlike the water that was falling fast and heavy on us. I wrapped my arms around him and we pulled each other closer as our lips and tongues met for the first time. It was electric. Shocks and tingles flew between our mouths in a way I'd never experienced before.

We pulled apart for a second, shaky, sharp breaths coming from our mouths. The feel of the warm air on each other's lips was enough to make me feel like I could let go and lose control in this kiss.

Wait, why had we pulled away? Why weren't we kissing anymore?

I pulled away further, so that Mark's face came into focus. His eyes were wide open, waiting for mine to find him.

"What's wrong?" I asked.

He seemed to smile at this question of mine and then put his hands on the sides of my face and pulled me in again for another kiss. This time, totally different to the first. The pulling away, I realized, was nothing more than a moment taken before changing gears. The calm before a storm. Because the kiss quickly went from soft and slow to everything but that. Fast. Hard. Hungry.

I whimpered as he moved his lips off my mouth and they trailed over my chin and neck. God, he was good at this. So, so good. Back up to my lips again, pushing inside my mouth. Open and wanting and demanding. Nice Mark was gone now. It surprised me, but fucking thrilled me too. Nice guys didn't kiss like this. Nice guys didn't wrap their fingers through your hair and tangle it and pull at it. Nice guys didn't slide their hands down to your ass and pull you closer. Nice guys didn't start walking you backwards to the house, completely wet and clinging to each other. Nice guys didn't grab onto you hungrily.

And as for me . . . I was definitely not being nice either, my hands pulling at his sticky shirt and wanting it off his body so badly that I wasn't sure I could contain myself. And then . . .

A slip on the wet soil. A tumble to the ground.

"Shit!" I laughed, pulling myself onto my hands and knees in the muddy soil. I looked over my shoulder at Mark who was laughing too, also pulling himself up. I was just about to turn around and kiss him again in the mud, when I saw his eyes zone in on my back, where my shirt had ridden up. His entire face changed in an instant. Everything that was there a few moments ago, was gone. Totally and utterly gone.

"What?" I turned and asked, looking at him. He didn't make eye contact now. "What?" I asked again frantically as his demeanor changed even more.

He stood up.

I stood up.

"Mark?" I asked, running my hands over my back, over my tattoo, where he'd been looking.

"What's wrong?" I asked, hurt and confused by this sudden change between us that I was struggling to understand.

"Sorry," he suddenly muttered.

"Sorry for what?"

"I shouldn't have done that," he quickly stated and started walking back to the house.

"Um . . ." I stood there in utter confusion. How had we gone from kissing like that, to this?

He strode up the steps to the veranda again and I got somewhat frantic. I chased after him.

"Mark. Stop!" I commanded.

He turned around and looked at me. His eyes were no longer filled with lust and want and desire for me. My heart broke.

"Frankie," his voice was slow and soft, but firm, "I'm really sorry. That should never have happened."

"Why?" I folded my arms across my chest.

He shook his head and then started wringing the water out of his shirt. The drops falling onto the ground felt so definitive. The end.

I nodded. "Okay." I couldn't hide the hurt in my voice, which made me feel like a total idiot.

"Good night, Frankie. Sleep well." He turned again and started walking into the house. He stopped, but didn't look back. "You should have a warm shower before bed, you don't want to get sick."

And with that, he was gone and I was left staring after him wondering . . .

WTF had just happened?

CHAPTER 42

"So, can I take him or what?" I asked Samirah, my arms folded.

She was still looking Harun over; he'd become quite fond of her, perhaps because of the scratches she gave him under the ear that made his back legs twitch.

"Um . . ." She sounded hesitant. "Ideally I wouldn't recommend traveling so soon after an operation."

I felt a little panicked by that. "Will it hurt him, though?"

"Well, not necessarily, but he might find it a bit uncomfortable."

"I'll give him his pain medication," I added.

She turned and looked at me. "Why do you want to leave so quickly, all of a sudden?"

I looked away. "No reason." I bit my lip, trying to push the feeling down: it was a mixture of anger and embarrassment over what had happened, or *not* happened between Mark and me last night.

"Did something happen between you and Mark? A fight? You looked like you were getting on so well."

"Mmmm, something like that. I mean, in a way. You could say it was something like that, it was, uh . . . Well, I don't really know what happened!" I stopped talking; the more I spoke the more pathetic I was starting to sound.

She eyed me curiously. She had this way about her. This strange mysterious way. Samirah definitely gave off the vibe that at any point, she might pull out a pack of tarot cards or a crystal ball and tell your future, or pluck some kind of spiritual guidance from the universe.

"That sounds . . . complicated?" She made it sound like a question.

"Apparently," I huffed. "So, can I take him?"

She reached down and gave him a firm pat on the head. "You know what, this guy's a toughie! He's going to be fine. As long as you drive carefully. Stop often so he can stretch his legs and make sure he stays hydrated and give him his pain meds and promise you'll go straight to a vet when you get home to have him checked out."

"Home . . .?" I said wistfully. And then a tear formed in my eye and I tried to blink it away. "I'm kind of between homes at the moment, it seems."

"Stay then," she said.

I shook my head. "No. I can't go back to the hotel."

"You can stay with Faizel and me for a few nights if you want?"

For a second I considered that, but then I remembered that look on Mark's face last night when he'd left me standing there, and how I'd felt. Mortified. He'd clearly decided halfway through the kiss that he no longer wanted to kiss me. Perhaps he realized that he was no longer attracted to me. That was surely the only reason he stopped. It was a familiar feeling that cut me to the quick. It was only in recent years that men seemed to find me attractive; before that it had been quite the opposite.

"I must go," I said.

"Are you sure?" she asked, all mysterious voice and piercing green eyes again. The same strange voice and eyes that implied she knew something that you didn't. And this time it rubbed me up the wrong way a little. I put my hands on my hips.

"Of course I'm going! Why would I stay here? The only reason I didn't go was because Harun over here swallowed the immobilizer and now that it's out and he's fine, I can go."

"Are you sure it was about the immobilizer?"

"Am I sure it was about the immobilizer? Um . . . You were the one that scraped that thing out of his smelly bowels, so yes, I'm pretty sure this has a lot to do with the immobilizer!"

She shook her head. "I mean, are you sure Harun swallowing your immobilizer was the only reason you stayed?"

"What? Pssshht! Hhhhmmmff!" I spluttered and stuttered. I was getting flustered by this conversation and the word "immobilizer" was starting to sound strange, since we'd said it far too much! "Yes! Why else would I stay? It's not like I like it here. This is not a place I would choose to be in so, YES! I am leaving. And YES, the only reason I didn't leave sooner, was because *he* swallowed my immobilizer."

Samirah folded her arms and eyed me skeptically.

"Why are you looking at me like that?"

"I'm looking at you like this because I can hear the words coming out of your mouth, but I don't think they match the words that are going on in your heart right now."

I scoffed. "My heart has words now, does it, doc? That seems very scientific."

"Science and medicine can only explain a small part of the way the world works. The rest, well, we have to rely on other explanations for it all."

"What kind of explanations?" I asked.

Samirah looked at me expectantly, leaning forward, as if she was waiting for me to have a profound epiphany of sorts. Well, if she was waiting for me to have some kind of massive, spiritual experience, she was sorely mistaken. There were no spiritual experiences to be had here; I had learned that a few days ago in the desert with the snake, and then again while lying on a stupid purple mat.

"Don't you think," she started again, "that you coming here has been a series of strange coincidences that can't really be explained by rational laws?"

"Huh?"

"You got stuck in an elevator, and because of that a series of things happened that led you to come here, and then you landed up with a dog you never intended to keep. And then while you were here, it seemed that something was conspiring to keep you here. Don't you think when you look back on the events of the last several days, that something inexplicable has been at work?"

"I don't believe in stuff like that," I said dismissively, even though I'd had that exact same thought a few times, but for some reason, didn't really want to admit to it.

"Well, I believe in that stuff." She sounded a little angry now. "I believe that in life, the unexpected happens and when it does, it can change us profoundly and change the course of our lives. It can move us to places we never imagined we would go, but then find we belong there."

"And why do you believe that?"

"Because it happened to me," she said, her voice taking on a small and fragile tone.

"What did?" I asked, my voice now matching hers because I could sense a shift in the atmosphere in the room. The air had taken on a heaviness, a thickness that was loaded with something I didn't understand yet. And even Harun could sense it, because he tilted his head up and looked over at her too.

She pulled her gloves off and tossed them onto one of the counters. "Seven years ago, I lost my husband in a car accident."

"What? You were married before Faizel?" That was hard to imagine, because they seemed perfect for each other, like they'd been together forever.

She nodded solemnly. "The driver of the other car was texting and didn't see the traffic light. Came out of the blue and smashed into the driver's side."

"Oh my God, that's . . . I'm so sorry."

She forced a small smile. "We were planning on having a baby." Her voice was soft now. "I was stuck in the car with him for three hours before they managed to get us out. He was dead that entire time."

I gasped. Put my hands over my face and mouth. "That's horrific."

She nodded. "I was so angry after that. I was consumed by it, all the time. Every time I saw someone on their phone, every time I saw someone not looking where they were going, someone driving badly, this rage used to bubble up inside me. I was angry with the entire world around me." She paused and took a deep breath. "The guy was checking his Facebook feed when he killed my husband. He killed my husband because he wanted to see how many people liked his post."

I lowered my head in shame. I'd done that before. "Where's the guy now?"

"In jail. I thought that would bring me closure and make me less angry. Which it did, but then the anger gave way to something much worse: fear. The fear was harder to live with than the anger. I became terrified of everything. I stayed at home, I stopped driving, I was too afraid to leave the house and go outside. Suddenly, the world was this terrifying place and I didn't think I could survive in it."

"I'm sorry," I said.

"I never thought I would find love again. I thought I was going to be alone and in my house forever . . . and then I came here."

"How did you hear about it?"

"There was a story about it on the news, and when I heard about it, this place with no phones that was small enough to walk around, it sounded exactly what I needed. And more than that, when I heard about it, I just had this feeling that I had to come here. I can't explain it."

I nodded. I could relate. I'd had that same feeling when I'd read about it in the paper, but I wasn't going to say that out loud.

"At first, when I came here, I was definitely running away from my old life. But after a while, I stopped running and I settled down, and that's when my entire life changed. I met Faizel and got a second chance at love that I never thought I would ever get. And now I've got not one, but two babies on the way at age forty! Do you know how hard it is to fall pregnant at this age, let alone with twins? It was all a miracle."

I stayed silent for a while and considered what she'd said. "I don't think it's like that for me," I finally concluded, breaking the silence. "I don't think I'm meant to be here. There's nothing for me here."

Samirah shot me a look. "What about friends?"

"Are we friends?" I asked.

She nodded. "We're definitely getting there, don't you think?" There was a strange beat between us and then she took a deep breath. "I haven't told anyone that story in a very, very long time."

I looked at her and a tear trickled down my cheek, I was so incredibly touched. I reached out and spontaneously pulled her into my arms for a hug. This was the second hug I'd given in days, and probably one of a few real hugs I'd given in years, other than hug emojis.

"Thank you, for everything you've done for Harun and for me," I said, pulling away. "Thanks for being my friend, in real life. I'll never forget you and this strange little town but . . . I don't belong here. I have to go." I gave her one last smile and then I left.

CHAPTER 43

⌒

$\mathcal{I}$ left Springdorp behind me forty minutes ago and passed that sign that I'd seen almost a week ago. But the second I drove past it, they started . . .

All at once, with this fervent intensity that made my head spin, things around me started buzzing and beeping. The noise disorientated me at first. I hadn't heard it in days and it took me a second to realize what it was. I looked at the seat next to me, my phone was plugged into the car charger and it was alive! Shaking and buzzing so much that it started to move sideways across the seat, like a crab. The onslaught of messages awakened it like Sleeping Beauty.

I pulled my car to the side of the road and grabbed the phone. I wasn't able to do anything with it for five minutes, while I waited for the notifications to slow down and finally stop. I glanced over at Harun in the backseat; he was sitting straight up now, his ear standing to attention. He looked agitated, cocking his head from side to side in nervous curiosity at the noise that was coming from the palm of my hand.

And then alarms started going off. Google reminders that I'd missed started shouting at me. I heard a deep growl behind me, followed by a bark and then Harun started scratching at the window, wanting out. I didn't blame him. I wanted out too. This felt like an invasion of my space. The car felt like it was heating up and the oxygen was getting sucked out with every notification that came through. I pushed the door open and climbed out, opening the door for Harun as I went. When my phone finally stopped beeping and buzzing and things settled down, I opened my Facebook page. I gasped. I had thousands of notifications there. Thousands of people had posted on my wall . . .

I scrolled fast and furious, not reading them even.

Then I went to Instagram and all my followers seemed to have returned, and more. I had about a hundred thousand more followers than I'd had before.

WhatsApp . . . it was lit up like a Christmas tree. Especially from Kyle. There were so many missed calls and WhatsApp messages from him I didn't know where to start and where to look and what to do, and for the first time in my life, I felt overwhelmed by it all. I felt lost in this massive web of messages and likes and shares. Like I was an insect trapped in a great big spider's internet web. I couldn't move. I couldn't breathe and then I saw it.

Kyle: I can see you're online now.
Kyle: Where are you?

And then my phone rang. It was him. I looked over at Harun and it seemed like he shook his head. I turned my back on him to take the call. I had to take this call . . . *Didn't I?* I'm sure Kyle was worried about me, even though he'd broken up with me. We'd been together for two years, of course he was concerned about me. My hands were shaking, my throat tight and dry and the sun was flaming down on me. Nerves had gripped me in some kind of nauseating, dizzying way as I raised the phone to my ear tentatively. I didn't even have a chance to say hello.

"Where have you been?" Kyle's words were fast and frantic.

"Uh . . . I've been . . . um, away."

"Oh my God! Do you have any idea what's been going on since your disappearance?"

"No."

"You're going to love it." Now he sounded excited.

I was confused. Where was the "Are you alright, Frankie?", "I've been worried about you, Frankie"?

"Since you've been gone Find Frankie is trending. I mean fucking trending like a mo fo. It's literally the hottest hashtag around. You've gotten two hundred thousand new followers and so have I. It's blowing the eff up. Genius! This was genius!"

"What's genius?" I asked.

"Going away like this! Everyone wants to know why you left and where you are. It's like a social media mystery and everyone's weighing in. And I totally get why you didn't tell me where you were, you needed this to be genuine and authentic and—"

"WAIT!" I shouted into the phone. "What the hell are you talking about?"

"Your plan to create all this mystery; you know what amazing content I've been generating over this?"

"That's not why I went away, Kyle," I spat into the phone.

But he didn't seem to be listening. He was rattling on and on about it all like this was exciting to him.

"Kyle! Kyle!" I tried to interrupt him, but he was like a steam train. "KYLE!" I shouted again.

"What?" he asked, as if he was angry and irritated that I'd silenced him. And then he sighed. "You're upset about the whole Paige thing, right?"

"Um . . . Yes!" This seemed like a stupid question.

"It's over between us," he said quickly. "I mean, when Find Frankie started trending and everyone was asking where you were, I realized what a mistake breaking up with you was, so I ended it with her so we can—"

"WAIT!" I cut him off again. "You broke up with her because I was trending?"

"You're huge, babe! Massive. Everyone's talking about you. Everyone wants to know where you are . . . Where are you?"

"I . . . you . . . it's . . . uh . . ." I didn't know what to say to him, this panic had seized me so suddenly and quickly that it made my rib cage tighten. "I've got to go!" I hung up, my breathing hard and fast. As soon as I did, the phone started ringing in my palm. Over and over again. I glanced over at Harun, who looked like he was about to launch at the thing and take it out of my hand. And then the slew of messages started.

Kyle: Answer the phone.

Kyle: I can see you're still online.

Kyle: Pick it up.

Kyle: We have so much to discuss.

Kyle: We need to figure out how to leverage this disappearance of yours into more content and figure out the best way of bringing you back for all our followers. So many brands want to partner with us already.

Kyle: This is what we've always wanted. We've never had so many followers before.

Never had so many followers before . . .?

"I can't believe this," I said, half under my breath to Harun. He moved closer to me and headbutted my stomach. I put my hand on his head, my mind swirling. My body felt prickly and strange and ready for fight or flight. I was shaking.

This was all too much. This was all too overwhelming. And Kyle . . . *Had he always been like this?* Talked like this? Had every single real-life event been turned into an opportunity to grow followers and create content? Did he even care about me? Had he ever cared about me? I turned to Harun.

"We have to go!" I said hurriedly. My phone was still buzzing in my palm and I scrambled to turn it off.

"Get in the car." I turned to Harun and pointed. He listened to me. I grabbed my phone and threw it onto the passenger seat and then closed Harun's door. I jumped in, wheel-spun the car around and pointed it back towards the town. Back towards the place we'd just come from. I looked into the rear-view mirror and gave Harun a little nod. He barked back at me and then I put my foot flat on the accelerator and the blue cheese sprang to life.

"Yes!" I laughed as the car flew forward so fast that it felt like we were barely touching the ground. God, I was so thankful for this car right now. I glanced at my phone, the signal had died and I finally felt like I could breathe again.

CHAPTER 44

*I*t was all so clear. Crystal clear. I had never felt so certain about anything before, even though I was currently experiencing the most uncertain time in my life. A time of tumultuousness and strange changes, but still, amongst all that noise, there seemed to be this silent sense of eerie calm that told me, unequivocally, that I was doing the right thing. I parked my car outside Samirah's and knocked on the door frantically. I wanted to get this out as fast as I could, in case a part of me took it back. She opened the door and the verbal dam broke through the wall.

"I'm back!" I started. "I drove out of town, and then my phone started buzzing and beeping and didn't stop and I felt like I couldn't breathe. Not metaphorically, but literally like my throat was about to close. It was just too much. It was so loud and bright and Harun was barking and I was panicking. And so, I'm back. Standing here on your doorstep." I took a breath. Samirah watched me in a way that told me she was waiting for me to get to the point. I cut right to the chase. "The assistant job? I want it. I don't know anything about being a vet's assistant though and, until now, haven't owned a pet, and I didn't even like Harun at first, but now I like him, and I think I can like other dogs too and I can learn. You can teach me, I'll do whatever . . . uh, except I'm not good with poop, but I'll do all the other stuff. And I'm going to find myself a little place here and stay a while. I don't know how long, I can't promise forever or anything, but for now I'm here." She smiled and I pointed a finger at her. "And *no*, it's not because of all those things you said to me. I'm not suddenly having some great spiritual awakening and realizing that I belong here. I'm just here. For now. And I'm on your doorstep. Looking for a job."

She tilted her head to the side like Harun might do. It was a curious look. She was trying to make sure I was being genuine and this wasn't some wild flash in the pan. Some spontaneous idea I was having that I would retract in a few minutes. And I didn't blame her, because to the untrained eye, this might have seemed like utter madness, but it was actually the only thing that made any sense to me right now.

Samirah kept looking at me silently for a while, but soon a small smile appeared on her mouth. Subtle. Just making the corners twitch. And then she started nodding.

"Okay," she said. "You can work for me."

"Oh my God, great. Great." I threw my arms around her and tried to hug her but pulled away quickly when I felt something.

We both looked down at the same time.

"Did your belly just kick me?" I asked.

"I think so."

Samirah grabbed her ribs and tensed her face up. "She's really going for it now. She must be excited."

"Me too," I gushed.

And then Samirah let go of her ribs and looked at me seriously. "It's not glamorous work."

I nodded. "That's fine."

"The hours can be long and unpredictable, and if there's an emergency in the middle of the night, you have to be here."

I continued to nod. "I can do that."

"And sometimes it's sad work too. Sometimes the animal doesn't make it, and sometimes you have to put them down."

I nodded. The nod was becoming a little smaller though. "I understand," I said, quieter this time.

"It can be smelly and messy too," she added.

"Mmmm." My enthusiasm was waning a bit, but suddenly I felt a big, wiry head at my side, pushing against my hand. Almost as if to encourage me.

"Okay, so that won't be fun. But I think I can manage," I said.

"The pay is not great either," she added. "You're not going to get rich doing this."

"It's okay. I just need enough to cover my rent and some groceries."

"Where are you planning on living?" she asked.

I shrugged. "Don't know." And then I giggled nervously. "Oh my God, is this insane?" I asked her, but didn't wait for a response. "It is! I know, but it also just feels . . ." I lost the words.

"Right?" she asked.

I nodded. "I can't explain it. But it does."

Samirah's smile grew and then she clapped her hands together excitedly. "This is great! I'm excited. And I think I might know a place for you to live."

"Really?" I asked.

"There're not a lot of places to rent here in town, but lucky for you I happen to know one."

"Really?" I couldn't believe my luck. This was all coming together so nicely.

"Come, let's go."

CHAPTER 45

Samirah and I pulled up to a small Karoo house. Another brightly painted one with a wraparound veranda built straight onto the small street. This place was so idyllic and quaint, the houses here were almost uniform, giving an impression of chocolate-boxy perfection. We climbed out, walked to the door and Samirah gave it a knock. I had Harun on the leash and as the door was being opened by an elderly woman, I shot him a quick look.

"Don't ruin this. Be on your best behavior."

"He'll be fine," Samirah whispered down to me.

Famous last words.

The cottage in question belonged to Mrs. Myra Marais, longtime resident of Springdorp. In fact, her family had settled in this part of the Karoo over a hundred years ago. She'd been born and bred here in this little corner of the world, and she had a small cottage at the back of her property that she was renting out for a very reasonable rate. She wasn't trying to make money, she said. She just wanted someone on the property so she didn't feel so alone, since her husband passed. My heart went out to her. And when she took me to the cottage, I hadn't expected it to be the way it was.

"This is gorgeous," I said, standing in the open-plan room looking out at the view. The cottage faced the desert. That feeling of endless expanse, sprawling out in front of you.

"Imagine the sunsets here," Samirah whispered to me.

"I can imagine," I said a little breathily. I remembered what Logan had said to me, about the desert seeping into you. A sudden noise made me look round. Two lazy-looking chickens walked onto the veranda clucking away to each other as if deep in conversation. As if discussing politics, or their husbands not ever looking after the chicks. I looked down at Harun to see if he'd noticed them, and he had. He was lazily watching them with his one eye as if they were just part of the scenery. Nothing to get worked up about, much like he hadn't gotten worked up at Mark's house about them. *Mark* . . .

"That's Bessy and Dotty. You must ignore them. Sometimes they come inside, but only because they like to be around people," Mrs. Marais said.

"That's okay, I don't mind," I replied. I was a vet's assistant now, after all. I was a lover of all creatures great and small. Furry and feathered.

"They give me two eggs a day for my breakfast every single day. Never let me down. Ever. Even when Dotty hurt her foot. You remember that?" She turned to Samirah.

"I do. She's a trooper," Samirah agreed.

"That she is," Mrs. Marais whispered. "That she is." As she said this, the two chickens wandered into the cottage, stepping inside as if they owned the place, and had done it a hundred times before. They were scouring the floor for morsels, pecking and clucking away happily.

I turned and smiled at the old woman. "It's kind of like Mark's house in a way. Right down to the chickens," I heard myself say, even though I hadn't actually planned on saying that. Shit, and now I was thinking about Mark again and what had happened between us the night before.

Samirah looked at me sideways, just a little, just enough to make me think that something was going on in that head of hers.

"Doesn't Mark have a cottage out back?" she asked. "I remember someone rented there once."

I shrugged. "I think he uses it as a storeroom now," I offered.

"Isn't Mark the nice lad down by the place you can rent those VCRs?" Mrs. Marais asked, showing her age.

I smiled at her again. "Yes, he is." Although "nice" was a questionable adjective to describe him. Moody, maybe. Unpredictable. A douchebag that kisses a girl like *that* and then storms away without an explanation.

"Such a pity," Samirah said.

"What is?" I turned to her.

"Such a pity you can't rent his place. No offence, Myra." She said that part with a strange tone again.

"Well, it's not like I would *want* to stay there anyway," I said a little too snappily, which caused Samirah and Myra to look at me in surprise. I shook my head at them both and then walked into the middle of the room. "But here, this place is perfect. This is where I want to stay." But as I said that, hell and pandemonium broke out.

CHAPTER 46

⌐

"*HARUN!*" I screamed as he rushed straight for the chickens, the leash pulling from my hand. They screeched and flapped and hopped around frantically as he raced after them.

"Dotty! Bessy!" Mrs. Marais gasped loudly, rushing forward with her walker and almost losing her balance as both the chickens jumped up onto the dining-room table, Harun hot on their heels.

Samirah jumped. "Sit, Myra. Sit." She pulled her down to the sofa and tried to calm her, but she was inconsolable.

"My chickens!" she wailed, sounding so pained, as if she were talking about her own children. It broke my bloody heart.

I watched in horror as Harun also jumped onto the table, skidding across it, sending things flying in all directions. The chickens jumped off the table and raced over to the other sofa. But they were no match for Harun, who jumped so hard onto the sofa, the thing toppled over. The chickens skidded out from under it, flapping and jumping and screaming their way free. I joined the chase. The cottage was so small and tightly packed, I was forced to push chairs away as I went. I tripped over the carpet and went flying, I could hear Mrs. Marais crying and whimpering as the whirlwind of destruction swept through her place.

"Dotty! Bessy!" She was frantic and Samirah kept urging her to calm down, "for her heart." *Shit!* This needed to stop, I couldn't give a poor old woman a heart attack. That would be terrible.

"HARUN!" I screamed again as he raced after the frantic flap of feathers. Finally, I caught up to him. I grabbed his leash and held it so tightly that my knuckles went white from the effort. I'd expected him to tear off again, continue the chase. But he didn't. As I grabbed the leash, he stopped. He simply sat down, and the chickens rushed out of the cottage and raced into the garden as fast as they could.

I looked at Samirah and Mrs. Marais. They were both sitting on the sofa. Samirah had her arm around the almost hysterical-looking old lady.

"I am so sorry," I said in a high-pitched tone. "He's not like that with chickens. I don't know what got into him. He's usually very—"

"Get out!" Mrs. Marais raised herself onto her feet. She was spluttering and coughing and pointing a wrinkled, bony finger at me now.

"Get out!" she repeated, low and shaky.

"B-But, the cottage?" I asked, and then looked at her with the best pleading eyes I could manage. But I realized instantly that my best pleading eyes were just never going to be good enough in this situation. I sighed and lowered my head, avoiding all eye contact now.

Samirah walked up to me and placed a hand on my back. "Maybe it's best if we leave. I'll call someone to help her clean up."

I nodded. "I'm so sorry," I said, exiting sheepishly, with Samirah close behind me. When we were back on the street, I turned to Harun.

"What the hell?" I threw my hands in the air, frustrated and angry, while Harun just sat there looking at up at me casually, as if he hadn't just totally destroyed someone's whole cottage and given them a bloody heart attack.

Samirah bent down to look at Harun's stitches. "He really shouldn't be running around like that," she said.

"Do you hear that?" I scolded Harun. "You know, that was the only cottage for rent in the entire town. And you just got us banned from it. You see how nice it will be when you and I are sleeping in the car tonight."

"Uh . . ." Samirah cleared her throat. "Technically, it's not the only cottage for rent."

I looked up at her and it took me a while to get what she was saying.

"What? Mark? Noooooo."

At that, Harun let out two big barks and started wagging his tail. Samirah burst out laughing. She reached down and patted him on the head. "Looks like someone had a plan all along," she said and then walked back to her car.

I looked down at Harun. Surely it wasn't possible? Was it? That he'd done this deliberately to get me to stay at Mark's? Dogs were just not that clever and couldn't think like that. Or could they? And then he tilted his head up to me and, I swear to God, he gave something that resembled a smug, self-satisfied smile before flicking his head like a diva might do and walking away.

"Satan's bloody Little Helper indeed," I shouted after him, but he ignored me.

"You can crash on my sofa tonight, if you want," Samirah said over her shoulder. "We can continue the search for a place tomorrow, I'll make a few calls." I climbed into the car and we drove off together.

"Do you mind if we make a small detour on the way back?" Samirah asked.

"Sure," I said, happy to be back in the cool air-conditioned car anyway and away from that poor woman. We drove for a few minutes until we came to an empty piece of land surrounded by a small fence.

FOR SALE.

"What's this?" I asked.

"This is the dream," she said in a soft, faraway voice.

"What dream?" I asked.

"The dream of starting an animal sanctuary for all the strays we get, and the wildlife that comes in injured that I have nowhere to put so I just land up . . ." She tailed off. "I didn't become a vet to have to put animals down," she said in a whisper. "There are not that many people living in town who can adopt. The nearest SPCA is miles away and it services such a large area it's often full . . ." Her voice had gotten a little shaky now. I turned and looked at her as she continued.

"Think about Harun—what would I have done with him if you hadn't looked after him?"

"You would have had to put him down?" I asked quietly, and then looked over at Harun in the back. My heart tugged in my chest.

"I need exactly R280,000 more to buy this place and then set it up with kennels and enclosures. And I just don't have that money. I've been saving for a while, but some people around here pay me in boxes of homemade biscuits."

We both stared at the land for a while. It was lovely. Open and vast and, unlike most land here, it had a massive tree in the middle of it. We didn't say a word to each other for a while as we looked at it together. I felt like I was sharing a moment with Samirah, and it made me feel closer to her. And then I felt like I needed to do something. I slipped my hand over her shoulder and gave it a gentle squeeze. She immediately turned and smiled at me.

"Thanks," she said.

I was about to ask for what, when she pulled off and drove away.

CHAPTER 47

*T*he sofa at Samirah's wasn't the most comfortable. It was old and small. But this was the only place I could go, and I was grateful for that. I lay there looking up at the ceiling. Harun was sitting on the floor watching me. He didn't seem to be settling down for the night. He seemed restless, with his eye glued to me.

"What?" I leaned forward and glared at him. "Why does it always look like you're concocting some devious plan in that brain of yours?" We had a little stare-off, but I gave up when I realized that he wasn't going to be answering me. I flopped back down and went straight back to the ceiling.

Boredom and agitation wracked my body, and I felt that same sense of total loneliness that I'd experienced when I'd first arrived. Perhaps it hadn't really gone away. Perhaps it had been here the entire time, sometimes closer to the surface, sometimes further. Right now, it was close. Very.

For some reason, crashing on someone's sofa made me feel alone and unwanted in a different kind of way. And, on top of that, God, it was so hot tonight. I got up, walked over to the big window and opened it. The curtain flapped about in the breeze, and I pinned it back then looked out over the street. It was dark and quiet. It was still strange to be in a place so quiet. But the breeze from the open window was welcoming. I walked back to the sofa and reached into my bag for my phone. Despite being so terrified of it a few hours ago, my hand now seemed to be aching for it. Perhaps I was just aching for something familiar to take the edge off.

I lifted it to my eyes and ran my thumb across the screen, something in me loosening a little. The light washed over me and I took a deep breath, as if trying to inhale its photons. I turned the phone around in my hands and looked at it. This thing contained my entire life. Every video I'd made, social post, Tweet, contact, message, everything that had happened to me in the last several years was contained in this small thing that fitted into my hand. It was like a box of memories and even if it didn't work, it still felt like one of my most prized possessions. The thing I would save in a fire.

Harun walked over to me and rested his big head on my stomach. The action totally melted my heart. It was as if he knew there was a knot of anxiety inside me and I needed help. I reached down and patted him on the head; he looked up at me with his ugly yellow eye. I sighed.

"You are the reason we're sleeping here, you know that?" I scratched his head, which made his back leg shake and the ornaments on top of the shelves rattle. He moved his head onto my lap even more, as if demanding more tickles. I obliged, but every time I stopped, he pushed my hand with his nose, as if he wanted me to use both hands. I put my phone down on the table next to me and scratched his head with both hands. But as I did, Harun made a sudden jerky move. I looked at him and gasped. He had pulled away and now had my phone in his mouth.

"What are you doing?" I jumped to my feet as Harun started reversing. One paw at a time.

"Drop it!" I commanded. But he didn't budge. I shook my head. "Please don't swallow it. That thing will definitely get stuck and there is no way it's coming out the other side!" He glanced behind him, and I followed his gaze. Shit! He was looking at the open window. Why the hell was he looking at the open windooooo . . .

"Noooooooo!" I wailed as he took one massive step and simply walked out the bloody window. As if he was on stilts. I rushed over and looked out. He was standing in the middle of the road now. Looking at me. Challenging me!

"Stay there!" I yelled. But Harun didn't stay. He started trotting down the road like a Lipizzaner horse. I ran for the front door just as a sleepy-looking Samirah emerged from her bedroom.

"What's wrong?" she asked.

"He's got my phone in his mouth!" I explained. "He climbed out the window and is now trotting down the flipping road."

"Better go and get him," she yawned and then started walking back to bed. "He shouldn't be moving around so much."

"I will!" I half-shouted as I rushed out the door and onto the empty road. Harun was sitting in the middle, about twenty meters from the house. The phone was glowing and the name Satan's Little Helper could not have been more apt in this moment. He really did look like some demon dog from hell with his glowing toothy mouth, and that one yellow eye that shone paranormally in the light of the phone.

"Harun." I walked towards him and held my hand out. "Give it back." But the more I moved closer to him, the more he moved away. As soon as I got close, he would simply rise up and trot to another spot, sit back down and glare at me over his luminous mouth. This went on five times before I realized that I was not going to get the phone from him this way. I threw my hands in the air, tired and frustrated and fed up with this strange game.

"Whhhhyyyy?" I wailed loudly. "Why are you torturing me?" He stood up and trotted off again. I watched and waited for him to repeat the same pattern of stopping after a few meters and then sitting back down, but this time, he didn't. He just kept on trotting.

"Harun! Wait!" I started jogging after him as he began to disappear over the curve of the road.

"You're not supposed to be moving around so much!" I shouted after him, concerned now for his health and the stitches. I tried to pick up pace, but I was too slow for his massive legs. He got further and further away, the light from the phone getting lost in the dark.

"Shit!" I gave up my foot chase and ran back to the house. I grabbed my car keys, fired up the blue cheese, and caught up with him.

"Please give it to me." I held my hand out the window, matching his speed. He ignored me and carried on walking. At some point he would stop walking, he couldn't walk forever, so I sat back in the car and made myself comfortable.

"I can do this all night, boy!" I said casually. But after another five minutes of walking, I started bringing out the big guns. Promises of Wagyu beef strips smeared in duck liver pâté. Pleas involving barbecue brisket . . . funny how he seemed to understand everything I said to him, except this. After another few minutes I looked around and took in my surroundings. I knew where I was! The road curved around a familiar bend, then a familiar old rusty windmill and then . . . Shit.

I knew where we were going. And this was the last place in the world I wanted to be.

CHAPTER 48

I stopped my car and watched as Harun trotted all the way up to Mark's porch. And then he dropped the phone to the floor, and simply lay down next to it.

"You have got to be kidding," I hissed. I looked around to see if there were any signs of life, but all was quiet and dark at the house and surrounds. I knew Mark slept on the veranda sometimes, but from here I couldn't see if he was there or not.

Probably not, I reasoned. I'm sure the loud, ridiculous rumble of my car would have woken him up. God knows this car was enough to wake entire villages on the other side of the world. Unless Mark was a seriously deep sleeper. I hoped not, because the last thing I wanted to do right now was find him on that porch.

What would he think of me? That I was some kind of creepy stalker. Like that guy from the Netflix show, *YOU*, narrating his inner monologue in that scary, monotone voice while he watched her naked through her window. I shuddered just thinking about it, and we all know how that show ended . . .

Harun stretched his paws out, then rolled onto his bloody back and closed his eyes to go to sleep, like this was a day spa and he was about to have a massage. The sheer cheek of it all!

"Un. Be. Lie. Va. Ble!" I crept up to the patio, walking as quietly as I could, but when my foot hit some gravel and it made a soft noise, Harun opened his eye and looked at me again. He wasn't sleeping. In fact, far from it. I could see by looking into that sly, yellow eye that he was up to something. I could almost hear it ticking away in that doggy brain of his—a brain that I'd clearly underestimated. Well, I wasn't going to make that mistake again. I waggled my finger at him and then mouthed the words, "Don't you dare!" I crept up the wooden stairs that led to the veranda and then, much like I'd done when I'd seen the snake, I froze.

Oh. My. God.

I shook my head; my eyes were as wide as saucers. I was completely unable to close them, even though this would have been a very appropriate time to do so. I put my hands over my mouth to stop noises coming from it. Again, I should have put them over my eyes, but didn't. Why wasn't I covering my eyes? If my eyes were covered then I wouldn't be seeing . . . *that!*

It's just a naked butt, I told myself, in a very cool and calm way. It's just a naked man's butt. Not like I've never seen one before. Not like I'd never touched one before. But no amount of cool and calm talking to myself was working. Because it wasn't just anyone's naked butt, it was Mark's naked one. It was attached to the man who had kissed me like *that* . . .

My knees felt weak just thinking about it. But then they turned to cement when I thought about what had happened next. *Close your eyes*, I told myself again. But just, simply, couldn't.

I was staring at it now. And it seemed to stare back at me, if that's possible to imagine. It was staring at me and mocking me.

You're getting none of this, it seemed to taunt.

A citronella candle was burning next to him. I could smell it, and the flame was dancing in the breeze, causing a little flicker of light to fall across it, making the whole thing so much more obvious.

I looked over at Harun again, very unimpressed by his actions. Very unimpressed that he'd brought me here to Mark and his sleeping behind. I mentally calculated the distance between me and the phone and realized that a few more steps would do it. I held my breath and took another small step. And another one, and another.

It dawned on me, though, that if I carried on standing, it would be easier to see me. So, carefully and quietly, I crouched on my hands and knees and started shuffling across the floor towards my phone.

"Hey, Harun. You cute little precious doggy," I whispered with a forced smile. He rolled over again and cocked his head to the side, as if he was objecting to what I'd just said. "You're right," I whispered. "You are not cute and little, what was I thinking . . .! Give me back my phone!" I reached out. My fingertips were so close now, I could feel the phone within my reach and I was going to get it and . . .

"NO!" I hissed, as Harun grabbed the phone once more and stood up. "Where are you goi— No . . . no . . ." I watched in horror. Absolute, shocking horror as he walked all the way up to Mark and then carefully, gently, placed the phone right on his . . .

I inhaled sharply and froze like a damn statue. I waited for Mark to wake up, only he didn't. How could he not have woken up? He now had a cell phone perched perfectly on one of his round and pert and, *oh soooo round* . . . I was almost breathless looking at it now. The phone was wobbling slightly on it, and the movement mesmerized me, especially because it was glowing and the light was casting all kinds of interesting dark and light shapes across the smooth and soft-looking planes of his ass.

Oh God!

I shielded my eyes! This time my hands did do the appropriate thing as he shifted his position, bending one of his legs in a way that made me see, *Oh God*, his balls! There they bloody were, squished and funny-looking under the weight of his body, just peeping out a little bit from between his legs, like a rabbit peeping out from inside its burrow. Surprisingly, the phone hadn't fallen off him. In fact, the whole thing was now in an even worse position: it had kind of slipped into the middle, and was balancing in between the two mounds, if you get my drift here. I hoped he didn't clench or something terrible like that.

I hung my head, torn between desperately wanting to look (for reasons I'm not proud of), but knowing that looking was so, terribly, terribly inappropriate. The kind of inappropriate that you could never tell a soul about, not even your best friend—"the other night I watched a guy sleeping naked" just sounded so wrong. I waited like that for a few more moments, head still lowered, and tried to decide what to do. I really did need my phone, and if I didn't take it, Mark would have some serious questions when he woke up in the morning, like: how did a phone get lodged between my ass cheeks in the middle of the night? Not an easy question to answer, really. I looked at Harun.

"I'm gonna kill you for this," I mouthed.

I weighed up my options; as far as I could tell, I really only had one. I needed to retrieve the phone and then get Harun and me out of there before Mark saw us. So, still on my hands and knees, I crept towards the sleeping Mark. I crept slowly, shuffling as silently as I could across the boards, my knees starting to feel the burn of it. I was not designed for sneaking and creeping like this and trust me, I felt utterly absurd doing it.

I reached the daybed and stopped. I was trying to breathe as softly as possible but my nerves were making that quite difficult. The phone (and his ass) was so close now, and I started reaching out for them . . . I mean IT! I was reaching for it. My phone. Nothing else.

My hand moved in slow motion through the air, getting closer and closer to him. I was trying to move as slowly as possible, and despite the fact that I have good upper body strength, the muscles in my arm were quivering. I bit my lip in concentration as my fingers finally connected with the oh-so familiar curves of my metal phone. I paused and took a moment before pulling it, but then—

"WOOF!" The ear-shattering sound of a deep, bellowing bark made me scream, flap, drop the phone, fall backwards and—

"OUUCHHH!" I wailed in pain as my face connected with Mark's as he woke up with a big jolt and jumped. We both scrambled to our feet and, *Oh shit!*

My eyes drifted down. I wondered if he realized that he was completely naked. Probably not, because if he had realized, he would have at least cupped his junk, so to speak. But he hadn't.

I willed my eyes to look away; they had been lurking down there for far too long. I moved them up his torso, surprisingly muscular. Small muscles. Cut and defined ones. Not big gym ones. And then I looked at his face and gasped.

CHAPTER 49

"*B*lood!" I said, pointing at Mark's face.

"What?" he asked, his hooded, sleepy eyes going big and wide and bright. Clearly, he still hadn't realized he was naked. How do you not notice that?

"Your nose is bleeding," I said, indicating it.

He touched his nose and pulled his fingers away. The tips were stained red and when he looked at them, the color drained from his face. He went as white as a cotton sheet.

"Oh crap . . ." He stared at his fingers.

"What?" I asked. Sweat beads were forming on his forehead and his lips had gone a ghostly white.

"I kind of don't like blood," he said, in a voice that was weak and shaky. "It always makes me want to fainnnnnnnnnn . . ."

"Oh my God!" I jumped up as Mark wobbled on his legs. Moving his weight from one foot to the other. His arms were reaching out for something to grab onto as he started to topple over.

"GOT YOU!" I yelled, rushing up to him, grabbing him around the waist. But he was heavy, and his body was sinking and . . ." Okaaaay, maybe I don't quite have you," I said, heaving and breathing loudly as I tried to hold him up. But his weight was pulling me down and I couldn't fight it. My legs were doing the splits dangerously as we both sort of slithered down to the floor slowly.

"Oh crap!" We were both on the floor now. Mark on top of me, me with my legs wide open, him in between. So inappropriate! #AwksAF

Why was I making hashtags in my head? #wtf

"Um . . ." I mumbled, against his chest. "You okay?"

I felt him take a big breath, and then heard him clear his throat as he peeled himself off me and into a sitting position. I quickly closed my very open legs.

"Fine. Sorry. Fine," Mark said, looking embarrassed. His once white cheeks were now flushed a bright shade of red, and he still had a little bit of blood trickling from his nose. I still couldn't tell if he hadn't realized he was naked, or if he just didn't care. But he was making no effort to cover the thing. I tried not to look. But it was hard. Wait . . . it wasn't *hard*. He wasn't hard, well, I hoped not. What I mean is, it was hard not to look. Not . . . *Oh crap*, why couldn't I stop saying the word "hard" in my head?

And that's when it looked like he finally, *finally* got it. Because there was such a fast scurry happening now, I could see it out of the corner of my eye. There was jumping, and cushions went flying and a blanket flapped in the air before he wrapped it around himself. Once the activity was all over, a deathly silence settled between us. It went on for ages, until he finally broke it.

"What the hell are you doing here?" he asked, sounding angry and accusatory.

"Mmmm," I mumbled, "that's kind of complicated."

I finally turned and looked at him. He was looking at his watch. "Two a.m. complicated?" He raised his eyebrows at me and I didn't know what to say. I opted for the truth.

"Harun stole my phone and then he ran all the way here. Which he shouldn't have done, because of the surgery. I had to follow him in my car and that's why I'm here. To get my phone . . ." I bent down and picked it up and then slipped it into the pocket in my gown. More silence between us. I hoped this explanation was vaguely believable, because when I heard it coming out of my mouth I barely believed it myself. It was right up there with "Sorry, ma'am, an alien stole my assignment."

We both looked over at Harun at the same time and I wished I knew what Mark was thinking. Whether he believed my story, or thought I was a complete creep. And then his eyes moved back to me and I stood up straight and uncomfortable as he flicked them up and down my body.

What was he looking at?

"Oh," I said flatly when I looked down. I was in my nightie and a thin satin gown. "I was in a hurry," I added defensively, just in case he thought I'd come here to seduce him. Not that I was wearing red lace or anything, but still.

"You sleep naked!" I snapped, trying to move the focus away from what I was wearing to what he was *not* wearing.

"It's not like I was expecting company!" he retorted.

"Still, you shouldn't sleep like that," I said. "Not here."

"It's my home. I can sleep naked if I want."

I gestured around us. "In case you hadn't noticed, your house is in the middle of the desert. Dangerous. No fences. Snakes, possibly jackals. And I would imagine that if you had to run away from a hungry predator, that thing," I pointed a little south of his belly button, "flapping about and all, it might attract . . . you know. They might think it was an animal running, a mouse or something—"

"MOUSE?!" He choked on the word and I realized my faux pas.

"You know what I mean."

He cleared his throat. "I hope I do, or else I would be very offended. Not to mention mortified."

"It's not a mouse," I mumbled, glancing at the sheet around him. "A meerkat, or a squirrel maybe, or a—"

"Just stop." He held his one hand up.

"Thanks." I breathed a sigh of relief, because I was running out of ideas here for tasty rodent treats that a predator might eat and clearly I was rambling too. He reached up and touched his nose again. It was still bleeding a little.

"You should probably . . ." I tailed off and pointed to his nose.

"Yes." He grabbed the top of it, squeezed, and then walked into the house and straight to the kitchen. He grabbed a tea towel, put some ice in it and held it on the bridge of his nose.

"You probably think I'm a bit of a baby for fainting," Mark said.

I shook my head. "No worries. Lots of people hate blood. I tried to give blood once at a blood drive and couldn't watch. I had to close my eyes." I offered this up to him, hoping it would make him feel a little better. He forced a small smile as if he appreciated the gesture.

"When I was young," Mark said, "I was trying to show off to these older kids in the neighborhood. I climbed up on my roof because they dared me to, and then because we watched *Jackass* so much, one of them suggested that I jump off the roof onto the trampoline . . ."

"Ooooh," I cringed, imagining what was next.

"Yeah." He nodded.

"And did you?"

"I did. And I totally missed the trampoline. Instead, I landed on the fence pole."

"Shit!"

"It was a small, thin pole and it pierced all the way through my upper arm." He pointed at a scar.

I winced at the sight of it. "What happened then?"

"It was terrible. I remember everything about it, especially the pain. And when I looked down and realized that it was all the way through my arm, I fainted."

"That must have been awful," I said, looking back at him.

"The other kids thought it was hysterical though. Thankfully one of them had the sense to call an ambulance."

"Kids can be jerks," I said, knowing this to be a fact.

"When I came round after fainting, I started to panic. I couldn't breathe, I thought I was having a heart attack. So they pulled me off the pole."

My eyes widened as I listened to the story.

"Turns out the pole was plugging a vein closed and when they pulled me off . . . there was just so much blood. I'd never seen so much blood in my life. It gushed out of me like a fountain. It covered me and poured onto the ground causing this literal pool at my feet. All I remember was all the redness before fainting again. I woke up the next day in the hospital. The doctors said I almost bled to death. I was lucky to make it."

"That's hectic," I said.

"I had nightmares about blood for years after that."

I smiled at him. "You have a really good excuse for hating blood then."

He forced a small smile at me too and then another pause. A loaded one. One that made me nervous.

"I'm glad you're here actually," he said quietly.

"Really?"

"I wanted to talk to you. I didn't like what happened between us last night and I wanted to explain. But when I woke up this morning, you were gone. I was worried that you might have left town."

"I did," I said. "And then I didn't."

He looked at me curiously.

"I have a job here now and looks like I'll be staying for a while."

"A job? Where?"

"With Samirah. I'm going to be a vet's assistant."

"That's cool," he said. "It'll suit you working with animals, since you're so good with Harun."

I tsked at that. "I would hardly call myself some animal whisperer. I didn't even like animals before Harun."

Mark grinned. "He's hard not to like."

"I know. No matter how hard you try," I said, and Mark gave a small chuckle.

"Where will you be staying?" he asked.

"Don't know. Haven't found a place yet," I said, and unintentionally glanced out the kitchen window at the small cottage out back. I could see Mark was also looking at it now, and I didn't want him to think I was hinting. *Was I?*

I turned back to him and smiled. "Samirah said I could sleep on her sofa for a while. Just while I find a place."

Mark nodded. "There're not many places to rent in town. When I first came here I really struggled to find a place."

"I guess this place doesn't get many renters."

Mark and I locked eyes and he looked like he wanted to say something, so I folded my arms and waited.

"Last night . . ." he started awkwardly.

"Yes?"

"Thing is, I hadn't expected that to happen between us," he said and then stopped. I leaned in and waited for more, but it didn't come.

"And?" I pressed.

He shook his head. "Nothing. I wasn't expecting that last night, and it just caught me off guard and I'm sorry if I made you feel . . ."

"Unattractive," I offered.

"Unattractive? What the hell are you talking about?" He looked shocked.

"I mean, I kissed you and then you stopped and walked away, so I just assumed that you thought I was—"

"NO! No," he cut me off. "I didn't think you were . . . Jesus, why would you think that? I mean, look at you. You're not . . . at all."

"Oh." I blinked.

"Me walking away had nothing to do with you, it was all me," he said quickly. "And besides, I kissed you back, if you remember?"

"So it's not me, it's you?" I asked sarcastically, not sure I believed him.

"Totally." He nodded. "I really don't think you're . . . I can't even say that word. It's terrible."

We stared at each other and my stomach tightened. I felt so vulnerable in that moment and I hated it.

"I'm sorry," he said softly. "For how I made you feel and for what happened and—"

I held my hand up to stop him. The more he talked, the worse I felt. "It's fine," I said quickly.

"Is it?" he pressed.

I took a moment to think about it, and then nodded. "It's fine. I'm an adult. You're an adult. Some shit happened, and then it didn't and now we're talking in your kitchen in the middle of the night and you are half naked."

Mark smiled at this, a smile so big and dazzling that I felt like I needed to look away, but couldn't.

"So . . . Friends?" he asked.

I forced a nod, because suddenly friends sounded like a bad word. "Sure." I looked into the dark. I felt I had to, or else I would give away my feelings, even though I wasn't totally sure what they were. I hadn't meant to do it again, but my eyes rested on his cottage once more. I stared at it while I tried to sort through the myriad of thoughts and feelings rushing through my mind. I heard Mark sigh and then footsteps coming towards me.

"I guess I could clean it out, if you want to stay there? But it's nothing fancy. It doesn't even have warm water. If you wanted to take a bath, you'll have to come inside."

"What? No. I wasn't hinting."

"You were looking at it though," he said.

"I was, but I wasn't trying to make you offer it to me."

Mark smiled. "I'm offering it to you anyway."

"Really?" I perked up.

"But you have to give me a day or so to clean it out. Can you stay at Samirah's for another night?"

"I'm sure I can. What's in the place, I can help you clear it out?" I offered.

"Nothing. Just old crap. Most of it needs to be thrown away."

"Cool, I can do that."

He shook his head. "I better do it."

"Shame, I wouldn't want to put you out. You're doing me a favor, so how 'bout I do you one?"

"Um . . ." It looked like he was considering this for a moment. What was there to think about though? Someone was offering to clean up. I would have jumped at that. I watched and waited for him to say something, he really did look deep in thought. This didn't seem like a super difficult question, though. Well, it shouldn't have been.

"Nah," he finally said. "I'll do it. Could be snakes in there."

"OH!" I went wide-eyed thinking about the last encounter I'd had with a snake. "Well, thanks. I really appreciate it. Otherwise Harun and I would be bunking in the car . . . Wait, it is okay to bring Harun?" I asked.

"Sure," he said.

"Thanks." I smiled, feeling very appreciative of his offer. "Has it stopped bleeding?" I asked, looking at his nose.

"I'm too scared to check," he said faintly.

I walked over to him and without asking, removed the paper toweling from his nose. No new blood had formed, and all the blood there had already dried up.

"Looks like it's stopped." I reached for a small cloth and ran some water over it, and then, very gently, lifted it up to his nose and wiped away the dry blood. "There," I said when I was done. "As if it never happened." I looked away from his nose and then up to his eyes. It was only then that I realized how close I was to him. There was a certain familiarity to the closeness, a certain feeling of comfortableness that existed there, because of what had happened between us last night. When you've already kissed someone, it's so much easier to just kiss them again. Our eyes locked and then . . .

CHAPTER 50

"*I*...I...better go," I blurted, as memories from last night flooded back again. Physical memories this time, though; like how my skin had felt hot when he'd touched it and how his lips and tongue had tasted. Memories that I didn't want flooding me right now, not since the "f" word had been dropped. Friends aren't meant to think about kissing.

He nodded uncomfortably and backed away. "Sure. Of course."

"Sorry about this whole thing, I don't usually make a habit of coming to naked men's houses in the middle of the night."

He smiled. "Yeah, that kind of thing usually lands a person in jail."

I gave a small chuckle. We were using humor to deflect now. How lame. But it was working, so what the hell. We walked to the car together, me in my satin gown and him still with a sheet wrapped around the bottom half of his body. Anyone watching us would've assumed we'd just had sex. Been at it inside. *Stop thinking about sex!* I climbed into my car and turned on the ignition.

"What the hell!" Mark said, jumping back from the vehicle.

"Yeah. That." I rolled my eyes. "It glows blue."

"I've never..." He walked around the car, taking in the endless blueness.

"It's a rental," I piped up, in case he thought this monstrosity was mine.

"It's very...blue."

"I know." I lowered my head in embarrassment.

"I mean, it is sooo blue," he continued, and he reminded me of what I'd sounded like when I'd first seen it. It was as if the awareness of the blue crept up on you. At first you were aware of its blueness. But the more you looked, the bluer it became until all you could think about was blue.

"It's weird, because of the position of the blue lights, it actually makes it look like it's hovering above the ground."

"I know," I said on a loud exhale. And then I thought about something else.

"Harun," I called out to the dog on the veranda. He appeared to have settled in quite nicely now. He opened his eye and looked at me, but didn't make a move.

"Harun," I called again. Still nothing. I made a move for the door handle and was just about to climb out when Mark stopped me.

"It's cool, he can stay here tonight. If that's okay with you?"

I considered his offer for a moment. "I mean . . . he did have a lot of physical activity coming here, which he really shouldn't have." I inspected Harun again, and I swear, his snaggletooth lip moved into something that looked like a small smile. As if this had been his bloody plan the entire time, which clearly it had. Little shit! Little black, wire-haired shit.

"It's really not a problem," Mark added. "And clearly he needs the rest." He turned and looked at him now, and the dog closed his eye. Manipulative too!

"Okay. Fine. I'll fetch him in the morning?"

"Crap, I just remembered, I have a meeting in the morning, for the town festival. It's at eight. I can take him with me and you can come collect him there, it's at the town hall."

"Oh, the festival." I nodded. This had come up a few times in the last few days.

He smiled at me. "The town hall is next to the church. On the main road."

"Aaaah," I said.

"You don't need GPS here."

"Nope."

"So come around whenever, I'll probably be there for a while. After you fetch Harun, you can come back here and hang out if you like, or whatever. I don't lock the doors, so . . ."

I smiled at him. It was such a sweet, small-town offer.

"I'll try to clean out that room tomorrow evening, so you can move in the following day. That cool?"

"Thanks again."

He shrugged. "No worries. That's what friends are for."

Dagger. Jeez, dagger in my guts. That word "friends" was giving me something that resembled painful heartburn. And then, just to add to the ailment, he turned and walked back to the house. I found myself staring after him, in a way I hadn't stared after him before. His entire back was on full display now. And it was taut, with tight muscles that rippled while he walked. Muscles contracting and expanding as his arms swung and shoulders moved. The two muscles running down his lower back that disappeared into the very thin, flimsy sheet, were the most distracting. I felt myself lean a little out the car window, closer to him, even though I was very far away. My head tilted to the side and my jaw loosened as I continued to look. A feeling of longing came over me. A longing to reach out and touch—

I snapped my head to the side when I saw the movement. I looked over at Harun. He was wide awake now and he was staring at me. And I swear to God, that bloody dog knew exactly what I was thinking. I looked away quickly, embarrassed, and then drove off. As I glanced in the rear-view mirror, Harun was still staring at me, looking pleased as bloody punch.

CHAPTER 51

*I*t was ten past eight on the dot when I arrived at the town hall. I hadn't intended to be there at that time, but I hadn't really been able to sleep when I got back from Mark's house. I'm embarrassed to admit that I was rather plagued by images of his naked body. The images seemed to have been seared into my brain somehow, as if I had taken a mental photo and posted it to my internal Insta account that only I could access #formyeyesonly.

It was difficult to get that out of my mind, to be honest, and by the time I walked over to the town hall it was all I could think about. I was also incredibly giddy from lack of sleep, so my mind was feeling a little unhinged. And it wasn't helping that everything I looked at reminded me: the painted picture of a hot dog on the wall of Jim's store, a street pole—okay, maybe not a street pole, that was my imagination really running wild there. I giggled to myself.

By the time I arrived at the town hall, I was almost in stitches; the lack of sleep was clearly getting to me. I usually had a good eight hours, tracked by my sleep app to ensure maximum REM and deep sleep. Who knew how much I was really sleeping now? But my laughter stopped abruptly when I walked into the hall.

It was packed. It seemed like the whole town was here. This made me nervous—I had never liked this kind of thing. Big, social gatherings in the past had usually ended badly for me. School dances and socials, sports days and even school assemblies. When I was a teen I'd avoided them at all costs, becoming a recluse wherever possible.

That's why I loved my online life. I could socialize without having to see people. It was so much easier to escape into that world than face the realities of this, clearly overcrowded, world.

I took a deep breath and reluctantly walked deeper into the throng. What made it worse was that everyone around me was having a loud debate about something; the noise in the hall was almost too much to bear. I couldn't make out the words that were being said, but they sounded passionate. I scanned the room, looking for Mark and Harun, or anyone familiar. I was feeling a little overwhelmed. So many people. I saw some movement and turned to find Samirah waving at me. I was so relieved I almost ran up to her.

"Hey, I didn't know you were going to be here," I said to her.

"You were fast asleep when we left, so we didn't tell you. What are you doing here?" she asked.

"I'm here to fetch Harun."

"Where is he?"

"With Mark." I scanned the room.

"What's he doing with Mark?" she asked.

"You know when he stole my phone last night and went for a walk with it?"

She nodded.

"He walked all the way to Mark's house." The chatter in the room got a little louder and I raised my voice to speak over it.

"What?" She gave a surprised smile.

"Yup, all the way there at two in the morning."

She laughed. "That dog. I think he's trying to tell you something."

"Like what?" I asked. The volume increased some more as the argument around got louder. What was so important that everyone felt like they needed to talk this loudly?

"I think you know," she said, all mysteriously again.

"What?" I asked.

"You know," she repeated.

"I don't know what you're trying to say." I raised my voice even more.

"Have you and Mark patched up your . . . disagreement?" she asked.

I shrugged. "Sort of. I guess." My cheeks flushed a little, I could feel them warm up.

Samirah smiled, long and slow and meaningful. "Is there something going on between you and Mark?"

"What! No!" I stuttered and shook my head. Fast.

"You can tell me if there is, we're friends." She was smiling too much now. As if she was taking great delight in watching me squirm.

"There is nothing . . . no . . . nothing. Besides, did you know . . ." I leaned in some more as the noise level rose again, and then rose some more. "MARK SLEEPS COMPLETELY NAKED!" I shouted over the noise but then . . .

SILENCE!

The only sound was my voice reverberating around the hall.

Naked, naked, Mark, Mark.

My face flamed a bright red and I went hot and sticky as every single person in the hall turned around and looked at me.

Naked, naked, Mark, Mark.

I know it wasn't possible, but those words seemed to be echoing around the hall. Bouncing off the walls over and over again as if they were on repeat.

Hundreds of pairs of questioning eyes were boring into me like laser beams. A few people were smiling, some looked shocked, others were murmuring to each other and then, I saw Mark. Standing there, just as red-faced as I was. Our eyes met and I gave him an apologetic shrug.

"Ooops." The word slipped out of my mouth, and everyone turned and looked at Mark. Then the crowd turned back to me. I tried to act normal and smiled. They eyed me suspiciously, and then turned back to Mark. A kind of ping-pong match took place as they glanced from Mark, to me and then back again. I noticed a few angry grimaces, mostly from the women—I even recognized some of them. Selma from the hotel, the other woman from movie night, the one who had silenced me at his gig. I couldn't bear it. Someone needed to speak. Someone needed to stop this awkward moment. Someone needed to do something to stop this, I felt like I was being crushed under the weight of all those staring eyes. Please, someone do something, say something, I mentally begged.

"I think we have our Margaret," Samirah's voice suddenly cut through the silence.

"Huh?" I looked at her and as soon as I did, her face pinched together in a frown, which led me to believe that I was going to regret whatever was coming next.

I turned and looked at the crowd once more. Their expressions had also changed. Some looked amused. Some were chuckling to themselves and others looked a little surprised.

"Hear, hear!" I heard that thick, familiar Scottish accent, and then a few more "hear, hears" rang out and the room erupted into loud, cheerful applause.

What had I just accidentally gotten myself into? And was this the moment that I finally realized I'd walked into cult town, and I had just become the human sacrifice?

CHAPTER 52

"What just happened?" I whispered in Samirah's ear. She looked at me and bit her bottom lip; was she trying to hide a smile?

"I might have just volunteered you for something," she said.

"I sort of got that. But what?"

"Uh . . . well, it's one of the characters in the reenactment."

"Nooooo." I face-palmed. The last thing I wanted to do was be a character in a cultish reenactment. Because let's face it, an entire town reenacting a historic event was either, a: the lamest thing on the planet, or b: a sign of very bad things. Like in that show *Evil Lives Here*, how they start each show by telling you about some horrific killer and then prefacing this with some ominous words. "But there had been signs . . ." Dot, dot, dot. Well, if this town was a serial killer, I would say that reenacting *anything* was a sign of something cultish and completely odd.

"What character?" I asked, eyeballing her.

She glanced over my shoulder. "You'll soon find out."

"Hello, lass!" The booming Scottish voice was behind me now. "Congratulations, you have just won the most coveted role in the reenactment. The one that every woman in this town wants."

I shook my head at him. "Who?"

"Margaret. The jackal slayer."

"The what?"

"Legend has it," Logan said, sounding very excited, "that when the Ackermans were on their long trek across the land to find this place, starving and dehydrated and barely hanging onto life, one night a jackal came and took one of their baby lambs. Margaret went out in the middle of the night and single-handedly fought the jackal off with a stick! It never came near them again."

"Wh-what?" I looked to Samirah. "That's ridiculous. How the hell could she fight off a jackal?"

"She was a brave, strong woman."

"And she was pregnant at the time too," Samirah added.

I rolled my eyes. "You guys, no starving, pregnant woman can fight off a jackal with a branch. I think that story has been grossly exaggerated."

"Exaggerated or not, that's what we reenact every single year."

My eyes widened. "Sorry, let me get this straight—you want me to act like a pregnant woman and reenact an imaginary fight with a jackal?"

"Exactly."

I burst out laughing at the sheer ridiculousness. "You've got to be kidding. No way in hell I'm doing that. Why would you even put me up for such a thing, Samirah?" I turned and glared at her.

Logan cleared his throat and then leaned in closer to me. "I think she put you up for it because of what you said you saw."

"Huh?"

He nudged me. "Let's just say that in the reenactment, Mark plays your husband."

"What?" I threw my hands in the air. "No! I'm not doing that."

"It's the most coveted role of the year. Every woman wants it."

I started shaking my head vehemently.

"Maybe Harun can play the jackal this year." Samirah perked up, sounding genuinely excited.

"Who are you playing in this thing?" I asked.

She patted her massive belly. "No way I can walk down the whole street this year, but last year I played sheep herder four."

"No, no, no." It was all I could say. "I've never heard of anything more ridiculous in my life." I looked around again for Mark. I expected him to be protesting as much as I was. Why wasn't he also loudly objecting?

"Who runs this thing?" I asked.

Samirah pointed to a man in the corner with a clipboard.

"He used to run a theatre before he moved here," Samirah added while I looked at him.

I didn't doubt that. The bright pink bow tie and French beret kind of screamed that.

I started walking towards him.

"What you doing?" Logan called after me.

"Quitting," I said over my shoulder as I walked. "Hi," I said loudly and abruptly as I reached the man with the clipboard and bow tie.

He gave me a once-over before answering. "Hello." He extended his large hand, bedazzled with golden rings, and I was forced to shake it. "I'm Ian," he said.

"Frankie," I replied.

"I know who you are." He smiled. "Everyone knows who you are." He gave me a wink and my face went a little red. "Thank you so much for volunteering to play—"

"I didn't volunteer." I cut him off. "In fact, that's what I'm here about. I want to quit."

He shook his head. "Sorry, once it's up on the board, you can't quit."

"Board?"

He pointed behind me to the handwritten piece of paper pinned to a board.

"Well, I'm sorry, I can't do it," I reiterated.

"Sorry," he said with a little sour-lemon edge to his voice. "Once it's on the board, it's final."

I scoffed and rolled my eyes. "That's ridiculous. It's not like I signed a contract."

"Well." He walked up to me. "In a way, you did. When your name is on the board, your name is on the board."

"Well, I never actually gave permission for my name to be on the board." I hadn't meant for that to come out at the volume it had, but it had and a few heads turned.

"Permission or not, it's on the board." Ian folded his arms in something that looked like a challenge.

"We'll see about that!" Also said too loudly, and now a few more people were looking.

Ian made a fast move for the paper and I was sure he was about to pull it off and hold it over my head like written gospel, so I threw myself at the paper and got there before he did. I blocked his approaching body with my back and rubbed my finger over my name. Pen! It had been written in bloody pen.

I glanced over my shoulder. Ian stood there, hands on hips. Glaring at me. I didn't like it. And I also didn't like the fact that other people had started to gather around him too. They all looked at me. I looked back at them and something unsaid passed between us all. A challenge!

I licked my finger very slowly and pointedly. A few people recoiled, but I wasn't going to let their disgust deter me. I turned back to the piece of paper and rubbed my wet finger over my name. Still nothing. I turned and looked at everyone, but this time they all seemed to be smiling. Bastards!

I turned back and, with my nail, started ripping at the paper, trying to rub my name off by pulling at the paper itself. All that did was make a total mess, as wet fibers curled up. But my name was still there despite this. I rubbed harder, and harder and . . .

"Oh shit!" The paper fell off the board and tumbled to the floor like a leaf. I stared at it for a while. I could hear a low-toned grumble around me, and looked up. This time everyone was looking at me with blatant disapproval. Shaking their heads and tutting loudly. I looked at Ian. His hands were to his chest, fingers splayed dramatically, mouth gaping open for added effect. He was acting as if he'd just witnessed some horrible crime. And then Samirah's face caught my attention: she gave me a worried head-shake and then her eyes darted down to the paper and she blinked several times, as if trying to communicate something to me.

A movement to my side made me turn to see Mark emerging from the crowd. He had a strange look on his face and I had no idea what he was thinking. Harun followed Mark out the crowd and then walked right up. Not to me though, to the piece of paper at my feet.

He bent his head and picked it up gently between his teeth. He gave me a disapproving look with his eye and then walked over to Ian and fucking handed it to him!

"You're kidding!" I threw my hands in the air and shook my head. This dog! This dog was basically ruining my life.

Ian reached down and took the paper from him tentatively, as if he was afraid that those teeth could nip him on the hand. (I wished they would.) He shook the paper, straightened it out and brought it up to his face. He then turned it around triumphantly and held it up in the air for everyone to see.

"Name is still visible," he said, glaring at me. I shook my head at him as he shot red, hot lava at me out of his big blue eyes. I could see that this had become a matter of pride for him. He probably didn't want me in his big production, but you could see that he was going to force me to do it, hell or high water!

Our eyes locked and he smiled at me. Self-satisfied, as if he had won.

#pissed

CHAPTER 53

"*N*othing to see here, folks!" Samirah took my elbow and led me away quickly. "Frankie is more than happy to play Margaret the Jackal Slayer in this year's spring festival," she added and then nudged me in the ribs. Hard.

"Owee," I winced.

She nudged me again. "What do you say?" she said, glaring at me.

I nodded, against my will. "Sure. Sure," I told the crowd as Samirah hurried me off to the corner of the room.

"Well, that was weird," I said, when I was away from it all.

Samirah stood in front of me and shook her head, and soon Faizel was by her side. Also shaking his head.

"What?" I asked them both.

"We take this thing very seriously," Faizel said. "You can't refuse a place in this festival. It's the most important event in this town. We are very proud of this place and this is the way we show it, and now you're a part of it too."

"I'm a part of it?" I asked, taken aback.

"Well, you live here now," Samirah answered.

"I . . . I . . ." It dawned on me. Like it hadn't dawned on me before. I lived here now. I, Frankie Paulson, was a part of something. Something real. Something that wasn't on Reddit, or Facebook. The thought suddenly, inexplicably, warmed my heart a little. But still . . .

"You still shouldn't have volunteered me though without asking," I said to Samirah.

"Hey, I'm pregnant. I have these hormones and my brain has turned to mush and you know . . . I don't know what I'm saying half the time."

Faizel nodded. "I can vouch for that."

I folded my arms across my chest, as something tugged in it. "I . . . I don't like being in things like this, not since . . ." I paused and Samirah and Faizel looked at me expectantly. I lowered my voice and leaned in. "I had a bad experience in a school play once, okay! It was mortifying. Everyone laughed at me. I can happily film stuff, or do a Facebook live video or IGTV, but this is too . . . *real*." I shook my head, feeling those old, horrendous feelings that I hated to feel. Someone had pinned the word "pig" onto my back during the play and the entire audience had laughed, even the teachers and parents.

At that moment, Mark and Harun appeared. My eyes immediately narrowed at Harun who came bouncing up to me as if everything was just peachy. He rubbed his giant head against my leg and I patted him, even though I was trying to be very angry with him. But that stupid wagging tail and big, pink hanging tongue was making it hard.

"He missed you," Mark said, an air of awkwardness in his voice.

"Well, he shouldn't have run off with my phone in the middle of the night, now should he." I bent down and took his huge face between my hands and looked at him. "You bloody naughty beast!" My attempt to scold him just sounded affectionate, which he clearly thought too, because his massive tongue licked the side of my face.

"Noooo!" I pulled back from him and wiped my cheek. "Gross, don't do that." I laughed and cringed at the same time. Then I stood back up and looked at the three of them.

"Looks like I'm playing the jackal-fighting pregnant woman in your weird town reenactment," I said, avoiding eye contact with Mark.

"It's not as weird as you think it'll be," Mark said. "First year I was roped into it I thought I was participating in some cultish ritual."

"That's exactly what I think!" I said, and our eyes locked for a moment.

"But it's actually cool." He smiled. "You'll enjoy it. It's just about the weirdest thing I've ever done, but it's cool."

"It is," Faizel said. "I'm playing the evil farmer who chased them away from the land."

I raised my confused brows.

"Legend has it that before they came here, they tried to settle on another piece of land but they were chased away by a farmer who, also affected by the great drought, tried to settle there too."

"Right," I said. "You know this is starting to sound like the story-line from a soap opera?"

"Wait until you see everyone in costume," Mark said.

"Sorry . . . costume? You have to dress up?" I asked.

They all nodded.

"Weirder by the second," I mumbled.

At that, Mark's eyes lit up. "You want to see something really weird?" he asked.

"Uh . . . I don't know," I said reluctantly.

But Mark smiled and nodded. "Trust me, I think you want to hear this." And with that, he took me by the elbow and pulled me away. The feel of his fingers wrapping around my arm made me flinch a little, but not in an unpleasant way.

"Where are we going?" I asked.

He gave me a slow, conspiratorial smile. "Wait and see."

"See what?" I asked, a bit alarmed.

"Shhhhh." He put his finger over his lips and gave me a wink, before he pulled up to someone. He tapped the man on the shoulder and when he turned, I tried not to stare. He was old and weather-beaten and wearing a cap that read "The Truth is Still Out There," clearly a reference to that old nineties TV show where those two agents ran around chasing little green men with bad hair. They had the bad hair, not the green men. He was also wearing these strange glasses that were sitting askew on his nose and taking up most of his face. The glass was encased in a thin, gold rim that was buckled and bent and were something a serial predator would wear. Most strange of all, though, were the flip-up dark lenses that were attached to the top of the frame. His clothing too was very questionable. His T-shirt had a huge radioactive print on it with the words "Fight Big Pharma" on it—I wasn't sure what it all meant—and on his feet—I tried not to gasp out loud—Crocs. Yellow Crocs. Old, worn, yellow Crocs.

"Frankie, this is your almost namesake, Frank," Mark said, with a little too much glee in his voice, which made me think he was up to something.

"Hi." I extended my hand for him to shake. He looked down at it, almost disgusted, and that's when I noticed that he was wearing silver gloves on both his hands.

"I don't shake," he said, and put his hands behind his back. It was awkward.

"Tell Frankie what you saw last night, Frank," Mark said and then poked me in the back a few times. Why was he poking me?

"Right," Frank said and then dug into his old jeans pocket and pulled out a very well-thumbed notepad and pencil that had been almost sharpened to death. He flipped the page open and started reading, while Mark continued to poke me in the back.

"At approximately 2:04 this morning, I was awoken by a loud rumbling sound." He cleared his throat.

"Frank lives at the end of town, just as you drive onto the dust road to get to me," Mark leaned over and said, a little quiver of excitement in his voice.

Frank looked confused. "I didn't think mentioning my whereabouts was necessary," he said to Mark almost angrily.

Mark nodded. "Sorry. Please, carry on."

Frank cleared his throat again. "Because the noise was unfamiliar to me, I went to the window to investigate further, and that's when I saw the UHO."

"The what?" I asked.

"Unidentified hovering object." He said it like it was a fact.

Mark turned and looked at me. "You hear that, Frankie? He saw an unidentified hovering object last night at two in the morning." He was smiling from ear to ear now.

I shook my head. "Sorry, I don't follow."

"Frank, why don't you tell Frankie what color the UHO was."

"It was blue," Frank stated.

I felt an extra-large poke in my back.

"Blue!" Mark said. "Imagine that, Frankie, a blue unidentified hovering object."

I finally got it, and when I did, it was so hard not to smile.

"The unidentified object was only visible for approximately two seconds before it disappeared around the bend in the road. It was traveling at a very slow speed, which makes me think it was here on an observation mission."

"Observation mission?" I asked.

Frank stopped talking and then looked around the room, to check if anyone was watching us, I presume. He leaned in conspiratorially. He was so close now and I could smell a strange smell coming off him, which if I'm not mistaken, was weed. This sort of explained a few things, although no drugs on the planet could explain, or excuse, yellow Crocs.

"Often the extraterrestrials will send a small recon craft first, for observation. Before they come."

My eyes widened. I knew who this was now. I remember Mark telling me about him. This was microwave, conspiracy-theorist man. Mark poked me in the back again and I could see he was struggling to stifle his laughter.

"What do they come for?" I asked. "These extraterrestrials?"

"Shhhhh." Frank raised his silver-gloved hand to his mouth and looked nervous. "I've said too much. I could put you in danger if you know their agenda."

"Agenda?"

He nodded and then looked seriously nervous. "The less you know, the safer you are." He gave me a strange little wink and then started backing away from us. "Welcome to Springdorp," he said, still walking away from me.

"Thanks," I nodded at him. He looked around the room once more, and then like he had rockets in his shoes, he turned and skidded away at speed.

I turned slowly and looked at Mark with wide eyes. "Well that was . . ." I stopped talking. I had no words really.

Mark nodded. "I know." And then we looked at each other, smiles stretching across our faces and we both started laughing.

A loud throat-clear broke the moment. Samirah, Faizel and Harun were standing there. Samirah passed the dog leash over to me and I took it.

"I think you should get him out of here," she said.

I looked to see who she was pointing at—it was poor Mrs. Marais.

"Okay," I said to them all. I turned to go but Mark stopped me.

"Listen, I have a lot to do, so I'm not sure when I will be home. I don't know if I'll get to the cottage today, sorry. Do you think you can stay at Samirah's one more night and I'll do it tomorrow?" he asked.

I glanced over at Samirah and she gave me a small nod.

"Thanks," he said.

I smiled, even though the idea of *not* staying at his place suddenly didn't make me feel that good. The idea of not continuing to share that laughter we'd just shared also didn't feel good. The idea of not being near him . . . also not. I started walking away but stopped and looked back at him.

"Shit," I mumbled softly to Harun. "I think I like him."

CHAPTER 54

I stood outside the cottage at Mark's house with Harun next to me. I'd gone back to Samirah's after the town hall, but then started to feel really bad that Mark had to clean this place out on his own. He was so busy, and also, I guess, I wanted to stay there sooner, rather than later. The only reason he didn't want me to clean it myself was that he was afraid of snakes, and I knew someone who was good with snakes.

I pushed the door open and let Harun off his leash. "Go look, boy," I said to him and peered through the door. The curtains were closed and the room was dark and smelled dusty.

"And?" I peered into the darkness to see what Harun was doing. I could vaguely make him out, sitting in the middle of the room casually. He seemed to be completely chilled, which told me that there was nothing lurking in there that shouldn't be. I walked inside and the first thing I did was open the curtains. The light rushed in, so bright and fast that I had to cover my eyes. The dust sprang to life. It glittered and glinted in the air around me like floating orbs. I swatted with my hands and opened the windows, letting some much-needed new oxygen into the room. Once the dust had settled, I looked around. I was shocked.

The cottage was cute and neat as a pin. A narrow bed, a little desk by the window and a small bathroom with a toilet and basin. Mark had implied this was some messy storeroom. But where was the storage? Where was the mess? The only storage I could see were three boxes on the floor that had been sellotaped shut. That was it. It was clear our definition of messy storage was completely different. I smiled to myself: the guy was clearly a neat freak. I could start staying in this room now, all I had to do was push the boxes against the wall and stack them. I moved over to one of the boxes and was about to pick one up when I noticed that the sellotape had peeled away a bit, the box flap sticking up just enough for me to peer inside. Something silver and shiny glinted back at me.

I shook my head: *nope!* I shouldn't look. That would be bad. But as I walked the box over to the wall, the flap opened and closed and opened and closed with my movement. And every time it opened, the silver flash blinded me. By the time I'd set the box down, my curiosity was seriously piqued. But curiosity killed the cat and all. I looked over at Harun. There were no cats here, and as far as I knew no idioms that involved dogs and curiosity. I pulled the flap up a little more, and more silver stuff flashed at me. Like some great treasure that wanted to come out and be found. I looked at Harun.

"What do you think, boy? Should I have a look inside?" I asked him and waited for his response. He didn't give me one. "I mean, what harm would it do?" I looked at Harun a little longer and when he didn't seem to object, I pulled the flap back with a nervous bubbly feeling in my stomach. The anticipation and flutterings of knowing that I was doing something I shouldn't was rather exhilarating. I'd never been much of a rule-breaker. A rebel. I'd always been a good girl. I wasn't the kind who stuck her nose into boxes she shouldn't.

I pulled slowly and peered inside excitedly, only to be sorely disappointed at what I found. A novelty silver-framed LP. Probably something he ordered to put up in the record store. I sighed and started closing the box again when the writing on the plaque caught my attention. My heart banged against my rib cage and I inhaled sharply and opened the flap again. This time I reached inside and pulled the framed record out, staring at the engraved words, my jaw dropping further and further open with each letter I read.

"Holy crap!" I said, when I'd read the name of my favorite band in the whole wide world. The band that spoke to me alone in my room when I was big and lonely and had no friends. The band that kept me company at night when I had no one to talk to, and the band whose posters had been up on my walls and ceiling. My first crushes. The band I had tattooed across my lower back, and refused to change, even though it was a crap tattoo, because they'd gotten me through the darkest times of my life. I read the words out loud.

"Presented to Step To That, in recognition of 1,000,000 album sales."

I smiled. Who knew Mark was such a fan that he'd bought himself a novelty album? I shook my head. No wonder this was hidden away. He was probably embarrassed by it. I put the record down and reached into the box again; might as well go for it now that it was open. A pack of photos caught my eye. I hadn't seen photos like this in years, the printed kind. I started flipping through them and it took me a few seconds to realize what I was looking at. And when I did, I gasped and dropped the pictures to the ground.

"What the . . ." I picked them up again and stared. These were photos of Step To That. The band. They were photos of them backstage, hanging out at a hotel, on a tour bus and . . .

The thought hit me and then left me. It was such a crazy thought that my brain wasn't able to process it. But then the thought hit me again, and again, and again as I stared at the face on the photo looking back at me. I brought the picture in closer, until it was almost touching my face.

No, it couldn't be . . .

Could it?

Brown eyes peering through yellow-lensed glasses.

Bleached white, spiky hair with a red and white bandana tied around the front.

Surely, it couldn't be?

A slim body wearing an oversized red baseball shirt.

Baggy jeans with silver chains hanging from the pockets, big purple platformed sneakers.

Large, silver loop earrings in both ears with matching silver necklaces.

Or could it?

Kneeling down on one knee, arms outstretched, fingers beckoning you through the photo.

Smoldering, yet innocent and intense look on face . . .

Could. Not. Be.

Could.

Not.

Be!

I heard a noise and looked up to see Mark standing in the doorway. His eyes dipped down to the photo in my hand and then a look washed across his face. It was easy to read. I did not need to be a facial expression reading expert to know what I was looking at.

Horror.

Absolute, eye-popping, jaw-dropping, red-cheeked horror.

CHAPTER 55

"*W*hat the hell are you doing here?" Mark asked angrily, his voice loud, almost a shout. I'd never heard it like that and it unsettled me.

"This is you, isn't it?" I held the picture up and scrambled to my feet. "This is you, right?" I waved the photo back and forth in the air.

"This is an invasion of privacy. What are you doing here?" he asked again, his voice getting even louder. He walked up to the box I'd been digging in, grabbed the platinum record and shoved it back in.

I waved the photo even more. "You are M.J. from Step To That, aren't you?" My voice was shaking now as I looked at him carefully. He looked very different now. Older, completely different style, longer hair, slightly bearded today (God, that suited him), but his eyes were the same chocolate brown that I'd stared into when I was young. It was him. My teenage crush. The voice I'd listened to over and over. That I'd swooned to and cried to and danced to and turned to in my most lonely moments. And my moments had been so lonely. On some days it had felt like his voice was the only voice that had said anything kind to me at all. *It was him!*

"M.J.," I said.

"Mark!" he corrected sternly.

He met my eyes for a moment, holding my gaze with an intensity that made my hairs prick up. And then, he broke it. It felt like he was ripping something away from me that, until that moment, I hadn't known how much I needed. He snatched the photo from my hand, so fast that the paper made my fingertips tingle, and also shoved it into the box. He took the box and started walking away. I followed him.

"Wait!" I called out, but he kept on going. He was moving so quickly that it was hard to keep up. I broke into a jog.

"It is you, isn't it? Oh my God. You are him! I can't believe this." Words started gushing out my mouth. "I knew you looked familiar. I mean, I should have seen it sooner. I stared at your face for years as a teenager. You were on my ceiling staring down at me, for heaven's sake. I should have seen it. Oh. My. GOD!" I squealed. "I can't believe this. You're M.J. The wild one."

"Mark!" He swung around and looked at me. His eyes zoned in on mine. This time they seemed cold. I stopped talking as his chilly gaze froze me. "I'm not that guy. The 'wild one.'" He gestured air quotes and spat those words out with venom. Slowly. One at a time. He turned again and carried on walking to the house. Even though he didn't look like he wanted to talk about it, I wasn't ready to drop this. *How the hell could I drop this?* This was not something you could drop!

"It's you! It's totally you!" I was quite hysterical now. "Oh my God. This is unbelievable. You were my favorite one. I had such a crush on you, to be honest. More than a crush. I mean, I once signed my name Frankie Taylor in my diary, God, that is so embarrassing to admit to now, especially to the actual person. But I had such a crush on you guys. I even have a STT tattoo on my back . . ." I paused for a moment. "Wait! You saw the tattoo the other night? Is that why you stopped . . . Oh God, of course it is. How embarrassing!" I reached around and touched my tattoo. It was an image from their album artwork, a heart with the letters "STT" in curly cursive through the middle of it. "I can't believe this! I mean, what are the chances? They must be a million to one. Billion to one. How many people are there in the world? That's how much the chances must be . . . to one. Oh my crap!" I stopped walking for a moment and put my hands on the sides of my face and shook my head. I was in physical shock. "Wow! Wow!" I started walking again. "You know you totally broke my heart when you left the band and it all fell apart? And it was weird that only you left, and your brother didn't leave too. I cried for an entire month, because the band wasn't the same without you. I was gutted when the band finally fell apart and even more when . . . when . . ." I stopped talking and gasped as the memory hit me on the side of the head.

"Oh shit," I said flatly, stumbling to a standstill. At that, Mark finally stopped walking and turned around slowly. His eyes were no longer icy. This time they looked like they were filled to the brim with pain. My heart broke.

"Oh shit. I'm so sorry. Crap! That was so insensitive of me." I shook my head, tears forming in my eyes. I took a step closer to him. "I'm so sorry, Mark. I would never have gone on like that, I wasn't thinking . . . your brother." I said that last part in a whisper and wished I could go back in time and stop myself from opening my stupid mouth in the first place. I felt so bad now.

Mark cast his eyes to the floor.

"I should never have gone in there and gone through your stuff. I thought I was helping you because you were busy, but it was wrong of me, sorry." My voice cracked. "And I'm so sorry about your brother.. When I heard what happened to him I . . . it was terrible."

There was a long, silent beat between us and it was filled with so much tension that it made the air feel sticky and thick. Pressing down on us. Finally, Mark looked up from the floor and made eye contact with me and, shit, his eyes were shining as if he was fighting back tears. My heart doubly broke.

"I'm so sorry," I whispered again.

He shook his head at me and then forced a small smile. God, that broke my heart even more. This man was killing me.

"Thanks for trying to help, but you really shouldn't have."

I nodded. "I know."

He looked at me for the longest time and then let out a sigh. As if he'd just resigned himself to something.

"I always knew someone would figure this out. I've been waiting for this day to come for years." He looked down at the box in his hands. "But you can't tell anyone who I am," he said softly. "Please." His plea came out desperate-sounding. "I put that behind me sixteen years ago. That's not me anymore."

"No one knows?" I asked and then a thought hit me. "Of course no one knows; well they don't know consciously." It made total sense now. Why half the town was in love with him and didn't know why, as Samirah had said. They probably also had had his poster up on their walls, or had looked at him longingly when they were younger. And when they met Mark, something about him stirred that up inside, even if they weren't sure what it was.

"No one knows. And I want it to stay that way." He said this rather emphatically and I nodded quickly.

"I won't tell anyone. I swear." And then I made a stupid joke that I shouldn't have made and it immediately tanked like a lead balloon in the space between us. Tanked so hard that I swear it should have actually made a noise. "Cross my heart, hope to kiss."

Mark looked at me and simply shook his head.

"Sorry, I didn't mean to, that was just one of my favorite songs." I shrugged at him apologetically. "God, that was lame, and so inappropriate. Sorry. I'm totally failing at this moment right now, but I got to be honest, I'm a little star struck here."

He shrugged back, and I swear I saw the tiniest smile flicker across his lips. "That's okay, baby girl."

I smiled back and then giggled a little, but tried to stop myself. It was a particularly stupid girly-sounding giggle too. Embarrassing. But I was just so fluttery inside. "Say you forgive me," I said back, naming yet another song title in this little game we'd suddenly found ourselves playing. I was relieved that the mood had lightened a little between us.

"Only if you go," he said, and my smile faded.

"You don't mean that really, do you?" I asked, a little worried that maybe we were no longer playing the song title game, even though that was the song from their second album, *Step Up To Me*.

He shook his head. "No. Don't go." He smiled at me and I was relieved. "Want something to drink?"

"That's not a song title," I said.

"No. It's not."

"So, you're actually asking me if I want a drink? IRL."

"IRL?"

"In real life," I quickly qualified.

"I guess I am."

CHAPTER 56

I sat on the veranda and waited for M.J., uh, Mark, to bring me a glass of something. He finally came back and passed me a beer. I took it and we sipped in silence for a while. I was grateful for the silence, to be honest. I had a lot to let sink in. This revelation that Mark was quite literally my childhood crush was just the strangest thing that had ever happened to me. But what else did I expect?

Things had been crazy since almost losing my life in that elevator, and then watching my whole life blow up in front of me. And then I came here and adopted a weird dog and was now starring in a reenactment. The past week had been this wild rollercoaster ride, that I didn't even remember getting on. My thoughts drifted to those two other women in the lift. I wondered if the one with the great eyebrows was okay. And the one with the smiley emoji shirt—was she smiling, or had her life also taken a strange turn like mine? I felt a kinship to them for some reason, even though I had no idea who they were.

"So, you know my secret," Mark said. I looked at him and felt a stomach flutter. The man in front of me was my childhood crush, and now that I was looking at him, I couldn't quite believe I hadn't realized it before. *And wait . . . I had kissed him!* I had kissed M.J. Taylor from Step To That! I sipped my beer quickly, mainly to cool myself down, because something was boiling inside me. I looked at Mark and he was picking at the label of his beer nervously.

"Why is it a secret?" I asked.

He stopped the nervous picking and looked up at me. "How much of our story do you know?"

"I know that at the height of the band's success, you left. And when they tried to bring out an album without you, it tanked and the band fell apart. And then your brother made a solo album a few years ago and that . . ." I stopped talking, I needed to tread lightly here. "It wasn't very well received," I said.

"It wasn't well received!" He gave a strangled, forced laugh. "That's an understatement if I've ever heard one."

I nodded. I remembered his attempt at a comeback. How the whole thing had backfired, and he'd been lambasted and ridiculed in the media. I remembered reading something online about it; the headline had been: "*The comeback we hope isn't back for good.*"

"They tore him apart in the press," Mark said, with an edge to his voice. "Tore apart his songs, his voice, his looks. They destroyed him. They pushed him to breaking point. They dragged his name through the media like it was dirt, they mocked him, they made him the laughing stock. And that's when he started down the path that led to that night."

I listened with horror to the story. To be honest, and I wasn't going to say this out loud, I'd been one of those fans who'd downloaded his album the second it came out. It hadn't been great. The magic that the band had when they were young was sadly gone.

"He was so high when he drove off the road that night that the coroner said he wouldn't have known what was happening, or felt it."

"I'm so sorry," I whispered again. And in my head, I scolded myself for reading all those sensationalized stories about him and his death. And the mocking in the media that had happened before it. *Washed-up ex-boy-bander with no talent*, I remembered seeing.

"He should never have tried to make that comeback," Mark said. "But he was so desperate for fame again. He hated me for walking away from the band and destroying it."

I sat up straight. "No. I don't think so."

Mark shook his head. "No, he did. He loved being a part of Step To That. It was his dream. He loved everything about it. The money, the girls, the fame, the touring, the screaming fans, he loved all of that. And I . . . hated it." He shook his head. "I couldn't do it anymore. I did it for as long as I could, I hung on for two years and finally I just couldn't."

"Why did you hate it?" I asked. It was so strange hearing this, because every interview I'd seen, every poster I'd looked at, he always had that smile on his face.

He shook his head and then let out a loud sigh. "You already know that my mum and dad had stores in the mall. My brother and I grew up listening to music in Dad's shop and watching MTV. When we were about ten, we decided we wanted to be musicians. My dad bought us a guitar and a small keyboard for Christmas, and we learned to play and started writing our own songs." He smiled at the memory. "They were so bad. We knew nothing about love and heartbreak at that age, but we were writing songs about it anyway, since that's what everyone on MTV was singing about. We started getting gigs, and when I say gigs, I mean we played in my dad's store and in the mall on holidays. That kind of thing. We started getting well known in our area and one year a local news station did a segment on us singing Christmas songs in the mall. I was fourteen and my brother was sixteen at the time." He paused and took a sip of his beer and continued. "I remember that day so well, a group of girls had gathered around and they were shouting and screaming so loudly, we were hardly able to play. Anyway, this producer saw the footage and a week later, the guy contacted us and wanted to know if we wanted to be a part of a band he was putting together. Obviously, we jumped, I mean, this was the dream." He stopped talking for a while and really picked at his beer sticker, pulling the whole thing off and then tossing it to the floor.

"Turned out it was a fucking nightmare," he said quietly. "The whole thing was completely manufactured and controlled. We couldn't be ourselves, at all. They even changed my name, Mark was too boring. They assigned us roles and we had to play them. We had to act and dress the part. I was the wild one, my brother was the shy one, Shane was the goofy one, Chris was the bad boy and Jack was the sporty one. They told us what to say and how to be and our lives were consumed with that." He looked up at me. "So I know a little about living a life that is controlled down to the second and completely false and manufactured, Frankie." He said that part with meaning, and that conversation we'd had over pancakes suddenly made sense to me. I nodded at him, took another sip of my beer, and it got caught in my throat. I coughed, feeling uncomfortable.

"I know a little something about putting on a show for someone else's benefit, not doing anything for yourself. Losing yourself in something that's not really yours. Not being your true self."

I opened my mouth to say something, but had no idea what. So, I closed it again.

He took a massive swig of the beer now. "Those were two years of my life I absolutely hated." He shook his head. "If I could take them back, I would. If I had a time machine, I would go back and say no to that producer and not become M.J. from Step To That."

"Wait. NO!" I said emphatically. "You can't say that. Do you know how much your music meant to me growing up? Do you know how many times I used to come home from school and be broken because I was the fat girl that had been teased all day and you were the only voice that made me feel better? Do you know how many times I listened to that song 'Special Girl' and wished, and hoped and pretended that someone was singing those words to me? Your music got me through high school. 'Special Girl,' *crap*, I must have listened to it thousands of times and . . ." My voice tailed off and got a little shaky, and I totally hadn't intended for it to happen, but tears pricked at my eyes. I looked down and twisted my fingers together, intertwining them nervously and anxiously as feelings flooded back to me. "All I wanted when I was growing up," I said quietly, "was to be that girl you were singing about in that song. I wanted to be the person that someone would say those things about." I shook my head. "So don't say you regret those years. Because then you wouldn't have made that song and girls like me around the world wouldn't have felt less alone." I forced myself to make eye contact with him. He was looking at me intently. "You can't regret that." I was almost on the verge of tears as I poured my heart out to him. "I wouldn't have gotten through high school if it wasn't for your music, so don't you dare say that."

He smiled at me. It started out looking somewhat forced, but soon I could see it wasn't. It spread across his face and into his eyes. "I won't then," he said softly, looking at me. "That means a lot. You saying that." He took another swig of the beer, a big one, downing the whole bottle in a few gulps.

"Is that why you came here?" I asked him. "Because of your brother's death?"

He shook his head. "I came here because I had no choice."

"Why?" I asked.

"The media is a fickle bitch, Frankie. It pulled him apart, and then after he died, it sang his praises. They must make up their minds." He turned the bottle around in his hands and started working on the label on the other side too. "I couldn't go anywhere without reading about him. Seeing his picture. Reading about us, and seeing my picture from all those years ago. And then the media started asking where I was and what I had to say about it all. I'd worked so hard to stay under the radar since leaving the band. And now they were after me too; they even implied that it was my fault, because I'd been the one who broke the band up and maybe if I hadn't—"

"Bullshit!" I jumped up, and sat down next to him. "You know that's not true. You know they only say things like that to sell papers and generate clicks."

He didn't look up at me. "Sure. I know. But still, it gets to you. I had to get away. So I came here. It was either here or a small town in America that is also a radio silent zone. But it snows there and as an Australian who hates the cold . . . it was here."

"And your parents?" I asked. "Don't they miss you?"

He shrugged. "I mean, I'm sure. But my sister is still there and they have three grandchildren who keep them busy and distracted, and they understood how much I needed to get away. Here, I can be myself. If people knew who I was, they would treat me differently, and it would start all over again. I needed anonymity."

"Sounds familiar," I said, crossing my legs uncomfortably.

"Did you also come here for that?" he asked.

"You could say I know a thing or two about people turning on you. I've also lived my life in the public eye, not nearly as much as you, though. I mean, tens of millions of people around the world know you, I'm only known by 350,000, so it's not quite the same." I looked up at him and our eyes met.

"But the same kind of experience," he said.

"I guess. Who would have thought?"

"We're both on the run," he said with a small smile.

"Looks like it."

"And we seemed to have run right into each other," he continued.

I nodded. "With a little help from Harun." I smiled at him as his eyes drew me in. I felt like my body was betraying me as it started to lean in. I think he was leaning too. He must have been, because suddenly I was sure his body was closer to me.

"Please," he whispered, low and desperate. "Please don't tell anyone who I am. Can you do that?"

I nodded. "I can."

He smiled again at me, and I found myself smiling back. Falling into his smile in a way that felt warm and right.

"I'm glad you're here," Mark said, pulling away from the lean a little.

Come back, come back, I screamed in my head.

"Me too," I said, even though I wanted to reach out and grab him by the shirt and demand he come closer again.

"Life is funny." He folded his legs and sat up straight.

"It is. Although I'm not sure I totally understand its sense of humor."

He looked at me and gave me that melt-in-my-seat smile again. How had I not known that smile? How had I not known that he was M.J.? Because now it was all I could see.

"You really signed your name with my surname attached to it?"

"Oh God." I face-palmed. "Forget I said that. Please."

He shook his head. "No way I can forget that."

"Sorry, it's so embarrassing."

Mark got up and walked into the house. Moments later he came back and gave me a pen and piece of paper. "Show me."

"No!" I pushed the pen away.

Mark laughed. "Come on. You can't be as embarrassed as I am right now. You know how I used to dress."

I laughed. "It was very fashionable back then, you know. I also had a pair of glasses with yellow lenses. I thought they were very cool."

"Did you now?" He leaned in again, and my body immediately reacted to it. "Show me your signature."

His voice and smell were pretty intoxicating and I found myself relenting. "Fine!" I signed my made-up signature that I'd signed so many times before and then handed it to him.

"I like how you put a heart above the 'I,'" he said, looking very amused.

I nudged him. "Hey, don't mock my little teenage heart!"

His smile faded a little and then he looked at me seriously. "I think it's cute. I wish I'd known you back then."

"No, you don't. Trust me. I was nothing like I am now. I hated the person I was back then."

He nodded at me. "I also hated the person I was back then." His voice was soft and thoughtful. "That's sad, isn't it?"

I thought about it for a while. "It is sad," I said.

"I'm actually glad someone knows who I am," he said, catching me off guard.

"Why?"

"It's hard keeping a secret like this. And I'm glad it's you who knows."

"Really?" I perked up. "Even though I signed my name and have you tattooed on my back?" I blushed and covered my face. "Wow, you have no idea how embarrassing that sounds right now."

His smile changed now. There was something else behind that small curve his lips were making. And, honestly, it kind of thrilled me.

"I'm not going to lie, when I saw that tattoo I kind of freaked out."

"That night when we were . . . ?" I didn't finish that sentence.

"Yeah. *That* night." His voice sounded soft and whispery now.

"That one," I replied, equally breathy. "Did you think I knew who you were and had stalked you here?"

He let out a chuckle. "Did you?"

"No." I shook my head.

"I didn't know what to think when I saw it, so I just . . . *ran*."

"That you did." I laced my fingers together. "That you did." I wanted to lean in and ask him if I kissed him this time, would he run again? But didn't.

"And you?" he asked after a few more moments of awkward silence, in which I'm sure both of us were thinking about that other night. Well, I was, anyway.

"What about me?"

"I've told you my entire family life story, what about you?"

"My family life story?" I asked, feeling uncomfortable now.

"Please," he said.

"Um . . . okay." I hesitated, not sure where to begin really. And then I took a deep breath and told him. "Well, my mother is on her fifth marriage, Dan the dentist is the latest love of her life."

Mark reclined in his seat and nodded; he looked like he'd settled in for the reading of a book, so I continued.

"So I had four stepdads growing up, none of them were horrible or terrible, but I guess none of them were . . . *Dad*. Not that I would know what a dad is, I've never known mine. He left when I was a toddler."

"Sorry. You said that," Mark said softly.

I shrugged. "Some of my stepdads really tried. Especially Ed the electrician."

Mark smiled. "Do you always do that with them? Dan the dentist. Ed the electrician?"

I smiled back at him and gave a small chuckle. "I can't help it if they deliberately went into careers that started with the same letter of their first names."

"I bet you can't do that with all of them?" he challenged playfully.

I thought about it for a while. "Well, there was Gareth the garage owner. That was my sister's real dad. He and my mom were married for about five years. I used to think he was my dad too until I overheard some mothers talking."

"You have a sister?" He uncrossed his legs and moved closer to me.

I nodded. "I do and she's . . ." A lump formed in my throat. "Perfect," I whispered softly.

"Where's she now?"

"Married to her high-school sweetheart and living in a really pretty house with roses and jasmine that grows along the white picket fence. She's the together one . . . I'm not, apparently. I'm the messed up one."

Mark smiled at that. "Apparently I was 'the wild one.' All these labels . . . Besides what's 'the together one'?"

"You know, the one that has it all figured out. The one who can't do any wrong, the favorite one."

Mark shrugged at this. "Sometimes people look like they have everything figured out, but they don't."

I shook my head. "Trust me, she does. She's always pointing out how figured out she is versus me. She's always telling me that I need to get a real job, or a real boyfriend or do something real with my life, as if everything in my life is fake or something." I rolled my eyes and looked over at Mark, but he wasn't responding the way I wanted him to. He looked at me pointedly and then leaned back in his chair. I leaned back too, deep in thought, thinking about my sister's words over the years.

"We kind of had a fight about it, just before I came here," I heard myself say to him.

"Does she know where you are?" he asked.

I shook my head. "Nah, but I doubt she'll miss me. Or even notice I'm gone. Neither will my mom, she's cruising the world with Dan the dentist and having the time of her life." I forced a smile. My mother had worked so hard when we were kids, we'd barely seen her, and when she'd retired I'd thought that maybe we would see her more, but she started her world cruising a few years ago and I'd rarely seen her since.

Mark sat forward. "Families are complicated."

I nodded. "Say that again."

"My brother hated me for years because I broke the band up and because when we were in the band, I was the more 'popular one,' and now that he's gone . . . I wish we'd healed all that. So if you can, don't leave things the way they are with your sister."

I nodded half-heartedly at this. And then we fell into a deep silence; I think we were both deep in thought.

CHAPTER 57

I woke up the next day in Mark's cottage. We'd spent the rest of the previous day cleaning it together; he'd put some new linen on the bed and I'd made a dog bed for Harun in the corner. We'd spent the entire time talking about everything. He'd told me more about his years in the band, his brother and his family. And I'd told him about my life, the Little Miss Daisy pageants, the food I turned to, the teasing, being in my sister's shadow. I told him about Kyle and our relationship and my social media life. *I told him almost everything.* It had felt comfortable and easy talking to him. And he was a better conversationalist than Harun, because he actually spoke back.

"So . . . first day at your new job," Mark said, through the door while I was showering in his bathroom. I'd come in that morning and he'd made me coffee and breakfast, which was really sweet of him.

"Samirah says I can take Harun to work with me," I said, as I wiped myself down from the shower and put on clothes. When I opened the door and walked out, Mark was standing so close that I bumped into him.

"Sorry!" I grabbed a hold of his elbow as an automatic reflex.

"It's okay," he said, also grabbing onto me. We held onto each other for just a little too long, until we finally let go and moved apart.

"We have rehearsals tonight," Mark reminded me.

At that I shook my head. "Rehearsals?"

"For the festival."

My eyes widened. "We actually have to rehearse this thing? Aren't we just walking down the street?"

He grinned. "This town takes the festival very seriously."

"It would seem," I said sarcastically.

"It's fun though. You'll like it. You'll meet everyone and feel part of something."

"I don't think the people around here like me. Not after movie night and then yesterday."

Mark shook his head, his hair falling into his face in a way that I was really starting to appreciate. I liked this casual version of him—this unpolished, unglamorous, version of him with the stubble and the floppy hair and those cute glasses that seemed just a little bit too big for him and the old worn shirts with bands' names on. He ran his hand through his hair and swept it back up, a gesture I enjoyed watching. The way he put it all back in place, only for it to fall back down again, like it always did.

"People around here are very forgiving, you just have to make a bit of an effort."

"Okay. I can do that, I guess." I gave a firm nod.

"I'm heading to the store now—do you want me to drop you off at Samirah's and then we can meet at rehearsals later?" he asked.

"Sure," I said, trying to hide a huge smile that was spreading across my face. This was all rather odd and strange and a little exhilarating too. Playing a weird kind of house together. Breakfasts and shared bathrooms and driving into work. In all the time I'd been with Kyle, I don't think I'd ever done this much with him. I'd done more things with Mark in the week I'd known him, than I think I'd done with Kyle in the entire two years. Well, things that actually mattered and meant something. That weren't just for show.

* * *

My first day as a veterinary assistant hadn't gone as planned. I'd been peed on by a nervous dog, scratched by a cat, and finally a rather forward parrot had hit on me and called me "sweet cheeks." But it had been nice working with Samirah, learning about the different kinds of care for the various animals, and what everything in the surgery was and what it did. I also realized that because this was a small town, her veterinary business wasn't exactly busy, but despite this, she really needed help because of her pregnancy. She'd explained that most of her work came from the nearby farms. When it was two in the afternoon we closed up for the day, unless there was an emergency. I walked over to Mark's store with Harun.

Turns out running a music and video store in a town with no television and radio was a much busier occupation than having a veterinary practice. When the customers came in, I watched how Mark talked about movies and music to them. His face lit up as he recommended a classic horror, or when he spoke about David Bowie's best album—in his opinion. It was nice to see. This breezy, bright side of him that seemed passionate about what he did.

His smile was adorable too, and the way he took his glasses off from time to time and polished the lenses on his shirt, and when he did that, how his shirt lifted up just enough to see a small flash of his stomach . . .

God, he had a nice stomach. Flat. Those defined lines that sort of snaked down into his jeans. That hinted at things to come . . . My face got a little hotter at my unintentional pun there. Or maybe it was intentional. Yes, crap! It was intentional. I was definitely thinking about his dick! I'd seen it the other night, and now it was all I could see when I looked at that little flash of skin on his stomach when he cleaned his glasses and . . .

"Shit! Oh my God, sorry." I quickly looked away, my face flaming red as he caught me staring at him. How long had I been staring? How long had he *known* I'd been staring? Oh, dear Lord, it had been a while. I knew that. I was officially a pervert.

"What are you looking at?" he asked in a voice that led me to believe he knew *exactly* what I was looking at.

I didn't look at him. "Sorry. Your . . . You were . . . lifting your shirt and I was . . . uh . . ." Was running out of words. Had no idea what to say to him.

"Were objectifying me?" he asked. That sounded so horrible. And creepy. But . . . It was kind of true.

"Sort of, I guess," I said, still looking as far away from him as possible. I could hear him coming closer to me, see the movement from the corner of my eyes. "Sorry," I quickly added.

He stopped when he got to the counter. I was on the other side of it, acutely aware of his presence now.

"Soooooo." He dragged that word out and I saw him lean over the counter a little towards me.

"Mmmm?" I replied, not looking at him, frantically twirling my hair around my finger nervously.

"What were you thinking?" he asked.

"Thinking?"

"Well, you were clearly thinking something while you were staring. What was it?"

I was thinking about your dick! No, I couldn't say that. That would be wildly inappropriate.

I shook my head. "Mmmm, nothing." I tried to sound innocent, even though I clearly had a filthy mind.

He leaned even more, and any second now, I was sure I was going to have to look at him, because focusing on that spot on the wall was making my eyes squint and sting.

"It didn't look like nothing." His voice had taken on a teasing tone. Wait . . . Was he flirting with me?

I forced myself to look at him, our eyes met and something, *something*, buzzed around us. The air seemed to have a weight to it, even a smell. We both leaned closer across the counter, our hands almost touching. We looked down and our fingers slid towards each other's.

Slowly. We stopped for a moment, mere centimeters apart. I could feel the warmth coming off his hands, zipping out the tips of his fingers and shooting over to mine, making them physically tingle. And then, as if someone had told us both to look up at the same time, we did. Our eyes found each other's and the tips of our fingers made contact. An electrical current ran into me, traveled all the way down into my toes.

"Frankie . . ." Breathy voice. Almost a whisper.

"Yes, Mark . . ." I whispered back.

"I—"

"HEY!" A voice broke the moment, and we both pulled away from each other as if we'd been caught doing something naughty.

"Zack!" I said, looking up.

"Frankie! How are you feeling after the other night?" he asked. "I was a bit wrecked the next morning."

I smiled. "I was okay."

"Hey, Mark." He turned to Mark and extended his hand. There was a brief, small pause before Mark shook it. Suddenly, everything was awkward AF. How had I gone from touching Mark's fingers, to Mark touching Zack's hand? I watched their hands as they connected. The shake was hard, and firm, and I imagined my fingers would have been hurt in the strong-looking clench.

"Zack," Mark said flatly.

"Mark." Zack mirrored Mark's tone, even though he'd already said his name and it probably wasn't necessary to say it again.

"Zack." Mark said his name again too.

Like I said, awkward.

"Is this your dog?" Zack asked, turning to Harun.

"YES!" I said too loudly and enthusiastically, because I was only too happy to shift the focus of this conversation away from firm hands and double name-calling.

Zack stepped closer to Harun, and I gave him a once-over as he came closer to me. He was definitely good-looking. Very. No doubt about it.

"What's his name?" Zack asked.

"Well, that's a funny story. He's had three names in the last week. Satan's Little Helper, Cujo, and now we have settled on Harun."

"Hey, Harun." He reached down to pat him and Harun let out a very ominous-sounding growl. "Seems like he doesn't like me." Zack stepped back.

"That's odd, he usually likes everyone," Mark said, looking at Zack through narrowed eyes. Zack glanced back at Mark over his shoulder and something competitive passed between them.

"I'm glad I ran into you.' Zack turned his attention back to me and smiled. Dimples. Cute and boyish and I admit, I melted just a bit.

"You are?" I heard myself say, perhaps a little too sweetly.

Zack nodded. "I was wondering if you would like to go out with me?"

My heart jumped. "Like, on a date?"

He smiled and gave a small chuckle. "Sure. A date."

I glanced behind him, Mark looked at me and then quickly turned around and placed a DVD back on the shelf. I tried to project my thoughts across to him, even though I knew that was impossible. I wanted Mark to look at me again. To shake his head. To tell me *not* to go on a date with Zack. Give me a reason not to say yes to this hot man in front of me.

But he didn't.

"Uh . . . um." I turned back to Zack.

"What about tonight?" Clearly, he wasn't taking no for an answer.

"Uh . . ." I looked over at Mark again and this time he did look at me. But not in the way I wanted. He shrugged, as if he didn't care. As if telling me to go. My heart felt like it physically slumped in my chest.

"Sure." I looked back at Zack.

"I'll fetch you at seven. At Mark's. I hear you're renting the cottage there."

"Uh . . . how did you know that?"

"Small town. News travels."

I nodded, a tightness in my throat.

"Great, see you then," he added, and then put his hand on my shoulder momentarily and gave it a squeeze. He walked out the shop confidently, shooting Mark a quick careless goodbye as he went.

CHAPTER 58

I was looking forward to my date as much as I was looking forward to an enema, to be honest. I wished I'd never agreed to it in the first place. The strange atmosphere between Mark and me since we'd left the store and come home was enough to make my skin crawl. I couldn't work out if he didn't like Zack, or didn't like the idea of me going out with Zack. But despite this, I still tried to look as hot as possible, obviously. I always found it hard to decide what to wear. I had to choose clothes carefully for my body, there were things that I needed to hide.

When I lost all that weight, my body and skin didn't exactly go back to the way they should be. As a result I can never, ever wear a bikini, thanks to the loose skin. I don't wear anything sleeveless either, thanks to the flappy skin at the top of my arms, and if I wear a tight dress, I always make sure I wear Spanx to make my stomach look flat and smooth. Of course, I'd never let anyone see this. As Kyle says, we must always project an image of perfection, and my body, despite being a fitness and beauty blogger, is not perfect. Not that I would let any of my followers know this. *Ever.* So, of course, I lie to them.

I stopped brushing my hair and looked at myself in the mirror. I leaned in. My brown roots were starting to show and my hairdresser was a million miles away. My usual appointment with her had been this week, but I was here. *Blonde—another lie I tell.* I'm not blonde. Far from it. I touched the brown roots with my fingers, and the hair there felt different to the blonde hair. It felt softer. I sighed and looked at myself in the mirror. I told my followers a lot of lies, now that I thought about it.

I also told them how much I loved myself. *All* of myself. How confident I was. How motivated and #blessed and #happy and at peace and striving for my goals I was . . . all the time. I looked at my phone, lying on the bed behind me. I had told a lot of people a lot of lies. Or led them to believe things about me that weren't really true. But Kyle always said that—

Wait.

Why did I keep thinking that? *Kyle always said?*

That's because he did always say. He was always the one saying, and doing, and saying how things should be done and I'd always gone along with it.

Why?

I turned back to the mirror and looked at myself. Suddenly, I wasn't feeling very good at all. My stomach tightened and knotted, and my feelings had nothing to do with the date. They were something else entirely. I finally emerged from the cottage at around six thirty and walked into the house; Mark was sitting in a comfortable-looking armchair, reading a book. He looked up at me and then seemed to silently study me.

"Are you wearing that?" he asked.

"Are we doing this again?" I said, remembering the night we went out.

He continued to peer over the top of his book at me, which made me feel uneasy.

"Something wrong with it?"

"It might be a bit formal."

"Oh, that again." I looked down at my dress and heels. "But I'm not walking this time."

"Mmmm, I know. But the heels might look like you're . . . you're . . ." He looked at me helplessly. I had no idea where he was going with this.

"What?" I asked.

"Heels sort of say . . ." He uncrossed his legs and leaned forward in his chair.

"They say what?"

"Nothing," he said, quickly looking back down at his book. "It's none of my business, actually."

I looked down at my sexy heels and twisted my foot from left to right, the glittery bits sparkling in the light. "You think heels are too datey? They make it look like I'm trying too hard?"

He shrugged. "Are you? Trying?"

"God. No! I wouldn't want him to think I was trying too hard. Or should I be?" I asked, taking a step forward.

"Should you try hard?" Mark reached for his glasses, slipped them on and looked at me again.

"Yes," I stated.

"If you want to. If that's what the vibe is?" Mark's eyes drifted over me and I felt goosebumps on my arms.

"I don't know what the vibe is!" I put my hands on my hips now. "What do you think the vibe is?"

"I thought it was a date vibe," he said.

"I mean, it's just a casual date, vibe. No other vibe intended, obviously." I looked at my dress again and sighed. "Yeah, this gives off too much of a vibe, right?"

Mark stood up now and his eyes ran the length of my body again. I shivered. "It definitely gives off a vibe."

"Okay, I'll change. And let's stop saying vibe!" I rushed off and put on a much simpler dress and flatter shoes. I rushed back to Mark who was now in the kitchen making a cup of coffee.

"And now?" I asked, giving a small spin.

He turned around, and his eyes drifted down to my feet. "Maybe the shoes are a bit too . . .?" He looked like he couldn't find the word.

"They're Gucci," I said.

"Exactly."

I nodded. "You think they're too fancy?"

"I didn't say that. You did," he replied.

I sighed. "You're right, too fancy and showy."

Mark didn't say anything, but nodded his head.

"Okay." I rushed back outside to change.

"Perhaps it's more of a pants and T-shirt thing," he shouted after me as I ran. And then I thought I heard him say something like, "the older and uglier the better," but I probably imagined that.

I emerged again in some jeans, a T-shirt and pair of sneakers, and wearing less make-up. And this time, when I walked in, Mark's eyes widened.

"What? Is it terrible?" I asked self-consciously, holding my shirt against me, hoping the Spanx had flattened that loose muffin-top of skin I had.

"No. You look . . . perfect." His voice was soft and low and suddenly all I could think of was that kiss under the sprinklers and how much I wanted to do it again, and how much I wanted him to tell me not to go on this stupid date.

"Thanks," I replied, my voice equally low and slightly breathy.

"You have freckles," he stated.

"I . . . uh, yes." I lifted my hands to my face awkwardly and covered my cheeks. Shit, clearly, I'd taken too much make-up off.

"They're cute," he said quickly. "I've never noticed them."

"I usually cover them," I mumbled, feeling self-conscious.

"You shouldn't!" He said it so matter-of-factly. I lowered my hands and our eyes met. I was overwhelmed with a desire to run across the room and throw myself in his arms. I took a small step towards him, hoping he would too, but he didn't. He turned away from me and busied himself in the fridge.

"Have a good time," he said over his shoulder, so casually that it sounded like he didn't care again that I was going.

"Okay." I stood there and looked at him, but he didn't look back.

"I don't think I'll be too late." I only said this because I was fishing for some kind of response from him.

"Cool. Take your time." He was still scratching in the fridge.

"You think?" I asked.

Mark turned and our eyes met again. "There's no curfew here, so come home when you want to."

I nodded at him. "But if I come home too late, that might give him the impression that this is a——"

"Date?" he interrupted. "I thought it was a date."

"What's a date, really?" I said with a chuckle now, feeling strange and awkward.

"Well, in my experience, it's usually when two single people decide to go out together to see if they're romantically compatible."

"Ro . . . man . . . uh . . ." *Romantic.* I couldn't get my mouth to say that word, for some reason.

"Candles. Flowers. Chocolates," Mark continued.

"Yes, I know what it means." I ran my hand through my hair. "But I doubt there are going to be any——"

"Hello?" A voice made us both turn. It was Zack. And he was standing there in the doorway . . . with a bunch of flowers. A big, red bunch of fracking flowers. My heart sank.

"Like I said . . ." Mark whispered under his breath.

"Wow, you look amazing." He stepped forward and held the flowers out for me.

"Uh . . . thanks." I took them and then Zack planted a kiss on my cheek! I tried not to pull away, as I kept my eyes firmly on Mark. Who rolled his. My skin felt hot and itchy and it wasn't from the kiss.

"These are really pretty, thanks." I swung my head and looked around the room. "I need a vase . . ." I glanced at Mark, who seemed to be eyeing the flowers with great suspicion. He held his hand out and my eyes traveled down to it. God, this was awkward.

"I'll do it," he said.

Tentatively, I handed my bunch of romantic red flowers to Mark.

"Thanks, man," Zack said. I couldn't help but notice that Mark rolled his eyes again before walking off towards the kitchen.

"Have fun," he called after us as he disappeared around the door.

"We will," Zack shouted and then shot me a very cute and dimply smile. But no matter how cute and melty his smile was, all I could think about was Mark's smile. I really didn't want to go on this date. But Mark wasn't exactly giving me a reason not to. So I went.

CHAPTER 59

I crept up the driveway, but it was hard to creep on it—being made from small stones that moved under the soles of your feet and all. I was home late. Despite the fact the date had totally sucked. Turns out that Zack only knew how to talk about his sheep. Conversation never seemed to move on from the dipping of them, the shearing of them, and why Karoo sheep were superior to other sheep. I'd not been able to shut him up, hence the fact I was coming home much later than originally anticipated. The lateness was in no way indicative of the fact I'd had a good time.

I was just about to take the curve that led towards the back of the house, when a light flicked on. It made me jump. "Crap!" I gasped in fright when I saw Mark sitting cross-legged in the daybed. The light shone down on him, making him look like someone in an interrogation room.

"You're home late," he said in a tone that didn't give much away.

"Am I? I hadn't noticed that . . . really?"

"How was your date?" Still, that tone.

"It was okay," I said dismissively.

He stood up and took a step towards me. Even though we were still far apart and it was dark, I could see there was an intensity in his eyes that made me stand a little straighter.

"Okay?" he repeated.

I nodded. "Yes. Okay." I don't know why I said this, it was just automatic. Like when someone asks you how you are and you say fine even though you're not.

"Okay . . . good?" He took another step closer to me.

"Sure." I nodded. "I guess. Sort of . . ." I also took a step towards him.

"How good?" he asked. He had stopped at the top of the stairs now, and I was at the bottom looking up at him. The light from the porch light framed him, making him look bigger and darker than he really was. He was looming over me, and so were his loaded questions.

"What do you mean?" I asked.

"On a scale of one to best-date-ever-I-am-in-love, where would you say it falls?" he asked.

"Well, I would say it was . . . uh . . ." I looked up at him and squinted. *Why the hell was he asking me all these questions?* What business did he have asking me how my date was, when he'd encouraged me to go?

I put my hands on my hips and then glared up at him defiantly. "Why are you asking me this? My date has absolutely nothing to do with you."

He continued to gaze down at me from his lofty vantage point, and then suddenly, with a loud thunk, he stepped down one of the stairs. I held my breath as he trod purposefully down the rest. One at a time. The sound of his feet on the wood created a kind of beat that was slow and screamed of anticipation. Something to come. Finally, his foot hit the ground and there he was, standing right in front of me.

"Thing is . . ." he said, softly this time. His tone had totally changed.

"Yes?" I urged. Something had shifted between us. I could feel and see it in the way he was looking at me.

"Thing is, Frankie, I know it has nothing to do with me, but despite that, I found myself sitting here all night, unable to go to sleep, wondering what you were doing and whether you were enjoying it and whether you were, were . . ." He stopped talking and looked pained.

"Whether I was what?" I asked.

"Whether you were kissing him."

"Why would you wonder if I was kissing him?" I asked. Heart pounding. Mouth drying up.

He stepped even closer to me. The light of the moon caught the side of his face and his eyes no longer looked brown in this light. They looked like a dark caramel. Warm. Like you could fall into them.

"Well, did you?" he asked. His voice was low and gravelly, and coupled with those caramel eyes, it was all making me feel very hot and fluttery inside.

"I . . . I . . ." Why was I stuttering? I was stuttering because the look on his face was stealing all my words and suddenly the entire night felt that much hotter than it had a few seconds ago.

Mark inched forward until there was hardly a gap between us now. "Because if you did kiss him, then I wouldn't be able to."

I sucked a breath in as his words winded me in the solar plexus. "You want to—?" I let the question hang in the air. I needed him to say it again. I needed proper confirmation that he had meant what I thought he meant.

"Kiss you," he repeated.

"You want to kiss me?" I managed in a whisper.

"It's all I've been thinking about all night," he said, and this time, his hand came up to my waist. Gently. I put my hand over his, slipping my fingers into his, to let him know that it was okay to touch me. It was okay for his hands to be on my body. I stared into his eyes; they were now a kaleidoscope of colors: caramels and chocolates with little flecks of gold around big black centers. I took his other hand, and without saying a word, I placed it on the other side of my waist. This hand wasn't as gentle as the first one was, and as soon as it came into contact with my body, his fingers dug into my skin a little. I heard myself let out a small moan which made the gold flecks in his eyes disappear into the black.

"Then kiss me," I said, the words sticking in my dry mouth.

CHAPTER 60

A small smile flickered over his mouth, but only for a second, because soon his lips were parting, as his face came closer to mine. I closed my eyes and waited. Waited for the moment of connection to come. The anticipation of those lips coming into contact with mine was enough to make me want to jump out of my skin. But when the lips didn't come. When I'd felt like I'd waited for an eternity, I opened my eyes.

"What are you . . ." I said, when I saw he'd pulled away. He was watching me with a smile now.

His smile grew and then he shook his head a little. "You're cute, that's all."

"Cute?"

He nodded. "So damn fucking cute, Mrs. Frankie Taylor, with a heart for a dot."

I blushed and put my hands over my cheeks, which suddenly felt hot. "I'm not going to live that down."

"Unlikely," he said, pulling my hands away from my face and then holding them. He moved closer. I looked deeply into his eyes as his face came right up to mine and finally, his features blurred together when he couldn't come any closer.

The kiss was slow and soft and short. It was more of a series of short little kisses, only lips. The short kisses soon grew longer though, until the spaces between them disappeared and it became one, long kiss. Deep. Slow. My fingers found a place in the back of his hair and his slipped around to the small of my back, pulling me closer to him. I held on as we kissed. He tasted sweet. Of chocolate and maybe a little bit of gin. His stubble was rough against my face, but in just the right way.

Soft and rough. Warm and deep. My hands left his hair and trailed over his shoulders, until they came to rest on his chest. He groaned against my lips, as if me just touching him there was driving him wild. The thought made me brave, so I ran my hands down even more, pulled at his shirt, and then slipped my hands into it. My fingers traveled up to his warm chest; it was smooth and firm and as the kiss deepened, I dug my nails into his sides, feeling his rib cage expand and contract beneath my hands. Another groan escaped his lips and this time, I heard myself whimper in response to it.

And then, everything was suddenly electric. As though a switch had been flipped. The kiss became fast, hungry. Devouring each other with lips and tongues and teeth. His hands slipped down my back, they cupped my ass, and then he pulled me into him. I could feel he was hard against me and this made me want to climb out of my clothes and climb right onto him. He pushed himself into me, moving his hips a little, and I swear, stuff in my head went fuzzy and fluffy around the edges until the angles and shapes of the real world fell away and it was just us. Outside. In the desert. Under the stars and . . .

"OH!" I exclaimed loudly when my feet were no longer on the ground. "Wh . . . what . . . Oh my God." I let out a loud giggle as Mark lifted me off the ground and started rushing me back to the house. "You're going to drop me," I laughed.

"Let's hope not," he said. I could hear he was starting to strain as he walked up the stairs with me, which wasn't very reassuring.

"Hi, Harun!" I said, as I reached the veranda and Mark finally put me down. Harun opened his one eye and looked at me as if he was totally disinterested in what I was doing. I looked back at Mark, whose breathing seemed a little labored.

"Fuck! Okay! Maybe I'm not cut out for sweeping you off your feet right now." He was smiling at me.

"I don't know . . . I feel pretty swept," I said, moving closer to him and placing both my hands on his shoulders. God, he really was tall and having to stand on my tiptoes to look up at him made him so much sexier.

"You do?" He raised a brow. "Swept?"

"Very."

We smiled at each other. It was a giddy smile. The kind you make when you feel like you're falling. Mark pushed the door open with his foot and took a step back. He held out his hand and I slipped my fingers through it and then let him lead me to his bedroom. The mood changed again when we walked in. The presence of the bed took impromptu spontaneous kissing under the stars to something else entirely. It added a layer of seriousness to it all. It added a layer of intention. The presence of the bed was the promise of sex. Mark must have seen me looking at it, because suddenly he took a step back.

"Uh, sorry, was that presumptuous of me?" His face fell and he looked at me with concern.

"It wasn't presumptuous." I stepped closer and kissed him this time. I tried to put everything I was feeling into that kiss. To convey to him that every second of that date, all I'd been thinking about, was him. And it had nothing to do with who he had once been. The boy on the poster on the wall. It was all about him. As he was. Now. The man I'd gotten to know over the last week. This kiss was about that.

The bedroom smelled like him. Full of amazing scents from fragrances that he'd acquired all over the world. I'm sure there was sandalwood and something you would imagine smelling in a souq in Morocco. This exotic smell had my head spinning and my body screaming. His shirt was the first thing to come off. During the kiss I'd found my hands gripping the bottom of it, pulling it up and then over his head. I'd had to put a stop to the kiss for a second, as I'd pulled it over his face. The absence of his lips felt catastrophic in some way. Like they were not meant to be away from mine. He clearly felt the same way, because the second his shirt was tossed to the floor, he kissed me.

Face between hands. Pushing me down onto the bed now and crawling over me. I put my hands on his chest and was struck by how perfectly smooth it was. As if running my hands over warm marble. He groaned a little as my fingers grazed his nipples, clearly he was sensitive there and I took great delight in grazing them one more time, just to see him squirm again.

But soon his squirm took on an urgency that I'd never experienced in my life before. No one, *no one*, had ever been this hungry and desperate for me. This pulling-at-clothes, fast-deep-kissing, hands-grabbing-and-squeezing desperate for me before. His breath came out in jagged little bursts, as did mine, as he fumbled with my T-shirt and started pulling it off and—

"Wait!" I pulled away from him suddenly, pulling my T-shirt back down. I'd been so swept up and away that I hadn't really remembered. *How had I not remembered?*

"What?" He crawled off me and sat back on his haunches, looking down at me. "Too fast?" he asked.

I nodded before I knew what was happening. Shit, I must be confusing him. I was clearly sending out a very mixed signal here. One minute I was telling him I wanted it, and then next I was telling him to stop. But I guess that's what happens when you let your brain take over.

"Are you okay?" he asked, looking very concerned.

"It's just . . . just . . ." I sat up and crossed my legs.

"What?" he whispered.

I shook my head. How did I get these words out of my mouth? How did I say this to him?

He leaned away from me. "You don't have to tell me. You don't have to give me a reason. We can just stop."

"I . . . I don't want to stop," I said, my voice shaking. "I do. But I don't."

There was a silence between us for a while and then I felt him stand up off the bed. I wanted to reach out and pull him back down, but didn't. I didn't look up at him either. But out of the corner of my eye, I could see he was pulling his shirt back on and then, I could see, he was adjusting something in his pants; he tried to hide this from me by turning around, but I saw. I straightened myself up and climbed off the bed too. Feeling a whole bunch of feelings, one of them being embarrassed.

"Do you want a cup of tea?" he asked.

I smiled. "You make tea a lot."

He shrugged. "My mum was British. Whenever we were upset or stressed, she would bring out tea. Said there was nothing a cuppa couldn't fix."

I nodded and we walked into the kitchen together. I sat at the table and watched him as he busied himself making the tea. He placed my cup down and then sat opposite me. I looked at the space in front of him.

"Where's yours?" I asked.

"I'm okay." He said that meaningfully, as if to imply I wasn't.

I lowered my mouth to the cup and sipped it slowly. It was warm and sweet and yes, it made me feel just a tiny bit better. But not much. I ran my fingers around the rim of the cup several times and then took a big, huge breath. A massive one. As if I was about to dive into a pool and swim an entire length underwater. I let all the breath out my body as I decided to tell him what was wrong. A knot tightened in my stomach, because I didn't really know how to get the words out, but I knew I wanted to.

CHAPTER 61

"So, you know how I told you I used to be . . . uh, big when I was younger?" I started slowly, forcing the words out of my mouth.

He nodded, rested his elbows on the table and leaned in. His body language told me he was engaged and listening to every word I was saying.

"I lost a lot of weight, right?" I said pointedly, hoping he would get where I was going with this and I wouldn't actually have to spell it out. Say the actual, difficult words. I still remember that night I'd said the words to Kyle. I still remember how he'd acted. It hadn't exactly been well received. Not that he said anything negative, but it was the way he looked at me after that, or didn't look, that left me feeling more insecure. Or the way that whenever we did have sex, I was never fully naked. Or the way he suggested I wear certain clothes when posting pictures, or pose a little differently.

Mark smiled at me. It was big and warm and genuine. "Well done. Not many people can do that, although I do still think you can eat a pancake from time to time."

"But you know what happens when you lose it, right?" I asked, taking another sip.

"What do you mean?" he replied, like he had no idea where I was going with this. He probably didn't. He didn't look like he'd been fat a day in his life.

"Uh . . . stuff kind of doesn't go back to the way it should be," I said softly.

"Stuff?" he asked.

I nodded.

"What stuff?"

"You know," I pressed. "Like . . . skin."

"Skin?" Still not getting it, clearly.

"It doesn't go back to the way it should be." I was starting to get a little frustrated now.

"How should it be?" he asked.

"Smooth. Stretch-mark free." I thought I was stating the obvious here.

"Who says it should look like that?" he asked.

"Uh . . . everyone," I said, blinking a little in disbelief.

He smiled. "Like everyone on Instagram? And maybe Kyle?"

"Well . . . yes!" I said.

Mark shrugged. "Well, I don't listen to what everyone says. I like to make up my own mind." He smiled at me, but I didn't smile back.

He leaned forward across the table. "To hell with what everyone thinks, Frankie. To hell with what Instagram and Facebook say and tell you to be and how to be it. To hell with all that crap. Isn't that what you told me a few days ago?"

I nodded a little. I had said that to him, which must mean that on some level I thought that too. For him though. Not for me.

"To hell with it?" I asked tentatively.

"And to hell with Tweeting some stupid opinion you have about something you barely know a thing about, and posting only the perfect pictures of yourself and waiting for people to like them before you like yourself and counting every single last one of your steps and seeing how many carbs are in a bagel and never getting a little lost because you're always on Google Maps. To hell with all of that." He paused for a while and then pulled my tea away from me and had a small sip. "It took me a while to learn that. To stop looking at what other people thought about me, for me to form my own opinion of myself." He passed the tea back to me and I sipped it too and nodded at him. A silence filled the room, and we sat in it for a while.

"Wait, did you stop me there in the bedroom from doing what I was planning on doing to you because you have stretch marks?" He sat back in his chair and ran his hands through his hair. It fell straight back to his face in that way that made me go a little crazy for him.

I nodded.

"Holy crap, Frankie, that's about as ridiculous as taking photos of breakfast and not eating it." And then he stood up and walked around the table towards me. I swallowed. Hard. He moved my chair and held out his hands for me to take. I looked down at them and hesitated, but then slipped them into his. He pulled me to my feet.

"Is that the only thing that stopped you?" he asked, almost sounding amused.

I nodded. "I didn't want you to take my clothes off and then . . . you know. Be disappointed."

"Who the hell would be disappointed?" He put his hands up to my face and held it, looking straight into my eyes.

"Well, my ex kind of was . . ." I trailed off.

"Your ex sounds like a total douchebag," he said. "And he was clearly an idiot too."

"Funny, you're not the only one who said that. My sister used to tell me that," I said.

"She sounds like a wise woman," he remarked.

"I had a boob job," I suddenly found myself saying. "A lift."

Mark blinked; I think he didn't know what to say. *Why had I even said that?*

"Kyle thought that—"

Mark held his hand up. "Kyle is a moron and I don't give a flying fuck what he thought." And then he reached out and kissed me again. This time, planting a soft, sweet kiss on my lips. "Besides," he pulled away from the kiss, "maybe I have a thing for stretch marks."

"Really?" I cringed.

"Maybe I have a thing for imperfections that make a person real, and not fake."

He kissed me again.

"Maybe I'm not into glossy appearances and performances and putting on a perfect show for everyone else. Maybe I'm into the opposite of all that." I could hear he was speaking from experience. "Maybe I've learned that physical appearances mean nothing. Not that I'm saying you aren't fucking gorgeous, which you are. But maybe smiling faces on posters and Instagram don't mean a thing. Maybe that's all a show and what I want is something real."

This time I kissed him. Fast and hungry and with so much wanting. He pulled away and smiled at me.

"So, can I take you back to my bedroom?" His smile was naughty and lusty and sexy as hell. In fact, he was just about the sexiest man I'd ever seen in my life. This scruffy version of him. This floppy-haired, stubbly, sometimes dirty-glasses-wearing guy. Not the perfect, polished guy that had hung on my wall as a teen.

I nodded and he pulled away from me and held his hand out. I slipped my fingers through his once more and they felt like they belonged there. I couldn't explain it, but my fingers really liked it there between his.

And with that, he led me slowly back into his bedroom. Back towards the promise of sex.

CHAPTER 62

*T*his time, everything was different. There was nothing fast and hungry and desperate about it. Instead, it was slow. We stood by the foot of the bed, eyes locked as he took his shirt off slowly and then dropped it back on the floor. He looked at my clothes and then raised a brow to me in question. The question was clear: *May I?*

I nodded, but reached behind me and pressed the light switch; the room went dark.

I felt Mark pull away from me, I heard a few footsteps, and then the light switched on again. I looked up at the light and then looked back down at Mark.

"I want to see you," he said softly, voice full of lust.

My heart beat a little faster from the nerves, but I nodded again. I didn't say anything else after that as he slowly reached down and took my hem in his hands and then, as if he was savoring the moment, he lifted the shirt up over my head and dropped it to the ground. He took a step back and his eyes drifted over me. My immediate reaction was to place my hands across my stomach, like I'd done with Kyle so many times before, or maybe put my shirt back on. But he shook his head at me and I resisted the urge.

"Beautiful," he said, and I could hear he meant it. The sound of desire was thick in his voice. He reached down and unbuttoned my jeans, and then pulled them, and the Spanx, down. He moved closer to me and kissed me again. First on the mouth, then on the neck, then down my neck. I moaned as the kisses worked their way down my chest, over my bra, stopping momentarily at my nipples. I groaned as he took one in his mouth through the fabric and pulled on it. And then he left my breast and kneeled down and started kissing my stomach. I gasped at the feeling—no one had kissed me there. No one had done that. His hands moved up to my ass and cupped it, and then he pulled me closer to him and, oh my God, he kissed me along my pantyline, and then his kisses moved further down. I held my breath for a moment, wondering if what I thought was about to happen was about to happen and then wondering those things you do in that moment like, *Shit, did I need to quickly have a shower? Did I need to wax?* My brain started thinking and working and . . .

"God!" I gasped and my brain immediately switched off the second I felt his fingers pull my panties aside and his tongue push its way in and give one slow, long lick.

He eased my legs apart with his hand, and with the other, pulled my panties all the way over—the feel of the elastic tugging against me gave a tiny little sensation of pain which only heightened my pleasure. His mouth was on me now. Slow and soft and every stroke deliberate and smooth. He definitely knew his way around, and he was taking his time. He was in no rush. I spread my legs a little more and looked down. Fuck, this was the hottest thing I'd ever seen before. Him kneeling on the ground with his head between my legs like this. I had to hold onto his head when I felt the feeling build. I had to grip his hair tightly in case I fell over as I shuddered. And when it was over and I was steady on my feet again, he stood up and our eyes met. I couldn't stop the stupid smile on my face.

"Well, that was . . ." I was breathy and smiley and giddy.

"Yeah, it fucking was," he said, sounding equally breathy. And then he pushed me back down onto the bed for the second time that night. And this time, I wasn't going to stop him. In fact, I was going to help him. My hands slipped between us and I tugged at the zipper of his jeans, and then pulled his underwear down, just enough for him to come bursting out. I wrapped a hand around him and he groaned against my mouth and moved his hips to push into my hand even more.

But soon, that wasn't enough. He reached for a condom by the side of his bed and I had a tiny moment of jealousy that hit me in the stomach, all cold and nauseous, as I wondered who that condom had been bought for. All the many conquests in town. It dawned on me, in that moment, that I better not expect anything out of this. He was clearly a player around town. *No expectations*, I said to myself. *No expectations*. But then he stopped. He raised himself up on his elbows and looked down at me. This time, he looked vulnerable. Much like I had a few moments ago in the kitchen.

"I don't do this often," he said to me.

"Okay," I said, not knowing how to respond.

"And when I do, I don't do it if I think it's going to be a one-off."

"Uh . . . okay." I wasn't sure what he was getting at here.

"I don't do one-night stands. That's not my thing . . . anymore." That last part gave me a little stab of jealousy again. Of course, he'd had one-night stands. Half the female population on the planet had wanted to sleep with him at some point. I bet he'd had groupies throwing themselves at him. Group sex. Orgies. Oh my God, stop thinking about that!

"I don't want this to be a one-time thing with you," he said. "If we do this, I would like to see where this thing between us goes. If that's okay with you?"

I smiled at him. God, he knew just what to say to make my heart beat fast and my chest constrict.

"Well, technically I am living here now," I said and then pulled him back down on top of me. "It would be hard to avoid you after this."

And that was all he needed. That was all we both needed. Because soon he was inside me and all thoughts went away. They flew out the window into the night sky outside. Swirled up to the Milky Way and through the stars and disappeared out of sight. His strokes were slow and deep and on each one, my breath came out in a little moan. He took his time. Kissing my lips and my neck as he went. But soon, he sped up. His thrusts were not as smooth and regular as they had been before and I could sense he was close. It felt amazing, all of it. It really, really did. But the truth was, I'd never been able to come just from sex alone. I was used to letting the guy finish like this, and I was always left wanting more. A more I didn't really seem to get. I guess I could have told them to help me a little, but I'd never really been that secure in bed that I could tell someone what I wanted and needed. So as much as this felt amazing with Mark, better than it had ever felt before, I knew I wasn't going to catch up to him, and he was clearly getting close. I could do what I did sometimes and fake it, but I didn't want him to feel like he wasn't performing, because fuck, he was. He really, really was but . . .

He slowed down. He pulled himself up onto his elbows and stopped moving inside me.

"What?" I gasped, looking into stormy black eyes.

He looked down at me for the longest time, as if he was trying to get a read on me. He brought his lips down to mine and instead of kissing me, whispered against my lips, "What do you need?"

No one had ever asked me this before. And the question was so strange that I barely knew how to answer it.

"I . . . I don't know," I finally conceded, my lips still against his mouth.

I could feel him smile against my mouth now and then in a low, almost-growl he whispered, "That's good. I'm going to have fun trying to work it out." He kissed me some more. He had completely stopped moving inside me and I was missing the feeling. But then, he rolled us both onto our sides, still inside me. He started moving again, and this time, he slipped his hand down between us and touched me at the same time. The sensation was instantaneous, mind-blowing, see-white-lights-at-the-back-of-my-eyes good.

"How's that?" he asked.

But I couldn't answer, the panting and moans that were coming out of my mouth made it impossible. He chuckled deep and low into the crook of my neck.

"That's all the answer I need," he said and pulled my earlobe into his mouth and sucked on it as he sped up. I writhed against him and moaned and for the first time ever, I was completely naked and I felt sexy as hell!

It was all so mindless after that. No thoughts, no more talking, no more kissing. It became this thing that was all about our bodies, and what they were doing and how they were making each other feel. My thoughts just shut off as the impossible started to happen deep in my belly. I grabbed onto the pillow in surprise as the feeling started growing inside me in steady waves. Rolling, swirling tides. I held onto the pillow for dear life as I came, he followed shortly after me, and when we were both done, we flopped into each other's arms. Satiated and sweaty and sticky.

"Well, that was . . ." I started talking and then giggled, which really hadn't been my intention, because who wants to giggle after the world's best sex? You want to be cool and sexy, but I was very uncool right now. I was all blushy and giggly.

"You're very cute after you come," Mark whispered to me. Oh crap! He was so cool after sex. "I'm going to have to do that again sometime soon."

My heart fluttered. My stomach clenched and I giggled even more. I put my hands to my mouth to stop the silliness, but Mark pulled them away and looked into my eyes.

"Don't," he said. "Don't be anything but you when you're with me."

His words stole the oxygen right out of my lungs. But then the moment was disturbed when we both heard a noise. We raised ourselves up on our elbows and looked in the direction of the noise. And there it was. Big and black and standing at the foot of the bed staring at us.

"Harun!" I scolded. "How long has he been there?" I picked up a pillow and tossed it at him. "Go away, we're naked!"

Mark laughed next to me and everything about this all felt so natural and right. Even down to that intrusive bloody hound!

CHAPTER 63

"*G*ood morning," I heard a voice whisper and I frightened awake. "What . . . who . . . OH!" I remembered. For a second there, when waking up, I'd actually forgotten where I was and, more importantly, what had happened the night before. But now that I remembered, I melted into the bed and let him wrap his arms around me.

"Morning," I whispered.

"Hi." His voice was low as he spoke against my neck, which caused the hairs to prickle from the warm vibration of his low, morning voice.

I giggled a little. "When I woke up, I kind of forgot where I was and what happened last night."

Mark stopped what he was doing and raised himself up on his elbow. He looked down at me with shock on his face.

"You forgot?"

I smiled at him and nodded.

"Wow! I am truly, madly, offended," he said, but he was smiling.

I laughed at the reference to his song lyrics.

"Was it that forgettable?" he asked, slipping his hand under the blanket and grazing it against my exposed breast. He pushed the blanket down and then kissed the place between my breasts.

"Well, was it?" he asked again.

"Mmmm," I moaned as he licked me. "I think I might need some reminding."

He pulled back and looked at me again. "Seriously? Seriously?"

He sounded incredulous now. "You need reminding, of that? Last night? What I did? Because I think I was rather good last night. Some of my best work, in fact."

I looked at him and laughed. "Yeah, you really 'worked it, worked it, worked it' last night."

Mark laughed now. "And I'm not going to ever live that down, am I?"

I shook my head. "Nope." I started singing, badly. "I'm gonna work it, work it, work it—"

"Babyyyy," Mark sang that word and I gasped and shook my head.

"I mean, I know it's you. But it really is you."

Mark hummed the song and I joined in.

"God, those songs were terrible," he said.

"Not to me. Not to millions and millions of adoring fans . . . Wait!" I raised myself up too and looked at him. "Wait, you must be really rich. Like seriously, seriously loaded. Like, Forbes rich list loaded. You guys sold like ten million albums!"

He smiled at me. A little coy, a little self-conscious.

"Is it totally rude to ask how much?"

"Totally rude."

"You know I can Google it, right?"

"I'd like to see you try," he teased.

"Maybe I'll walk all the way to the mountain and climb it."

He smiled at me for a moment, but then it faded slightly.

"I'm not being serious, you know that, right? I don't actually care how much you have, in case you think I do. I was just joking and curious for totally ridiculous reasons, because I've probably never been in the same room as someone so loaded," I quickly said, in case he thought that. "I really don't care. Really."

He shook his head. "I don't think that." He smiled at me, but I could still see it was a little forced.

I sat up fully in bed now and looked him in the eye. "You forget, I kissed you before I knew who you were. This . . ." I indicated the bed, "has nothing to do with who you were. Sure, I was a total groupie and I was insanely in lurrrrve with you when I was fourteen. And I probably fantasized about this moment right here a million times"—I blushed now just thinking about it—"but what happened last night has nothing to do with you being a part of a famous and totally hot boy band who I happened to be obsessed with once upon a time and have tattooed on my lower back."

I leaned in and kissed him, and he kissed me back, chuckling against my mouth.

"I hope not," he said, pulling away. "Most of my other relationships had something to do with that."

"I think I understand that. My last relationship was directly related to how many followers I had, and then didn't have."

"I hate your ex, by the way!" Mark said and I smiled.

"Thanks," I replied with an even bigger smile.

Mark paused. "Are you sure you're over him though?"

I thought about this for a while and, to be honest, Kyle breaking up with me seemed to have been the last thing on my mind this past week and a bit. I'd almost forgotten about it, and it made me wonder just how into him I really had been.

"I think with us, if I look back, our relationship was more of a business arrangement. I know that sounds ridiculous, but it was. It wasn't built on us, it was built on what we could give others. So yes, I'm over him," I said with a smile. "So, truly, madly, over him."

"Good." Mark kissed me. Long and slow and sexy. Threading his fingers through my hair and pushing me back down onto the bed. "Because I have a confession to make," he whispered against my mouth.

"What?" I asked.

"I kind of truly, madly, like you."

"You do?"

He stopped kissing me and pulled away again. "And when I say 'like you' I mean that in the real-life sense. No double-tapping, swiping-right stuff. Real like. In real life."

"Real life like."

"Exactly."

"I like you too," I said, pulling him back down and kissing him hard and fast now—I needed him. But then—

"HARUN!" I pushed him away as he came climbing onto the bed and pushed his way between us.

"Can I call him Satan's Little Helper now?" I asked Mark as he rolled around between us with his belly in the air, pushing us further and further apart.

Mark laughed. "You know you landed up with a lunatic dog, right?"

I looked down at Harun. Tongue out of mouth. One eye. Snaggle-tooth from hell. And then I reached down and scratched his belly. "Totally," I said, as he wiggled back and forth, scratching his back on the duvet.

An alarm clock beeped next to the bed and I looked at it. "I've got to get ready for work."

"Me too," Mark said, climbing out of the bed totally naked. God, he was yummy.

"You know," I said, thinking about it, "this is the first real job I've had in years."

"And how does it feel?"

"Good!" I nodded. "It feels good to actually be a part of something real, you know?"

Mark smiled. "I do know what you mean. Real life is actually more than it's cracked up to be."

"I guess it is." I smiled to myself, because I was feeling all warm and fuzzy inside. And it wasn't just because of Mark. It was also because of Samirah and Harun and my new job and new place in this town. I hadn't felt this connected in years, and ironically, it was the most disconnected I'd ever been.

CHAPTER 64

"*Y*ou look happy this morning," Samirah said. She'd been eyeing me suspiciously since I'd arrived.

I shrugged. Trying to act as casual as possible. But Samirah always seemed to have a knack for things like this.

"Not particularly," I finally said, trying to brush it off.

"Dottie's high-as-a-kite catnip cat has just vomited half a dead mouse on your shoe and you're still smiling from ear to ear like the Cheshire Cat!"

At that, I couldn't help but smile even more. But then I tried to hide my smile, something I shouldn't have attempted, because her eyes widened when I did.

She slid up to me suspiciously. "Is it Zack?" she asked.

"Zack! Wh . . . No! No. Not him."

"But everyone saw you on a date with him last night."

"What? How?"

"Small town. Get used to it. News spreads here like snotty germs at a kindergarten."

"Yuck!" I didn't think I liked her analogy that much.

"What else did people say?" I asked.

"They said it looked like you guys were really hitting it off. Lots of talking."

"He did most of the talking," I quickly corrected her. "Just to be clear about that, he talked, I was forced to listen."

"So, it didn't go well?"

"Not really," I conceded.

She folded her arms and looked me up and down. "Interesting."

"What?"

"This isn't the face and demeanor of someone who had a bad date. This is the face and the demeanor of someone who . . ." She gasped "Oh my God! You and Mark. *You and Mark!*"

"Shhhhhh," I hushed her.

She looked around. "Why would I shush? There's no one other than me to hear this. And it's not like it's a huge shock."

"Why isn't it a huge shock?" I asked, feeling a little warm in the cheek.

She clocked me and tilted her head to the side. "You told half the town that you saw him naked."

I pointed at her belly. "Can't babies hear you in utero? Isn't that a thing? You wouldn't want your babies to hear you talking about naked men now would you?"

She laughed. "That is great deflecting."

"I am not deflecting."

She eyed me. "So, are you guys a . . . *thing?*"

My face went bright red, and I started nodding.

She laughed at that and then leaned in some more. "Tell me everything!"

"Hey!" I held my hand up at her. "We are so not there in our relationship yet."

"Aren't we?" she asked, looking disappointed.

I shrugged. "I haven't really had many friends. In real life anyway. I'm not used to this."

"Well, get used to it. You're living in a very teeny-tiny town now. You sneeze, everyone knows about it and talks about it. Besides, I make a really good friend. You know what my name means?"

I shook my head.

"It means good companion."

I smiled at her. "I can see that."

"Besides, you probably won't be able to make too many other female friends around here, since most of the ladies in this town are going to be so jealous of you and Mark."

"Me and Mark . . ." I let those words hang in the air.

"You are a 'me and Mark,' right?" she asked.

I smiled. And then nodded. "I mean, I think so. He said he wanted to see where this went."

"I think it's great," Samirah said. Suddenly her landline rang and I jumped. I hadn't heard a phone ring in days, so the noise caught me off guard. She walked over to it. "I can see it. You and Mark!"

"You can?" I asked, as she picked up the phone.

She gave me a nod and then quickly added, "But then again, I saw it a mile away ages ago. And apparently so did Harun."

"You did?" I stepped forward, but she was talking to someone else now.

"Hello, this is Samirah." She listened intently to the caller and started nodding. "We can be there in about twenty minutes," she said and then clicked her fingers at me and pointed at a bag in the corner of the room. I rushed over and picked it up.

"Don't worry, Zack, we're on our way." She hung up and we sped into the house, where she grabbed her car keys.

"Wait, did you say Zack?" I asked. "As in Zack I went on a date with, Zack?"

"Yup. One of his sheep is having a problem delivering."

"Delivering what?"

She turned. "Its lamb."

"Oh! I see." I nodded. "And this is at Zack's farm?"

She smiled at me. "It's actually quite convenient, if you think about it."

"What is?"

"Well, you're going to have to tell Zack about you and Mark now, because maybe he thinks you guys are dating."

"Shit!" I looked at her and my eyes widened. "I hadn't thought of that."

Her smile grew. "I can see this is going to be an interesting delivery!"

CHAPTER 65

"I'm so glad you're here," Zack said as he ran up to the car.

"Where is she?" Samirah said, climbing out and doing her very pregnant version of a run.

"Here." Zack pointed and charged ahead. I followed behind them both with the bag Samirah had instructed me to bring.

"How long has she been in labor?" Samirah asked as Zack let us into her pen.

"I'm not sure, but the lamb is stuck. And my hands are too big, I can't get the leg out."

I stopped and gaped before I went in. The noise the sheep was making was one of the most awful I'd ever heard. It frightened me and made me question whether or not I could actually do this. Samirah shot me a look over her shoulder. "Come. It's okay," she said, as if she knew what I was thinking. I nodded and walked up to the sheep who was standing in the middle of the pen.

"Wh . . . what's that?" I pointed in horror as the sheep turned around.

"That's the lamb's head," Samirah said.

"Oh my . . . oh . . . gross!" I almost heaved when I saw it like that.

Zack gave me a sympathetic look, followed by a smile. "I know, first time you see it!"

"Help me get her to the ground," Samirah said.

Zack pulled the sheep down. It protested loudly but was finally on the floor.

"Help me down," Samirah said, clicking her fingers at me.

"Oh. Yes!" I rushed over to her and she grabbed my hand and after a few tries, she managed to get down to the ground next to the sheep.

"What do you do?" I stared in horror at the little, dead-looking face. "Is it even alive?"

"For now. But not for long." Samirah patted the ground next to her and I lowered myself.

"I need gloves," she said to me.

"Gloves!" I shook my head. This was all too much. The closest I'd ever come to a birth of any kind was watching that blogger online who had filmed her birth in a babbling brook in the forest, not the nitty-gritty parts though, and posted it; she had trended for the whole bloody week with her #spiritualbirth.

She held her hand out to me and I rummaged through the bag, until I found the gloves, but when she put them on, I turned away.

"I can't watch this! Oh my God!" The sheep seemed to agree and gave out a scream.

"Hold her down, Zack!" Samirah shouted. "And calm her, Frankie!"

"Calm her?" I asked.

"Go round and talk to her, this is going to hurt. She needs to keep calm."

"She's an animal, what shall I say to her?" I asked.

"If you still think they're just animals after everything you've been through with Harun . . ." She let the words hang in the air.

I thought about that for a moment. "Okay." I nodded in agreement. "I'll go talk to her."

I crawled around to the front of the sheep. Zack was holding her down while Samirah was busy with . . . *that*.

"Hi there," I said to the sheep's face. Her eyes were wide like saucers and she looked scared and in pain and my heart went out to her. I carefully laid my hand on her forehead and leaned in. "It's going to be okay. Samirah over there is a very good vet. She's also almost a mom and she's going to make sure your little baby lamb comes out all white as snow and stuff like that. You know?"

The ewe's eye drifted towards me, and I swear, it wasn't my imagination, she looked like she was actually listening to me.

"You know that song, right?" I patted her head again. "Mary had a little lamb, little lamb, little lamb. Mary had a little lamb her fleece was white as—"

"GOT IT!" Samirah suddenly shouted. The ewe gave one almighty bleat and then before I knew what was happening, Samirah was putting a wet-looking, lifeless lamb in front of the mother.

I gasped. "Is it dead?"

Samirah shook her head. "No. Wait and see."

"But it's not moving." I felt so panicked looking at that wet, lifeless little creature lying there.

"Just wait," Samirah said again.

The mother began licking the baby's head. I waited with bated breath and suddenly, the baby stirred and opened its eyes.

"It's alive!" I wrapped an arm around Samirah. "It's alive! You're amazing," I said, giving her a squeeze.

We stood there and watched as the mom licked the baby. Slowly and surely, it sprang to life, raising its little face and even moving its front feet around on the ground. I suddenly felt very emotional. Overcome with such a rush of joy that I felt tears spring to my eyes.

"It's beautiful," Zack said, coming up next to me. The three of us stood like that shoulder to shoulder and watched the mom and baby doing what could only be described as cuddling.

"It is," I said, and then turned to look at him. I expected him to be looking at the lamb but instead his eyes were glued to me. He had a look on his face and . . . *Oh dear.*

Samirah gave an awkward-sounding throat clear. "I'll just go to the car and wait," she said, walking away and leaving Zack and me all alone.

Zack turned to me. "What say we go for a drink to celebrate this tonight?"

Oh shit! I'd never done anything like this before, in person anyway. If an online date didn't work out, you never spoke to the person again, or had to see them again. You just swiped and blocked them. But now the person was standing in front of me, asking me out on another date.

He took a step closer and I shuffled back a little.

"Uh . . . thing is, Zack," I started. Oh crap, this was hard! Especially because he was looking at me like that, and he did have dimples! Mark didn't have dimples, but he was Mark and right now, all I wanted was Mark.

"Thing is?" he asked, looking at me as if he knew what was happening.

"Thing is . . . Mark and me," I said.

"Oh. I didn't know you two were?"

"We weren't. Not until, uh . . ."

"After our date?"

I cringed. That sounded so bad. I shrugged. "I, we, yes. After the date we just realized that we had feelings and we—"

"Feelings?"

I nodded. "I'm sorry. I didn't know it would be like that, or I would never have gone out with you."

I looked at Zack. I was waiting for him to say something. Something horrible. But I didn't mind what he said right now, as long as he ended this awkward moment.

But then Zack smiled. I blinked a few times.

"It's okay," he said.

"It is?" I asked.

"I mean, it's not great. Take a girl out on a date only for the other guy to slide in."

"He didn't slide," I quickly corrected.

He smiled. "Oh, he slid. Trust me. Mark is a slider." But he said it in a playful tone and I smiled back.

"You're not mad?" I asked.

"It was one date." He walked up to me and laid a hand on my shoulder. "It's cool. I kind of thought something was happening between you guys, or was going to happen, so I guess I walked into it knowingly."

"What? How?"

He laughed. "The guy practically challenged me to a duel when I came to ask you out," he said.

"He did?" I said, thinking back to the video store.

He looked down at the ewe again; the lamb was trying to stand up on its feet.

"It's cool. We're even. I can't be too angry with the woman who helped save my prize ewe and deliver her lamb."

"I suppose you can't," I said.

CHAPTER 66

I climbed back in the car, Samirah was busy disinfecting her hands and passed me a wipe. We sat in silence for a while, wiping our hands together.

"That was . . . *amazing*!" I said. "I mean, it was the most incredible thing I've ever seen or done before in my life. Legitimately, best thing I've ever done. Ever. Hands down!"

I looked at her and started laughing a little, only I was sort of crying too.

Samirah smiled at me. "Yeah, it's pretty awesome!"

"Thank you!" I said to her.

"It's a pleasure."

"No, I mean it. Thank you for giving me this job, for making me feel at home, for looking after Harun for . . . everything."

Samirah tilted her head to the side playfully. "Told you I was a good companion!"

I laughed. "You are!"

"Uuurgh." She reached down and grabbed her belly. "Not a good time to be kicking!"

"I can't believe you're going to go through that," I said, indicating out the window of the car.

"Well, hopefully not! I'm not planning on getting stuck halfway."

"God, can you imagine it!" I said.

And then Samirah did something that I'd never seen. She looked . . .

"Are you crying?" I turned in my seat.

She shook her head in fast movements. She bit her lip and then turned and looked at me with wet, shiny eyes.

"What's wrong?" I asked, feeling nervous. Samirah was always so calm and collected and seeing her like this unnerved me.

"I've seen thousands of animals give birth. It's the most natural thing in the world. I'm a doctor, and yet . . ." She paused and took a deep breath. "I'm completely scared, okay? I'm so scared to give birth! Is that wrong of me? I've wanted a baby for so long, and now that they're coming, I feel bad, because I'm more frightened of getting them out than them actually being out. Which just makes me feel like a terrible mother already and I haven't even become a mother yet. Which must make me a really, really terrible mom, right? I'm not technically even a mother yet and I'm already a bad one because a part of me just wants the babies to stay in there and not come out at all because I'm so scared of that part!" She was talking fast in a high-pitched panicked tone.

"No!" I reached out and put a hand on her shoulder. "You're going to be a great mom. Seriously great!"

"I don't know, Frankie. After what I just saw I feel like crossing my legs and never letting them out. That doesn't make me a very good mom, does it?"

I laughed now.

"This is not funny!" she said, but was also smiling.

"It is," I said, chuckling a little while I held onto her shoulder.

Samirah started chuckling too, a few tears rolling down her cheeks. We sat there in the car together and then, something amazing happened.

"Look." I pointed as the little lamb rose up onto its feet. The little lamb that *we* had just saved.

Samirah and I watched as it stood up on shaky legs and fell down. The mother nuzzled it, giving it encouragement. It tried again and fell again. It repeated this a few times until it was finally standing. Its little legs wobbled beneath it, shaking and trembling as it took its first steps.

I heard Samirah breathe out next to me and I swiveled in my seat to look at her.

"Think about that. First steps. First time they call you 'Mom.' First hugs and kisses."

Samirah smiled. "Yeah, it's going to be pretty amazing, right?"

"It is. And Faizel is going to be a great dad too."

"He is." She seemed much more relaxed now. Smiling from ear to ear.

"Just get the hard part over and done with, make sure you get a big epidural, and after that, it's going to be amazing."

"Sounds like you want kids one day?" Samirah asked.

I shook my head. "I've never really thought about it before. My mother wasn't the best mom. She tried, I guess. She did her best. She worked really hard to put food on the table and to pay school fees, but she was very critical of me, you could say. She treated my sister and me very differently, as if my sister was better than me or something."

Samirah looked at me for the longest time. "It makes sense then that you would go looking for admiration and affirmation online from strangers," she said quietly.

I smiled at her. "Are you a psychologist too?"

She shook her head. "No, I'm not. But for the record, you'd make a great mom."

"Nah, I don't think so."

"Look how you took care of Harun, you're maternal!"

I smiled wryly. "Trust me, that surprised me."

"I'm sure a lot of things have surprised you lately," she said in that mysterious, sagey voice of hers again.

There was a pause in the conversation. A serious one.

"Can I ask you something?" Samirah enquired in a soft voice.

"I guess."

"What were you thinking about at meditation?"

"Um . . ." I paused for a while before I spoke. Trying to figure out whether or not to tell her. I met her green eyes and she gave me one of those kind smiles of hers, the kind that you knew meant she cared. And I knew I could tell her. "I was thinking about when I was younger how I was bullied a lot. The kids teased me nonstop because I was much bigger than I am now and it was . . . *awful*."

A meaningful silence filled the car.

"That kind of thing really stays with you." Samirah broke the silence.

"You too?" I asked.

"Try being a darker-skinned Muslim girl at a mainly white school."

We looked at each other for a while; it didn't feel like we needed to say more. Explain further. We each understood being treated as an outsider in our own ways.

She gave me a smile. "You know, my mother used to say to me that true beauty is defined by how we treat each other, it has nothing to do with what we look like on the outside."

"Wow. I wish someone had told me that when I was growing up," I said. "Things might have been different for me."

"Things were exactly how they were supposed to be," Samirah said.

"What do you mean?" I raised my brows at her.

"You were meant to go through what you went through, because it made you stronger," she declared.

"Did it? Really?"

"Well, look at you. Leaving all that crap behind. Independent woman in a new town with a new job, starting a new adventure."

I nodded. "I hadn't thought about it like that. I sort of just thought I was running away in fear."

"You did in the beginning. But look at you now, you're running towards something unknown, fearlessly. You just helped a sheep give birth!"

"I guess I did." I beamed at her. "We've totally become friends, haven't we?"

She placed her hand on my shoulder and gave me a squeeze this time. "Totally. And I didn't even officially friend you or like one of your posts!"

Her words, although said in an irreverent way, held more weight than I think she knew. Because when I thought about it, Samirah was the first friend that I'd made offline in years. We hadn't agreed to be friends by clicking a button and sending thumbs ups and hearts each other's way. It had just happened naturally, and it was real. More real than anything I'd had in years. Maybe ever.

I thought about my other so-called friends, who'd all abandoned me when I'd needed them most, ghosted me when I'd reached out . . . Real friends don't do that. Only fake ones.

Fake friends and a fake life.

I was starting to think that, the longer I stayed here. Because when you do something real, like save a baby lamb, it puts things into perspective. It really highlights what's real and what's not. Real was over there in that pen, jumping about on its new legs with glee. Real was sitting next to me in this car, trusting me enough to tell me her deepest fears.

That was real.

The other stuff—@TheKyleWhite101, #powercouple, @FitspoFrankie —well, I was starting to think that wasn't.

CHAPTER 67

*W*e woke up together in Mark's bed the next morning, and the next morning, and the morning after that, until a whole week of waking together had gone by. We would have breakfast together at the kitchen table, with Harun looking on, hoping to steal something off our plates when we weren't looking. Turned out Mark was also a coffee connoisseur and each morning he would brew me a different blend. And after breakfast on most mornings, we grabbed a shower together and had hot, wet, sometimes very clumsy shower sex. And after that, Mark would drive me into town and drop me off at Samirah's and he would go off to the store. And everything about that was perfect!

The pace of life here was slow and lazy and many days we would simply be off work for the whole afternoon and find ourselves with nothing to do but lie in bed, talking and reading and watching Mark's favorite movies while I got a crash course in cinema and music. I watched and enjoyed movies that I never thought possible, even ones in black and white. We'd settled into this comfortable, effortless way of falling into bed at night, making love, waking up and then, after work, taking Harun on long walks through the desert followed by gin on the veranda, followed by talking late into the night and playing board games by candlelight when the electricity went out, which was pretty often. We even did quiz night and I officially joined Risky Quizzness. It was such fun. Turns out I have a serious gift for general knowledge, all that endless Googling and my need to know everything had finally come in handy! I was amazed by how much fun I was having without my phone and online life. I hadn't thought about it once or craved it. For the first time in a long time, my life was balanced in a way it had never been balanced before. Work, friends, alone time, exercise.

Our routine began to feel so normal and natural. These weeks had completely changed my life, and I was really starting to feel a part of something. I'd also gone to book club, after being asked by Natasha for the hundredth time while doing my grocery shopping. I had gone back to meditation, and had a much more successful attempt at it; I'd popped round one afternoon to share a coffee with Logan at the hotel restaurant; and to top it all off I'd bought a box of dye and dyed my hair brown to match the roots that were showing. And what really surprised me was how much I loved it! I also found myself going for long jogs in the desert, exercising for no reason other than I enjoyed it. I hadn't really enjoyed exercise in years, despite the fact I had been @FitspoFrankie. I exercised this time not to track it and log it and post about it, but for me, and me alone.

My days felt so full of stuff now. Real stuff. With real people. I'd even discovered my love of reading again. I hadn't read in years. I had associated it with the lonely time, but now I was enjoying those moments alone where I could get lost in a book.

But the highlight of the week was definitely the rehearsal for the festival. And I must admit that, as much as I was rolling my eyes about this whole thing, I was actually enjoying it. There was this sense of community and camaraderie that I'd never experienced in real life before. And it was far better than anything I'd ever experienced online. Sure, the whole thing was completely ridiculous if you had to zoom out and look from the outside. A motley group of us walking down Main Street, trying to reenact scenes from this great trek that the Ackerman family had taken to get here. Ian and I were also getting along well, despite our shaky start. He'd spent extra time working with me, teaching me the moves I needed to perform when fighting off the jackal with a stick. I'd laughed the entire time he was teaching me, but laughed even more when Faizel let go of the sheep he was meant to be herding, who then made a bolt for it. He chased the thing down the main road for ages before finally catching up to it, drenched in sweat. But what was really nice about the rehearsals was that I was meeting people and was starting to feel at home in this small place. I was making connections here. Little dots in my life were being joined together to form a web of things that I hadn't known I'd wanted, until now.

And at work I was learning so much from Samirah. It had been great, except for that day when a stray feral kitten had come in. It had been picked up on the side of the road and Samirah had spent an hour on the phone, calling people in town and asking them if anyone wanted a kitten, then she'd called the SPCA which was three hours away, but they were sadly full. She'd even contemplated keeping it herself, but couldn't, what with her five dogs. I'd then offered to take it home, only to discover that Mark was deathly allergic to cats—red-faced, gasping-for-air allergic—and I'd had to run him to the town doctor for a shot of strong antihistamines. By the end of the day, after trying absolutely everything to home it, we were left with no other option. I'd cried the entire time. So had Samirah. And, when it was over, we'd sat on the veranda drinking tea and talking for hours about the sanctuary she wanted to start, so that kittens like this one could get a chance at life. I'd gone home that night and cried while Mark had held and comforted me.

And then, before I knew it, another week rolled past. Another week that Mark and I spent together, another week with Samirah, another week I'd spent submerging myself in the town and all its strange happenings. But this weekend was different. We couldn't go fynbos picking and gin making, because on Sunday it was the festival. And today we had to go and try on our costumes.

CHAPTER 68

"*S*eriously, is this it?" I asked, looking at myself in the mirror. "This is it?" I turned around to get a better look at myself. My dress was long and heavy, hanging all the way to the ground. My feet were squeezed into pointy boots that were more uncomfortable than heels, and I was wearing a bonnet that, when I looked at it, I couldn't help but say "Under his eye" in my head. I looked terrible. But Mark looked worse in that long jacket with the puffy shoulders that made him seem like he didn't have a neck.

"What the hell?" I burst out laughing when I saw him. "We look terrible."

Mark smiled at me. "Nah, I think you look sexy as hell." I laughed as he walked over to me and laid a hand on my waist.

"Back off, I still need to pin her in." Ian came over with a pin and pushed Mark away. "But before I pin you in, you need something else."

"What?"

"Here." He passed me a small cushion.

"What's this for?"

"Margaret was pregnant." He put a hand on his hip, holding the cushion out for me.

I laughed and shook my head. "No. I draw the line at that."

"This is a true-to-life reenactment!" He sounded like he was getting worked up again. Truthfully, these last weeks spent with him, I was really starting to appreciate him. Sure, his obsession with this yearly reenactment was perhaps a bit much, but I guess it showed passion. He had a passion for his town and its history and heritage. So did everyone here. Everyone who lived in this town seemed to have a deep connection with it, and they wanted to celebrate that. So, bearing that in mind, I guessed I could shove a cushion down my dress.

"Fine," I conceded. "But don't make me look like I'm fat!"

"Honey, you could never look fat," he said to me and I smiled to myself, because that just wasn't true.

"Okay, wait here, I'm coming back with more pins," Ian said, passing me the cushion.

I took it, maneuvered it to my stomach area and looked down. I hadn't seen myself like that for years and a little feeling started nibbling at me.

"God, you look hot," Mark said, obviously picking up on my thoughts. He came up to me and kissed me. I totally melted into it. The kiss started to escalate and soon it felt like one of those kisses that needed to end with something other than *just* a kiss.

"Come." Mark dragged me by the hand into one of the small changing rooms. He closed the curtain and pushed me up against the wall. The kisses became hot, heavy and thick with passion. I giggled against his mouth.

"We can't do this here," I whispered. "I'm getting pinned."

"To the wall." He pushed my arms behind my head into the wall, and I gasped.

"Shhhhh," he whispered, bringing his lips down to my neck, only to realize none of my neck was available to kiss. He pulled at the tight, high-necked dress I was wearing.

"Crap, this thing is . . ."

"Not designed for making out," I added.

"NO!" He abandoned my neck, reached down and tried to get under my collar. But the ruffles and layers made it impossible.

"Holy crap, how many layers are there? They are so heavy."

I giggled more as he tried, with both hands, to pull the layers of the dress up.

"There is too much of this stuuuufffff," he moaned, giving up and then turning his attention to my top. He eyed it and then just reached out and put his hands over my boobs. I laughed.

"Can you even feel that?" he asked.

I shook my head. "No."

He squeezed. "This?"

"Nope."

"How many layers are under here?"

"A lot."

"No wonder everyone was so chaste in those days—it's not that they weren't having sex, it was that they couldn't!"

I pulled him in for another kiss. "Thanks for trying," I said.

"Pleasure."

"HEY!" We heard a voice from outside. "You guys better not be doing what I think you're doing in there."

Mark pulled the curtain aside. "No such luck."

"Well, I should hope not. You know people actually have to wear those clothes again next year," Ian said with an amused smile. "Come on, I need to pin you."

I sighed and walked back into the room. Ian and I then spent the next few minutes pinning me into my dress. Mark sat in the corner and watched me with eyes that were so dark and filled with lust, they kept making me blush, and because of that, I had to keep looking away.

Ian laughed. "You guys," he said.

"What?" I asked.

He sighed. "What can I say, young love is a hot and heavy thing."

Love.

The word seemed to hang in the air and made us both uneasy.

"Ooops." He stopped and glanced from Mark to me and back again. "You haven't gone there yet, the whole *love* thing. Have you?"

Mark and I looked away, and kept very silent.

"Oh dear, seems like I put my foot in my mouth." Ian stood up and backed away from us. "Sorry for making things awkward," he said, but he was smiling, as if that had been his intention all along.

Mark and I finally gazed up at each other again and I held my breath. It dawned on me that we hadn't really discussed what was going on between us. We'd just fallen into this routine and relationship without actually defining what it was, or asking where it was going. It felt good, but were we still just seeing where this would go, like Mark had said that first night together? Or were we past the "just seeing" and had we arrived at the "seen" bit?

I turned my attention to my dress. This was probably something we should talk about at some point.

CHAPTER 69

*W*e woke up on Sunday morning to the sudden, violent scream of the bloody alarm. It sent us both flying out the bed; falling and jumping and tumbling. Our alarm hadn't been set for this early in, well, ever.

We raced through showers, breakfast and scrambled into our outfits. When we were done, for the first time since waking up, a small, calm silence settled between us. Memories from the other day, from trying on our costumes, came back to me. I think they must have come back to Mark too, because he was looking at me in the exact way that I was looking at him. Harun was watching us from his perch on the sofa. As if waiting for us to do something, or speak.

"You look . . ." I started, then stopped.

Mark nodded. "You too."

I smiled. "How do you know I wasn't going to say you looked ridiculous?"

He smiled back. "I'm pretty sure you were."

"Hang on, I thought you said I looked sexy in this." I paused. "Remember, you said that, when we were trying these on?" Hint alert. Me steering the conversation very deliberately, and I don't think very subtly either. At least I hadn't come out and said, *Remember what Ian said about young love! Hahah! So funny . . . But do you? Love me? Do you? Cos I think I might be falling for you . . .*

I waited for Mark to speak. But I think he was waiting for me, because he raised his brows. I raised mine right back, and I think I heard an exasperated sigh coming from the peanut gallery on the sofa.

"We better get going?" Mark said. It sounded like a question. What was he asking? Would you rather stay here and cuddle and tell each other how we were both falling in love?

"Sure. If you think so?" I asked straight back, popping the ball in his court again.

He nodded. "Well, we can't be late. Especially since you are the star of the show," he added jokingly.

I shrugged. "I can't believe it. I've only been in town for three weeks." Double hint. So pointed. Telling him how long I'd been here.

"Really?" He sounded surprised.

"We met three weeks ago," I said very pointedly.

"Feels like longer," Mark replied, with a smile.

"Does it?" I asked.

And then, he walked up to me. Slow strides. This was it. The moment I was waiting for us to share. We had spent every single day together for more than two weeks, one of which had been spent almost entirely in bed—it was time to say how we felt. I could feel it on the tip of my tongue, desperate to come out. And I wanted to hear it from him too. I mean, I felt it. I felt it when he kissed me and held my hand and we made love, but I wanted to hear the words. Hear that he was feeling for me what I was feeling for him.

But he didn't say anything. Instead, he kissed me. It was an amazing kiss. It made my limbs weak and my chest flutter with a fast breathlessness and I could sense that he was putting his words into the kiss. I could feel them. But . . . I also wanted to hear them.

* * *

The whole town had gathered at the church at the end of the main road. The atmosphere was electric and everyone was in high spirits. Many of us were in costume, ready to reenact the great trek that the family made when they found this little place and settled down. It was rather miraculous, actually, a family walking for weeks through the desert with all their livestock and everything they owned in the entire world, looking for water and a new home. When you thought about it, this entire town had been built on the back of the bravery and determination of one family.

Faizel was there with his sheep. An old ox wagon had been pulled out of storage, two horses tied to it, ready to pull it down the road in the procession. The streets were lined with residents who were not a part of the reenactment, and for the first time since arriving, I saw the 1950s couple. God, they really were cool and gorgeous. They looked like they had just stepped out of another era. She was wearing a red, polka dot, retro dress with a really cinched waist. Her hair was bleached blonde like Marilyn Monroe and it was piled on her head in huge curls that looked like they wouldn't move, even in a gale-force wind. Red lips, gorgeous cat-eye glasses and pushing a baby in a vintage pram. Her husband looked like he'd walked off the set of *Mad Men*. A dapper suit and tie, with a red triangle of fabric peeping out of his jacket pocket. They looked amazing, and I could see why living in a place like this would suit them. I scanned the crowd further, and there she was: the reclusive writer with her sharp, bobbed black hair and black-framed glasses that really stood out against her pale skin, which looked like it never saw the sun. She was wearing black. From head to toe, and to be honest, a cloud of misery hung around her head. Perhaps that was just her artistic persona? The somber, brilliant reclusive writer, who brought masterpieces into the world every decade or so. I saw Jim and Natasha standing there on the side, giving me a massive wave and a thumbs up. This was nice, I admit. It was really good to feel part of something like this, even if it was still possibly—no, definitely—the silliest thing I had ever done before. Although, Samirah and Mark might point out that taking photos of my breakfast and not eating it was probably sillier.

"You ready?" Mark whispered in my ear.

"Uh . . . I guess. I mean, I'm not totally sure what I'm meant to do."

"Don't worry, no one really knows what they're meant to do. We basically just all walk down this road to the spring and have a big party."

"So why did we rehearse all that stuff?" I asked.

Mark shrugged. "For fun, I guess." He smiled at me. And I kind of got it. This wasn't really about being historically accurate, no matter how much Ian said it was and how much we were all dressed up. This was really just an excuse for the whole town to come together in celebration. And honestly, this place and its people were something to celebrate.

CHAPTER 70

The atmosphere in the crowd as we all walked down the street together was amazing, fun and funny and so full of joy. And when we came to the part of the road where everyone was meant to stop and I was meant to step out of the procession and say my few lines and swing my giant stick around, recreating this mystical jackal fight, I was more than happy to do it. Even though I giggled all the way through. But the crowd loved it, everyone burst into applause and then we all started walking again. Faizel's part was next, when he reenacted the moment when he chased the Ackermans off his land. And within half an hour, we were all at the end of the road, walking towards the spring that the town was named after.

Even though I'd been here for a few weeks, I'd actually never seen it before. And when I did, I finally got why the Ackermans were so thrilled to have found it. It really was like an oasis in the desert. In the middle of all the sand and dust and dryness was a cluster of huge rocks. They looked out of place, as if dropped from the sky. In between the rocks, as if they were holding it all in, was a pool of bright green water. Perhaps the brightest and greenest water I'd ever seen. It was hard to imagine how this little miracle of water had happened out here, but it had.

"And now for the—" Ian's voice shouted at us, but he stopped abruptly when there came a loud and unfamiliar noise. We all turned our heads: it sounded like cars. Many, many cars.

And it was. *Where had all those cars come from?* And those vans? I counted five cars and two vans and they were coming towards us. Everyone was watching in utter confused horror as the cars finally came to a stop and people started pouring out of them. I looked at them all, trying to figure out what was going on. And that's when I saw it. It looked strange and out of place and so furry-mammal-in-the-zoo. *People walking towards us with cell phones in the air.*

"What the hell?" I heard someone near me say.

"What's going on?" someone else said.

And then, out of the crowd, a face appeared and I recognized it immediately. I blinked several times, fast, because I wasn't sure I could believe what I was seeing.

"Oh my God, Jess! What are you doing here?" I said, as my sister came running up to me. But she didn't say a word, not one, until she got all the way to me and threw her arms around me. Why was she hugging me like this?

"Frankie! Frankie!" she said into my shoulder. Wait, was she crying? And why was she calling me Frankie?

"I'm here," I mumbled, totally taken aback by this strange show of emotion. She pulled away from me, grabbing onto my shoulders, tears in her eyes.

"We've been so worried about you."

"You have?" I asked, unsure of who the "we" was.

"And I'm so sorry," she gushed. "I am so, so sorry."

"For what?" I asked.

"That day you called me, I should have listened to you. You were going through something and I shouldn't have brushed it off. I'm so sorry. Maybe if I'd listened to you and tried to understand, you wouldn't have disappeared."

I smiled at her. "It wasn't that that made me leave," I said to her.

"Oh God, I've been so worried about you. We filed a missing person report with the police but they said you were an adult and that you'd probably just gone off. We didn't know where you were or what to do and then Kyle—"

"Kyle?" I cut her off. "What about Kyle?"

"He's the one who found you. He hired a private investigator who tracked your phone to your last known location and came here and found you."

"Who came here?" I asked.

"The private investigator. He took photos of you and brought them back. I was so relieved when I saw them. I had started to think that maybe you were . . ." She burst into tears now. "That you were . . ." She sobbed and covered her face. "I was just so happy to see you were alive."

"Wait, you thought I was dead?"

She nodded, biting her lip. Fighting the tears.

"Kyle hired a private investigator to find me?" I asked, still struggling to take this in.

My sister smiled at me through her tears. "Maybe I was wrong about him," she said. "He really loves you, it's not all for show."

I shook my head. "No, trust me, you've been right about him this whole time. Everything he does is for show and I don't think he ever really . . . uh . . . KYLE?" I exclaimed, when I saw him over my sister's shoulder walking towards me.

"Frankie!" he said loudly, and then he turned to the person who was walking next to him. "Are you getting this?" he asked. The guy next to him nodded.

What the hell?

And then he started running towards me, dramatically. I looked over at Mark and Samirah and everybody around me and shrugged. They all shrugged back as general confusion fell on all of us.

"Frankie!" My sister stepped out the way as Kyle and his cronies were now right in front of me.

"Kyle. Wh-what the hell is going on here?"

"What's going on here is that we are live streaming this to one million people around the world."

"Live streaming what?" I looked around, completely confused.

"Hashtag Find Frankie. And we found you!" He turned to the guy who was holding the phone and spoke directly into it. "And thank you to Huntsman Private Eyes, for helping in the search. If you are looking to find someone you love, look no further than Huntsman. Your hunt is their business." He shot the phone a huge, supermassive Explosive™ smile.

"Uh . . ." I gaped at that. It sounded like an advertising slogan. "What the actual fuck?" I mumbled to myself, but I think a few people heard me. I looked over at my sister in horror—she was smiling at me. This was all so strange. I felt like I was still asleep and dreaming. This couldn't be real, could it?

And then Kyle turned back to me and his very false-looking, bright white, veneered smile waned. (Had his smile always been this fake-looking, or was I only noticing it now?)

He looked me up and down. "What the hell are you wearing? What's wrong with your hair? Wait, have these people kidnapped you and . . ." He turned back to the guy with the phone and started talking directly into it again. "Well, I found her, but she's wearing some really weird clothes, everyone is, and this looks a little culty. If you're watching this and you know anything about cults, put your thoughts in the comment section below and hit me up and let me know what you think's going on here."

"Wait! What is going on here?" I shouted. "And how do you have the internet?"

He turned to the camera again. "And thank you to our internet partner, WebActive, who donated one of their state-of-the-art satellites for us to get internet to this remote part of the world. No part of the world should be disconnected, so trust WebActive to keep you connected."

Logan stepped forward now, looking big and intimidating. "Do you know it's illegal to use the internet here? It interferes with the ASO satellites."

"Kyle, you can't do that. You heard him. It's illegal," I said, in a pleading tone.

Kyle looked back at the camera. "Definitely some kind of cult, but the important part, the part that you've all been waiting for, is that we have found Frankie and I couldn't have done it without you all. All my new followers who supported me through this time and gave me helpful suggestions and strength." Kyle walked straight up to me and pulled me into his arms, giving me a huge hug. He held on so tightly that I felt crushed.

"You've put on so much weight," he whispered into my ear. "But you can lose it again. It will make for great content too. Your weight loss journey."

I pushed him away. "Kyle . . . What . . . Why . . . It's . . ." I was struggling to get the words out. This situation was wordless. I didn't think I had any at all. "What about Paige?" I finally managed to say.

Kyle hung his head, then turned to the camera guy and indicated for him to come closer. Then he looked back at me. "I'm sorry, Frankie. That was a mistake. The worst mistake I've ever made. I have already shared that with all our followers, and they have reached out and forgiven me and told me that the only way to make it right was to come here and find you and bring you home. And so, that's what I'm doing. Bringing you home. To me. And to our millions of followers."

My mouth dropped open. "Millions?"

He nodded. And now it genuinely looked like he had tears in his eyes. And it had nothing to do with finding me. "I know. It's what we always wanted. It's what we've worked so hard for, and now we have it."

I shook my head in disbelief. "Millions. Millions of people?"

"Look." He passed me his phone and I started scrolling through our social media accounts. The phone felt good in my hand. As if my hand had missed it. My fingers moved instinctively over the keys like they knew how to do this in their sleep.

Instagram: 560,000 followers.

Twitter: 150,000 the hashtag #FindFrankie trending.

Snapchat: 334,000.

My vlog on YouTube . . . Fucking trending!

Facebook: Live video, 1,098,987 people watching . . . Right now!

My eyes widened and I looked at him. And, for a second, everything came back to me.

I wanted to be a somebody. A real somebody. And now I was.

Kyle nodded at me. "I know. It's everything we ever dreamed of."

I found myself nodding a little. My head just did it, even if I wasn't sure I wanted to. Well, maybe there was a part of me that wanted this. Millions of followers! Millions of people thought I was somebody. Millions of people had tuned in to find me and had been worried about me and wondering where I was and . . .

"Oh my God, what the hell is that?" Kyle took a step back as Harun stepped forward and started growling at him.

"Harun. Stop!" I put my hand on his head and tried to calm him, but he continued to growl at Kyle.

"What the hell is that?" Kyle looked repulsed.

"It's my dog," I said.

Kyle looked at him for a while. "It's the ugliest dog I've ever seen in my life . . ." And then he stopped talking and stared at Harun for a long time. Then he pulled his phone out and started looking for something. When he'd found it, he held his phone up to me.

"Ugly dogs of Insta. It's not a massive hashtag, but it's popular. We could totally make a profile for him, we could make him the most popular ugly dog on the internet, it's actually . . . Jesus, it's genius if you think about it. Everyone likes an underdog and this," he indicated Harun, "this is an underdog if I ever saw one. Imagine the memes we could start. They would go viral." I looked over at my sister again and started shaking my head at her in utter disbelief. Had Kyle always been like this? She looked about as confused as I felt right now.

Kyle took a step closer to Harun and this time, Harun's growl became a bark. Kyle stepped back and clicked his fingers at someone, a girl wearing a strange pink plastic dress. "Take some pics of him. Get him an IG account. Let's get the ball rolling."

I looked at the woman he was talking to. Young, pretty, lilac hair, contoured face, matt lips.

"Who is that?" I asked.

"This is Andy, she's our new social media manager."

"Heeeeyyyy." Andy dragged the word out as if she had no energy to use her voice and lips and actually make words with them.

I turned back to Kyle and looked at him in disbelief. "We have a—"

"Social media manager," he blurted, not hiding his excitement. "We've made it, Frankie. We've made it. And now there is only one thing left to do . . ." He turned again and looked into the camera. "All you guys, my amazing fans, took a poll and 95 percent of you agreed that I should do this, and so, I am . . ." He turned back to me and then started dropping to his knee.

"Wait . . . What are you . . .?" I looked around, shocked. The entire town was here and they were all looking at me. And Mark was looking at me too. He looked pale and strange and I didn't know what to do. I felt backed into a corner with Kyle down on one knee and phones in my face.

I turned back to Kyle. "Don't . . ." I shook my head. "Don't."

"Frankie . . ." He looked up at me and smiled. This big, put-on smile. I looked around again, everyone was still watching. Everyone. Mark and Zack and Samirah and Faizel and my sister and Logan, and, and . . . *I was completely overwhelmed.* I wanted to turn and run, but couldn't.

Mark and I made eye contact and he shook his head, and then hung it.

"Ma—" I made a move for him, but Kyle grabbed my hand and pulled me towards him.

"In front of you and all our fans who are watching this . . ." Kyle reached into his pocket and pulled out a ring box. He held it in the air and then turned to face the camera again.

"And of course, I would like to thank Shimany Jewelers for this amazing three carat sapphire ring, you can find a link to their website below this video, use the promo code #Frankieisfound to get a 10 percent discount off your purchase."

"Wait! Wait!" I waved my hands in front of me. "Time out. Time out!" I made a big "T" in the air.

"Finally," I heard Samirah say. "You let that go on long enough."

"Hear, hear," Faizel said. And then, a general "hear, hear" bubbled up from the people around me. *My people.*

The people who I'd gotten to know and care about over these last few weeks. Who had all welcomed me in—well, not necessarily at first, but now dressed in these silly clothes, surrounded by them all, I kind of felt a part of a community. IRL!

A living, breathing community that didn't meet online and slide into your DMs and WhatsApp group. And with them all standing behind me and my sister now looking down at Kyle in utter disgust, I felt strong enough to do what I was about to do. What I needed to do. And should have done two years ago.

CHAPTER 71

"*K*yle!" I exclaimed loudly, as he gripped my hand tightly in his and looked up at me from that ridiculous bent knee.

"Frankie," he said in a sickly sweet voice that made me feel a little nauseous.

"Get up off the floor." I tugged at his arm and tried to pull him up, but he didn't budge.

He gritted his teeth and spoke like a ventriloquist in a hissed voice. "What are you doing?"

"I'm asking you to get up off your knee and put that ridiculous three-carat whatever away." I pulled my hand again and managed to extricate it from his grip.

Kyle gave a nervous giggle and then turned to one of the phones that was right in our face. "She's just . . . taken aback," he said, and then smiled into the phone.

"Yes! I am taken aback," I said. "That's a good way to put it." I folded my arms and took a step away from Kyle.

He smiled at me and turned to the camera again. "She just needs a moment. God only knows what she's been through these last few weeks. I'm sure it's been very traumatic. If any of you have been through a similar experience, let me know in the comments and tell me how you dealt with it."

"WHAT are you GOING on about, KYLE?" I threw my arms in the air getting frustrated. "I am not traumatized. I wasn't kidnapped. I have not been abducted by a strange cult. I am here by choice!"

Kyle shook his head tightly at me, as if he didn't want anyone to see. "You don't know what you're saying," he said.

I laughed. "Kyle, I know exactly what I'm saying. Today, I know more about what I'm saying than I did weeks ago when I wanted to say something." I stopped talking and thought about that sentence. That didn't exactly make sense and I could see a few people around me scrunching up their faces as they too tried to work that out.

"What I mean is, I am perfectly sane right now. More than I've ever been before. And everything is so clear to me now too."

He blinked a few times as if he was very confused. "What's clear?"

"Get up, get up, get up." I walked over to him again and pulled him to his feet. "And put that thing away." I pointed at the ring box that he was holding in his hands. "I am not going to marry you, Kyle. And if you really take a moment to think about it, you don't want to marry me either. Really marry me. You want to marry me because it makes good content and hundreds of thousands of people took a poll and told you to do it!" I spat the words out and Kyle looked at me as if I was mad. "Kyle . . . you and I, what we had, it's not real, is it?" My voice got a little softer and gentler, but this only made the cameras come in closer. I tried to swat a few away with my hands as if they were flies.

"What we had was a business arrangement, not a relationship. It was for show. For everyone else. We never did anything just for us. There was no 'us,' Kyle. It was all about *them*." I pointed at the cameras now.

Kyle looked confused. Poor guy. It was clear he had no idea what I meant. He clearly had no idea how a real relationship or friendship worked, and I did. I'd had the privilege of experiencing that these last few weeks.

"Kyle, you don't love me. You love the likes."

"I . . . I . . . do love you, Frankie," he said, more to the camera than to me, which made me see that he was still playing for all the viewers. Was he even capable of being real? Having a real conversation? For a moment? Maybe I needed to take a different approach.

"You made me get a boob job!" I pointed at him and everyone around me gasped. "You didn't love me for me. You cherry-picked the things you liked about me. You constantly told me what was wrong with me, or what I was doing wrong."

"Self-improvement, babe. I was trying to motivate you towards your Personal Explosive Smash Through™." He turned to the camera again. "If we are not having powerful daily Smash Through Experiences™, we are not growing."

"Oh my God!" I threw my hands in the air. "If I hear you say the word 'explosive' or 'smash through' or 'breakthrough' or 'hashtag personal damn growth' again, it will be too soon. Besides, it's all crap, Kyle. All of it."

Kyle looked at me sternly now. As if this was the thing that had finally made him think. He started shaking his head. Looking almost wounded.

"Frankie, if we are not constantly striving and pushing the boundaries of our own goals, we will stagnate and not ever step into our purposes, smashing through the doors of challenge that surround us."

"Uh . . ." I blinked my eyes at him quickly, and then looked over at my sister. She was shaking her head in utter confusion.

"It's all in my book," he said, turning to the phone again. "Explosive, Personal, Smash Through In Ten Steps™, dropping in two weeks' time." He smiled at the camera and then looked back at me and shrugged, as if to say, *Duh*. Like I was meant to have any idea what the hell he was going on about.

"I . . . I . . . It's . . . You . . . We . . ." I stuttered frantically trying to grab onto some words of sense. But there was nothing sensible about anything that was going on around me, so I said the only thing that came to mind. "You had pec implants!"

A huge gasp rang out around me, and everyone's eyes zoned in on his chest. For the first time that day, it looked like a real emotion actually washed over Kyle's face. He looked mortified, and truthfully, I felt a little bad.

"Keep going, keep going," our social media manager whispered at me. "People are loving this, you must see the comments."

I swung around and glared at her. Looking straight into the camera now. "I don't care about the comments. I don't care about the likes and the shares and the heart emojis and hashtags anymore."

She gasped at me. As if I'd stabbed her in the ribs with something. She took a step back, almost recoiling. As if she'd never heard anything more disgusting and disturbing in her entire matt-lipsticked life.

I put my hands on my hips and looked around, taking in the whole scene. The townsfolk all behind me, dressed in their reenactment clothes. I caught some eyes I knew as I scanned the crowd; Ian gave me an encouraging nod, Natasha gave me a thumbs up, as did the rest of the ladies from book club.

I turned back around and looked at all the phones. And then I sighed loudly and walked up to Kyle. I put my hands on his shoulders and gripped them tightly. He looked confused.

"I'm sure there is someone perfect out there for you, who shares in your passion and daily motivational quotes and will enjoy spending hours and hours and hours taking photos of you at the gym holding a protein bar, read your book and love it, but that person is not me . . . *anymore*."

Kyle hung his head and I honestly felt sorry for him. "Hey!" I squeezed his shoulders a little harder. "Think what great content this will make. You, recovering from a break-up like this. Think about all those people out there right now who are posting you sympathetic emojis and broken hearts. Think about how you can turn this whole thing around and use it to motivate people one day. Your Break-up, Smash Through™! Think about that, Kyle." And then I let go of his shoulders, turned and started walking away. But then I stopped and swung around again, pointing an accusatory finger at everyone.

"And as for you lot, you heard the guy, it's illegal to have the internet here. Get out of here. All of you." I saw my sister's face drop and then I quickly corrected, "Not you," I said to her. "I want you to meet someone. Come." She ran up to me and I turned back to the crowd and scanned it for Mark, but he wasn't there. I scanned it again, and again and sudden panic rose up inside me. When had he gone? I hope he'd seen me turn Kyle down and didn't think I was now engaged to him.

I turned to Samirah now. "Where is he?"

I swung around, feeling frantic and lost and . . . *then I heard it.*

Every single person heard it. We all turned at the same time and looked towards the stage.

CHAPTER 72

I rushed over to the stage where Mark was busy tuning and strumming his guitar in front of the mic. The sound was loud, floating through the speaker. When I finally reached him, I was totally out of breath. A few people had run with me, including Faizel and my sister.

I stood in front of the small stage and shouted, "I didn't say yes to him, by the way!"

"She didn't. She didn't," Faizel added, equally loudly.

"I swear. I didn't say yes to him. I didn't even know he was coming. Please believe me," I pleaded, looking at Mark. I couldn't help the tears that were welling up in my eyes now. I was waiting for him to say something to me, something bad, something . . .

"I know," he finally said, smiling. His voice came to me loud and echoey through the speakers. And anyone who wasn't watching this, was definitely watching now.

"You know?" I asked.

He nodded at me.

"Then . . . Then . . . why did you leave?" I asked.

His smile grew. "Are you kidding? That was the cringiest thing I've ever seen in my life." Mark looked around. "Sorry, Kyle. No offence, mate." I smiled. He sounded so Australian right now and it made me laugh. And then a tear slipped out my eye and down my cheek. It wasn't a sad tear.

"What's going on?" my sister asked next to me. "Who's that?"

I turned to her just as Samirah managed to waddle up to us.

"He's right, though," Samirah said, totally out of breath, reaching for Faizel's shoulder to steady herself. "Cringiest thing I ever saw in my life, and I like big romantic gestures!"

"It really was." I nodded in agreement.

Mark gave his guitar one loud strum and everyone turned back to him. "As cringe as it was, though, it did make me realize something."

"What?" I asked.

"It made me realize that I hadn't really told you something, yet. Something I should have said to you this morning."

I smiled and my heart started skipping beats. A whole lot of beats. "What haven't you told me?" I asked expectantly.

"Something fairly important." He looked cute and coy now. "And it made me think of doing something equally cringe." He strummed the guitar again, and a small crowd had now gathered around us. Andy was there with her phone in the air, and a few other phone wielders from Kyle's posse too.

I looked at the phones and then back at Mark. "They're still live streaming," I said, in case he was about to do what I suspected he was about to do.

He shrugged. "I know. And I'll probably regret doing this . . ." He looked up at the people filming. "But fuck it! Right?"

"What are you doing?" Faizel asked.

"The grand love gesture," Ian said, coming up behind me.

"Who is that?" my sister asked, pointing at Mark. I was just about to answer her when we were all stunned into silence by Mark singing.

The song.

My favorite song in the world. The song that had gotten me through the darkest times of my life. That had spoken to me when no one else had. And he was singing it, *to me*. Despite the fact he didn't want anyone to know who he was, he was singing it to me.

This beautiful, soft acoustic version of the song rang out around us and started drawing an even bigger crowd. His eyes were locked on me, though. Only me. As a teen, I'd imagined this moment a million times over in my head, and now, it was actually happening.

And it wasn't because I was a someone with a million followers; he didn't care about that. He just cared about me. Not the me who was somebody to everyone, but the me that was only a somebody to a few people.

"Oh my God," I heard my sister say next to me, and then felt her hand on my shoulder. "It's him! It's him! M.J.!" she squealed behind me.

And then I heard more voices and murmurs. Because it was absolutely unmistakable now. Undeniable. His voice was the voice that we'd all listened to growing up, there was no getting away from it. The second he opened his mouth and sang that song, we all knew exactly who we were listening to.

"It's him!" Ian gasped.

"Who?" Samirah asked, sounding genuinely confused.

"M.J. Taylor. OH. MY. GOD!" he replied in a high-pitched, excited voice. "I should have seen it."

And then like dominoes, more and more voices joined in the conversation.

"Wait, is that who I think it is?" someone else said.

"Oh my God, he sings exactly like the guy from Step To It." The whispers round me were getting louder and louder.

"It's him! Isn't it!"

"That's M.J. from Step To It!"

"It has got be him!"

"WHO?" Samirah asked again, much louder than she had before. "Who is he?"

"I didn't know he could sing like that," Faizel said, clearly as oblivious as Samirah was.

I felt two hands on my shoulders and turned. It was my sister, wide-eyed. "Is what I think's happening, really happening now?" she asked, hardly able to contain her excitement.

"What's happening, could someone tell me?" Samirah piped up angrily now.

"SSSHHHHH!" Several people glared at us and then put their fingers over their mouths. I turned back to watch Mark and that's when I felt Harun next to me. I looked down at him and gave him a pat. This was all happening because of him. He'd been steering me in this direction, to this exact moment in time, since I'd met him. In fact, since leaving that elevator and almost losing my life, something had been steering me here. I looked back up at Mark as he sang, watching me with a cute, but slightly embarrassed smile.

"Oh my God! He's singing to me," I whispered to myself and then grabbed my sister by the hand and looked over at Samirah. She grinned at me.

"He's totally singing to you," she said excitedly. "Now this is a romantic gesture I can get behind." And then a few people around me started singing along, and soon, the entire place had been turned into a giant sing-along. Even the people on phones were singing. Some of them had even lowered their phones to watch what was clearly a historic moment unfold in front of them.

And then, when it was over, when he'd sung the last lyric and strummed the last note, he put the guitar down and looked at me from the small stage. The crowd had gone deathly silent. And I swear, you would have heard a pin drop as every single person in the crowd held their breath. Mark looked slightly pleased with himself, in a totally adorable way. Not smug, but cute and self-assured. As if he knew damn well that singing that song to me had made my heart melt.

"So?" I heard Samirah say.

"So?" I looked at her.

"Are you just going to stand there like the cat got your tongue, or are you going to do something?" She pushed me forward with her hand. Mark jumped off the lip of the stage and landed in front of me with a thud. We stopped a few feet away from each other.

"Uh . . . that was . . ." My voice was soft, I didn't want everyone to hear me, so I stepped closer to him. I took his hands in mine. "Amazing," I whispered through a smile so big my face felt like it would break in two.

"Not completely cheesy?"

My smile grew. How was that even possible?

"Cheesy in the best kind of way." I stepped closer, until our faces were almost touching. "You know everyone here knows who you are now? And possibly a million people on Facebook."

He shrugged. "I don't care."

"You don't?"

He shook his head. "I only care that you know how I feel about you."

My heart zigzagged in my chest. "How do you feel?" I asked, still desperate to hear him say it.

He pulled my hands up to his chest and held them tightly against his body. I glanced behind me quickly. This massive public show was not how I'd imagined this going down. I'd imagined something far smaller, maybe just the two of us in bed, whispering to each other. Not this. But here we were. I looked back at him. He was smiling at me in a way that completely and utterly took my breath away.

"Frankie . . ." he started.

"Mark?" I said encouragingly.

"I think I might . . ." He paused and looked at me for a while.

"You think you might, what . . .?" I asked, leaning in a little.

"Well, that's wrong. What I meant to say was that I *know* I might . . ."

"Know you might, what?" I asked.

He chuckled now. Low and coy and sweet. I found myself chuckling back, feeling just as coy as he was looking right now.

"Truly, madly . . ." he said, and then paused, biting his bottom lip as if he was about to laugh a little, his cheeks had gone a soft shade of pink.

"Like me?" I asked.

He nodded. And then, suddenly, he shook his head. My heart instantly dropped.

"What?" I asked, my voice shaking a bit.

"No. I think I might truly, madly . . . *love you*." His face flushed a bright shade of red as he said it and my heart thumped in my chest.

"Seriously?" I asked, giggling stupidly. I mean, this was all so completely cheesy but also amazing and cute as hell. And I was swooning so much, that I thought I might fall over. "You do?" I asked again.

He nodded at me and then I found myself nodding back at him. Our heads got closer and closer as the nodding intensified.

"I . . . I . . . love you too." The words got stuck in my throat as happy tears welled up in my eyes and he pulled me into a kiss.

CHAPTER 73

After Mark's and my very public declaration, things carried on as normal. The people with the phones were eventually ushered away by the police that arrived after ASO had called them. Kyle was amongst those ushered away; the last time I laid eyes on him he looked like he was recording a very tearful vlog for all his followers, no doubt about me. Even though they were gone, I was pretty sure that Mark was trending now and millions of people around the world had just seen that video. But he didn't seem to care. And no one else in town seemed to care that much either. There was an initial rush of people who couldn't believe it was him, but soon the rush was over and everyone went back very quickly to treating him as Mark the guy from the video store. No one cared that our festival had been disturbed either, because as soon as all the phones left, the town carried on as normal.

Some people had jumped in the spring as tradition would have it. Mark and Faizel were playing some songs, Zack had roasted some lamb on the spit and the whole town was eating and drinking together. I'd had to fill my sister in on everything that had happened to me in the last few weeks, finding it hard to believe how much had changed in such a short time. The party went late into the night, and by the time it was over, I was well and truly spent. The day had been long and possibly one of the best of my life. I had loosened my dress, pulled the top half down and was wearing a small T-shirt as Mark, Jess and I made the walk back to where she'd parked her car. People were waving goodbye to me and calling me by my name now, as if I'd always been part of this town.

"This place is amazing," my sister said as we walked up the road. "I can't believe you found it."

"I'm glad she did," Mark said, and Jess blushed. She was still blushing every time Mark said anything to her; she too had had many Step To That posters on her wall. Although she had preferred Shane "the goofy one."

"She'll stop that blushing soon," I chuckled at Mark. "I hope so anyway."

"Or I won't," she said, holding her cheeks. "Which would be totally embarrassing."

She put her arm around me as we headed towards her car.

"Are you sure you don't want to come with us now?" I asked, as we reached her big suburban SUV.

She shook her head and then yawned. "I think I'll go check into the hotel. Thanks for booking me in, by the way," she said to Mark, who had asked Logan to organize a room with Selma earlier.

He shook his head. "No worries," he said.

"I need a bath and I need to crash because I've been driving all day and I'm exhausted."

"I'll come over for breakfast in the morning," I said to her. She looked at me sideways. "Oh, I eat breakfast now. It's my new thing," I joked.

"You seem to have a lot of new things now." She reached out and ran her hand through my brown hair. "I love it, by the way," she said.

I reached up and touched it self-consciously. "Thanks."

We stood and looked at each other for a while, and then she pulled me into her arms again. "I'm so glad you're okay. I was so bloody worried. Mom was beside herself too, she was even going to fly back home from Barbados with Dan, but then Kyle said he found you and I said I would go with him."

"At least Kyle was good for one thing, I guess," I said, and gave her an extra squeeze.

"You need to phone her and let her know you're okay," she said, pulling away from the hug.

"I will." I nodded.

She turned and looked at Mark and immediately blushed again. Her hands flew up to her face and covered her cheeks. "So embarrassing," she said, fanning herself. She opened her car and started to climb in.

"I'll see you at breakfast at nine," I said. "The hotel is on this road, a few blocks up." I pointed. "You can't miss it. This place is really small."

She smiled at me. "I saw it when I drove in."

"It was nice meeting you," Mark said.

She nodded, her cheeks going pink again. She climbed in and closed the door. I gave her a wave and then blew her a small kiss. She smiled right back at me and then drove off. Mark and I watched her, and when she was gone, he put his arm over my shoulder and looked at me.

"What say we get home?" he asked.

I nodded. "Please." It had been a pretty action-packed day and I also wanted a bath and bed. When we made our way to the car, we'd had to walk all the way up the main road, and by the time we got there, we both fell into it, utterly exhausted. I looked at Mark, and he looked at me. And in that look, I could see that something between us had changed. The confession of our feelings had made this feel super real. And full of possibilities.

I started the car and we both laughed when the blue glow surrounded us.

"Don't you have to take this car back at some stage?" he asked.

"I leased it for a month, so I guess in about a week, but . . ." I patted the steering wheel and couldn't believe I was about to say this out loud. "Maybe I'll ask them if I can buy it."

Mark laughed. "Really?"

"Sure, why not? It's what got me here in the first place so it's special, in some way." I looked in the rear-view mirror to see what Harun was doing on the backseat. He was just sitting there, looking at us again. He always seemed to be thinking something through.

Mark reached over and grabbed my hand. "I'm glad it brought you here," he said, pulling me into a kiss.

"Mmmm." I pulled away. "Did you smoke?" I asked, blocking my nose.

"Faizel and I shared a cigar after our set."

I cringed.

"It was disgusting," he admitted. "But manly, don't you think?"

"No." I swatted the air around us.

"Yeah, Samirah hates it too when we do it."

"How often do you do that?" I asked.

He shrugged. "Once, twice a year. On special occasions."

"Well, keep it that way, and warn me next time you're about to do it, so I don't almost kiss an ashtray."

"So, you're planning on staying here then?" he asked a little tentatively.

"Uh . . . if that's okay."

"It's fine. It's good," Mark quickly corrected. We looked at each other and leaned in.

"God, I really want to kiss you right now," I said, and then remembered. "Oooh, I have mints in the glovebox."

"Great." Mark opened the glovebox and reached inside. But instead of pulling out mints, he pulled out the envelope.

I stared at it. I'd forgotten that I'd shoved it in there because I was tired of always seeing it in my bag. I hadn't thought about it in days either, but now that I was looking at it, the raw emotions that I'd felt hit me all at once again.

"What is it?" he asked.

"It's from my dad."

"Your biological dad?" he asked. "The one who left you?"

I nodded.

"What is it?"

"Don't know. I can't bring myself to open it." I took a deep breath. "He died. A couple of months ago. This is what he left me."

Mark turned the envelope around in his hands. "I can see why you're struggling to open it."

"It's the closest I've been to him in years," I said, a tear forming in my eye.

He grabbed the flap between his fingers and looked up at me. "May I?"

"Okay." I nodded.

Mark pulled the envelope open. I watched intently as he did, his fingers moving in slow motion. When it was open, he tipped it over and two pieces of paper fell out.

We looked at them in his lap. "Which one do you want to look at first?" he asked.

I picked up one of the pieces of paper and opened it.

It was a handwritten note. In my father's writing.

I started to read it.

"*Dear Frances, I know I wasn't there for you when I was alive. And to be honest, I sometimes think it was best. I'm not father material. I never was* . . . Oh my God," I gasped loudly. "That's, uh . . . Wow. I don't know what to say, that's . . ."

"Not what you were expecting?" Mark asked.

"No." I looked up at him, tears forming in my eyes. I'd not been expecting that at all. Or maybe I'd just hoped for something different.

"Do you want me to read it?" he asked.

I nodded, unable to talk through what was a very strangled throat. I pushed the letter over to him. Mark started reading again and I braced myself for more words that I really didn't want to hear.

"*The doctors tell me I don't have too much time left. This cancer is a real bastard. But as I lie here, I find myself thinking about you, and wondering what my life would have been like if I'd been a different kind of man. I find myself wondering all sorts of things. That's the thing about death . . . it makes you think. But there is nothing I can do to change anything. I can't go back in time and be your dad. And to be honest, I probably wouldn't if I could."* Mark paused as those words sank in.

I put my hand to my chest. That was harsh. And it fucking hurt.

"You okay?" Mark asked.

I shook my head. "Not really. But carry on."

"You sure?" He reached out and wiped a tear from my face. "You don't have to read this, we can burn it if you like?"

"No. Carry on." Mark stared at me for a few moments, concern etched across his face. But he finally looked back down at the paper.

"I can't go back and give you any of the things you probably needed from me in life, but I can hopefully give you something that you need from me in death. Please find my enclosed cheque."

Mark reached down and picked up the other piece of paper and turned it over in his hands.

"It's not much. I'm not dying a rich man. But it is everything I have, and I'm leaving it all to you. Do with it as you like. I know it doesn't make up for anything, but I hope it will bring you some happiness. Do something with it that makes you happy. Regards, Timothy (Dad)."

Mark passed the cheque to me and I turned it over in my hands: R320,000.

I looked down at it for the longest time. The name and numbers were written in that same scribbled handwriting that everything else was written in.

I held it up and looked over at Mark.

"What are you going to do with it?" he asked.

"I don't know," I admitted. Truthfully, I'd barely spent any money since arriving here. It surprised me how little one really needed to be happy. How little shopping one needed to do. How little one really needed to do your hair and make-up and nails. And then a thought hit me . . .

"Oh my God!"

"What?" Mark asked.

"We've got to drive to Samirah's." I put my foot down and pulled off, tires screeching.

Mark screamed and Harun barked.

"Sorry, I forgot how fast this thing was." I drove it at a more regular speed until I reached Samirah's. I rushed up to the front door and banged.

"Samirah," I called.

She opened the door, looking exhausted. "Crap! Frankie, I'm climbing into bed and the babies are kicking and Faizel smells like an ashtray and—"

"Feel like calling a certain estate agent?" I said, thrusting the paper towards her.

"What?" she asked, looking down at it.

"What do you think?" I asked excitedly.

"What do I think of what?" She was still trying to catch up to me here.

"It's an inheritance from a father I never knew. He said I should do something with it that makes me happy, and I literally cannot think of anything I would rather do than buy that land and build that sanctuary."

"Wait . . ." Samirah's eyes widened. "What?"

"So . . .?"

"Frankie, I can't." She pushed the cheque back to me. "This is so thoughtful and amazing and generous and kind, but I could never do this. That is my dream, not—"

"No. That's where you're wrong." I shook my head. "It's what I want too. This is what I want."

I pushed the cheque back to her and she looked at it for the longest time.

"You sure?" she asked.

I nodded. "More sure than I've been in ages."

She paused. Holding her breath for a moment and then . . . "This is amazing!" She threw her arms around me and the two of us jumped up and down on the spot together.

"Wait. No!" She pushed me away quickly and suddenly. "No jumping. Please, no jumping. I swear they're going to fall out." She grabbed her stomach and we both laughed.

CHAPTER 74

I went to meet my sister that morning at the hotel restaurant. But our breakfast turned into lunch, as we sat and talked for hours and hours about everything. We *really* shared our feelings with each other. I spoke about how I'd felt growing up, and for the first time ever, she seemed to understand it. She also apologized for never standing up for me when I was being bullied, said she should have been strong enough to do that. By the end of lunch we were holding hands and sharing tears like we'd never done before. Logan kept the tea coming and we kept on talking. And when it was time for her to leave, I had a request.

"Will you do something with me?" I asked a little nervously.

"Anything," she said.

"I want to post one more thing on social media, and I'm going to need . . . support," I said quietly.

She nodded. "Whatever you need."

I smiled at her. "I'll follow you out of town to where we can get Wi-Fi and then . . . you'll be there with me?"

She pulled me into a hug. "Of course."

We left Springdorp behind us, and then drove for another forty minutes until we reached that sign I'd come to know so well over the last few weeks. And when we passed it, we pulled over onto the side of the road together. I climbed out of my car and passed Jess my phone. I'd already taken the photo and written the message—all I had to do now was press post. I'd been thinking about it all night and working on it, and honestly I was still in two minds about it, but deep down inside, I knew it was something I needed to do.

Jess read the message and when she was done, she looked up at me, tears in her eyes and smiled. "This is perfect," she said. "Do it."

I nodded at her, trying to draw all the courage in the world towards me to post that picture of myself that I'd taken last night; stretch marks and floppy skin and no make-up and all. My finger hovered over the button for a few more seconds and then I pressed it.

Dear followers,

I have a confession to make to all of you. I'm not who you think I am. I've been misrepresenting myself, and now I want to get real. I am not perfect, far from it. I have stretch marks, don't actually eat breakfast, hate making smoothie bowls, and there have been many days in my life that I didn't like myself that much. No motivational quote can change that. I have been selling you this image of perfection and a perfect life, but that is all for show. I recently heard some very wise words that I want to share: true beauty is defined by how we treat each other, it has nothing to do with how we look on the outside.

This might seem like the most contradictory message, especially coming from me. But it's the truest thing I've heard in years. So I want to show my true beauty today by finally getting honest with each and every one of you and showing you all my true self. I thought that being a someone to everyone was the most important thing in my life. That being liked and friended and followed and thumbs-upped was everything. But it's not. There is more to life than that and it's taken many years to work that out. I also want to tell you all that you are good enough just the way you are. Imperfections and all. I used to think that being prettier and having bigger boobs and being thinner and blonder and more contoured were the things that mattered most, but that couldn't be further from the truth.

Love and friendship and family, and even an ugly, one-eyed dog, trumps all of that.

This will be my very last post because I am officially becoming a Wi-Fi refugee. I am putting down my phone and living life. Real life. So goodbye, and I hope each and every one of you finds the happiness that I'm finally finding—stretch marks and all!

Love Frankie

CHAPTER 75

❧

Four months later

$\mathcal{W}$e were all there. Samirah, Faizel and the bouncing babies Fatima and Ahmed, Mark, myself, and Harun. This had unofficially become our Sunday afternoon ritual. A ritual we'd fallen into without much thought. Without someone arranging it, or coordinating it. It had come naturally, like the way the desert breathes out in the evenings. Living out here, I'd quickly come to understand that the desert was also a living entity with feelings and moods, just like us.

We were seated on the veranda, stuffed after our barbecue. Fatima and Ahmed were in their carry cots, fast asleep after their bottles of milk. Samirah and Faizel always sat on the swing chair, gently swaying back and forth; Mark and I always sat on the daybed. All of us had a coffee in hand, sipping it. Sometimes we would chat, saying a million things to each other, and sometimes, like today, we would all be still. Wrapped up in our own pleasant thoughts, just sharing this moment of closeness and connectedness without saying a word.

It dawned on me in that moment, the spiritual awakening that I'd been trying so hard to have out there in the desert that day, I'd kind of had it. It wasn't some lightning moment, some blast from above. It was more subtle than that. And maybe that's actually how they're meant to be. Something that subtly, over time, leaks into your consciousness. At first, you don't really know it's there, the feeling lurks somewhere just out of reach. But gradually, the feeling becomes a little stronger and more crystal clear until one Sunday, sitting on a veranda in the middle of the Karoo, you realize with every fiber of your being that you are meant to be here. That the strange and peculiar series of events that had started with the elevator had brought you here. To this moment. To this daybed. This place. These people.

I inhaled sharply at the thought and the others looked at me. I couldn't help the blurry tears that came to my eyes. They smiled at me, no words spoken, as if they understood the moment I was having and were respecting it. Giving it room to breathe and fully form. I reached over and took Mark's hand. Usually on days like this Harun lay at our feet on his blanket, but today I could see he was restless. In fact, he'd been like this for the last few weeks. Not able to rest and relax, which he was usually so good at.

"What's wrong, boy?" I finally asked, after the second time he'd paced the length of the veranda. The only words that had been spoken for at least ten minutes.

"He seems restless today again," Samirah noted.

I nodded. "He does. Come here." I extended my hand to him. He looked at it for the longest time, before walking over and placing his massive head in it. He relaxed and the full weight of his head was too much for one hand. I reached down and placed another hand under his chin.

"What's wrong?" I asked, as he closed his eye and nuzzled into me. He kept his head in my hands, eye closed, breathing in deeply, as if inhaling my smell. And then, he pulled his head away and took a step back from me, and suddenly, I could feel him going. I sat up straight.

"What's wrong?" I asked again, as he took another step back.

I stood up, panic seizing me for some reason.

He took another step back. And then, deliberately, slowly and carefully as if he was trying to take a mental image of everyone, he looked at all of us. Samirah first, then he ran his eye over Fatima and

Ahmed. Then Faizel and then his eye drifted over to Mark. He seemed to linger there a little longer. As if he was trying to make sure of something. And then he looked back at me and took another step backwards.

I stepped forward. "What are you doing?" I asked. The tears had already come to my eyes, and I had a sense I knew what was happening. He looked at me with that one yellow eye that at one point I'd feared, but over time had come to love and rely on. And then he barked. Short. Loud. He wagged his tail and lowered his head, in what looked like a small bow. As if his performance had come to a close and the curtain was falling. And then, he turned and ran.

"WAIT!" I screamed, running down off the veranda and into the desert where he was headed. "WAIT! What are you doing?" I ran as fast as I could as Harun raced ahead of me. The sun was starting to set, casting shadows here and there, and every now and again, Harun would completely disappear into one and then reappear in a shaft of light somewhere else, as if magical.

"Where's he going?" Mark shouted, coming up next to me. It felt like we ran for ages, my legs scraping against bushes and shrubs, but I didn't care. But at some point, I couldn't run anymore. My legs and lungs would simply not carry me any longer. Mark came to a stop next to me, and soon Samirah followed. We all stood there together, out of breath, and watched as Harun became smaller and smaller and smaller, running off into the now fast-setting sun.

I shook my head as he reached the horizon. The point at which he would completely disappear from view. I inhaled so sharply that the breath felt like a dagger in my tight throat, and then I burst into tears. Loud and unbridled.

"COME BACK! COME BACK!" I yelled.

At that, Harun stopped. He turned around and looked at us.

"WHERE ARE YOU GOING?" I shouted so loudly that I tasted metal in the back of my throat.

I felt an arm come up around my shoulder: Mark. I felt another arm, it was Samirah. We stood there arm in arm, staring at the dog in the distance. And then I heard it. Three loud barks. So definitive, so final like a . . . *goodbye*.

He was leaving me. The thought hit me in the ribs and the head and the heart and my legs. I felt the thought like a pain that ricocheted through my entire body. A pain that was sharp and dull and ached at the same time.

"He's . . . he's . . . leaving me . . ." I stuttered and stumbled in between the guttural sobs and moans as I held my chest because it felt like the heart inside it was going to break and smash. "Why is he leaving?" I wailed.

"Perhaps his work here is done," Samirah said softly. There was warmth and love in her tone, but there was also truth to it. I recognized that truth immediately, even if I didn't want to admit it.

Harun gave three final barks, and then he turned and disappeared over the horizon, out of sight.

"NOOOOO!" I wailed so loudly that I'm sure I woke the desert itself up. Mark pulled me into his arms and I wept into his shoulder. I felt a hand on my back, Samirah rubbing it in small and steady circles. I pushed Mark away.

"He can't just leave me," I said frantically and then started running again. Sore legs and screaming lungs, I ran and ran and ran. I looked over my shoulder. Samirah and Mark were still standing there. They hadn't moved and looked like they were simply waiting for me to return. As if they knew nothing could be done, running was futile.

I ran until I couldn't run anymore, until the sun finally went down and the world around me started getting blacker and darker. I stopped and then fell to my knees, gasping for air and sweating from the effort and the achy nausea that was surging through me. I sat there, catching my breath, waiting for the world to stop spinning from lack of oxygen.

Finally, I heard footsteps behind me. It was Mark. He held his hand out for me. I took it reluctantly and he pulled me to my feet.

"He's gone," Mark said softly to me as we walked back towards the house.

"He's gone," I repeated thoughtfully. And I think I understood what he meant. I think I understood what Samirah meant too. Harun had come into my life, and for a brief moment, he'd been my dog, but now, after he'd done what he was meant to do . . . *he was gone*.

He didn't belong to me.

He belonged to the world.

He wasn't mine.

He was much, much greater than that.

CHAPTER 76

One year later

I must have watched and waited for Harun for months after that. But he never came back. He was gone. Only, he wasn't really gone at all. He was in everything I did. He was in every single moment of every single day of my new life, because it was him who'd helped steer me towards this new life.

Mark and I got married out here in the desert in front of his house. It was a small wedding, only friends and family. My mom and Dan the dentist had flown in from Bermuda for the wedding, my niece had been my flower girl. Samirah and my sister had been my bridesmaids. I didn't even wear a wedding dress. I just wore my favorite casual sundress. There were no decorations, no proper seats for everyone. Just some hay bales and bright picnic blankets. We did it at sunset, my favorite time in the desert.

It was not an Insta-worthy wedding, it was not a Tweet-worthy, post-worthy wedding, but it was the most special day of my life. For a moment, like catching a shadow moving in the corner of your eye and turning around only for it to be gone, I swear I saw Harun sitting at the horizon. I liked to imagine him like that. Out there in the world, bringing other people together like he'd brought me and Mark together. I imagined him moving from place to place, the most unlikely cupid, creating love and connections wherever he went.

That is how I thought of Harun in my quiet moments, when I missed him the most. But I also had a lot to keep me busy too.

Our animal sanctuary was up and running. It was nothing fancy, but it was perfect and our first inhabitant was a one-eyed ostrich with a deformed foot that was totally moody and hateful, but sometimes reminded me of Harun. I was very fond of it, despite the fact that he tried to bite me every time I was there. As Samirah had said, so fortuitous that the first animal we took in had one eye! "All the better to see you with," she had joked. More soon followed. We got a feral stray cat whose back leg had been lost, so it made it hard for her to hunt and catch food. When she'd arrived, she was skin and bones, but now she was healthy and happy, even though she never let Samirah or me get close enough to touch her. A tortoise with a broken shell arrived, and Faizel had worked some DIY magic, managing to make it a cover for the part that was missing. And then our first dog arrived. I'd been waiting for this moment since we opened, I suppose silently hoping that Harun would have shown up, or a puppy that looked like him. But it wasn't him, or his puppy. It was a small, fluffy white thing. A runt from a litter on one of the nearby farms that under normal circumstances would have probably been drowned.

"Severe angular limb deformity," is what Samirah called it. Something that could perhaps over time be corrected with surgery, but it would never be perfect, and she would never walk normally.

I think Knuckles, as we affectionately called her, because it looked like she was walking on her knuckles, stayed at the sanctuary for exactly three nights before I brought her home and told Mark that we had a new pet.

Little by little, the sanctuary filled up with all kinds of animals that wouldn't have had a chance at a life, if we weren't here. And when I locked up at night and left to go home, I always got this tiny feeling inside . . . I felt just a tiny bit closer to my dad. For the first time ever.

But perhaps the strangest thing to happen to me since Harun left, was the message I'd gotten almost a year after the elevator accident. It was from the girl in the elevator who'd been knocked unconscious. I was out doing my monthly shopping in the next town over—there were just some things you couldn't get at Jim's, and once a month I made the two-hour drive to the town that had an actual small shopping mall. It was on these drives that I usually turned my cell phone on and FaceTimed my mom and sister. This had become our routine and I looked forward to it a lot. Sometimes I would go to my dormant social media accounts, and have a look at what was happening there. By the way, my very last post is by far my most popular post of all time. Kyle had launched a successful, motivational book about getting over a break-up and Finding Your True Smash Through Self™. He was back together with @Paige_Dreams_ and the two of them looked happy. Well, if their huge, live-streamed Insta wedding was anything to go by, or those gorgeous pics from their honeymoon in Bali. I sometimes also Googled Mark on those trips, to see what people were saying about him. His singing that day had caused a worldwide media storm, but on that same day ASO had also released a statement reminding everyone that using Wi-Fi was strictly prohibited and that perpetrators would be prosecuted to the full extent of the law if they did. This seemed to have kept most reporters and media away; there had been a few people who'd come to town looking to interview Mark, not to mention a few groupies. But they never found him. Everyone in town either pretended that they had no idea where he was, or they gave the wrong written directions. After going around in circles for a few hours with no GPS, most people gave up.

But on this specific shopping day I'd noticed a message in my Facebook inbox from a name I didn't recognize. When I'd clicked on her profile to see who it was, I'd recognized her immediately. The woman from the elevator. And that's how I found myself sitting in a coffee shop in Joburg, telling my entire story to the two women I'd shared an elevator ride with almost a year ago to the day. It was clear that Becca's life had changed as much as mine had, and by the time

I'd finished telling them my story, the coffee shop manager was glaring at us with irritation, because we'd been there for so long and they were trying to close up now.

"Do you guys want to come to my place?" Zoe said, the big red scar on her forehead moving as she talked. She'd been the one who'd invited us here, and was the one who had the last story to tell.

"Sure." Becca got up and pushed her chair in. She was a famous writer. I'd actually read one of her books when I'd tried to become a #bookstagrammer. I'd even posted this cute picture of her book lying in a pile of carefully cut-out pink hearts. I smiled to myself. That life was a long time ago.

"Let's go," Zoe said, moving towards the door. I couldn't wait for her to tell us her story, because I had a feeling that hers was probably going to be the craziest of all!

ACKNOWLEDGMENTS

I'd like to thank our wonderful veterinarian, Myra Marais, for all her suggestions and for keeping my fictitious dog alive in this book.

Discover Jo's uplifting rom-com guaranteed to make you laugh and cry,

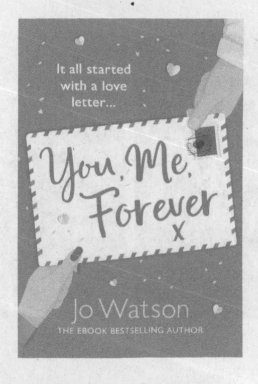

Available now from

Don't miss Jo's glorious,
laugh-out-loud standalone
office rom-coms!

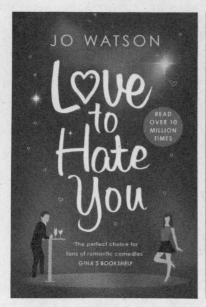

HEADLINE
ETERNAL

For laugh-out-loud, swoon-worthy
hijinks, don't miss Jo's
Destination Love Series!

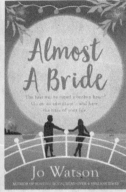

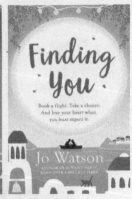

HEADLINE
ETERNAL

FIND YOUR HEART'S DESIRE...